# A LADY OF TRUE DISTINCTION

## GRACE BURROWES

GRACE BURROWES PUBLISHING

A Lady of True Distinction

Copyright © 2019 by GRACE BURROWES

All rights reserved.

*A Lady of True Distinction by Grace Burrowes*

*To those who wander alone*

# CHAPTER ONE

"Hawthorne, be reasonable. I know you dislike Mrs. Summerfield, so please allow me to pay this call with you."

Hawthorne Dorning continued walking toward the mounting block rather than do violence to a brother who meant well. "To dislike a woman who has never done me any harm would be ungentlemanly. Shame upon you, Valerian, for implying such a thing." Moreover, Valerian was wrong, not that Hawthorne had time to correct him.

Valerian kept pace easily, though Thorne was two inches taller. "Since your distant and misspent youth, have you ever once stood up with the lady at a local assembly?"

"I have not." Thorne had watched, though, as Margaret Summerfield had stood up with his brothers and half of his neighbors. She was neither a coquette nor a snob, and she moved with an easy grace on the dance floor.

"Have you ever been seated beside her at the interminable dinners that pass for socializing in these bucolic surrounds?"

"Again, no." But then, Thorne excelled at avoiding invitations to those dinners.

"Have you tarried with Mrs. Summerfield in the churchyard, flirting discreetly while you pretend to discuss the weather and the crops?"

Thorne had stood in the churchyard many a fine morning, enjoying small talk while from the corner of his eye watching Margaret hurry her nieces into a waiting coach.

"I do not flirt, discreetly or otherwise."

A groom stood at Gowain's head, though the gelding would have napped in the spring sunshine all day.

Valerian snorted, which inspired something like an equine frown from Thorne's gelding. "What do you call it, then, when you smile knowingly at a young lady, lean near her, and nearly whisper confidences that cause her to blush and giggle?"

"I cannot help that my attempts at conversation are more discreet than yours or Oak's." Thorne checked the snugness of the girth, because Gowain loved nothing better than to hold his breath while being saddled. When the horse exhaled, the girth was looser than safety required, which afforded an enterprising steed all manner of opportunities.

"We're on to his tricks, Master Hawthorne," the groom said, stroking Gowain's big russet nose. "He likes to keep us on our toes, does Sir Gowain."

"Captain!" Thorne yelled, which had the dog on his feet and trotting across the drive as Thorne swung into the saddle.

"You're taking your hound calling with you, but not your most charming brother?" Valerian asked.

"Captain needs the exercise, or he'll chew more slippers to bits, while you can at least be trusted around my footwear—for the most part." Thorne took up the reins and turned the horse down the drive. "Don't wait luncheon for me."

"I wasn't about to. Please give the lady my regards. She's not that bad, once you get to know her."

"If I got to know her, she'd have to get to know me, and I very much doubt Mrs. Summerfield is interested in that challenge." She'd never said as much, but Thorne had concluded long ago that his interest in Margaret Summerfield was unreciprocated. He'd consigned his fancies to the category of youthful infatuation and not looked back.

Thorne cantered down the drive, Captain bounding at Gowain's heels. In the interests of concluding this task as quickly as possible, he cut across the fields rather than taking the lanes to Mrs. Summerfield's estate. The eastern boundary between Dorning Hall and the Summerfield property was a stream that, on his best day, Gowain could not clear in a single leap. He nonetheless tried, creating a great splash and much thrashing about as he landed short of the far bank.

"You never make that jump," Thorne said when they'd scrambled up the bank. "Why must you insist on doomed bravado? Your behavior is foolish and unbecoming, horse, and one of these days you'll regret your histrionics."

Gowain, of course, shook like a dog when he reached solid footing, then trotted on as if only rider miscalculation had resulted in the indignity of mud on a fellow's fetlocks. Captain chose to tarry in the stream, resulting in a very wet dog following Thorne onto the Summerfield front steps.

"You stink," Thorne said, waving his riding crop. "Go away."

Captain wagged a sopping tail and looked expectantly at the front door.

"Get thee gone, beast. You are not presentable."

The front door opened, and where a smiling butler or cheerful housekeeper should have stood, Thorne beheld Mrs. Margaret Summerfield.

"Mr. Dorning. Good day." A small hesitation followed that greeting, then she stepped back. "Do come in. Dog, you will wait here."

Captain sat, his gaze crestfallen.

"His name is Captain. We came by way of the stream, and he indulged in a swim." As if any female cared one whit what a smelly dog got up to when loose in the countryside.

"Hammond," Mrs. Summerfield said as a footman took Thorne's

hat, spurs, and riding crop. "Have some water brought for Mr. Dorn-ing's friend, and if Cook has a bone, that would likely also be appreci-ated. Mr. Dorning, I'm in the blue parlor at the moment. My nieces are exploring the Asian steppes in the green parlor."

She marched off, and even the brisk tattoo of her heels radiated impatience with her caller. Nothing about Margaret Summerfield was silly or insubstantial. Her features were angular, her brows darker than her blond hair and dramatically swooping. She moved with purpose rather than grace, and Thorne could not recall her smiling in his direction since she'd worn pigtails.

If even then.

Her house, by contrast, bore the welcoming scents of beeswax and lemon oil, the signature fragrance of a well-maintained abode. Here, though, an undernote of something—spearmint? cedar? Thorne could not decipher the olfactory subtlety—added an extra touch of freshness.

The manor smelled of sunshine and joy, while the lady of the house marched along like an artillery sergeant anticipating rain before a battle.

"Do we attempt conversation over a tea tray," she said, "or will you state your business and gallop on your way?" She opened the door to a parlor done up in various shades of azure, cream, and gold. The room was light and airy, and the daffodils on the sideboard a pretty complement to the color scheme. The entire drive was lined with blossoming red, white, and yellow tulips, and more daffodils had graced the sideboard in the foyer.

"What makes you think I come on business, Mrs. Summerfield?"

She took a sniff of the flowers. "You last presented yourself in my parlor when you wanted to discuss damming the stream to create a water meadow. Before that, you broached the idea of trading rams to improve the quality of your wool. Prior to that, you sought to breed a mare to my stallion. Business, Mr. Dorning, and here you are again."

On the most pressing business of all.

"I do have a proposition for you," Thorne said. "A business proposition. Might we be seated?"

His request occasioned another small hesitation, as if his hostess had to consider whether allowing him a seat was truly necessary.

"By all means, make yourself comfortable."

Something thumped against the inside wall, followed by a muffled shriek. "Has warfare broken out on the Asian steppes?"

"Very likely. If I am not vigilant, they will soon try to sneak their ponies into the library."

"My siblings and I had better luck secreting our cavalry mounts in the conservatory, but then, Papa was usually distracted by his latest botanical experiment, and Mama was invariably out socializing."

Mrs. Summerfield took a wing chair, but such was the authority with which she settled onto the cushion, that Thorne was put in mind of a queen assuming her throne. She was not a small woman, neither was she slender.

They might have danced well together, had he the fortitude to request such an honor.

Another thump sounded through the wall, while the lady remained unruffled.

"There were rather a lot of you for your parents to keep track of," she observed. "I have only the two nieces to manage, and they often defeat my best efforts. What brings you here, Mr. Dorning?"

She wasn't ringing for a tea tray, a small mercy.

"Nine children are a lot," he said, "especially when seven of them are male. Now, we brothers must all find our way in the world, though Dorning Hall is essentially a glorified farm."

"Very glorified. Between tenancies, the home farm, and other properties, the Dornings must own thousands of acres."

She traced a seam on the armrest of the chair. The upholstery was a pattern of cabbage roses rioting amid swirling greenery, while the carpet was a pastel blue reminiscent of a still pond under a summer sky. Had the brisk, businesslike Mrs. Summerfield designed this pretty room, or were the appointments a relic of some predecessor's good taste?

"The Dornings are the largest landowners in the area," Thorne said. "We are far from the wealthiest."

Her hand went still. "One wondered if you'd rebuild your dower house."

The dower house had been struck by lightning during one of Dorset's more spectacular autumn storms. Rebuilding was out of the question.

"We are salvaging what we can, but the fire did a thorough job on the beams and the interior. The family is turning our sights in other directions."

A thunder of footfalls from the next room suggested six infantry regiments, rather than a pair of little girls, were at war.

"How do those new directions bring you to my doorstep, Mr. Dorning?"

"I am here more or less as a supplicant, a neighbor in need." He'd rehearsed this speech for half the night, convincing himself the words would sound amused if not charming. "The Dornings are embarking on a new venture, converting our botanical riches into commercial products. Lord Casriel conceived this enterprise. We brothers are to carry it out. As the closest thing to a land steward that Dorning Hall has, care of the actual fields and plants falls to me."

"I wish you the joy of that undertaking, Mr. Dorning. Your father certainly bequeathed you a wealth of specimens to support your endeavor."

Every English manor had gardens for herbs, medicinals, and fragrances. The more ambitious had color gardens, scent gardens, glass houses, walled gardens for kitchen produce, conservatories to preserve tender specimens during cold weather, and exotics for additional cachet.

Dorning Hall's botanical resources were enormous and varied, true enough. Fat lot of good that had done anybody for the past thirty years. Mama had despaired of Papa's compulsion to collect plants, and yet, Papa had gone on collecting just as Mama had gone on having babies.

"Competing with the London shops will be difficult," Thorne said, veering away from his prepared remarks. "My brothers fail to grasp how difficult."

"You will need capital."

He rose, better able to think on his feet. "Most assuredly, and it's not as if the Dornings enjoy an intimate acquaintance with the London markets, the London banks, or the London public."

Mrs. Summerfield remained serenely situated in her chair. "And you think I am?"

She made an occasional foray into London. Nobody in this corner of Dorset could undertake travel without every neighbor wishing them a safe journey.

"I think you are the best-smelling woman I have ever sniffed."

He'd surprised—and mortified—himself with that admission, but he'd apparently surprised her too.

"Thank you, I think, though as an acting steward, you are more likely to encounter the scent of a hog wallow than damask roses. What exactly is it you've come here to ask me, Mr. Dorning?"

"I don't go around sniffing women," he said, pausing by the daffodils. "But your fragrances have captured my attention. I can close my eyes and know if you're among the congregation on Sunday morning on the strength of your perfumes."

"And here we thought you were napping."

Sometimes he dozed, soothed by the scent of her in the next pew behind him. "You are as likely to arrive at the village fete wearing something lemony as you are wearing a sandalwood scent, and both will be exquisite. I cannot predict what perfume you will choose, but your selections are like different signatures written in the same hand. I know them to be yours without knowing how I know them to be yours."

Now she got to her feet. "I am flattered, Mr. Dorning. The word exquisite has probably never been applied to anything about me, though I fail to see—"

"Somebody on this estate is a genius at developing scents," Thorne said, facing her. "Somebody has a combination of skill and artistic insight that eclipses any olfactory talent I have ever encountered. I want to hire that person."

This time when she hesitated, she didn't appear to be consulting an inner sense of etiquette to determine which courtesy the moment required, but rather, she appeared flustered—intriguingly flustered.

"I am sorry, Mr. Dorning. While your comments are flattering, and I agree with you—the scents I wear are unique—I am not in a position to grant your request. I'll show you out."

*No, you will not.* "My brothers believe any old lotion or salve will sell, provided Oak can design a pretty label for it. They believe all lavenders are the same."

"All lavenders are different," she retorted. "The same parent plant will produce different fragrances in its offspring, depending on the conditions where they are cultivated. Rainfall, sunshine, the soil quality, density of planting, even the crop that last occupied the same plot can affect the results."

"Did your herbalist teach you that?"

They were face-to-face, and though Thorne did *not* go around sniffing women in the usual course, he did inhale through his nose: jasmine hiding under a veil of neroli with a hint of green tea, but the rest of it...

"I again wish you well, Mr. Dorning, but I am not in a position to assist you."

"I will beg, if you require that indignity of me." More unrehearsed foolishness, though for his family, Thorne would make a fool of himself ten times over. "Who blends your scents, and what must I do to gain access to his or her expertise?"

God, she smelled wonderful. Distractingly, maddeningly wonderful, though her gaze offered no quarter.

"I cannot assist you. I'll see you to the—"

A loud crash, suggesting porcelain dropped from a great height, came from the next room along with a shout.

"Aunt Margaret, come! Please come quickly!"

Thorne was out the door three steps ahead of the lady, who followed at an indecorous dash.

PLEASE LET them be unharmed alternated in Margaret's mind with Why must the children create havoc now? When she crowded past Mr. Dorning into the family parlor, her lament switched to I will kill them ere they gain their majorities.

"What is going on here?" she snapped.

"I'd say"—Mr. Dorning sauntered over to the glass-fronted porcelain cabinet—"somebody's army sought a good vantage point from which to ambush advancing forces. Is that what you're doing up there?"

A white-faced Greta peered down at him from the top of the cabinet. "I'm a t-tiger of the vast Asian steppes."

"You are a girl who will go without supper tonight," Margaret said. "That vase belonged to your Grandmother Summerfield."

The vase, which had been stored atop the cabinet for safety, lay in pieces on the hearth.

"Better the vase than a child's skull," Mr. Dorning said, as if children routinely climbed seven-foot-tall furniture unassisted. "How did you get up there?"

"She climbed the doorjamb," Adriana said. "I gave her a boost."

"Loyal of you," Mr. Dorning observed, holding up his arms. "Down you go, child."

Greta shrank back against the wall as if she were in truth a distressed wild creature. "I can't."

"You cannot spend the rest of your life atop the furniture, my girl." He swept a graceful bow. "Mr. Hawthorne Dorning, at your service. I occupy myself clearing ditches, laying hedges, stacking hay, riding the fields, and am otherwise engaged in manual labor. That must be our secret, for as an earl's son, I'm supposed to be a gentleman. The result, though, is that I am quite strong enough to get you safely down."

The effect of this odd speech—the longest Margaret had ever heard from Hawthorne Dorning—was to catch Greta's attention.

"Hawthorne is a funny name. I'm Greta."

"What you are is stuck, young lady." The situation seemed to amuse Mr. Dorning.

"You could have broken your neck," Adriana said, just as Margaret thought the same words. Adriana took Margaret's hand. "I told you not to climb that high."

"Ah, but you did give your sister a boost," Mr. Dorning said. "Perhaps you will assist her to clean up the mess, once we get her down from her aerie."

Margaret's heart was thumping, her mouth had gone dry, and she was on the verge of summoning footmen—though what could they do?—when Mr. Dorning held up his arms again.

"Down you go, Miss Greta. *Now.* I promise not to drop you."

He knew how to blend a casual assumption of obedience with a comforting hint of amusement. Plucking children from dangerous heights was just another chore to be tended to, along with the ditches, hedges, and tenant calls. He did not, however, know the lengths Greta went to avoid contact with strangers.

The girl sat up, so her stockinged feet dangled down the front of the cabinet and her head nearly touched the molding. Mr. Dorning put his hands on her waist—gracious, he was tall—and then he hefted Greta to his hip, stepping free of the shattered vase.

"The next order of business," he said, tapping Greta's nose with one gentle finger, "is an apology to your aunt. You gave her a fright."

Greta stared at the floor. She darted a glance at Adriana. She gazed up at the top of the breakfront. She remained snuggled against her rescuer, when Margaret had been certain Greta would scramble free at the first opportunity.

"I should not have climbed on the furniture... again." She rested her head against Mr. Dorning's shoulder. "I am sorry."

*What am I to do with you?* Margaret had asked that question any number of times. She wasn't about to ask it while Mr. Dorning toed through shattered porcelain.

"Both of you wait for me in the schoolroom," she said as Mr. Dorning set Greta on her feet well clear of the wreckage. "We'll discuss this later."

The girls were running for the door before she could remind them to bid a civil farewell to their guest.

"Were you ever that lively?" Mr. Dorning asked as small feet pelted up the corridor.

"I had no sister to inspire me to great feats of foolishness. I apologize for their lack of manners, Mr. Dorning."

He used the side of his boot to scrape the porcelain into a pile. "Don't be ridiculous. They are barely of age for the schoolroom. It took years to put the manners on me and my brothers, and in the case of our youngest, the project is not yet complete. Greta must be quite nimble to have climbed to the top of the doorjamb."

"She's a terror. I get on better with Adriana." Anybody would get on well with Adriana, while Greta... Greta was a dear, lovable, exasperating challenge.

"That might change. I thought my father the dullest man in the realm until he took me with him to hike the fells in the Whinlatter region. I was about twelve and a perfect age to be outdoors for weeks at a time. My height meant the guides treated me as if I were older. I had a grand adventure and have been wandering around out of doors ever since."

The memory inspired him to smile, which was no help at all for Margaret's tattered composure. Hawthorne was the largest of the seven Dorning brothers, though they were all sizable specimens. Margaret occasionally came across Mr. Oak Dorning out sketching, and Mr. Valerian Dorning was a hopeless flirt.

More than Margaret avoided most of her neighbors, she avoided

Hawthorne, and he'd apparently been happy to avoid her as well. And yet, his smile was startlingly sweet and a little wistful.

*He would be an excellent father.*

Ridiculous thought. "I regret that our drama of the day involved you," Margaret said, taking a path toward the door. "Thank you, though, for plucking Greta to safety. The footmen would likely have fetched a ladder, scratched the wallpaper, and taken all day to do it."

Mr. Dorning ambled along at her side. "You will make the children clean up the mess, or at least try to?"

"I should, shouldn't I?"

"To put right what we have put wrong is a relief, which leads me to ask: Have I put matters between us wrong, Mrs. Summerfield?"

*I have underestimated him.* Many people had a fine sense of smell, but they ignored it. Their noses busily collected all manner of information—the milk was going off, the stain on the carpet was brandy that had probably spilled the previous evening, the iron had been too hot when applied to a man's starched cravat—but those perceptions were ignored.

Mr. Dorning did not ignore his perceptions, apparently.

"I prefer to keep to myself," Margaret said. "I am aware of no source of ill will that should affect our neighborly civilities." She sounded like a dratted lawyer, implying a truth opposite the plain meaning of her words.

He paused with her by the front door and collected his spurs from the sideboard.

"Might I call on you again? Perhaps you cannot share recipes with me, or allow me to hire away your herbalist or housekeeper, but even an occasional consultation regarding scent-making could be helpful."

"Surely the late countess had her own recipes, Mr. Dorning."

He sat on the chair intended for the porter, crossed an ankle over a knee, and strapped on a spur. His movements were easy, a man comfortable in his own body. Charles had never had this sort of relaxed grace, though he had been accounted an excellent dancer before his illness progressed.

"The housekeeper might have a few recipes of my late mother's somewhere," he said, affixing the second spur. "That is a good thought. My sisters might even know where those recipes are. I'll ask them."

He rose, and if he meant to say more, Margaret could not afford to give him the chance. She passed him his hat and crop and opened the front door.

"I'll wish you—why on earth is *he* paying a call now?" Bancroft Summerfield's coach and four was tooling up the drive, leaving a plume of dust in the spring air.

"I don't recognize the equipage," Mr. Dorning said. "The offside leader is flirting with lameness, though."

Margaret wanted to slam and lock the door, but it was too late for that. "I never did offer you tea, Mr. Dorning. Might you stay for a cup?"

The coach in the drive rocked to a halt. Two footmen hopped down from the boot, the first scampering forward to hold the leaders' bridles, the second setting the steps before the coach door.

"Say you'll stay, please. I was most rude to neglect to offer you refreshment."

Mr. Dorning set his hat and crop back on the sideboard. "You have something I want, Mrs. Summerfield."

She could not give up her recipes, but neither could she face her brother-in-law alone. "Name it."

"I'd like your waltz at the spring assembly."

Margaret was too relieved to be dumbstruck. "You have it, provided you can look harmless and friendly for the next half hour."

A man as robust as Mr. Dorning should not have been capable of simpering, but Mr. Dorning managed it convincingly.

"Mrs. Summerfield, I *am* harmless and friendly."

*Hah.* "Bancroft Summerfield is neither. My apologies in advance."

# CHAPTER TWO

In Hawthorne's experience, Mr. Bancroft Summerfield was one of those neighbors whose purpose was to annoy the entire shire and thus provide a topic upon which all agreed, even those who could not agree on anything else. Hawthorne avoided him, though in some circumstances—church services, company dinners—that strategy was impossible.

"He's always in a hurry," Mrs. Summerfield murmured as Bancroft bustled forth from his coach.

"Important men have many demands on their time," Thorne murmured.

Mrs. Summerfield sent him the same look his siblings wore when he sat with the dowagers at the assemblies. *Are you daft?* The elderly always had the best gossip and the naughtiest jokes. Why not sit with them?

"Bancroft, welcome," Mrs. Summerfield said, curtseying when her brother-in-law's brisk progress brought him to the front door. "I believe you know Mr. Hawthorne Dorning. He arrived not five minutes before your coach turned up the drive."

She declined to extend her hand to her caller, which was curious between family members, and she'd told a deliberate falsehood. From Margaret Summerfield, that was downright odd.

Thorne endured the civilities and trundled back to the blue parlor, dutifully inquiring after Bancroft's plans for planting—it was that time of year, after all—and how lambing had gone for him.

"How does one answer such a question?" Bancroft replied, taking a wing chair before his hostess had invited him to sit. "Lambs arrive. They either thrive or they don't, and I cannot concern myself with the particulars. One has a steward to whom such an inquiry might be better directed. Are we having tea?"

Bancroft attempted an air of bluff good cheer, but that little speech was a dig at Thorne—an earl's son as likely to mend stone walls as clear ditches.

"Tea would be appreciated," Thorne said. "Spring mornings can be deceptively chilly. Is that a new coach, Summerfield?"

Mrs. Summerfield gave the bell-pull a tug.

"My coach is not new. I've had it since Yuletide. Honeywill's workmanship, finest coachmakers in London. What brings you to dear Margaret's doorstep on this fine day, Dorning?"

*None of your bloody business.* Thorne never lied, but he could choose among relevant truths. "Mrs. Summerfield and I occasionally have business, as neighbors do. Fences, water rights, herds and flocks, that sort of thing."

"You may bring those concerns to my steward in future," Bancroft said. "Margaret has quite enough on her hands managing the children. You must not expect her to play the part of a country squire in addition to her other responsibilities."

Bancroft beamed at Mrs. Summerfield as if she should thank him for meddling.

"Nonsense, Bancroft," she replied, twisting a gold ring around the fourth finger of her left hand. "A pleasant chat with a neighbor is no hardship. The acreage here is hardly extensive, and you live a good twelve miles away."

"Nonetheless." Bancroft held up a gloved hand. "Nonetheless, I take a sincere interest in this household, as dear Charles would have wanted me to do. If you'd rather not deal with Mr. Dorning, all you need do is send me a note, my dear."

That offer was odd and blunt to the point of rudeness. The tea tray arrived, which inspired Bancroft to criticize the temperature of the tea (not hot enough), its strength (too strong), and the quality of the tea cakes (too small and on the dry side). Thorne was on the point of excusing himself when Bancroft paused in the middle of a diatribe on the dishonesty of coachmen to peer at Thorne's boots.

"Are those spurs I see, Dorning? I know we're in the country, but spurs are not worn indoors."

"Abject apologies," Thorne said. "An oversight. My sisters would be ashamed of me."

"Well, get thee hence and remove them, sir, at once."

Thorne would have cheerfully obliged, but Mrs. Summerfield was gripping her tea cup much too tightly. Bancroft wanted a moment alone with his sister-in-law, who apparently did not want to be alone with him.

"I'll be careful of the upholstery," Thorne said, "and I'm sure we'll both soon be on our way."

"Don't let us keep you," Bancroft replied. "If you're to mind all of Lord Casriel's tenancies and farms, I'm sure you have someplace else to be."

Thorne took a leisurely sip of hot, aromatic tea. "We don't start planting until next week. I'm happy to enjoy my neighbor's company and these excellent tea cakes a little while longer."

Bancroft's smile faltered. "As it happens, I cannot afford to tarry here. I am preparing to leave for London, Margaret, and wanted to alert you to my plans. The Season calls, and I need a few adjustments made to my coach. The bumpkins here in Dorset cannot be entrusted with so fine a vehicle."

*Oh, for pity's sake.* "You'd best have your groom pick the stone from your offside leader's right front hoof before you leave," Thorne said, holding out his tea cup for a refill. "A stone bruise can easily abscess, particularly if a horse is made to travel any distance with the stone in his shoe."

"Point noted, Dorning. Will you be going up to Town this spring?"

*Not if you'll be there.* "Lord Casriel and his new countess are tending to the social chores on behalf of the family, and my brothers Sycamore and Ash yet bide in London. I will enjoy the glories of spring in Dorsetshire, thank the heavenly powers."

"Perhaps I'll call on the earl while I'm in Town," Bancroft said, rising. "The demands on one's time are without end in London. One must retire to the country in defense of one's health, but first, one must attend to the obligations of one's station. My dear, I will call upon you when I return, and you may write to me at the town house if you need anything."

He kissed Mrs. Summerfield's cheek, bowed to Thorne, and took himself off.

Thorne's hostess sank back in her chair, saying nothing even after the front door had banged shut.

"Your Charles was such a decent fellow," Thorne said. "Bancroft is every bit as handsome as Charles was, but it's hard to believe he and Bancroft sprang from the same roots. Have a tea cake. They're quite good."

Mrs. Summerfield took a sip of her tea. "Not too dry?"

Thorne passed her a cake flavored with lemon and ginger. "Of course not, and the tea is neither too hot nor too strong, but Bancroft is a tribulation in breeches. Why didn't he ask to see his nieces?"

"He doesn't care about them, a consolation if ever there was one." She dipped her cake into her tea and took a bite.

Bancroft's call had apparently exhausted Mrs. Summerfield's usual reserve. "You don't care for him," Thorne said.

"He is, as you say, not the best company. In some ways, he and Charles were chalk and cheese."

Thorne would have bet money that she loathed her brother-in-law. "At least he's off to London for the nonce. The entire parish will wish him Godspeed."

A smile blossomed, first in Mrs. Summerfield's eyes, then subtly over the rest of her features. The change was remarkable, turning a severe countenance mischievous. She wasn't pretty in any typical sense, but when she smiled like that, she was...

Not quite alluring, but certainly interesting.

"I wish him Godspeed as well," she said, "but he's too much of a pinchpenny to spend the whole spring in London. He will, though, be gone for weeks, you're right. What a lovely thought."

She finished her tea cake. Thorne finished his tea. "Have you devised a suitable punishment for your ruffian nieces?"

"An illustrated essay on tigers for Greta, I think," Mrs. Summerfield said. "For Adriana..."

"A poem," Thorne suggested, "and it has to rhyme. In my youth, I regarded poetry as a purgatory devised especially for restless boys. Adriana looks like she enjoys verse."

"You can tell that by looking at her?"

"She is watchful, and poets must be perceptive if they are to turn their talents to good effect." He had another tea cake because the social call he'd been dreading had become oddly enjoyable. "You will keep your promise?"

Mrs. Summerfield set down her cup and saucer. "My promise?"

"About the waltz. I like to dance, but so few women can accommodate my height. I feel as if most of them would have an easier time if they stood on my dancing slippers and let me galumph about."

"Is that why you sit out so many sets among the dowagers?"

She'd noticed him hiding among the fans and turbans, had she? "In part. I also like the company of my elders."

"And you get on well with children."

This was apparently not well done of him. "I like children."

"I will keep my promise, Mr. Dorning. I apologize again for Bancroft's rudeness. It's not personal."

Well, yes, some of it had been—quite personal. Thorne rose rather than make that impolite observation.

"I'll look forward to our waltz, and if I should see a pair of small figures trudging along the bridle path, their worldly goods bundled into their kerchiefs, I'll know that poetry and literary punishments got the better of two intrepid little soldiers."

Mrs. Summerfield accompanied him to the front door. Whereas previously Thorne had had the sense she'd wanted to make certain he was departing, now her company felt almost friendly.

"Thank you again, Mr. Dorning, for enduring Bancroft's call with me. That was gallant of you."

Thorne bowed over the lady's hand. "I do know how to sabotage a coach, madam, as does my brother Sycamore. We could render Bancroft's return to the country much more difficult than he anticipates."

"Good to know."

Thorne had been joking. The lady had been in earnest. He parted from her on the front steps of her house, where she waited as he swung into Gowain's saddle and trotted off to Dorning Hall. Two questions followed him, much as Captain lolloped at Gowain's heels.

First, why wouldn't Mrs. Summerfield even discuss sharing her perfume recipes? Thorne was prepared to make the exchange lucrative for her, but she hadn't let him get even far enough to mention remuneration.

The other interesting aspect of the visit was none of Thorne's business, but had piqued his curiosity. Nobody liked Bancroft Summerfield, but he was merely a busybody, an officious pest, and every neighborhood had a few of those.

Mrs. Summerfield not only disliked Bancroft, she was afraid of him, though Thorne could not for the life of him think why that should be.

"OAK, my dear, you have outdone yourself," Valerian said, leaning closer to peer at the canvas. "You've taken an old pile of rocks and turned it into a promise of moonlight trysts and fervent kisses."

Oak poured turpentine into a glass jar and one by one deposited his brushes into the jar. "But will the ladies see it like that?"

"God help us, with this botanical venture we are dependent on the opinions of females, aren't we?" This plan to turn Dorning Hall into a glorified emporium of herbal potions was Casriel's. As the title-holder, he'd been loath to engage in trade per se, though not out of snobbery.

The Dorning offspring, raised by a passionate amateur botanist in bucolic Dorsetshire, simply had little business expertise outside the streams of commerce generated by a large rural estate. Casriel had come up with an enterprise that relied upon the family's ample agricultural resources to take advantage of London's enormous urban markets.

Or that was the theory.

"Casriel's scheme depends on the very weather," Oak retorted, swirling his brushes. "We are dependent on the roads, on the French taking years to get back on their feet, on my art, Ash's charm, and your ability to keep us all organized."

"And on Thorne's hard work." Of all the younger brothers, only Thorne had inherited the previous earl's love for the land itself. "Is this image of the abbey ruins a bit gloomy?"

Oak left the brushes to soak and went about his studio gathering up the odd scrap of paper and paint-speckled cloth. "When trying to minimize costs, a nightscape that lends itself to monochrome prints makes sense."

"But what I see as romantic, the ladies might see as eerie. I see a place to meet a lover, while the ladies might see a place for brigands to lurk."

Oak corked his jug of turpentine. His studio, an eastern attic on the topmost floor of the cottage he and Valerian shared, was both airy and cluttered. An open window let in the brisk air, and a rubbish barrel was nearly overflowing by the door.

"I can always sell it," he said, considering his painting. "Let's ask Thorne what he thinks."

"We don't have to ask him," Valerian said as the man himself came cantering up the drive. "Thorne, being Thorne, will oblige us with his unsolicited opinion."

Oak snatched a rag from a table littered with jars of paint, boxes of pigment, more brushes, and lengths of wood and wiped his hands. "And Thorne will usually be right."

Thorne had been right that building an herbal manufactory from the remains of the dower house would take months rather than weeks. He'd been right that London apothecaries weren't interested in adding yet another bottle of lavender water to shelves already crowded with versions of the same product.

"Thorne is very good at telling us what won't work, I agree," Valerian said. "I wish to heaven we had some idea about what *will* work."

Other canvases were displayed around the room, a few on easels, more on the walls. Oak had to paint the way Thorne had to ride their acres and Willow had to commune with his canines.

"Shall we go down to lunch?" Oak asked. "I forget to eat when I'm painting."

"Forgetting to eat is unnatural," Valerian said. "But then, you are exposed to paint fumes and other noisome smells far too regularly. Doubtless, your wits have become addled."

"Your store of insults has become stale," Oak said, tossing the rag at the barrel and missing. "You forgot the part about what few wits I was born with. Where has Thorne been?"

"Paying a social call."

They took the stairs down through the house. Complaisance Cottage had eight bedrooms and wonderful views, being situated on a hill overlooking Dorning Hall. Thorne's household—the steward's cottage—occupied the other side of the hill. Both residences relied upon the Hall's stables, kitchen gardens, and home farm, though the earl and countess would have the family seat itself to themselves.

If they ever bestirred themselves to come down from Town.

"Are we ready for planting?" Valerian asked.

"What do you think?" Oak replied.

Thorne looked forward to planting, to the backbreaking labor of turning cold, damp earth for seeding, to the inevitable machinery malfunctions that he always managed to repair after liberal applications of profanity and ingenuity.

"Do you ever get tired of it?" Valerian asked as they filed into the dining room.

Oak went to the washstand in the corner. "It?"

"Planting, clearing the damned irrigation ditches. Spring assembly. Shearing, laying hedges, haying, weeding, midsummer assembly. Weeding, weeding, weeding. Planting the winter crops. Corn harvest. Autumn assembly. Penning the sheep. Moving the sheep. Orchard harvest. Clearing the damned ditches again. Yuletide. Winter assembly. Lambing. Sheep to pasture. Planting…"

"Life in a nutshell," Thorne said from the doorway, and clearly, that life pleased him. "I made progress with Mrs. Summerfield."

He swiped his fingers through the soap and scrubbed up a lather on his hands. Thorne had calluses on his calluses, while Oak's hands were those of a skilled artist.

"When I am around Mrs. Summerfield," Oak replied, "I have the sense that the male gender generally has disappointed her somehow. Pretty woman, though. Can't deny she's attractive."

"You think a bowl of apples is pretty," Thorne said.

"How did you make progress?" Valerian asked, taking his turn at the wash basin. "You went there to steal her herbalist to make us perfumes, and you've come back smelling like your horse."

Thorne took a bowl and plate from the sideboard, served himself some lentil and potato soup, and sat to the left of the head of the table. Oak took the foot, leaving Valerian to sit across from Thorne. If

Ash were on the property, he'd sit beside one of his brothers rather than take the place at the head of the table.

"I went there to begin a dialogue with her," Thorne said, taking a ham and cheese sandwich from the tray in the center of the table. "Matters took an interesting turn when Bancroft Summerfield showed up."

"Bane-croft," Oak muttered, taking a sandwich for himself. "I don't like him, and I can't say exactly why."

"He excels at the subtle insult," Valerian said. "'Such a pity you can't rebuild the dower house, but materials have become so dear, haven't they?' That sort of thing."

"Tell us about Mrs. Summerfield," Oak said, tossing a bit of salt into his soup. "How exactly did you make progress? What is your objective where she's concerned?"

Thorne dipped a corner of his sandwich in his soup. "I'm considering courting her."

Valerian prided himself on his manners, but only a swift application of his table napkin to his mouth prevented him from spluttering ale all over his meal.

# CHAPTER THREE

"Who was the tall man?" Adriana asked.

"Mr. Hawthorne Dorning is our neighbor," Margaret replied. "Fenny, you have time for a cup of tea with Mrs. Blevins."

Miss Fenner, a young lady of enviable patience and good humor, popped a curtsey. "My thanks, ma'am." She was out the door as if late for the upcoming assembly rather than going below stairs for a chat with the housekeeper over a quick cup of tea.

"Mr. Dorning was very strong," Adriana announced. "He had dark hair. My papa had dark hair."

Greta was at her desk, pencil poised over a piece of foolscap. When absorbed in a task, she had the ability to ignore everything, including Margaret's lectures and threats.

Margaret had wood fires burned in the nursery, an extravagance, but she believed the children were healthier for it—and wood smelled ever so much nicer than coal. A slight mustiness in the air suggested the carpet needed a thorough beating, and a lingering scent of chamomile indicated Miss Fenner had recently washed her hair.

"How is your poem coming along?" Margaret asked.

"I finished it," Adriana replied, skipping a circle around the hearth rug. "Do you want to hear it?"

"No." That from Greta, who hadn't even looked up.

"Why aren't you ever nice?" Adriana retorted. "I said I boosted you onto the cabinet. I admitted it. I am being punished too. You should be nice."

Greta aimed a look at Adriana that portended pigtails dipped in inkwells and a favorite doll going missing. Warfare in the nursery was serious business, though Miss Fenner assured Margaret such behavior was normal. Adriana was more articulate with verbal slings and arrows. Greta had the gift of greater strategy.

"Uncle has dark hair," Greta muttered, hunching closer to her paper.

"What was *he* doing here?" Adriana asked, skipping another circle. The nursery was large, a good twenty feet by twenty feet, but one skipping child made the room too small.

"Bancroft is your uncle. He calls because he is family." Blast the luck.

Adriana came to a halt. "Mr. Dorning is handsome."

He wasn't, particularly. His build was that of a plowman—rangy and muscular. He moved like a man comfortable traversing the fields and woods, not like a mincing aristocrat. His eyes were his most arresting feature, shading violet when he was out of doors and a deep blue otherwise.

He was tall, strong, sensible, and dealt easily with fractious children. His eyebrows might grow fierce and his features craggy as he aged, but his rare smiles would still have the power to charm.

Not that Margaret had any use for charming men.

"He is strong," Greta said, frowning at her paper. "He is not afraid of a broken vase."

Margaret peered over Greta's shoulder. "Is that why you did not jump down? Because of the broken porcelain?" If so, thank heavens, because a seven-foot leap could have resulted in injury. Bancroft would have used that pretext for any number of harangues.

"I was too high," Greta said, shading in a stripe on a tiger stalking across her page. "I should have climbed back down, but I couldn't."

Margaret risked a pat to Greta's shoulder. "I'm glad you didn't try to jump or climb down. Mr. Dorning's assistance was timely and easily rendered."

Greta bore the pat, still focused on her tigers. Two beasts prowled among what was doubtless supposed to be a lush jungle. Their proportions were all wrong, with bearlike shoulders, enormous paws, and fangs that defied practical use, but what struck Margaret was their eyes.

These were furious tigers.

Adriana began hopping one-footed in a random pattern. "You should not have climbed onto the cabinet, but you would not listen to me."

"I wanted to see from high up, like a grown-up. The big tiger is Grendel."

"A fine name for such a grand fellow," Margaret said. "And the other tiger?"

"Cyclops."

"Does he have one eye?" Adriana panted.

Greta took up an eraser. "She does now."

"Can a cyclops be a she, Aunt Margaret?"

"Of course. If women can be two-eyed or blind, they can certainly be one-eyed."

Greta liked that answer. Her smile was slight and fleeting, but she was a logical child for all her fanciful imagination.

"Uncle stopped by to tell me some news," Margaret said.

"Bad news?" Adriana asked, going still. "Is he moving here?"

He'd threatened that in the past and threatened to move Margaret and the girls from Summerton to the Summerfield family seat. A pointed reference to the precise wording of Charles's will had stopped those threats, for now. Charles had been the girls' guardian prior to his death, and his wishes regarding their welfare were still controlling.

"Your Uncle Bancroft will soon be off to London for a few weeks."

"He will come back," Greta said. "He always comes back."

Margaret tried to present Bancroft in a positive light to the children. He was their uncle. If anything happened to her, God forbid, he would become their sole guardian. That too, was a function of Charles's will.

"You can write to him," Margaret said. "A lady maintains correspondence with her family."

"I will write to Mr. Dorning," Greta said. "I will thank him for helping me. I can draw him a tiger with pretty eyes."

That pronouncement was more socially appropriate than any Greta had made to date, though of course a young lady ought not to correspond with men outside her family.

"I will write to him too!" Adriana said. "I will draw him a dog. He has a dog."

"You need not write to him," Margaret said. "I will see him at the assembly, and I can convey your gratitude."

She hated stifling Greta's overture, but writing to Mr. Dorning was not well advised.

"A note of thanks is always appreciated," Greta said, doubtless parroting Margaret herself. She set aside her illustrated essay and took out another piece of paper. "A lady maintains her despondence."

*Oh, did she ever.* "True, but Mr. Dorning is not related to you, so you are limited to enclosing a note of thanks inside my own letter to him." Some people begrudged even a widow that much latitude. Thank heavens country manners were more permissive than the London variety.

"Then you must write him a note," Adriana said, dashing to her desk. "And I can send my picture with your letter too."

The last person—the very last, possible person—Margaret should be extending cordial overtures to was Hawthorne Dorning, and yet, they were to share a waltz. She could plead a sore ankle or a megrim, though the assembly was one of few social outings she allowed herself. If she missed the assembly, that would cause talk, and talk was to be avoided at all costs.

"Uncle is away to London." Greta's observation should have been apropos of nothing. With the uncanny intuition of the very young, she'd instead lit upon a salient fact.

"We will write to Uncle and to Mr. Dorning," Margaret said.

"Mr. Dorning's letter first." Adriana helped herself to three pieces of paper.

"Aunt must use ink, and we have none," Greta said.

"Aunt can write a practice letter. We always write practice letters."

"Very well," Margaret said. "I will write a practice letter, then we will clean up the mess in the green parlor. If your efforts are satisfactory, we can take a walk down to the cottage to inspect the daffodils."

An air of peaceful industry settled over the nursery, though Margaret's practice letter was a surprising challenge to draft. She could not tell Mr. Dorning to eschew future calls, though it would be better if he did. She could not tell him that he was the neighbor she most enjoyed spending time with, though that would also be true.

He had a quiet competence that solved problems without a fuss and took difficulties in stride. Charles had been such a man, though he'd lacked Hawthorne Dorning's robust physical presence. Taken on his own, Charles had been a fine specimen of manhood, well mannered and attractive.

Next to Mr. Dorning, Charles's memory was that of a riding horse compared to a draft animal. The one, when healthy, was serviceable and handsome, as domestic animals went. The other was powerful in its own right.

Domestic by choice, rather than breeding.

"You aren't writing anything," Greta said.

"I'm thinking."

*Mr. Dorning, Thank you for rescuing my dear Greta from certain peril...*

Too dramatic.

*Your call was most appreciated...*

Too friendly.

Margaret sat on a hard chair, pencil in hand, for some moments, then jotted a few lines along with a quick, *My thanks—Mrs. Charles Summerfield.*

Copying the note using the ink in Miss Fenner's desk was the work of a moment, and then it was time to liberate the captives from the nursery.

Margaret left the house with the same sense of relief she always felt when she gained the out of doors, especially when her travels took her through the garden, past the glass house, and into the wilder reaches of her property.

The cottage beyond her garden might once have been a game-keeper's or steward's home, but it sat empty now. Margaret used it as her herbal and her retreat from life's challenges.

The day was a buffet of spring scents: Manure had been spread on somebody's fields upwind, trees unfurled their leaves into an increasingly strong sun. No flowers bloomed in the garden yet, but the Holland bulbs were making a show, overlaying the smell of damp, turned earth or the occasional brush pile set to burn.

"Will Mr. Dorning call again?" Adriana asked, swinging Margaret's hand as they left the garden proper.

"Not anytime soon," Margaret said. "This time of year is very busy when a man's responsibility is caring for the land." She'd been daft to give him a waltz, truly.

Greta seized her by the other hand. "The first daffodil might have bloomed. The sun makes them do that, and it's a sunny day."

A beautiful day, and that Greta would take Margaret's hand made it only more so. But then... Greta had not objected to being held by Mr. Dorning, not even a little.

"Perhaps the first daffodil has bloomed," Margaret said. "We can take turns sniffing it, but we must leave it to thrive with its sisters."

As Margaret must content herself with sparing Mr. Dorning a single unremarkable waltz.

THORNE WAS ASTONISHED to realize that Oak had been right. Oak was often right, though he seldom ventured opinions on contentious topics. The topic in question—Margaret Summerfield—stood across the assembly room, taking coats and caps from her neighbors as they filed in the door.

To each arrival, she handed out a smile, some teasing, some sweet, some kind. How had Thorne not noticed that Margaret Summerfield was attractive, and especially when she smiled?

And the lady was hiding behind a mundane, helpful task that prevented her conversation from progressing past superficial socializing. Did she do this at every assembly, and if so, why?

"Staring is rude." Valerian passed Thorne a cup of punch that savored of apples and brandy.

"She's pretty," Thorne replied, taking a cautious sip of his drink. "And I'm not staring, I'm appreciating. Our publican has once again done the impossible and managed to turn a lowly libation into an incendiary brew."

"Which means all the young sprigs will be laid out on the green within an hour, leaving thee and me to keep the ladies happy."

Valerian looked harmless with his lacy cuffs, elegant coat, and charming smile. Thorne knew better.

"You have that look," Valerian murmured.

"This is my I-took-a-bath look. You are simply accustomed to seeing me covered in dust, chaff, and horsehair."

"You look like you're planning something. You wore the same expression when you decided to dam the stream to create a water meadow below the yearling pasture. The same look as when you decided to breed Tatiana to Mrs. Summerfield's stud."

"Both projects turned out splendidly. What's your point?"

"Courting a woman who doesn't care for you is not only very uphill work, Thorne, it embarrasses your siblings and is annoying to the lady."

Something, or somebody, annoyed Margaret Summerfield. Thorne's money was on her brother-in-law.

A large group had arrived, all gathered around the door. Thorne passed Valerian his drink. "Consume that at your peril." He crossed the room, took the place beside Mrs. Summerfield, and reached for the next coat. "Mr. Mortenson, good evening. I see you brought the entire family."

Four young ladies and their mama smiled and blushed and passed over bonnets and coats. For the next few moments, general greetings meant Mrs. Summerfield could not shoo Thorne off, though as soon as the new arrivals ebbed, she made the attempt.

"Thank you for your assistance, Mr. Dorning, but I can manage from here."

"Is that the Summerfield family motto? 'I can manage from here.' Dornings adhere to the same creed, for the most part."

"The Summerfield family motto is 'No peace without justice.' Hardly original, but pithy."

"You don't have an herbalist," Thorne said. "I asked Mrs. Weller at market on Thursday, and she revealed your little secret."

Mrs. Summerfield's hands, which had been busy untangling the ribbons of a bonnet, went still, then resumed their task.

"Mrs. Weller ought not to gossip about other people's affairs."

"She said your gift with fragrances surpasses genius and approaches divine inspiration." And at eighty-three years old, Hannah Weller was not given to exaggeration. "The salve you made for her rheumatism has given her 'the hands of a sixty-year-old,' to quote her."

"Arnica, comfrey, a few other herbs for scent. A brisk application of heat to the affected joints by virtue of friction on the skin. Most medicine operates on the mind rather than the body."

"However the medicine works, she sang your praises, while you try to hide your abilities. Is that modesty, Mrs. Summerfield, or something else?"

She hung the bonnet on a peg and picked up another from the several on the table before her. "Perhaps I don't want every old woman in the shire importuning me for results I cannot deliver."

Fair enough, and this was not courting talk. "All I want from you is a single waltz, but if this gathering runs true to form, we'll be made to wait the entire night for it. May I fetch you a glass of punch?"

"Please."

Thorne did not care for the tension she conveyed in even a single syllable. He took the bonnet from her and untied the knot in the ribbons.

"All you need do, ma'am, is tell me to absent myself. I have two sisters and many brothers. I also had two parents very much concerned with ensuring I learned my manners. I am trying, in my bumbling way, to converse on some topic other than the weather with a woman whom I have long esteemed. If my company is unwelcome, you simply say so. I will not take offense, sulk, pout, or brood. I will, however, request that you honor the gift of your waltz."

Tonight she wore the scent of orange blossoms, a light, happy fragrance said to presage marital thoughts. Undertones of honey came through, along with a hint of freshly scythed meadows.

"If you would fetch me half a glass of punch, Mr. Dorning, I would be grateful."

"Have I given offense?"

She moved on to another bonnet. "I am much concerned with raising my nieces, and before that, I was in mourning. I have never been a handy conversationalist."

As a younger woman, she'd been as ready with platitudes and chitchat as the next lady, from what Thorne had observed. He brought her the drink—half a glass—as well as a plate of food from the buffet.

Would she have told him if he had given offense? He hoped so.

"Shall we sit?" he asked. "The late arrivals have slowed to a trickle, and they can hang up their own bonnets and caps." The musicians, a pair of fiddlers and a concertina player, would take ample advantage of the buffet and the punchbowl before the dancing began.

"The room is already growing warm," Mrs. Summerfield said. "Let's find some peace and quiet before the melee starts."

She led him outside to the church steps. Others had taken the same notion. A few people were ranged around the benches on the green. Some couples perched in the village's shop doorways. The full moon was rising in the east—assemblies were always timed to take advantage of moonlight—and the night offered a hint of spring's mildness.

"Mr. Merryweather tarried in the forge late today," Mrs. Summerfield said, wrinkling her nose as she settled onto the hard stones. "Mr. Havers has apparently cleaned out his loafing shed."

Thorne took a whiff of the evening air, catching only faint hints of the scents Mrs. Summerfield read like copperplate text. Merryweather was the blacksmith, and his labors put a subtle tang of sulfur and ash on the breeze. Havers worked a large tenant farm directly west of the village and kept a dozen milch cows.

"Is your sense of smell like Oak and colors?" Thorne asked, coming down beside her. "We can't take Oak anywhere that he isn't peering at the sky, scanning the horizon, or studying mud puddles. He lives through his visual perceptions of life and can recite a description of commonplace surrounds that notes every detail and hue you forgot you saw."

"Something like that. I cannot ignore scents or flavors, but especially scents."

"You have a gift, then," Thorne said. "Like a musician, artist, or master chef. Are your nieces similarly astute?"

She held the plate out to him, and Thorne took a slice of bread that had been baked with the dough rolled up around some sort of cheese, tomato, and basil combination. He hadn't noticed the basil when he'd chosen that snack. He couldn't ignore it now.

"You don't know Greta and Adriana, Mr. Dorning."

"I know them to see them at market." Though he seldom had, come to think of it.

Mrs. Summerfield took a nibble of a cinnamon bun. "They can be difficult."

"My mother claimed that boys were awful, but girls were worse, and that was one of her more cheerful pronouncements on the topic of motherhood."

"She had the raising of *nine* children, Mr. Dorning."

"Are Greta and Adriana awful?"

More of the cinnamon bun disappeared. Mrs. Summerfield tore off one bite at a time at a methodical pace. The din from the assembly rooms grew louder, and the moon rose higher.

"Greta is a lady of particulars," Mrs. Summerfield said. "She was named for a Danish great-aunt, and Charles likened her to an old woman, unwilling to be touched, unwilling to eat anything she dislikes, irrationally intolerant of certain fabrics, but able to recall the oddest details no matter how long ago they occurred. She can also quote people verbatim at the most inopportune times."

"She seemed like a perfectly normal little girl to me, but perhaps she does take after her aunt in a few regards."

Mrs. Summerfield gave a slight shiver. She wasn't wearing a cloak or shawl, which had made sense when escaping the close confines of the assembly rooms, but she was apparently chilly now. Thorne slipped off his coat and draped it around her shoulders.

"Am I like a crotchety old woman, Mr. Dorning?"

"Perhaps Greta shares your inability to ignore certain details. A hundred people are in those assembly rooms, getting ready to drink and stomp their evening away. Not a one of them went into that building thinking, 'Merryweather worked late at his forge today.' You, however, could not avoid that conclusion. Nobody likes rough wool against the skin, but perhaps Greta can't ignore it. Maybe what most people regard as a food they don't enjoy is for her a gustatory torment she'll be tasting long after she's gone to bed. Like you, she cannot help the gifts she's been given."

Mrs. Summerfield set the plate aside, though the food wasn't half gone. "You think she's *like me*? I'm only her aunt, Mr. Dorning."

Thorne at first worried that his observation had been yet another conversational blunder, but no. Mrs. Summerfield looked as if he'd passed her a bouquet bearing every beautiful scent in the shire. Pleased, uncertain, *shy.*

"I inherited my height from an uncle," he said. "All the Dorning men are tall, but I'm the living image of Uncle Thomlin, who was also the tallest of his brothers. Oak's artistic talent came from an aunt. Why shouldn't Greta get some of her unique abilities from you?"

"Because I am not related to the twins by blood, Mr. Dorning."

True enough. The girls were not Summerfields by name, but rather, the offspring of a deceased Summerfield sister and her spouse.

"One can influence children by virtue of how they're nurtured. Oak's talent was fostered because Aunt Ida took an interest in him. If Greta and Adriana notice that you have a keen sense of smell, they will become more perceptive about the scents they encounter too."

"You have a point." A point that clearly pleased her.

A violin began to warm up with ascending scales, and the couples on the green drifted toward the assembly room doors, but Thorne wasn't nearly ready to abandon the only topic that had made Margaret Summerfield smile.

"Tell me more about your nieces," he said. "They appear to be great good friends, for all their differences."

"They are," Mrs. Summerfield said, picking up the plate. "I worry about that, about them becoming enemies. They have spats and skirmishes and are again thick as thieves fifteen minutes later. I have no siblings, so this is all quite terrifying to me, but the governess is one of eleven and says we're muddling on exactly as we ought."

Thorne let her chatter about her nieces, who sounded like a pair of hoydens in training to him, though all the while he was also aware of the question he needed to ask when the moment was right.

Mrs. Summerfield had told him in very certain terms that she could not part with any recipes, then she'd sent him a recipe for a concoction of lavender water, one of the most common, humble, useful scents in the herbal. From one perspective, that was no gift at all—every housekeeper likely had half a dozen such recipes—but for Thorne, it was reason to be encouraged.

Margaret Summerfield had sent him a recipe, and that was both a gesture of trust and a foundation upon which he could build.

# CHAPTER FOUR

Even as Charles's illness had progressed, he'd been mannerly, but he'd never lent Margaret his coat on a brisk spring evening. The pleasure of that gesture went beyond the mere comfort of warding off a chill.

When Mr. Dorning had surrendered his coat to her, he'd surrendered a piece of his privacy as well. He was an astute man—more's the pity—and he would know exactly what a garment would tell a woman with her sensitivities about its owner.

His wardrobe was likely lined with cedar and hung with lavender sachets, a bracing, masculine combination. He'd probably polished his own boots prior to the assembly, for the hint of boot black was stronger than if the boots had merely sat outside the wardrobe while their owner dressed.

Mr. Dorning apparently eschewed the use of heavy starch, because that, too, left only a faint trace on the scent of his coat. His shaving soap was intriguing, having elements of both roses and spices, perhaps a hint of nutmeg, but hard to pinpoint among all the scents wafting around the village green.

Margaret could have spent the entire evening sniffing his coat, the collar, the cuffs, the pockets, and even the armpits, though God forbid Bancroft got wind of such behavior. Instead, she passed Mr. Dorning his coat before they returned to the assembly room.

"My thanks," she said. "I'll find you when the waltz comes around."

He bowed, and she affixed her assembly smile to her face—a little gracious, a little gay, but not too much of either. She was a widow and had to navigate between social hedges. Charles had made her promise that she'd remarry, but Charles had also declined to leave her clear title to Summerton or sole guardianship of the girls. Both of those decisions complicated the topic of remarriage.

"There you are." Valerian Dorning was speaking to his brother, who was still at Margaret's side. "I was forced to consume your glass of punch, Hawthorne. You are in my debt."

Margaret had no siblings, no relatives at all, and thus undercurrents between brothers baffled her, and yet, she sensed unspoken communication between Valerian and Hawthorne. Valerian was staring at Hawthorne's chest, for example. What did that mean?

"Mrs. Summerfield," Hawthorne said, doing up his coat buttons, "Valerian is apparently without a partner for the first set. Perhaps you'd take pity on a poor feckless lad and stand up with him?" The poor feckless lad was the best dancer in the shire, according to every chaperone or mama to remark on the matter.

"I would be delighted to."

Valerian offered his arm as Hawthorne finished buttoning his coat, and insight dawned: Valerian, the family dandy, had noticed his brother's coat was unbuttoned. The night air was much cooler than the assembly room, meaning a man would have no reason to unbutton his coat in the out of doors.

Oh. Oh, how *interesting*. Hawthorne Dorning had transgressed strict propriety for Margaret's comfort—which was quite gentlemanly of him—and he didn't care who knew about that or what conclusions they drew.

Which could be a problem.

As a smiling Valerian bowed and Margaret curtseyed, her pleasure refused to fade. Charles had been endlessly gallant. He could
have had many failings instead of a very few, and Margaret would
always treasure his gallantry.

"May I say," Valerian murmured as they joined hands and raised
their arms, "you look positively radiant this evening, Mrs.
Summerfield?"

"You may say nearly anything, Mr. Dorning. I am not constrained
to believe you."

The figure had them turning to their corners, bowing and prome-
nading, then they faced each other and linked hands again.

"Thorne looks like a sturdy, sensible fellow," Valerian said.
"Don't make the mistake of thinking he's just another charming
bachelor."

Valerian was the charming bachelor, but to Margaret, his smiles
were too well timed, the look in his eyes too *My, you are a fascinating
creature!* He was the fascinating creature, and he knew it.

"Do you imply that Hawthorne is not charming, or that he's not a
bachelor, Mr. Dorning?"

Logic turned his smile lopsided, into more of a grin. "He's both,
but he's also a man of tender sentiments and great loyalty. You
mistake him for a widow's plaything at peril to his happiness."

One characteristic Margaret had learned about family was that
family meddled. Witness Bancroft's behavior. He was the only other
relative the girls had. He hovered, implied, and generally made a
nuisance of himself, though Margaret sometimes wondered if he
could have told Greta from Adriana were Margaret to dress them the
same—and they were far from identical in appearance.

Though she never did put them in matching attire. They were
twins, not dolls.

When next Margaret was chasséing at Mr. Dorning's side, she
kept her voice down. "Are you a pot to call kettles black, Mr.
Dorning?"

He missed a step. "I beg your pardon?"

"Miss Fenner is well acquainted with the governesses, companions, and spinsters in the neighborhood, among whom you have a certain reputation. Perhaps you'd best concern yourself with your own behavior, rather than interfering with your brother's socializing."

When the figure called for the couples to step close, Mr. Dorning smiled down at her, his eyes crinkling at the corners, and yet, he spoke through clenched teeth.

"Thorne took off his blasted coat. Next, he would have been feeding you with his fingers in front of half the biddies in the village. I would not want to see either of you become the brunt of talk."

*Feeding me with his fingers?* Charles had never done that either. "Your concern is appreciated, Mr. Dorning, also misplaced. In the years since Mr. Summerfield's death, I have comported myself more than properly. A little picnic on the church terrace hardly imperils my reputation."

The dance steps moved Margaret down the line and Valerian up the line, though in a few more figures, she would face him again.

Were Bancroft not leaving for Town, Margaret might have been a little more circumspect, but truly, how much more circumspect could she be? Hawthorne Dorning was a gentleman and a neighbor. That he'd share a few snacks with her at the assembly or pay an occasional call was hardly remarkable.

Except... both were remarkable, and that Margaret looked forward to waltzing with him was more remarkable still.

THORNE DID NOT CONSIDER himself devious, though a man raised with eight siblings had to learn a bit of strategy. Asking for Margaret Summerfield's waltz was a case in point. Any dance with her would have been an opportunity for conversation, some casual touching, possibly even flirtation. The waltz, however, was the final dance of the evening and the only one that allowed a couple an opportunity for a true discussion.

He had the sense she was small-talked out—he certainly was—and even fatigued after having stood up for nearly every set. The musicians set a slow, lullaby tempo, and the relatively few couples on the floor swung into the pattern.

Thorne liked to dance, and as an earl's son, he'd been taught early and well how to partner a lady. Margaret was taller than most women, and thus dancing with her was more pleasure than duty.

"Tired?" Thorne asked as the fiddles lilted in close harmony.

"Quite. You?"

"I might be late to services tomorrow." The revelers who'd failed to exercise caution at the punchbowl would stay home with megrims, head colds, and other vague ailments. "May I ask you something, Margaret?"

"Mmm?"

She hadn't objected to his use of her given name. That was progress, though she might not have noticed that familiarity, which was... not progress.

"Why did you refuse to share your herbal recipes with me, then send me one the same day?"

"Might we discuss that later?"

Fine idea, when twirling lazily down the floor with her was such a pleasant way to end the evening.

"Shall I call on you?"

She stared at his cravat, which was doubtless no longer the subtle tribute to fashion that Valerian had tied for him hours ago.

"I walked here with the Dinwiddies," she said.

Such was Thorne's preoccupation with maintaining a proper distance from his partner—and no more than a proper distance—that her inference took a moment to sort out.

"I will gladly walk you home," he said. "I'm sure Oak and Valerian can find their way to Dorning Hall without me."

They'd learned years ago not to bring a coach to the assembly unless the weather required it. A toddle home by moonlight helped clear the head and prepare the body for rest. Besides, the distance was less than two miles, and hitching up the coach for such a short jaunt was a ridiculous imposition on the staff.

"That will save the Dinwiddies having to escort me up my driveway."

A good half mile, that drive.

Thorne let the rest of the dance pass without conversation and focused on enjoying closeness to a woman who fit him bodily and who didn't feel compelled to chatter or ask what he'd heard from *the earl in Town*. Casriel was a conscientious correspondent, but also newly married. The earl's younger brothers heard little from him besides admonitions to get the herbal business on solid footing sooner rather than later.

The music came to a close. Thorne bowed, Margaret sank into a deep curtsey, and as Thorne raised her up by the hand, he was struck again by Oak's observation about her beauty. She was a strawberry blonde, not the most fashionable hair color. She was blue-eyed, which again wasn't particularly remarkable on an Englishwoman. Her curves were subtle, and yet... she was attractive.

Some of her allure was her scent, which still tempted Thorne to discreet sniffing hours after she'd arrived at the assembly. Some of it was her manner. Margaret Summerfield didn't indulge in the touches intended to cause a man to notice her. No mannerisms with her fan, no affectations with her gloves, shawls, or parasols. She didn't titter, giggle, laugh, or raise her voice.

She was a *quietly* fetching woman, and she'd invited him to escort her home.

The evening was mild by the standards of Dorset in early spring, and the moon was still well up in the sky. The way home was easy to see, the roads dry, and for the first part of the journey, the Dinwiddie offspring provided steady chatter that gradually slowed.

"We'll bid you good night," Mrs. Dinwiddie said at the foot of Margaret's drive. "Ralph, give me your arm. I vow I am too old for these entertainments."

"Mama, you say that at every assembly," one of the daughters remarked.

"And I echo that sentiment, being several years Mrs. Dinwiddie's senior," Mr. Dinwiddie replied, giving his wife his arm. He bowed to Margaret, winked at Thorne, and led his brood on down the lane.

"I love this time of year," Margaret said. "The world is waking up, even at night."

"The work is expanding to exceed the available hours of daylight," Thorne countered. "Now will you answer my question?"

Margaret set a slow pace up the drive as the Dinwiddies' chatter faded on the night air.

"The recipe I sent you was not mine, but it's a good, simple formula. The scent remains fixed for years, which isn't always the case."

"A scent can change over time?" This was not exactly news to Thorne, but also not something he'd considered. "Do scents ever need time to improve?"

"Sometimes a recipe needs time to mature, as spirits acquire flavor by aging in the right barrels."

Which raised another consideration. "Is the vessel used to store the concoction also a consideration?" Ye gods, this was growing complicated.

"Of course. If everything from wine to whiskey to brandy is affected by the wood chosen for the storage barrels, why would you expect a perfume, say, to behave any differently?"

"I don't drink perfume."

"Glass or ceramic is usually a safe bet."

"I cannot afford bets, Margaret. When it comes to this botanical business, my family cannot afford bets."

The manor house loomed around the next curve, towering maples casting it in moon shadow. The trees weren't entirely leafed out, and Thorne wondered if new leaves had a scent Margaret could detect.

"I don't understand, Mr. Dorning. Cannot afford in what sense?"

"My family calls me Thorne, or Hawthorne if they're being peevish. My brothers and I have been charged by the earl with turning the vast botanical riches of Dorning Hall into a profitable concern. We have raw materials in quantity, thanks to Papa's avocation, but Grey fails to realize that every large estate has many of those same ingredients."

"Is the earldom in difficulties?"

Conversations held by moonlight had a confessional quality, though Thorne would rather have seen Margaret's expression when she posed that question. He trusted her discretion, but what answer was she expecting?

"My father was not a sound manager, though neither was he a profligate spender. He focused on his botany and expected the land rents to cover our expenses, as they have for centuries. Peace on the Continent has changed much, though, and Casriel knows little of complex commerce. Every street corner in London already has an apothecary shop with fully stocked shelves. Wedging our way onto those same shelves, when all we have to offer is lavender water and chamomile lotion, will not be quick or easy."

"Can you open your own shop?"

"That will take money, as will creating the products to ship, as will getting them to London. I had hoped..."

He'd hoped not to talk business all the way up the drive, for one thing.

"You had hoped to bring some unique products to the equation, a few spectacularly impressive scents or soaps."

"Well, yes, except I know more about how to shear a fractious ewe than I do about what constitutes a spectacularly impressive scent. The fragrance you're wearing is lovely."

She slipped her arm free of his. "Orange blossom isn't that unusual."

"But you aren't wearing the typical orange blossom scent. You've tinkered with it somehow, and the result is richer without being heavier."

"You say the nicest things, Mr. Dorning, but I have lost my recipes. I'm sorry."

She was sorry—the reluctance in her voice was genuine—but she was also being untruthful. A woman kept her favorite recipes in her head, at least some of them.

"What if I brought you some recipes to look over?" he said. "Could you advise me as to the probable results?"

She walked along beside him as the quiet deepened. The moon was past its zenith, the trees closer to the house darkened the way, and yet, Thorne was in no hurry to wish her good night.

"Your family expects you to make this venture successful, don't they?" she asked.

"I expect myself to make the venture successful. My brothers are good fellows, and they each bring something to the table. Oak can design beautiful labels, Ash is a very competent accountant, Valerian knows fashion and fashionable people, and Grey, as the earl, gives us a certain cachet."

"Cachet does not create a popular product. What of your youngest brother, Sycamore?"

"He has his hands full with a fancy club, though he can find everything wrong with any suggestion the rest of us make." *Fancy club* being a euphemism for a high-class gaming hell.

Margaret led him to a bench situated beneath one of the maples immediately before the house. "In the first place," she said, taking a seat, "I'd focus on men's fragrances rather than women's. The market for ladies' products is full of fancy French nonsense, and ladies are seldom as free with their coin as men can be. Then too, a man's product is expected to cost more than its feminine variant."

Thorne sat as well, not because the evening was pleasant and he was in the company of a woman he was considering courting, but because those basic facts hadn't occurred to him, and he'd been wrestling with Grey's brilliant proposition for months.

"Focus on *men's* products?"

"You are the Dorning *brothers,* aren't you? Why wouldn't you make products for men? You are men, and you use scents, soaps, pomades, colognes, and so forth. What you know about women's products would probably fill a teaspoon. Then too, your father probably chose plant specimens from a male perspective, not for your mother and sisters."

"How does one gather herbs from a male perspective?"

"Say you are an older fellow with thinning hair." Margaret untied her bonnet and set it beside her on the bench. "You will use your lavender oil, cedar, thyme, and rosemary to create a salve to treat baldness or to make sachets for a man's wardrobe. If you are a lady who tends to have a flushed or choleric complexion, then that lavender will be better used in a skin tonic. Your father was likely more concerned with baldness than women's ailments, and his herbal will reflect that."

Thorne resisted running a hand through his hair. "There is a cure for *baldness?*"

"Not a cure, a treatment, and as with all treatments, results will vary."

Ye gods, a treatment for baldness. "To be honest, I'd thought the market for fragrances broader than the apothecary market."

"Meaning people will spend more money to look and smell beautiful than to be healthy. You are probably right, especially in London. Lord, I'm tired."

"That is a polite reminder that I'm keeping you out when the hour grows late," Thorne said, rising. "I'll see you to your door."

"Please sit for a moment, Mr. Dorning."

*Hawthorne. Please call me Hawthorne.* He sat.

"Medicinals are unpredictable," Margaret said. "I suggest you leave them to the apothecaries and quacks. In my experience, very few patent remedies are worth a farthing. If you'd like me to look over some scents intended for men's soaps, pomades, or colognes, I am willing to do that. I can suggest herbals that include recipes of that nature, and I can explain how to follow the recipes."

"I will accept that generous offer, and on behalf of my family, thank you."

"I do have a request."

"Name it."

"You will not associate me in any public way with your venture. Don't even tell your family. I'll help you as much as I can, but only on an informal basis. Agreed?"

Secrecy sat ill with Thorne, but a legitimate reason to spend more time with Margaret suited his plans well.

"Agreed. I will call upon you by way of the fields rather than come up the lane for all to see, if you prefer."

"I'd like it if you brought me the scent of the fields rather than the dust of the road."

Still, she remained beside him on the bench.

"Margaret, shall I take my leave of you here?" To walk away while she sat alone in the dark also sat ill with him.

"I'm trying to get up my nerve."

Thorne's senses, already attuned to the lady's tone of voice, scent, posture, and words, sharpened further. "I beg your pardon?"

"Oh, you heard me. I'm telling myself that a farewell kiss to your cheek needn't mean much, that a pleasant waltz and a little chat about flowers isn't a very great thing, but to me, it's... I would like to kiss you, Mr. Dorning, to thank you. Or something. I think I would. I haven't kissed anybody for quite some time, but as best I recall, it can be pleasant, interesting, and—"

Thorne scooted around on the bench so she'd not be taken by surprise. He gave her the space of three silent heartbeats to change her mind, offer disclaimers, or break into song, but she merely sat on the bench, regarding him silently in the moonlight.

So he kissed her.

# CHAPTER FIVE

---

"You have foregone Terpsichore's vernal charms, Mr. Hartley?" Bancroft asked.

The steward rose from the estate desk, a gratifying hint of the flustered scholar about his demeanor.

"I wanted to send a report up to London with you on Monday, sir. I thought you could read it in the coach." He capped the ink and set it on the standish. "There will be other assemblies."

Rural assemblies were as predictable as death and as irksome as taxes. Bancroft closed the door and approached the desk. Hartley shuffled aside without being asked.

"Reading in coaches makes me bilious." Bancroft sat, leaving Hartley to wander the room.

"Do you know how long you'll be gone, sir?"

"I do not, but I do intend to spend the rest of the evening communing with my accounts. If you leave now, you might catch the last waltz with the local beauties."

Hartley's peregrinations took him to the bookshelves, where monthly reports marched along in a tidy if not always cheering row.

"Then I would have to work on your report on the Sabbath, Mr. Summerfield, and that I am unwilling to do."

"Hartley, you don't dance, you avoid the assembly, you eschew music, you won't even scribble a report on the Sabbath. Have I employed a Dissenter?"

"No, sir. Merely a conscientious second son who values his employment."

Bancroft was a second son, which had to figure among the most diabolical purgatories ever devised. "Planting has progressed to your satisfaction?"

"We have only the Biltmore farm yet to go, sir, and we save that one for last because the land lies low and takes longer to warm up and dry out in spring."

"Fascinating. You have your eye on that property, don't you?" Jeremy Hartley was ambitious, which was a fine quality in modera-tion. Bancroft had promised him a life estate on one of the tenant farms if Summerfield House could be made profitable in five years. Years one through three hadn't achieved that goal, and year four wasn't looking to reverse the trend.

"I keep my eye on all of your properties, sir. That's what you pay me for."

Of all the employees, servants, and pensioners on the Summer-field estate, Hartley alone enjoyed a generous salary, though he did earn it.

"I value your hard work," Bancroft said, opening the household wage book, "but have you any idea which trait I respect in you even more highly than your diligence?"

"I hope I bring many useful attributes to my work," Hartley said, drawing himself up. He was in every way an unremarkable man. Medium height, medium-brown hair, medium intelligence.

"Your loyalty is your greatest asset," Bancroft said. "To Summer-field House, to the tenancies, to me. I leave my estate in your capable hands, Hartley, confident that when I return all will be running smoothly. Fetch me that abacus, would you?"

The tenants weren't warm toward Hartley, but they respected him and did not circumvent his authority by pestering Bancroft directly about repairs, improvements, and other annoyances. Bancroft was called upon to open the Hall on Boxing Day and preside over summer and fall picnics. Charles had been a more creditable country squire, but had he been less vigorous in the prosecution of his rural duties, he might have lived longer.

Charles had also been far too openhanded with the tenants, neighbors, and womenfolk, bequeathing Bancroft a spectacular muddle to sort out. Though to give the devil his due, Charles had been well liked.

"Summerton is good land," Hartley said, stretching up to get the abacus down from on top of the bookshelf. "So is much of Summerfield House. Bad luck happens, but over time, good land will always be worth the effort to care for it. We can't eat coal, my father always said."

"A veritable oracle, your father. I won't worry for the property while I'm gone, but I'm also not larking off to London completely free of care. Would I be imposing too greatly to ask you to take on another small duty while I'm gone?"

"Of course not, sir." Hartley set the abacus on the corner of the desk. "Name it." If Hartley had possessed a tail, it would have been wagging.

"My dearest relations, that is to say, Mrs. Summerfield and my nieces, are not twelve miles distant, and I have not been as attentive to their situation as I ought to have been."

Watchful, yes, but attentive, not exactly. If one of the myriad Dorning bachelors was sniffing about Margaret's skirts, the time had come to rectify the oversight.

"Mrs. Summerfield strikes me as a woman of sound judgment," Hartley said, winding the clock on the mantel. "Her property seems to prosper."

"The property, in point of fact, is not hers. Summerton belongs to my nieces."

Hartley closed the clock and tucked the key beneath it. "Then the late Mr. Summerfield knew what he was doing. That estate is the best of the land your family owns. It doubtless turns a fine profit and could be earning even more."

The same conclusion Bancroft had reached even before Charles's death. He'd asked his brother to deed him that property, and Charles had laughed, saying the estate was spoken for.

Laughed, the blighter. "How could it be earning more? And do have a seat."

Hartley folded himself into the chair before the desk, crossing an ankle over his knee. Ask him about the land, and he became less the sycophant and more the sage.

"What you probably notice first about Mrs. Summerfield's estate is that it's beautiful," Hartley said. "The hedges bloom with honeysuckle. The gardens burst with color. She has a stream that never runs dry and a bluebell wood. Her land has just enough roll to it to drain well without eroding."

*Get to the point.* "All apparent to the casual observer." Not that Bancroft had noted any of these details.

"That farm could be so much more," Hartley said. "She could grow wine grapes on those hillsides, soft fruit, orchards, anything besides yet another field of corn. Her wood is overgrown, her hedges should be replaced by walls, and why she let the Dornings dam up the stream is beyond me."

Dornings again. The eleventh biblical plague. "When did this happen?"

"Shortly after I came to work for you. Hawthorne Dorning wanted to create a water meadow and figured out how to engineer it by damming up the stream between the two properties. The stream still flows, but he also has his water meadow."

"Water meadows are old-fashioned." Which was the extent of Bancroft's knowledge about them.

"If you can run water over a field all winter, you can bring on the grass much earlier in spring, improve the grass you do get, and create a larger hay crop. We haven't any water meadows on our land here, and I don't see a way to create one. A water meadow can also help with flood control or irrigation schemes, not that Mrs. Summerfield has either of those problems."

"And Margaret allowed Mr. Dorning to do this?"

"She didn't really have a choice, sir. Water is considered a common nuisance, and every landowner has the right—generally—to manage it as best he can. Dorning could have built his water meadow without her permission, but that's not how the Dornings deal with their neighbors."

And thus did the conversation wander to the crux of Bancroft's agenda. "I don't know the Dornings well. An earl's sons and a mere squire don't move in quite the same circles. We have different market towns, different churches, and Dorning Hall has never been noted for its neighborly entertainments. What do you think of Mr. Hawthorne Dorning?"

Bancroft's property was much more impressive than a mere squire's farm, and the Dornings likely hadn't a spare groat between them. Bancroft hadn't spoken honestly, though: Margaret held a life estate in the property she occupied, and the remainder went to the children. For now, the property was more or less Margaret's and certainly not Bancroft's.

"The Dornings as a family are much respected," Hartley said. "They are good neighbors, hard workers, and responsible with their land."

Not what Bancroft had wanted to hear. "And Mr. Hawthorne Dorning?"

"Not afraid to get his hands dirty. All the Dorning brothers pitch in, sir. They are known for it. Whether it's stacking hay, laying a hedge, or clearing a ditch, they work side by side with tenants, and Mr. Hawthorne Dorning most of all."

"He's a big brute." And like his brothers, his eyes were an odd color. More Saxon blue than the rest of the Dorning tribe, but unnaturally vivid.

"Knows what he's about too," Hartley said. "The tenants look up to him, and I've been known to discuss the occasional hypothetical with him over a pint."

Arguing agriculture. How splendidly English—and boring. "That is all quite interesting, Hartley, but I do not trust Hawthorne Dorning's motives."

Hartley sat up. "In what sense, sir?"

"When I paid my farewell call on Margaret, Dorning was strutting around her foyer, making himself quite at home. I do fear he has more on his mind than another water meadow. The greatest injustice in all of the legion of injustices incorporated into English law is that I could not offer dear Margaret the sanctuary of holy matrimony." Not that Bancroft for one moment had been tempted.

"You're good to be concerned for a widowed family member, Mr. Summerfield."

"I *am* concerned for her. Today a water meadow, tomorrow who knows what Dorning will charm out from under Margaret's nose? She hasn't shown any inclination to marry anybody, but she's merely a woman. Dorning could spirit away half her lambs, and she likely wouldn't know it."

Hartley was blessed with the gift of deliberation. He considered a problem from all sides, set it aside, then considered it again. The beauty of such a trait was that he did not make quick leaps of insight and could thus be led.

"She has competent farmers," Hartley said slowly.

"Probably true, but Dorning is an earl's son, and you know how pragmatic the yeomen can be. Dorning is in a position to do them favors. You said it yourself—the Dorning brothers pitch in. If, as one of Mrs. Summerfield's tenants, you had a choice between championing the cause of a widow who is amply provided for, or winking at a scheme concocted by an earl's son, which would you do?"

"I'd have a word with the widow, sir."

"An honorable course, but you are not well acquainted with Mrs. Summerfield. She has raised stubborn independence to a high art, and it's honestly not for her sake that I worry. Charles provided well for his widow, but every lamb of hers that wanders onto Dorning property is in effect stolen from my nieces, and it's their welfare that concerns me most greatly."

How benevolent that sounded, how convincingly avuncular. Bancroft would never slight his nieces' best interests, but they were a pair of bothersome little females. All they needed was a bit of a dowry and the ability to make congenial conversation, and they wouldn't need either for more than ten years—which in Greta's case was fortunate indeed.

Bancroft would do well enough by them, when the time came.

"So what, specifically, are you asking me, sir?"

"Keep an eye on Mrs. Summerfield's situation in my absence, much as I would were I not making my annual sojourn to the capital."

Increasingly, that pilgrimage was less to enjoy the very expensive social whirl and more to search for an heiress of great fortune and modest intellect. One intelligent female in the family was more than enough.

"Should I call on Mrs. Summerfield?" Hartley asked.

"You certainly can call on her. Ask her how planting is going, or lambing, or something of that ilk. Be charming."

A hint of shrewdness came into Hartley's brown eyes. "Charming, sir?"

"She's a widow, she lives alone with two small children, and her only family will be far away. A bit of harmless flirtation, an offer to look over her acres, a suggestion about a water meadow of her own... nothing *untoward*, of course."

"Of course not, sir. Never that."

"I'm glad we understand each other." Bancroft shuffled the pages on the blotter into a pile and held them out. "You can finish this report in the library, Hartley." A sepulcher at this time of night, alas.

"I'll have it ready for you by the time you leave on Monday."

Hartley rose, and Bancroft waited until he was nearly at the door, hustling off to execute yet another task for his employer.

"One other thing, Hartley?"

"Sir?"

"Those Dornings. I realize they are beloved by all and a titled family and all that other, but I also know how the nobs can be. They smile and invite you to the open house, while they run their hounds through your best cornfield. We might be well advised to keep an eye on Hawthorne Dorning, don't you think?"

"Yes, sir. I think that exactly."

"Good man. I'll leave you to your report."

HAWTHORNE DORNING KISSED like spring stealing across the land. His fingers slid into Margaret's hair at her nape, an easy touch, but nonetheless intimate. He had warm hands, and he moved as if he had eternities to cradle the back of her head and gaze into her eyes.

Blast the timing. Darkness provided privacy, but Margaret wanted to see those magnificent Dorning eyes when Hawthorne made the decision to kiss a babbling widow good night.

And yet, darkness was appropriate. Scents were magnified by darkness, sounds too. The stable was upwind, bringing both a tangy whiff of horses and the sound of stock contentedly munching hay. The greening aroma of farmland awakening to the growing season underlaid everything, while Hawthorne Dorning's scent wrapped Margaret in masculine fragrances.

His mouth touched hers, and she was hard put not to seize him by the hair and prevent him from moving away.

Ah, but he came back, a more lingering caress of mouth upon mouth. Tension eased in Margaret's belly—Hawthorne was a very competent kisser—and she allowed herself to return his kisses. She relaxed into the moment and into him.

Hawthorne Dorning knew how to hold a woman so she felt snug, warm, and cherished, and so she was also abundantly aware of male strength and restraint. Margaret explored under his coat, finding warmth and muscle in abundance.

With Charles, she'd always been so careful, so mindful of his frailties, for all he'd looked hale and healthy.

Hawthorne pulled away enough to rest his forehead against Margaret's. "This could become—"

"It can't become anything," she whispered, hoping to stem whatever gentlemanly reservations he'd been about to state.

And yet, she wanted more. Even a ruralizing widow of modest means who must do nothing to jeopardize the welfare of her dependents was allowed to want more. Margaret put her longing into her kiss, and by slow degrees, Hawthorne answered her yearning.

She took a taste of him, he smiled against her mouth, then did likewise. His flavor was sweet and cinnamon-y, like an apple turnover, and erotic, like nothing Margaret had experienced as a wife. The sudden blossoming of desire took her by surprise, as a mild day in late January insisted that spring would come, despite snow, despite barren trees, despite the sun making only a brief appearance.

The sunshine on those startling days of reprieve was so bright as to hurt the eyes, but ah, the heart was warmed.

"We have to stop," Hawthorne whispered. "We stop and you go into the house. Then I walk home, pausing for a long swim in the creek."

*Delightful man.* Margaret resumed kissing him, and while he accommodated her, she could also sense that he'd made up his mind, and when the formidable portcullis of his will had been lowered, not even moonlit kisses could prevail against it.

Margaret eased her mouth from his and subsided against him. His embrace was pleasure of another order, for he held her close, his cheek resting against her temple.

"I had forgotten," she said. "I had forgotten the joy of being awake in springtime." Because she no longer wandered the woods and hedges looking for plants, no longer spent long, sunny afternoons in her herbal.

"I forgot my name for a few moments. Do you seek a dalliance, Margaret?"

He might have been asking if she preferred sugar with her tea, but the question was significant. "Not on purpose, though I have been widowed for several years, and twenty-six is not exactly ancient. Here you are, willing to be kissed. Here I am, not quite sure how to answer the question."

"I kissed you first."

*Lovely man.* "So you did, and quite well, I might add."

They shared a moment, surprised and pleased on Margaret's part. Hawthorne was apparently content to hold her rather than rush off to the charms of a frigid stream, but what was he thinking?

"Shall I call on you?" he asked. "By way of the fields?"

"You shall." *And I will receive you for so long as Bancroft remains in London.*

And then?

Some of Margaret's joy ebbed into sadness. *Then,* she'd very likely bid Mr. Dorning a fond farewell and revert to being the neighbor he never saw. At a future assembly, his engagement to some blushing young lady would be announced, and Margaret would wish the couple well.

"Into the house with you," Mr. Dorning said, rising and drawing Margaret to her feet. "I will scour Dorning Hall for herbals and bring you whatever I find."

That provided him a reason to come calling, and she had offered to look over his recipes, hadn't she?

He walked with her to the foot of the manor's front steps, the gravel on the drive crunching loudly beneath their feet. Valerian Dorning's warning, about Hawthorne not being a widow's plaything, further dimmed the evening's glow.

Where did that leave them? Where did Margaret want that to leave them? "Thank you for a lovely evening, Mr. Dorning."

"Hawthorne," he said, brushing a kiss to her cheek. "Thank you for a lovely evening, Margaret."

He was making some statement, not about the evening. Margaret stole a final quick embrace and then skipped up the steps and slipped inside the house. She peeked out the window to see Hawthorne still waiting at the foot of the steps.

She'd forgotten this, too, that a gentleman waited to ensure the lady was safe. She lit the carrying candle from the sconce, threw the bolt on the front door, and made her way up to bed. When she reached her bedroom, she again peered out the window and saw a tall, masculine form striding across the meadow, making a straight path for the stream that divided Summerton and Dorning Hall.

# CHAPTER SIX

---

Grey Birch Dorning, Earl of Casriel, did not particularly enjoy London, even in spring. He very much enjoyed the company of his countess, Beatitude, and she had decreed that their first Season as a couple would be spent putting on a proper show in Town.

She was entitled to her revenge, after all. Years of making up the numbers, pretending not to hear gossip, ignoring drunken overtures, being friendly but not too friendly, observing propriety but not too much propriety took a toll on a woman.

Grey's one condition for their London stay was that he and Beatitude remain at home on the occasional evening. No dinner guests, no card party, no musicale or soiree, just the two of them doing whatever they pleased. Tonight, they pleased to while away their evening in his estate office, both of them catching up on correspondence.

"Jacaranda says Worth is thinking of putting up a guest house on his brother's property in Cumbria," Beatitude said, turning a letter sideways. "She invites us to visit there."

"My sister invites us to visit a house her husband hasn't yet built on land he doesn't yet own," Grey said, removing his spectacles. "Marriage has made a formidable woman fanciful."

Also happy. Jacaranda and Worth were glowingly happy.

Willow and Susannah were glowingly happy.

Sycamore in his gaming hell was happy, though his joy was of a rather more bellicose variety. He delighted in collecting the vowels of the high and mighty and in watching them fret over debts of honor as other mortals did.

Beatitude rose from the couch and put on Grey's eyeglasses. "You are worried," she said, studying him. "Something is bothering you."

Having a wife was an adjustment. Grey had learned how to shield himself from the constant scrutiny of his brothers, but Beatitude saw everything Grey attempted to protect her from, and she loved him all the same.

"Planting has gone well," Grey said, putting Thorne's report aside. "No deluges, no late frosts, no oxen going lame just as the land is ready to be turned. Thorne sounds happy."

For Thorne.

Beatitude subsided into his lap. "But?"

"But I told my brothers last year to plunder the botanical riches of Dorning Hall and set themselves up in business. I'm not charging them for use of the land, conservatory, glass houses, or gardens."

She looped her arms around his neck. "You are waiting to take a portion of the profits, as your brothers are waiting."

"But what else are they doing besides waiting?" Grey asked, nuzzling his wife's neck. She smelled good, of gardenias and early bedtimes.

"The dower house had to be dismantled, Grey. That was quite a project."

"True."

"Some sort of herbal should be built on Dorning Hall property. That's another project."

Beatitude's fingers winnowing through his hair were soothing, also muddling. "They've started on the building, but only started. I've half a mind to jaunt down to Dorset—"

Beatitude kissed his cheek. "The only place you're jaunting for the upcoming week is up to bed with me at night and down to breakfast the next morning. We are hosting a ball next Wednesday, lest you forget."

That ball would be staggeringly expensive, something Grey had kept to himself. Beatitude was entitled to make one bold statement regarding her remarriage, and the wood and stone salvaged from the dower house had—for the first time in years—put Grey a little ahead financially.

But only a little. One bad harvest, and he'd be once again scrabbling for every groat.

"Grey, we have been in Town less than a month. Do you really hate it here so much?"

"Right now, Town is my favorite place to be. In fact, this very chair in this very room fulfills all my fondest dreams, provided this very countess fills my lap." He kissed her back on the mouth. How he loved her mouth.

"You are worried about your brothers."

Grey sat back. He loved his brothers, too, and Beatitude wasn't wrong. "I told them: Here's carte blanche to make free with the biggest botanical farm in the realm. Help yourself to the lot of it, but generate some revenue and get out of my house. They went as far as the next hill and haven't done much else."

Beatitude shifted so she was straddling Grey's lap. She'd already changed into a dressing gown, and thus not much came between Grey and his wildest dreams.

"How are they supporting themselves?"

"Ash is working for Sycamore here in Town. Valerian impersonates a dancing master or tutor of deportment. Oak sells a few paintings, and Thorne takes a modest salary as my steward. Oak, Valerian, and Thorne have little in the way of monetary needs because they still live at Dorning Hall, more or less."

"So you have made significant progress launching your brothers. Ash is entirely out from under your roof, as is Sycamore. Thorne is the best steward you could find anywhere and pulling his share of the load at Dorning Hall. Oak and Valerian are malingering, but they, too, are in a better posture than they were a year ago."

She untied Grey's cravat and massaged the back of his neck.

"I can't think when you do that, madam."

"You can't worry. We're going shopping tomorrow."

"Now, I'm worried. What are we shopping for?"

"I won't spend a penny, but if we can send back some genuine intelligence to your brothers, such as the latest fashion in rose water, the most popular nerve tonic, then we might inspire them into making progress with their herbal products."

"A nerve tonic sounds appropriate. How many people did we invite to this ball?"

"We invited everybody who's in Town, as is polite. What is your alternative plan, Grey? If your brothers can't make a go of this botanical business, what is your strategy?"

"Send at least three of my brothers to Peru."

She looked him in the eye, and because she was wearing his spectacles, the effect was interesting. "You are worried, and when you worry, you do something about it."

Never, ever would Grey consider deceiving his wife. "I'm considering selling some land."

"That would break your heart."

"And put enmity between me and my brothers and probably be a stupid decision in the long run, but the land is not as profitable as it once was, and I cannot change that." He gently peeled the spectacles free from Beatitude's ears. "Thorne will consider it a personal failure if I have to sell a single acre. No Earl of Casriel has parted with so much as a square yard of Dorning Hall land for centuries."

"Warn him," Beatitude said, climbing off Grey's lap. "Fire a shot across Thorne's bow, and if he, Oak, and Valerian are dawdling, then perhaps they will apply themselves more diligently to their challenges. I have a challenge for you, my lord."

Beatitude also had good advice. A frank letter to Thorne was in order, but not tonight.

"I am ever your servant, my lady."

"Race me up the stairs."

She bolted from the room, and Grey gave chase, making very sure not to catch her until she was nearly at the bedroom door.

MARGARET WAS absent from services on Sunday, though Thorne was certain he'd left her in good health Saturday night. He spent the balance of his Sabbath scouring Dorning Hall's attics and library and by late afternoon still hadn't found what he sought.

"You should be looking in Grey's study," Valerian said, strolling between the library's half-empty shelves.

"No, I should not. I respect my brother's privacy. Why isn't anybody dusting this place?"

"We're between housekeepers."

Thorne extracted a biography of Dr. Johnson from amid volumes of poetry. "Again?"

"The last one tippled. Grey thought to economize until he and Beatitude come down from Town."

"If he wanted to economize, he should have closed up the house properly, given most of the staff leave, and—why does this library have no sense of order?"

Valerian took Dr. Johnson from him. "Because this library, with the exception of all things horticultural, was of little import to the late Earl of Casriel. The present earl has had other matters to tend to. If you seek recipes for tisanes and simples, why not look among Papa's notes? Grey wouldn't toss them out, and—"

"I cannot bloody find Papa's notes, and I never knew Papa to be all that interested in fragrances. He pursued botany from a masculine perspective." Thorne came across one of the volumes for which he'd been searching, a dimly recalled, wonderfully illustrated bound treasure.

Valerian paged through Dr. Johnson's life story, releasing a musty, dusty scent that resonated with the library's general airlessness.

"Thorne, the logical place to look for Papa's notes is Grey's study. Grey maintains a sort of shrine to Papa's memory there, though you have to look closely to see it."

Thorne moved on to the next row of shelves. "And you have looked closely among another's possessions? Isn't there a word for that?"

Valerian wandered to the other side of the shelves, so two rows of books stood between Thorne and his brother.

"I am not a spy. I am merely a younger sibling. Ash and Sycamore understand the limitations of that status and would not judge me for taking an interest in my brother's affairs."

"If I were to take the same interest in your affairs, you'd attempt to bloody my nose, not that you'd succeed." Where the hell could the damned books be?

"*Recettes du Jardin*," Valerian said, blowing dust off a slim volume. "By Madame Celestine Verlaine."

"Give me that."

Valerian passed the book over between the shelves. "Have you considered how this looks, Thorne?"

The book stank of mildew, and if it had been permitted to wander away from Papa's botanical treatises, it was probably of little value. "How what looks?"

"Are you courting Mrs. Summerfield, or trying to winkle her skills from her while pretending to enjoy her company? When you fix your mind on an objective, you become cavalier about the means you use to reach your goal."

"Does the pot call the kettle black, Brother?" Thorne asked, holding Madame's herbal at arm's length and shaking it gently. "You want your boots repaired, you compose an ode to Olivia Smithers's eyes. You need a few more monogrammed handkerchiefs, and all of a sudden, I see you walking halfway home from church with Caroline Isaacs."

Valerian looked disproportionately offended by Thorne's question. "Pots and kettles have nothing to do with anything. I don't want to see you make an idiot of yourself."

Thorne came across his quarry hiding among the American political pamphlets. "Forgive me if I look askance at your solicitude."

Valerian came around the end of the row, so Thorne was hemmed in by bookshelves on either side, the wall at his back and Valerian's scowl before him.

"If you mean to woo Mrs. Summerfield, then woo her. Bring her daffodils and poetry, ride out with her to the abbey ruins, and picnic with her by the stream. If you're interested in a business arrangement involving recipes and fragrances, then tell her what you're prepared to pay for her expertise and what you expect for your coin."

Valerian made sense, but Thorne was not in the mood to be lectured. "We haven't all that much coin."

"Do *you* have the means to support a wife and children? For I do not, and until I do, I will neither walk a lady home by moonlight, nor waltz with her in a manner fit only for courting couples."

That poverty and honor kept Valerian from courting a wife had not occurred to Thorne, though it should have.

"Mrs. Summerfield is very skilled at concocting fragrances," Thorne said. "As an earl's son with a gentlemanly occupation, I am of suitable station to pay her my addresses. I can offer her a commodious home in the steward's cottage, I am happy to be a doting step-uncle to her nieces, and I believe the lady might look with favor upon my suit. Why are you quibbling at a mutually advantageous match that hasn't become a fully formed courtship, much less an acknowledged possibility yet?"

"Because a woman does not want to be wooed for her recipes, and a man should not surrender his freedom for a mess of rose-scented bathwater. I told her not to trifle with you. I see my sermon was delivered to the wrong party."

Thorne advanced on his brother, though Valerian did not yield a single step. "You told her what?"

"Not to trifle with you. You've been trifled with before, and it did not end well."

"That was years ago."

"You stayed drunk for most of your second term at Oxford and over a woman you thought was a widow. Your arm took a year to mend. Grey was worried about the example you set for Sycamore."

"You exaggerate about a youthful folly." One that still gave Thorne nightmares.

"Pure Dorning stubbornness," Valerian retorted, poking Thorne in the chest. "You did not stop to think Mrs. Plumley might have a husband, did not stop to wonder if she considered toying with university boys her favorite diversion, did not worry for an instant that she might extract payment from you for the letters you wrote, or turn her husband loose on you when you could not pay."

"I *would* not pay." Too late, Thorne had learned that the Comely Mrs. Plumley was something of an institution, and a notorious one at that.

"Stubbornness and pride," Valerian mused. "What could possibly go wrong when those two attributes collide in an earl's impoverished son? Dear me, I must ponder that conundrum while my brother steals a widow's perfume recipes and makes besotted sheep's eyes at her in front of half the shire." Valerian made kissing sounds and sauntered off in the direction of the fireplace, a cavernous hearth sporting a bed of old ashes and a dusty set of andirons.

*Besotted sheep's eyes?* "I do occasionally smile at my neighbors," Thorne said, following him. "If anybody qualifies for the title of Mr. Sheep's Eyes, it's you."

"Grey expected us to have products to sell six months ago, Thorne. How much more patient can he be?"

How odd that Valerian would ignore a taunt. "Grey is very patient and also—sometimes—an idiot. He expected us to have the whole dower house torn down, sold, and shipped off in one summer. He wants the family wing disassembled in a few months' time as well. He has no idea what developing a commercial enterprise will take, and we haven't even built a proper herbal because we've been too busy selling bricks and stone."

At a tidy profit, thank the heavenly choruses.

Valerian propped an elbow on the mantel and rubbed his fingers across his forehead, a posture reminiscent of their late father.

"We haven't even begun to develop products either, Thorne. All we have are some pretty paintings Oak has done, while Ash has left his card at a few London apothecaries. We've done nothing here at the Hall, and if you waste the next six months courting a widow under false pretenses, Grey will have no choice but to exile us from the property."

Valerian was *worried*. Not meddling, not spying, not lecturing for the sheer pleasure of annoying a sibling. Thorne thrived on the responsibility of caring for a patch of ground. Oak's art had begun to be noticed and even produced the occasional sale. Ash was racketing about London with Sycamore, and Will trained dogs for no less personage than King George.

Jacaranda and Daisy were content with their spouses and children, while Valerian...

Had charm when he cared to exhibit it.

"We should have sent you to London," Thorne said. "Ash is probably moping the Season away, or wasting his days fretting over Sycamore, which has never been a productive enterprise. You are hectoring me about courting protocol because if I muck up the agricultural aspect of this venture, you are left with nothing."

"If you muck up the courting, I am left with a brother who should have known better and other siblings whose expectations are blighted. Grey has been patient long enough."

Offended dignity colored that remark, but also an admission: Valerian was relying on Thorne, which had been a theoretical burden prior to this discussion. For Valerian, who had to flirt himself up mended boots and embroidered handkerchiefs, the need for a profitable business had passed from the theoretical realm while Thorne had been hawking loads of building stone and overseeing the autumn harvest.

"I won't fail you," Thorne said, "but if you bring up the lovely and duplicitous Mrs. Plumley again, I will flatten you on the drive and gallop Gowain over your remains." Valerian alone knew the extent of Thorne's indiscretion where Mrs. Plumley was concerned, and had Valerian not kept a close eye on Thorne—spied on him—as the drama had unfolded, Mr. Plumley would likely have done much worse than merely break one of Thorne's arms before Valerian had arrived on the scene.

Valerian saluted him from the cold hearth. "I found a half-dozen notebooks in Papa's hand that appear to be crammed with instructions for making this tea or that tonic. They are on the sideboard in the foyer, which brings me to my next inquiry."

"I live to satisfy your curiosity."

"Nothing all that interesting of a botanical nature was ever kept in this library, so why have you been rooting around like a truffle-hunting boar, and what have you found?"

Thorne ambled for the door, his pace relaxed. "Just some light reading. I'm off to pay a call on Mrs. Summerfield. Perhaps you might sketch us an architectural plan for our herbal?"

Valerian pushed away from the mantel and set an equally unhurried pace for the door. "I know little about how to build an herbal. I'm sure we'll need stills, ventilation, a large hearth or two, decent lighting, and worktables, but I have no insight into the exact proportions or configurations that make for an ideal—"

Thorne was a fraction of a second too slow. Valerian had the two little books in his hand even as Thorne reached for the door latch.

"Give those back, Valerian."

Thorne was the best pugilist in the family, in part because of his size and sheer muscle, but also because when his determination was aroused, no mere physical blow deterred him. Pain became an incidental cost to pursuing an objective, and not much else mattered. He had Mr. Plumley's instruction to thank for starting him on that lesson, and nobody had landed a meaningful blow on him since.

"*Children's books*, Thorne?" Valerian's puzzlement was more bothersome than his needling.

"Greta and Adriana, Mrs. Summerfield's nieces, are in want of diversion," Thorne said. "You and I both know the power of a good tale, and these were among my favorites."

Valerian passed the books back, his expression nearly somber. "Be careful, Thorne. They are little girls, and they know nothing of your commercial ventures. Trifle with their aunt, and I will have to beat you, though Bancroft might have you waylaid in an alley first. Use those children to pursue your objectives, and I will make Plumley's beating look like a mere schoolyard scuffle."

Valerian fluffed Thorne's cravat, refolded the creases in his lapels, and bowed him through the door.

# CHAPTER SEVEN

"We should get a tiger," Adriana announced, petting Cicero, the largest of Margaret's house cats. He was orange, long-haired, and friendly... up to a point. Margaret had never seen him swipe at one of the girls, but he hissed at the occasional footman.

"What would we do with a tiger?" Greta asked, considering her sketch.

"Roam the jungle with him," Adriana retorted. "A tiger would keep us safe, like the tigers who live in the temples. He'd eat anybody who came to do us harm."

"Adriana is fanciful." Greta's expression turned her statement into a question.

"Adriana has a powerful imagination," Margaret said, pausing by the nursery window. "A fine quality in anybody who'd seek to take on the problems of the world." No sense of smell was needed to know that the day would be gorgeous. The canopy of the home wood was luminous with new leaves. The daffodils in the garden were shining yellow harbingers trumpeting the arrival of a beautiful spring day.

"I want to roam in the woods," Adriana said, peering over Greta's shoulder. "You are getting better at drawing. It's not fair."

"I practice. You hop around on one foot much better than I do."

Which, of course, inspired said hopping.

"If we have another dry day today, we can walk in the woods tomorrow," Margaret said. "We can refresh our bouquets and check on the bluebells." The woods and hedges had been calling to Margaret more loudly than ever in recent days. After winter's unrelenting bleakness, spring was for enjoying, for exploring and learning the secrets of the countryside, not for wandering about in a house that felt increasingly oppressive.

"I love the bluebells!" Adriana bellowed.

"It's too early for bluebells," Greta replied. "Aunt Margaret said."

"Then why are they blooming in the garden?" Adriana switched feet, which managed to make her hopping louder.

"Because," Margaret replied, "the garden offers protection from the elements, lacks trees competing for the sunlight, and will be warmer for having stone walls beside the bluebells to soak up the sun's heat during the day."

Adriana hopped over to the window. "Who is that?"

A man rode up the drive on a fancy chestnut. Margaret's first thought was that Hawthorne Dorning had at last come to call. Monday and Tuesday had passed with no sign of him, and Margaret's impatience had grown by the day.

Which was silly. He'd asked her to look over a few recipes, nothing more. Whatever pleasure she'd taken in a single kiss, *nothing more* was exactly what she should expect. She would explain that to him if it became necessary.

Though if that *was* Hawthorne Dorning, Margaret wondered why he'd come up the drive. She'd asked him not to call by way of the lanes, and her request had been in earnest, even as she had resented the need for discretion.

Greta joined them at the window. "That is Mr. Hartley's horse. His name is Benjamin, after Benjamin Franklin because he doesn't mind storms."

Greta likely had no idea who Dr. Franklin had been or what his connection was with storms, but having heard this snippet of equine biography somewhere, she'd never forget it.

"Mr. Hartley is Uncle Bancroft's steward," Adriana said, both feet on the carpet. "Uncle went to London, so why is his steward here?"

Any change from routine provoked anxiety in either girl, and in Margaret. They were just old enough to recall Charles's passing and the great upheaval it had wrought. She was certain they recalled, in some manner without words, losing both parents to influenza as well.

"I don't know why Mr. Hartley has stopped by," Margaret said, "but callers are always welcome. Adriana, you have sums to do, and Greta, your sketch is far from complete. Make a good effort today, and we'll have a long ramble in the woods tomorrow." Which seemed ages away when the sun was shining so benevolently.

Miss Fenner burst through the door, looking slightly flushed. "Mrs. Summerfield, you're to have a caller. That handsome Mr. Hartley is on the steps as I speak, and he wasn't at the assembly, though I did see him at church on Sunday."

*Handsome* Mr. Hartley? "Perhaps once the children are settled to their tasks, you can join Mr. Hartley and me in the parlor. Ambers can sit with the girls in your absence."

Fenny ruffled a hand over Adriana's braids. "Truly, you want me to join you, ma'am?"

"Perhaps Mr. Hartley is here with exactly that hope in mind," Margaret said. "We know he can have no personal interest in calling upon me."

Fenny clapped her hands briskly. "Children, to the parapets! We have lessons to learn and battles to wage with the forces of ignorance."

The girls trooped over to their desks, and Margaret, with a similar lack of enthusiasm, made her way to the guest parlor.

"MR. HARTLEY, GOOD DAY," Margaret said, dipping a curtsey.

Jeremy Hartley was handsome, if a lady favored regular features, sandy-brown hair, and a pleasant smile—which Margaret did not. In half boots she'd be the same height as Mr. Hartley, though his riding boots gave him a slight advantage over her house slippers.

He bowed correctly. "Mrs. Summerfield, good day. I trust my call comes at a convenient time?"

Of course not. If Margaret was to be housebound for the day, she at least wanted to linger by windows undisturbed.

"A friendly call is always well timed. How fares the Summerfield family seat?" She could not ask him about much else, because that estate was his entire occupation and his family did not bide in the area.

"I am happy to report that planting is all but finished—always a field or two that requires a little more time, isn't there?—and we're getting ready for shearing right on schedule. The price of wool is holding steady, but the first to market always has an advantage, as Mr. Summerfield often states."

More than three years after Charles's death, Margaret still associated references to Mr. Summerfield with her late husband, not his younger brother. The mental adjustment—oh, *Bancroft* Summerfield —was particularly irksome when Mr. Hartley referred to *his* Mr. Summerfield so cheerfully.

"Shall we be seated, Mr. Hartley? I would not want to take up much of your time, but a cup of tea and a biscuit shouldn't take long."

He sat in the chair Charles had preferred, angled to face the sofa and get a good amount of light from the window.

"How do you go on here at Summerton?" Hartley asked, his smile oddly concerned. "I know it's not a large property, but you've been handling the reins now for several years. Buildings can fall into disrepair before you know it, tenants are always complaining about maintenance, and hedges have a way of encroaching on even the best-maintained fields."

"I like broad hedges, Mr. Hartley."

He crossed an ankle over a knee, a posture a gentleman did not assume before a lady unless they were quite informal with each other. "I wasn't aware you enjoyed shooting, ma'am."

"I enjoy knowing the hares, pheasants, grouse, and songbirds have shelter. My acreage is sufficient that I need not begrudge the beasts their homes."

"Ah, but that generous sentiment means the foxes, badgers, deer, and other pests also have more places to shelter." He shook a finger at her. "We can't have that, can we?"

His gesture was meant to be playful, though the effect on Margaret was curious. She had a lovely life on a peaceful, pretty patch of ground. Her nieces were a greater blessing than anybody knew, as was the relative solitude the Summerton household enjoyed. She had great good health, as did the girls, and her household enjoyed material comfort anybody would envy.

And yet, Mr. Hartley's admonition, meant to be lighthearted despite its condescension—left her ready to shriek at him to leave. He was Bancroft's emissary, and thus his motives were suspect.

"If I were to cut my hedges back as you prefer," she said, "or enclose my properties as so many have, then I'd eliminate many of the medicinal herbs that bring so much ease and comfort to so many. I have sheep enough, Mr. Hartley, but only one healthy patch of winterbloom that my late husband propagated for me from seeds he imported himself. Would you hack it to the roots to make room for another bullock?"

His brows knit, as if she'd come out with one of Greta's apparent non sequiturs. "Certainly not, ma'am. If the flowers are of senti-mental value, then of course they should stand."

Winterbloom was not a flower, though from September to December it provided a lovely display of color.

A footman brought in the tea tray, thank heavens, or Margaret might have been forced to endure a panegyric to the enclosed common. Bancroft had gone significantly in debt enclosing fields at the family seat that Charles had allowed to remain in common use.

The result was doubtless greater profit for Bancroft, though the lack of free grazing for cows, sheep, and pigs had cost the village six families, and others were considering emigrating as well.

"You will be pleased to know that I've taken an inspection tour of your properties," Hartley said when Margaret had plied him with China black and tea cakes.

She set her tea cup down rather too quickly and got a slosh of hot liquid across her fingers. "I beg your pardon?"

"No need to thank me," he said, smiling at his boot. "Mr. Summerfield feels badly that he's left you to muddle on here with so little help from the family estate. Unfortunately, we have had much to do at Summerfield in recent years. I am charged with rectifying Mr. Summerfield's oversight, though, so you must apply to me should you have any questions about the tenancies or the management of the land."

*Stay off my land.* Margaret blotted her smarting hand with a table napkin. The burn wasn't serious, though her fingers had turned pink.

"Mr. Hartley, while I appreciate your interest in Summerton, I assure you we are managing quite well. No further inspections of my property will be necessary. I daresay you will confuse—if not offend—my farmers and tenants by presuming to appear on their lands unannounced."

"Not *their* lands, Mrs. Summerfield, *your* lands. The sooner the tenants grasp that distinction, the better off you'll be. A few blunt discussions with me, and they'll know that taking advantage of a widow—"

"Mr. Hartley, my husband left me and the girls this property precisely because it was the best-managed real estate he owned, and he tutored me thoroughly as to how it should be run. If you interfere with my tenants, or sabotage my authority, you will be seen to disrespect Charles's memory."

That she had to call upon her late husband infuriated her, but Hartley was not the problem.

Bancroft was. Charles had indulged Margaret's distrust of her brother-in-law, but only in a limited fashion.

Hartley held out his cup for more tea.

Margaret poured carefully.

"Mr. Summerfield was quite clear with me, ma'am. I am to make myself available to you with an eye toward assuming the burden of managing your tenancies. He feels remiss for not having effected this transition sooner, and I must agree with him. For a woman to be tasked with the details of a large agricultural enterprise is less than ideal. You have a household to run and nieces to raise, and Mr. Summerfield is only trying to do his duty by you."

Olivia Smithers was the village cobbler. Having no sons, the blacksmith, Mr. Merryweather, had apprenticed his oldest daughter. Hannah Weller was the village herbalist and midwife, her daughter the most competent seamstress in the shire. Women managed businesses all around Mr. Hartley, but they were invisible to him.

As Margaret longed to be.

"I understand, Mr. Hartley, that you are trying to do your duty by your employer, but your loyalty to Bancroft and my loyalty to my husband's express wishes are in conflict. I will honor my husband's wishes, and you will refrain from trespassing on my land."

The word *trespassing* had him sitting up straight. "Mr. Summerfield wants his nieces to inherit a property in good repair, ma'am. You cannot fault him for that."

Bancroft was making this gambit as the opening foray in a war that would end with all of Summerton's income in his hands, and thus all of the girls' options—and Margaret's future—controlled by him as well.

"Mr. Charles Summerfield desired the same end. Since his death, the family seat has become sunk in enormous debt, while Summerton continues to run profitably. Forgive me if I reject Bancroft's attempts to meddle, Mr. Hartley. He might mean well, as you doubtless do, but good intentions do not a young woman dower."

Or a widow protect. Not in this case.

"May I call on you again?" Hartley asked. "Mr. Summerfield will be gone for some weeks, possibly months, and he did most sincerely ask me to keep an eye on matters here in his absence."

What Hartley lacked in discernment about his employer, he made up for in loyalty—blast the man.

"You may call upon us, of course, but come up the drive as any other visitor would, rather than conducting pointless inspections of that which does not concern you. If I have immediate needs, I can rely on my neighbors for assistance, as I always have."

Hartley finished his tea and set the empty cup on the tray, then rose. "Those neighbors are not family, ma'am, with all due respect. The Dornings got you to agree to use the stream to fill their water meadow, but that means you can't attempt the same improvement."

"My land doesn't lie properly for a water meadow, Mr. Hartley."

He considered her, not with the genial, condescending smile of a helpful gentleman, but rather, with the shrewd gaze of a man familiar with complicated enterprises and hard decisions.

"Your woods are full of deadfall, and that lumber could be sold for a pretty penny."

While the delicate and precious medicinal plants sheltering in those woods would be trampled by heedless sawyers.

"I use the wood for my hearths here at Summerton, Mr. Hartley, and I donate to our elderly households as well. As you doubtless know, the deadfall piles up in years when we're afflicted with high winds and excessive rains, then we'll go for more years without losing a single tree. Charles explained that and much else to me. I'll see you out."

Hartley clearly hadn't expected to meet with resistance. He'd probably anticipated gratitude or at least compliance with his orders. He was not visibly angry—Bancroft had likely sent him out on many a misinformed mission—but neither was he defeated.

"Would you like me to include anything specific in my report to Mr. Summerfield, ma'am?"

How sporting of him to admit that tattling to Bancroft was the next item on his busy schedule.

"Tell your employer the truth, of course. Tell him that you've observed Summerton to be a superbly managed piece of land, and you see no further need to insert yourself into the goings-on here."

Margaret led her guest to the front door, certain he'd tell Bancroft anything but that.

"I can convey that assurance to Mr. Summerfield, ma'am, though I do see a few areas for improvement. He will still insist that I come by regularly and monitor progress."

*On what blooming authority does Bancroft monitor my flocks and fields?* "I will do as I see fit with my property, Mr. Hartley, and you must do as you see fit with your responsibilities as well."

Miss Fenner chose that moment to bounce down the stairs, smiling as if Father Christmas were making an early spring call upon the household.

"Mr. Hartley! We missed you at the assembly. You aren't leaving so soon, are you?"

"I am indeed on my way, Miss Fenner. A pleasure to see you, of course."

"If you have time to admire our Holland bulbs," Margaret said, "Miss Fenner could use a breath of fresh air before returning to the nursery, I'm sure."

That provoked a smile from Mr. Hartley that Margaret had not seen before. Truly friendly instead of practiced and polite. When he smiled like that, Mr. Hartley did have a certain handsomeness.

"Please say you will stroll with me," Fenny added. "I enjoy nothing so much as fresh air and sunshine, but the children must earn their outings, and progress today in that direction has been limited."

She was dissembling. The children had had a very peaceful morning, while Margaret felt as if an enormous spring storm was boiling up in her heart.

"I will leave you to enjoy the garden," she said. "Mr. Hartley, please respect my request to leave my tenants in peace should you call again."

Bancroft's plotting aside, the way Mr. Hartley regarded Fenny confirmed that more calls were in Margaret's future. That made her so angry that she no sooner had made her farewell to Mr. Hartley than she snatched her cloak from its peg and marched down the corridor to flee out the side door into the woods.

A BLUEBELL WOOD was a magical place, not only for its visual beauty, but also for the fragrance the flowers imparted. Thorne had often stolen into the Summerton bluebell wood as a boy, but had forgotten what a lovely place it was, even when the flowers had yet to bloom. A few brave blossoms had opened at the center of the clearing, their deep periwinkle hue a pretty contrast to the new green of the grass.

A figure stormed up the path from the direction of the manor house, cloak whipping, steps thumping against the hard-packed earth.

"Mrs. Summerfield." Thorne rose from the log he'd perched on. "Good day."

"Mr. Dorning." Her curtsey conveyed annoyance. "Good morning. You have refrained from using the lane, for which I should thank you, but I do not usually receive callers in my woods."

"You already have a caller," Thorne said, making no move to approach her. "Jeremy Hartley's gelding is tied to your hitching post."

Some of the ire drained from her posture. "That's why you're lurking in my woods? Because you sought to avoid Mr. Hartley?"

"You asked for privacy about our undertakings, but I had not realized what a busy place Summerton is."

She looked about the wood, as if to ensure no fairies or elves lurked within earshot. "Busy in what sense?"

"Monday, the vicar graced you with a call and stayed for more than an hour. Yesterday, Mrs. Weller came by. I saw her walking up your lane, and knowing what a friendly woman she is, I did not tarry. I hoped Hartley's schedule allowed only a polite call."

A section of the lane was visible through the trees, down a gentle slope and across a pasture. Thorne had sat upon the downed tree and read his father's notes and the French herbal, but they'd made little sense to him.

"Hartley came by to spy for Bancroft. I ought not to have said that. I'd invite you back to the house, but he will dispatch a report of your call to London by express, and Bancroft will install footmen in my servants' hall before I've sat down to supper tomorrow."

This presumption clearly vexed her. Exceedingly. "How can Bancroft direct your staff?"

Mrs. Summerfield knelt beside the few blooming flowers and sniffed. "My nieces are the daughters of my late sister-in-law. Charles was their guardian." She did not pluck the bluebells, but instead left them to blossom with their companions. "He gave guardianship of the girls to me, directed that they should be raised at Summerton, and then appointed Bancroft co-guardian, to be consulted on major decisions affecting their well-being, though I am to have custodial authority of them in their minority."

The arrangement was unusual, but not unheard of when a man's will was carefully drafted. The widowed Duchess of Kent had legal custody of her daughter Victoria, and that dear child was in line for the throne.

"So Charles left Bancroft room to meddle," Thorne said. "Might we sit?"

She paced over to the log and took a seat. "Bancroft lives to meddle. As often as he can, he reminds me that I am not a blood relation to the girls. He never asks to see them, but he muses about blood being thicker than the peculiar fancies of a dying man, and twins are always difficult. How a self-absorbed bachelor would know anything about raising children, much less twin girls, escapes me."

Dorset sheep were famous for the frequency with which they

gave birth to twins, and to Thorne, the girls neither looked nor *felt* like twins—not that little girls were sheep.

And not that talk of family squabbles was advancing the purpose of Thorne's excursion. "What exactly did Hartley want?"

"To undermine my authority as owner of Summerton, while claiming to be gallant and helpful. At Bancroft's direction, Mr. Hartley has done me the very great favor of riding over my lands, inspecting my farms, and likely interrogating my tenants. He told me I need not thank him." She scuffed a boot through the grass. "Mr. Dorning, I wanted to dump the teapot over his head."

*Call me Hawthorne.* "Why now?" Thorne asked the obvious question. "Charles has been gone almost four years. Why encroach on your authority now?"

She looked out over the clearing, toward the house. "Charles left Bancroft a solvent estate in good repair. Bancroft took a notion to enclose the commons adjacent to the estate village. Building miles of stout fencing is enormously expensive. Charles's father had enclosed some of the common land, and the estate had barely recovered when old Mr. Summerfield died. Charles said we had enough enclosed land, and the villagers needed the open land that remained. He was right."

Thorne's father had refused to enclose any land adjacent to the village, and Casriel concurred with that decision, as did Thorne.

"So Bancroft is cash poor?"

"Destitute would be my guess. Summerton, by contrast, operates at a tidy profit."

She turned her face up to the sun, which beamed down with subtle warmth. A moderate breeze would turn the day brisk, but here in the bluebell wood, the elements were kind.

"That profit belongs to you," Thorne said.

"And believe me, I use the solicitors my own family hired to manage my funds. I could not do the same with the girls' dower portions, but I receive regular reports and forward them to my lawyers. Charles put the money in the cent-per-cents, and there it will stay until Bancroft can finagle a way to steal from his nieces."

This recitation left Thorne wanting to stand his brothers to a pint at the posting inn. Dornings argued, teased, squabbled, and occasionally engaged in fisticuffs with one another, but they weren't prone to this sneaking, mean-spirited contention.

"I'm sorry you are beset by a traitor in the person of the one man you ought to be able to rely on," Thorne said. "The law is on your side, though, and the girls are thriving in your care."

"They are," she said. "I should not air the family linen like this. I do apologize. Bancroft's objective is to bother me, and I must deny him that satisfaction. You brought books."

Thorne had considered bringing her flowers. The Dorning Hall conservatory always had a few specimens in bloom, but flowers would have been a presumption.

"I brought recipes." He passed over his father's notebooks and the French herbal.

She leafed through the French volume first, then set it aside. "Nothing remarkable there. Heavy on the lavender, but then, French lavender is good quality."

With Papa's journals, she took more time, even getting up to pace as she read, then coming to a halt in a slanting beam of sunshine. Her strawberry-blond hair turned to copper and golden highlights as she stood, head bent, finger tracing down a page.

She belonged here, in this greening wood, birds flitting through the canopy, a few bluebells teasing at her hems. If Thorne could have characterized the scent of the place in one word—damp earth, new grass, a hint of cedar and flowers—he would have used the word *renewal*. The clearing smelled of hope, resilience, and beauties yet to bloom.

"These notes are all very interesting," she said some moments later. "I would like to study them at greater length, but nothing that I've seen will yield a recipe I could comment on knowledgeably, Mr. Dorning. I'm sorry."

Thorne had waited while she'd leafed through six entire note-books. "*Nothing* is of any value? My father was one of the most learned and avid amateur botanists in the world. Surely something among those notes must point in a useful direction."

*It had to.*

"That could well be," Margaret said, pacing back to the tree. "But I cannot comment on those notes. They all relate to medicinal tonics, lotions, and plasters. Hannah Weller might be able to help you if that's the direction you seek to take your enterprise."

Thorne rose, resisting the impulse to kick the downed tree. "I seek to take our enterprise in any profitable direction that I can achieve in the next ninety days. If Dorning Hall is not to supply London with tonics and plasters, then we're eschewing half the products we could easily manufacture."

She stood toe to toe with him, adding a whiff of orange and clove to the olfactory bouquet of the clearing.

"I will not involve myself in any undertaking purporting to deal with medicinals, Mr. Dorning. I know fragrances, I enjoy them. Medicinals are beyond my purview. Too many people dabble in medical lore without the proper knowledge, and much harm results." She shoved the journals at him. "What are those?"

The two children's books lay where Thorne had left them on a boulder in the dappled shade of a sturdy beech tree.

"Those are for the girls." The children's stories became an awkward offering, given the lady's refusal to assist Thorne with medical products. London's myriad apothecaries did a booming business in patent remedies, tisanes, and liver pills, alas for the Dorning brothers.

"You brought books for the girls?" She picked up the one with the better illustrations. "Why?"

"Because rainy days require books, and England has more than its share of rainy days." The late earl had said as much, and when in a magnanimous mood, he'd read to his children on gloomy afternoons.

Mrs. Summerfield subsided onto the tree trunk. "These illustrations are marvelous."

While this meeting in the woods was a complete waste of time. Every rural household made up a few remedies—willow bark tea, mustard plasters, comfrey salve, chamomile tea, calendula tinctures. Thorne had little idea *how* those concoctions were put together, though, much less which ones could be made cheaply in quantity and which were harder to create.

"You are frustrated," Mrs. Summerfield said, closing the book of adventures.

"I am *worried*," Thorne said, taking the place beside her. "Casriel lit upon a fine notion—develop the herbal resources at Dorning Hall —but he was sparing with the details. Months later, and I am still vague on the details myself. I have lived my entire life at Dorning Hall. I know where every rosemary border or patch of mint is planted, but I don't know what to do in order to—"

She put her hand on his arm. Only now did Thorne realize that for the lady of the manor to go abroad in the spring sunshine without a parasol, bonnet, or gloves was unusual. Hartley's visit had upset her even more than she'd allowed Thorne to see.

"I must be careful," she said, hugging the book to her chest. "Bancroft is poised to meddle, and if he got wind that I was associated with your venture, he'd find a way to use that against me."

What hold could Bancroft possibly have over a woman as self-possessed, practical, and secure as Margaret Summerfield seemed to be?

"He'll interfere with the children?"

"All he has to do is bring a suit in Chancery, and the expense and scandal will ruin me. I hold a life estate at Summerton, but I can't sell the property because the remainder goes to the girls. I have cash enough for my needs and a bit put by, but I have a widow's mite compared to what a protracted lawsuit would entail. Besides,"—she hunched in on herself, as if the clearing were suddenly chilly—"Bancroft would win. The judges would find in his favor, and I'd be lucky to see the girls once a week from across the churchyard."

The situation at Summerton was complicated, and Thorne did not like complications. He liked even less the idea that Bancroft Summerfield was making Margaret's life difficult.

"What if you remarried?" Thorne asked. "What leverage would Bancroft have if you became Mrs. Hawthorne Dorning of Dorning Hall?"

# CHAPTER EIGHT

Long, long ago, as a schoolgirl with a head full of fancies, Margaret had fallen asleep whispering the words *Mrs. Hawthorne Dorning* to her pillow. In a darkened room, while she dreamed of a strapping youth with a blazing smile, those words had been daring, sweet, and silly.

In this sunny glade, the words were still daring and sweet, but Margaret was no longer that fanciful girl. Perhaps the words weren't silly either.

"I beg your pardon, sir?"

"I should beg your pardon," Mr. Dorning said, rising. "That was no sort of... no sort of anything." He crossed the clearing and almost tromped on the few bluebells in bloom. "I did not expect to have this discussion with you today."

"Did you expect to have it with someone else?" He'd never married, never courted a woman that Margaret knew of, and yet, he was well liked and much respected. Of all the Dornings, Hawthorne was the first to put his hand to any difficult communal task, the first to help a neighbor beset by accident or illness.

"I did not expect to raise the topic of holy matrimony with

anybody for quite some time," he said, "but then Willow took a lovely wife, Casriel found his countess, Ash is admiring a lady from afar, and a man gets to thinking."

"About *me?*" The notion was so endearing—and so ironic—Margaret couldn't help but smile.

"Of course about you," Hawthorne said, retracing his steps. "About matrimony, and perfumes, and tisanes, and,"—he looked up at the ash and beech branches entwining overhead—"about armies marching across the Asian steppes."

He'd brought books for the girls, and now this...

"They are good girls, Hawthorne Dorning. The best, and should you find the prospect of becoming a step-uncle unappealing..."

He cocked his head, as if waiting for her to switch back into English. "I like children. Like them a lot. When my niece left Dorning Hall for her fancy school, I moped for three months. My only consolation was that Casriel was moping worse than I and needed cheering up with an occasional cuff on the back of the head."

"You like children." Memories of Hawthorne with this or that tenant's son on his shoulders while he walked between windrows of raked hay, or at his side when he laid a hedge came to mind. He did like children. He was patient and had the knack of making children feel included and useful instead of in the way and bothersome.

Even Charles hadn't had that gift.

"You want my perfume recipes."

"I do. I haven't made a secret of that. What do you want, Margaret?"

Another woman might have been put off by his honesty. Margaret treasured him for it—more irony.

"I want for Charles not to have died so young. I want Bancroft to charm his way into the good graces of some heiress so he'll leave me and the girls alone. I want..."

*What did she want?* Hawthorne was an earl's son and thus undeniably eligible. He had no vices that Margaret knew of, and he cared deeply for the land. He liked children. He valued her expertise with perfumes, which she'd all but set aside when Charles had died.

Another loss to lay at Bancroft's feet. Another complication.

"I never thought to remarry," she said. "I am content with my life at Summerton. I envisioned myself raising the girls, setting aside a little coin each year, minding my own vine and fig tree, as it were."

"Never having any children of your own?"

The question hurt, more than he could know, but then, Margaret had kept much about her circumstances private. Only Charles had had all the facts, and he'd taken those confidences with him to the grave—she hoped.

"I'm happy to have the raising of the twins." Overjoyed, even as she lamented that a young couple had died and would never see their offspring grow up.

"And that's all you want? To live out your days with Bancroft sending spies to call on you, ignoring his nieces unless he can use them as pawns, pretending that your ability to concoct fragrances isn't—what did Hannah Weller call it?—just short of divine inspiration?"

Bancroft was a problem, true. Hunting for an heiress amid Mayfair ballrooms was expensive work, and even were he successful, he'd have to contribute something to the bride's settlements. His management of Summerfield had got off to an impecunious start, and large estates did not reverse course easily.

"What about you?" Margaret asked, rising. "What do you want?"

She made the mistake of allowing her gaze to stray to Mr. Dorning's mouth. That tender, adept, smiling, clever, kissable male mouth...

"I enjoy copulation," he said, "if that's what you're asking. Enjoy it a lot. I'm not looking merely for a business partner, Margaret, but neither am I looking for somebody whose entire role is to sit at the far end of my dinner table. I contemplate taking a wife, and it did occur to me that you and I would suit quite well, in many regards."

They would suit. They were both practical people, and the idea that Margaret *could* be a business partner of sorts... Though how practical was it to recall a man's kisses when trying to think clearly about his courtship overtures?

Bancroft would object to the marriage, strenuously, if given the chance.

"I must consider this," Margaret said. "I must give the notion of marriage to you careful thought, and you are not to badger me for a response. I can promise you nothing, Hawthorne, other than that I will ponder my options."

And ponder what marriage with a man who liked copulation *a lot* might mean.

"Good for you," he said. "The decision wants careful consideration, and if you do look with favor upon my suit, we must negotiate the terms upon which the marriage will go forward. I realize I am not my titled brother, or my charming brother, or the one who's clever with numbers, or the fellow who can take on a London club and turn it into a profitable venture. I am not—"

Margaret put her fingers over his lips. "You are the one who works hard, who never complains, who behaves well under all circumstances, who is loyal to his loved ones, and who knows how to kiss a woman so she dreams delightful dreams and stares out of windows, hoping to see you riding over the hill."

"Am I indeed?"

He wasn't blushing, but he'd taken to staring at the bluebells across the clearing. His eyes were the color of the little blossoms.

"You are all of that, and you are the man I'd like to kiss right now." *Before I lose my nerve.*

He took her in his arms and turned so he could half-sit, half-brace himself against the fallen tree. "As it happens, I am abundantly willing to be the man you kiss."

He tucked Margaret into the vee of his spread legs and bussed her cheek. "Your turn, Mrs. Summerfield, and I've been dreaming delightfully of you too."

CASRIEL HAD MADE A LOVE MATCH, as every gossip in the shire felt bound to remark whenever the subject of the earl's marriage came up within Thorne's hearing. Willow had made a love match, as had both of Thorne's sisters. If Lady Della Haddonfield ever brought Ash up to scratch, their union would be one of sheer romance writ large.

As Thorne wrapped his arms around Margaret, he wondered if half a love match was better than no love match at all.

He'd admired Margaret Summerfield from a respectful distance for years, even when she'd been plain Miss Margaret Mallory living quietly with an elderly aunt. Margaret had a spark about her not of wildness, but of *wilderness*. Sunlight loved her, her smile spoke of blue skies, and her way of moving wanted fields to hike and wooded trails to wander.

Thorne had had nothing to offer her as a mere youth, then he'd gone off to university. On summer holidays, he'd watched her at the assemblies as she danced with every other bachelor. By the time he'd come home to Dorset to stay, she had married Charles Summerfield, and Thorne had wished them both well. The happy couple had gone on an extended wedding journey—a relief, that.

Dorning Hall had needed a steward and as much free labor as the brothers could offer. Life, season by season, had gone on.

And now, Thorne was to again kiss the lady he'd once pined for—or be kissed by her. Margaret gradually let him have her weight. She was no sprite, which suited him wonderfully, for he was the family plough horse. Her arms came around his waist, inside his coat, and she rested her cheek against his chest.

"I had forgotten," she said. "I have forgotten so much, as if I'd brewed a potion to becloud my memories."

"What have you forgotten, Margaret?" Thorne could guess, but he wanted to hear her say the words—and he wanted to take down her hair. He settled for stroking her back as desire stirred and a breeze teased at the wildflowers.

"I had forgotten the sheer pleasure of a sturdy embrace," she said. "The warmth of a man's body. The sensations of nearness, and"—she paused to sniff at him—"the trust that goes with intimacy. You use lavender soap with a dash of peppermint. Peppermint is easy to overdo."

Thorne kissed her on the lips rather than let her pursue that thought. "I hope my kisses are flavored with joy. Care to investigate?"

She did investigate, setting a leisurely pace while she plundered Thorne's mouth—*she tastes sweet*, was the extent of his discernment—and pressed close everywhere they touched. Thorne let himself become aroused, for Margaret was certainly waxing enthusiastic. She stroked her palms over his chest, then went a-viking around his waist and over his hips to clutch him by the bum.

*Why didn't I bring a blanket?* The thought formed in Thorne's mind as Margaret drew away, finishing the embrace with a glancing caress to his falls.

"Refreshing your recollections?" Thorne asked.

That was the wrong thing to say. Margaret's smile faltered, and she took a step back. "I'm sorry. I miss Charles, in many ways, but our union... This is awkward."

Thorne did not dare touch her, because what she had to say mattered, and the moment might not arise again.

"Margaret, I'm glad your marriage was happy. I'm glad Charles was a proper and doting husband to you. You deserved that, and I'm sure you made him a wonderful wife. Speak of him as you need to, miss him, wish he hadn't died. I am attracted to you and I respect you, but that you loved Charles and cherish his memory must never come between us."

"You mean that."

"Of course." Especially the part about being attracted to her and respecting her.

She took the place beside Thorne on the log. "Charles and I were friends, good friends. Still, I did not expect that our marriage would be anything other than a cordial union, pleasant for all concerned. Perhaps we'd have a child of our own—Charles wanted a child—but that wasn't meant to be. I never expected he and I would grow as close as we did. I don't think he anticipated that either."

"So you lost not only your husband, but also your best friend when Charles died." Thorne's best friends were his brothers, and one by one, life was stealing them away. Far better to lose them to life than to death.

"Yes, exactly, and we didn't foresee the girls coming to live with us. Charles was a doting and devoted uncle, but then influenza orphaned the girls, and he became their guardian."

"And you became a sort of mother." Margaret apparently inhabited that role naturally, right down to the slight lack of confidence that troubled many a loving parent.

"That word..." She unbuttoned the top three buttons of her cloak. "Bancroft hovers at my elbow, waiting to pounce. He might allow me to raise the girls in peace if I'd wink at his plundering of their bequests. I refuse to wink. That is all the money they will have in the world, and a lady cannot count on marriage to provide security for her entire life."

"I'm not wealthy, Margaret." That had to be said as well. "I have some savings. I have a livelihood. I can support you and the girls modestly without taking a penny from your estate. Casriel might deed me one of the farms that's losing money, but I can't promise that. The steward's house at Dorning Hall has eight bedrooms and comes with some acreage for a garden if you want to rent out Summerton."

This discussion was a far cry from romantic dreams, but Thorne treasured the fact that he and Margaret could speak frankly. She owned property. She understood the demands of caring for land. She grasped the economics of a rural lifestyle.

And she smelled like some exotic Spanish orchard, of juicy oranges and warm spices. Thorne permitted himself to take a whiff of her hair and wrap an arm around her waist.

She rested her head on his shoulder as if they, too, were good friends. "I am not wealthy either, but I have longed to wander Dorning Hall's fields of herbs and botanicals. I recall seeing your father hiking about, a specimen sack over his shoulder. He and Hannah Weller had rousing arguments, but he also listened to her when she disagreed with him. He got on particularly well with Hannah's grandson Lucas, and Lucas adored the earl."

Thorne hadn't known that. He'd known only that Papa disappeared into the countryside for whole days, and sometimes went on walking expeditions elsewhere in Britain. He'd sent seeds and plants all over the world and received them from foreign parts as well.

"So you'd like access to Dorning Hall's plant stores and conservatory written into the settlements?"

"I don't know. I need time to think about this, Hawthorne. I must consider the girls first and foremost. I must not be swayed by selfish inclinations."

A reference to Bancroft lay in what Margaret wasn't saying, but so too, did reason for encouragement. Her selfish inclinations apparently swayed in Thorne's direction.

A faint sound of trotting hooves drew Thorne's eye to the drive. Jeremy Hartley was departing the premises, though he'd far exceeded the fifteen minutes considered polite.

"Your visitor has taken himself off," Thorne said. "Shall I leave Papa's notebooks with you?"

"Please. I will take good care of them, I promise, and thank you for the loan of the children's books too."

He'd meant them as a gift. "What do you miss most about your marriage to Charles?"

Margaret sat up. "Oh, everything. He was there, a bulwark against all tribulations, and I tried to be that for him as well. I could not haggle with the tenants or decide to whom to rent Summerfield House for the shooting season, but I could keep him comfortable. I could remind him to rest and take his illness seriously. He even listened to me half the time."

*I can do that—listen to you at least half the time.* "My parents were not particularly well suited," Thorne said, "but when Mama died, my father said he missed even her nagging. He could tell from the sound of her footsteps whether she was angry, happy, busy, or content, and he missed that too."

"Marriage is an odd undertaking. When it works, it's wonderful."

Had it ever *not* worked between Charles and Margaret? "I can pledge my utmost commitment to making our union successful, Margaret. I'm not afraid of hard work."

She scooted off the log and collected the various books and notebooks. "If I know anything about you, it's that you are industrious. Give me a week."

Seven days to decide his fate. Thorne cast around for a lure that might tempt her to say yes, in addition to his kisses and his modest income. Every bachelor had an abundance of kisses to share, though the Dorning Hall botanicals were also apparently attractive to her.

"I'll call on you next week," Thorne said, rising and dusting off his backside. "Until then, perhaps you might give some thought to how an herbal manufactory should be designed."

She brushed at her skirts. "I beg your pardon?"

"If Dorning Hall is to enter the business of selling botanical extractions commercially, we'll need a facility to produce those products, won't we? The herbal at the Hall itself sits beneath the family wing, which Casriel has taken a notion to tear down. We have stone and some timber salvaged from demolition of the dower house, and we can use that to build whatever it is that one builds when producing fragrances and whatnot."

"Whatnot." Margaret bent and plucked a single bluebell. "You think to take the London markets by storm with *whatnot* distilled by *whatever-it-is* means, using recipes that you haven't yet devised."

She was amused. "I not only think it, Casriel and my brothers expect it."

She kissed his cheek and passed him the flower. "Until next week, Mr. Dorning."

And off she went down the woodland path, leaving Thorne with a single fragrant little flower and a whole bouquet of hope.

"WHEN I AWOKE THIS MORNING, I did not foresee a proposal of marriage from Mr. Dorning," Margaret said. "And yet, I had the sense that Hawthorne has considered the matter carefully and is making a sincere and well-intended offer."

Hannah Weller adjusted the towel she'd wrapped around the blue porcelain teapot. "I saw you dancing with him at last week's assembly, my dear. He was considering something, all right, and so were you."

At eighty-three years of age, Hannah said precisely what she thought. Margaret had always relied on the older woman's honesty, painful though that had sometimes been.

"Bancroft is off to Town," Margaret said. "Hunting an heiress, no doubt. Mr. Hartley did not attend the assembly, and I thought I was free to enjoy myself a little. Mr. Dorning walked me up the drive at the end of the evening."

Hannah's cottage sat at the edge of the Summerton acres just outside the village. The smell of the place was marvelous. Every species of herb and flower ever collected in Dorsetshire contributed to the scent, as did myriad spices and exotic fragrances.

"He walked you up the drive," Hannah said, lifting the lid of the teapot. "Then he bowed politely and wished you good night?"

"We shared a kiss, then he waited at the foot of the steps until I was safely inside the house."

"Lady Jacaranda put the manners on her brothers, a thankless task, no doubt. What did you think would happen when you allowed a bachelor of sound mind and even sounder body to kiss you?"

"That he'd go home and go to bed, then get up the next morning and attend services. I don't know, Hannah. I am so absorbed with raising the girls, minding my tenants, and avoiding Bancroft's notice that I didn't think Mr. Dorning's overtures meant anything."

Hadn't allowed herself to think that.

Hannah poured two cups of tea—mugs, not delicate china. "You pined for Hawthorne Dorning once upon a time."

The scent of chamomile and lemon wafted up from Margaret's cup. Hannah always knew what to serve, and this combination was both soothing and bracing.

"Every girl in the shire chose a Dorning to pine for," Margaret said. "I liked Hawthorne because he was quiet without being bashful. He's a doer, not a talker, and he never once teased me about being a Long Meg. This could use just a touch of cinnamon."

"I agree, or possibly ginger."

"Ginger is too sharp, unless you use a very high-quality ginger. What should I do, Hannah? Bancroft will be against the marriage and could try to use it to take the girls from me. I cannot lose those children, not to Bancroft Summerfield."

Hannah wrapped ancient hands around her mug. "If there were no children, would you marry Hawthorne?"

"Yes."

"In ten years, the girls will be of marriageable age, twelve at most. Then you will be, what? Not yet forty years old. Consider that another forty years of life might remain to you after the girls find husbands. If you pass up Hawthorne Dorning's offer now, you will have traded ten years with the girls for fifty years with him. Is that what you want?"

"I am all they have, Hannah. What I want doesn't matter."

"Have a biscuit. You wonder whether Mr. Dorning can intimidate Bancroft into doing the right thing and leaving the girls with you."

"That's part of it." Margaret took a nibble of a sweet, pale biscuit. "You used lard instead of butter."

"Lard gives a lighter texture."

The spices absent from the tea were present in the biscuit—cinnamon with a hint of ginger—and yet, for Margaret, the combination didn't work. Lard did not taste the same as butter, for all it did result in a lighter texture.

"I promised Bancroft I would never dabble in medicinal herbs again."

"You did not dabble. You learned everything I know, read everything you could find, and experimented with every plant you could dig up. The old earl said you were a genius."

The old earl was gone and had apparently never mentioned Margaret's abilities to his sons. "His lordship also said Lucas should study medicine in Edinburgh."

"Drink your tea, Margaret. It's best consumed hot."

Margaret rose, leaving the tea at the table. "I would have to tell Hawthorne about Charles, Hannah. Bancroft won't remain silent, and I owe a man planning to marry me that much honesty."

*At least* that much honesty.

"Bancroft is an idiot, and he's an idiot who will bide in London until the shopkeepers refuse to grant him any more credit. You have time to marry Mr. Dorning, and if it becomes necessary to explain a few particulars about your first marriage, then you can choose the time and place for that after the vows have been spoken."

"A marriage should be built on trust. Charles trusted me, and I trusted him."

Hannah dipped a biscuit into her tea. "And then dear Charles turned about and gave Bancroft the keys to your nursery."

That had been an unwelcome posthumous surprise, but as the solicitors had pointed out, Charles had died young, and the girls' parents had died young. If Margaret should expire, better for Adriana and Greta to be wards of an uncle than left to the mercies of court-appointed guardians—assuming the courts didn't appoint Bancroft in the first place.

Margaret wandered the room, pausing before a sketch of Lucas Weller. The likeness was good, catching Lucas's merry and gentle nature. Margaret had seen the drawing many times, but now, Lucas's kindly expression gave her the sense he was commiserating with her.

Another death at much too young an age. "He was so dear. I've never asked you who drew this."

"Oak Dorning. I believe he drew it from memory. He brought it by in that frame about a month after Lucas died."

The frame was rustic wood, which suited Lucas's open features and tousled dark hair.

"Hannah, I am tempted to marry Hawthorne Dorning." Lucas would not have begrudged her that happiness, nor would Charles. "I face a constant battle with Bancroft, whose brilliant management is running Summerfield House into the ground. He sent Hartley to sniff about my hedges and inspect my fields, and that was not an exercise in familial concern."

"Hartley is competent." A substantial compliment from Hannah, who regarded stewardship of the land as a biblical vocation.

"Hartley cannot raise a crop of pound notes, which is what Bancroft needs. He's in London trying to woo an heiress, or I'd have no reprieve from his meddling."

Hannah dipped the second half of her biscuit into her tea. "Hawthorne Dorning is an earl's son, an outstanding farmer, and a gentleman. How can Bancroft argue that the girls are worse off with Hawthorne for a step-uncle than they are in your sole care?"

That question sliced to the root of the dilemma cleanly: Bancroft would posture and pontificate, but marriage to Hawthorne could strengthen Margaret's hold on the girls rather than diminish it.

"I feel as if I'm overlooking some obvious impediment," Margaret said, touching her fingers to Lucas's cheek. "My life has been a series of stumbles that have nearly sent me to my knees. If not for Charles..."

But Charles *had* come along, the marriage *had* been happy, and the girls *were* in Margaret's custody.

"You don't need my permission to marry a worthy man, Margaret, but you do have my blessing. The Dornings are fine fellows, and Hawthorne is not hard on the eyes either."

And he *enjoyed* copulation. Even recalling that admission and the frank humor with which he'd made it caused Margaret to blush.

"I will give this matter more thought," she said, resuming her place at the table. "The bluebells are starting to bloom. Have you noticed?"

"I thought to check on them tomorrow, if the day holds fair. Will you take the girls to see them?"

"Lately, we are in the woods almost daily. Since Charles's death, I have not allowed myself to wander the hedges or to collect any but the most mundane specimens. I experiment with scents, but I don't lose myself in foraging as you and I used to. To be out of doors at this time of year, away from the house for some part of every day, is good for me. I'd lost sight of that."

"Perhaps Mr. Dorning has what you seek."

*What do you want, Margaret?* He'd put that exact question to her and, in so doing, had helped her form at least part of her answer: She wanted a man who valued her happiness and who allowed her to be a part of his happiness as well. She wanted a partner, a friend, and a lover whom she could esteem for all the rest of her days.

And yet, she hesitated. "He'll call upon me in a few days. He'll expect an answer."

"That doesn't mean you have to give him one. Bancroft has barely arrived in London. You have time, Margaret. For once, you have the luxury of time."

Margaret turned the talk to the vast and far-flung Weller family and half an hour later took her leave. As she made her way home, Hawthorne Dorning's question circled in her mind: What did she want?

She wanted him. The other factors—an ally, a companion, a partner, a friend—all mattered, but undeniably, Margaret also wanted *him*.

# CHAPTER NINE

"Did you ever know Charles Summerfield to be ill or grievously injured?" Thorne asked.

Valerian passed him a letter from the stack he was sorting. "We all came off our ponies from time to time. That one's from Grey. If he's returning to Dorning Hall, you will please warn us."

"I don't mean a typical boyhood mishap." Thorne peered at the letter, not particularly eager to open it. "I mean an illness or disability that followed him into adulthood."

"He had scarlet fever," Oak said, ambling along the library's bookshelves. "I recall Mama sending over baskets of oranges, apple cider vinegar, lemons, and honey. We were not permitted to play at Summerton for most of one spring."

"Brother Oak sees all," Thorne murmured. "Give me that letter." From the far side of the desk, Thorne recognized the familiar scrawling penmanship.

"I thought Charles had St. Vitus's dance." Valerian held the letter up to the window's light and peered at the direction. "I rejoice to inform you that the infant Sycamore yet lives."

"Maybe Charles had both," Oak said, snatching Sycamore's letter from Valerian and passing it to Thorne. "That can happen. First the scarlet fever, then you think it's gone, and next thing you know, more fevers and aches. We haven't had a letter from Jacaranda for a while."

"She and Worth are visiting in the north," Thorne said, tucking away Sycamore's letter. Sycamore knew that no correspondence at Dorning Hall remained private for long, but he was nonetheless blunt to a fault. If property for opening an apothecary was not to be had, Thorne wanted to learn of that before Valerian did.

"Last I heard," Valerian said, "the king's mail reached even Cumbria. We also haven't heard from Ash."

Oak resumed wandering along shelves he'd had more than twenty years to peruse. "Cumbria is beautiful, I'm told. The light is different from what we have here, more like the Low Countries, but the terrain is dramatic. I'd like to see that."

"While we," Valerian said, "rather than fret that you've caught an ague tramping in the hinterlands, would like for you to remain safe and warm and happy among those who—this one's for you."

Oak ambled back to the desk and took the letter without looking at it. "What has Grey to tell us, Thorne?"

"When I read the letter, I'll let you know. Sycamore is trying to find us a commercial property well situated to distribute our products. Perhaps he's had some success. To the best of your recall, Charles Summerfield recovered from his fevers, didn't he?"

Thorne hadn't paid much attention to Summerfield. Charles had been a genial, well-liked young man, but for most of his youth, he'd attended a church closer to the Summerfield family seat. Besides, Thorne had been too busy either trying to get a glimpse of Margaret Mallory, or telling himself to stop longing for what could not be.

"You'd best ask Hannah Weller about Charles's health," Oak said. "She is the local historian of illness and injury, and she will regale you with tales of infirmity until the biscuits are gone and the tea is cold. I hope to be half as sharp when I'm her age."

Valerian had set aside three epistles addressed to Grey. "What's in your letter, Oak? You can tell us the nice way, or we'll just beat it out of you."

An empty threat. Oak was as fast as the wind with his fists or on foot, and if Oak's privacy was forfeit, Thorne's would be next.

Oak made a show of studying his epistle. "The letter is from Hampshire."

Valerian steepled his fingers on the desk, like a patient headmaster. "The direction told me that."

Valerian should have been a spy. The notion dropped into Thorne's head all of a piece and made such perfect sense, he nearly blurted it out. Valerian had the self-possession, the easy manners in all company, the keen powers of observation, the ability to put puzzles together.

A pity there was no demand for spies in Dorset. None at all.

Oak strolled to the window that overlooked the back garden. A tidy, formal expanse that Mama had insisted be preserved from the craze for reconstructed nature. Papa had indulged her, likely because sculpting entire landscapes to look like paintings cost exorbitantly.

"I asked Worth to nose around for me," Oak said. "I am good at restoring old paintings, and I am a creditable portraitist. Worth has mentioned a neighbor from time to time, a lady who lives not far from Trysting. She has a significant collection that needs work. I have the ability to restore it. She's writing to let me know that I have the post— or that she has declined my services."

Well, damn. Sweet, quiet, industrious Oak had stolen a march on them all. "What of our labels and advertisements for the botanical business?" Thorne asked.

Oak tried to open the window, which squeaked and groaned, and eventually yielded a whole six inches.

"I have done myriad sketches and paintings for that purpose," Oak said. "I can continue to support the endeavor from Hampshire."

"Hampshire?" Valerian rose from the desk. "You're off to bloody Hampshire?"

"Bloody Hampshire is for the most part a day's hard ride or

not-so-hard coaching from us," Thorne said, slitting open Grey's letter. "Before you accept the offer, Oak, please do Grey the courtesy of informing him that you're considering a position. He's still the head of this family, and he might hear of other posts while in London. His access to London gossip means he might also know something of your prospective patroness that you should be apprised of."

"Nobody knows much about her," Oak said, bracing his backside against the windowsill. "Even Worth, who is legendarily interfering when it comes to ladies without champions, doesn't know much about her."

Valerian snatched up his three letters. "And that fascinates you? This woman has alienated her neighbors, has no proper society, and you're ready to drop everything and abandon us to become her artist in the attic?"

"He hasn't accepted anything yet, Valerian," Thorne interjected. "Your display of concern—which only looks, sounds, and feels like a jealous tantrum—is unwarranted."

The silence that sprang up had a familiar, uncomfortable feel. Ever since Willow had taken a bride, the Dorning brothers had been in a state of unrest. Thorne expected his sisters to marry—Daisy, though among the younger siblings, had married before any of her elders. Jacaranda was too managing not to have a household of her own and had gone into service as a housekeeper with that objective in mind.

Along Worth Kettering had come, and Jacaranda had promptly had a husband to manage too.

"Things change," Thorne said. "Sycamore is thriving in London, Grey has taken a countess, Willow has never been happier. We wish them all the best, and if Oak should become God's gift to some Hampshire recluse's attic, then so be it. I will miss him, but rejoice in his good fortune."

Valerian recovered his aplomb between one breath and the next. His visage shifted from scowling to genial. His posture changed from that of a man righteously charging into a melee, to the languid saunter of an aristocratic ornament.

"You are quite right," he said, "as you are with obnoxious frequency. I stand rebuked and offer Oak my sincerest apologies. Best of luck, dear boy. May all your attics be full of priceless nudes."

"Bugger yourself," Oak muttered, heading for the door. "It's a fine day. I'm off to do some sketching."

"Why every young man should learn to sketch," Valerian said as Oak's footsteps faded down the corridor. "So he can make a polite exit from any company and claim the siren song of nature's beauty compels him to seek the out of doors. He'll get in a spot of fishing, have a fine nap at the abbey ruins, and dream of pigments and portraits."

"What the hell ails you?" Thorne asked.

"I have developed the ability to read correspondence that has yet to be opened," Valerian said, taking the spot at the window. "Grey's letter chides us all for not having products to send to London. We do have products, of course, bundles of lavender, bales of peppermint, but those are wholesale goods. And to the extent we simply turn them over to shop owners or market vendors, we part with substantial coin we might be keeping for ourselves. Grey would know that if he stopped gazing fondly at his countess for so much as a day."

Grey was more than fond of his countess. He'd defied the weight of common sense, financial imperative, and patriarchal duty to marry his dear Beatitude.

"Perhaps Grey is informing us of impending uncledom." Thorne broke the seal and scanned the contents.

"He will," Valerian said darkly. "He's a Dorning. It's only a matter of time before the union is fruitful."

"So what news did the post bring you?" Thorne said, skipping past all the Town gossip. "You have three epistles, none of them local. None of them in a hand I recognize. You make a great noise about Oak seeking a position in Hampshire, while you quietly carry on your own campaign to leave the Hall."

"We've already left the Hall."

Thorne cast his gaze around the library. "And yet, every day, we're back under its roof. Consulting with the staff, collecting the post, dwelling here in spirit while we sleep elsewhere."

He went back to reading, because glowering at Valerian in the midst of this discussion was pointless. Valerian had a scheme afoot, but he'd part with the details only when he damned pleased to.

"The widow in Hampshire has been corresponding with Oak for two months," Valerian said. "I suspect her means are limited."

"That is none of our..." Thorne reread the sentence at the bottom of the page, certain he'd mistaken Grey's meaning, but no. "I must kill my brother."

"It's not my turn to be killed. If you kill Sycamore, we might inherit his gaming hell, and Ash probably has a notion how to run it. Kill Grey and Willow becomes the first earl in the realm to prefer dogs to people. Thank heavens Lady Susannah prefers Willow to almost—Thorne, *what is it?*"

"Grey has gone mad," Thorne said, passing over the letter. "He thinks to sell the pasture and fields bordering Summerton. He further notes that Bancroft Summerfield has conveniently presented himself in Town, and Grey is considering approaching him with an offer to sell the land."

"Having Bancroft for a neighbor doesn't suit, I take it?"

"Dorning Hall needs that water meadow, Valerian. It's our best hay, our only guarantee of early grass, and the means by which I drained the pasture below the mares' field. Bancroft can flood our mares' field, destroy what little profit the home farm makes... This is the last parcel of land Grey should sell."

"But the only one for which he's likely to find a willing buyer knocking on his very door."

And therein lay the difficulty. "I am to call on Margaret Summer-field in three days' time. I cannot go to damned London. I can send an express, which Grey will put off reading until Beatitude jollies him into it. Then he'll dismiss my reasoning as old-fashioned clinging to every acre for the sake of tradition, which I most assuredly am not. Without that water meadow... Bloody bleating hell, I must leave for damned London at once."

First, Thorne would have to write Margaret a groveling note, which would take only the rest of the day to do properly. She would be most unhappy to find Bancroft holding land across the stream from her, and she would blame Thorne for allowing that to happen.

As well she should.

"I find," Valerian said, wrestling the window open the rest of the way, "that it's time I made a pilgrimage to the capital. My manly humors want exercising, which one cannot accomplish here amid the splendors of Dorset. My wardrobe needs refreshing. I should have a look in on Ash and Sycamore, knock their heads together for old times' sake."

"They'll be touched that you'd make the effort." *I am touched.* Valerian could not afford a new wardrobe, and he could exercise his manly humors with any number of local widows and probably had. "We also need a place of business, or Grey's brilliant scheme dies aborning."

"That's easy," Valerian said, shooting his cuffs and fluffing his cravat. "If we're selling products aimed at men, we need to be on Bond Street."

"Of course we do, but Bond Street is some of the most expensive rental property in the whole of London."

"Details, details. My first order of business will be preserving your water meadow from the clutches of Bane-croft. Leave it all in my capable hands and keep your appointment with Mrs. Summerfield."

He marched out the door before Thorne could embarrass them both with effusive thanks.

MARGARET ALLOWED herself three days to pretend she'd accept

Hawthorne Dorning's proposal, but a letter from Bancroft put a stop to her nonsense. He'd been in London less than a fortnight and had already made the acquaintance of a Miss Emily Pepper, whom he described as the well-situated only child of a *very successful* cloth nabob.

"I should be happy for Bancroft," Margaret muttered, passing the deck of cards across the table.

"I've never found Mr. Summerfield to be all that objectionable," Miss Fenner replied, shuffling the deck with deft hands. "He's a bit thick-headed about some things, or so Mr. Hartley implies—not that Mr. Hartley would be disloyal to an employer—but we're all thick-headed from time to time, aren't we?"

Mr. Hartley's name found its way into most conversations with Fenny these days. "What *does* Mr. Hartley say about his employer?"

"Oh, the usual. Mr. Hartley understands Mr. Summerfield's position, which I think is quite kind of him."

She shuffled again, the sound of the riffling cards plucking at Margaret's nerves. Hawthorne Dorning was due to call on her today. She'd put on her favorite day dress, banished the children to the garden, fortified herself with a calming pot of chamomile tea, and resorted to playing cards to pass the time.

*I would rather be working in my herbal*, except she hadn't permitted herself that joy since Charles's death. She'd dusted, reorganized, and updated her stores, but she hadn't *worked*.

"Mr. Hartley does seem to be a very sensible gentleman," Margaret said, "but what exactly does he see as Bancroft's position?"

Fenny dealt the cards using a hair too much force. One of the cards—the eight of clubs—skittered across the table straight into Margaret's lap.

"Sorry, ma'am."

This conversation rattled the utterly un-rattle-able Fenny, which suggested her loyalties were already unraveling after only two calls from Mr. Hartley.

Margaret arranged her cards from highest to lowest, as she'd taught the girls to do. "About Bancroft's position?"

"Why, he's the younger son, ma'am. Nobody expected him to inherit, and thus all that business about where to plant potatoes and where to put in corn escaped his notice. Mr. Hartley says a bit of patience is needed, is all, and Summerfield House will soon be in excellent form."

Charles had been self-conscious about his illness, but his own brother had known the truth since adolescence. If Bancroft had no idea which crop went into which field, the cause was sheer laziness. Land didn't farm itself, and the best steward was still an employee who took direction from the owner.

"What else does Mr. Hartley say about Summerfield House? The girls could end up inheriting that property, too, and one likes to be kept informed."

Hell would flood with rose water before Bancroft allowed his nieces to inherit the family seat. He had two by-blows already, quietly being raised by their mothers. Margaret made it her business to know that the boys were adequately cared for and had put in writing to their mamas her willingness to provide additional funds if needed.

Charles would have done as much, if not more.

"To be honest, ma'am," Fenny said, "Mr. Hartley and I find other subjects to discuss besides his duties at Summerfield."

"Poetry?" Fenny was a closet poet and a good one. She had Byron's sly humor, an enormous vocabulary, and a gift for treading the line between wit and cynicism.

"Mr. Hartley is hopeless when it comes to poetry, but willing to learn. Do you have any sevens?"

"Alas for you, not a seven to be seen." Sevens were good luck, not that good luck mattered when a woman was intent on refusing a very tempting marriage proposal.

Shrieking in the garden had Fenny putting her cards down. "Mr.

Dorning must be here. The pickets you posted are sounding the alarm."

On the path below the window, Greta stood on one side of Mr. Dorning, Adriana on the other. He knelt beside the dry fountain and passed over a small package to Greta.

Adriana, bless her kind heart, let the occasion pass rather than start a war based on the unfairness of a parcel given to her sister.

"How do I look?" Margaret asked, rising to study herself in the pier glass.

"You look anxious," Fenny replied, gathering up the cards. "Just recall that Mr. Dorning is likely more nervous than you are."

Nervous was not in his nature, which was one of the reasons Margaret had noticed him as a youth. The other boys had been boisterous, shy, arrogant, self-conscious, and all manner of obvious about their emotions. Hawthorne Dorning had a self-possession that had been evident even in adolescence. He was friendly without being effusive. Hardworking but not a Puritan. Physically robust but not crude—never crude—but oh my, he had a way with a kiss.

"Let's greet my guest, shall we?"

"Ma'am, before you go down, there's something you should know."

"If you give notice today, I will write you a glowing character after I bury your dismembered body. At least give me some warning, Fenny."

"Of course, ma'am, but I know Mr. Hartley doesn't call here to court my favor. He probably thinks he's being subtle, asking me to walk to the stream with him, wondering aloud why your farmers rotate through four crops instead of three, when three crops have served Dorset well for centuries, and so forth."

Bancroft was too proud to grow turnips, apparently, which meant Summerfield House did without winter fodder. Charles's father had instituted a modest acreage of turnips, and Charles had been planning to expand on that.

"You," Margaret said, leading the way from the room, "being a mere empty-headed governess, have little insight into why the farmers do as they do."

"Precisely, ma'am, but Mr. Hartley is not stupid. He's very bright, in fact, and I'm sure he's reporting all that he sees to Mr. Summerfield."

"I assumed as much, but I am disappointed for your sake. You fancy him, don't you?"

Fenny was silent until they gained the back terrace. "I love your girls, Mrs. Summerfield, love them to pieces, but children grow up, and then it's off to another post for me, probably one that's not as comfortable as Summerton. Governesses are supposed to be young and pretty, but not too pretty. I manage the not-too-pretty part well enough, but eventually youth will elude me. What becomes of me then?"

The perennial question of the sensible woman, a query that had progeny of its own should she have offspring: What will become of my daughters?

"You don't have to receive Mr. Hartley if his attentions are unwelcome, Fenny."

Over by the fountain, a rapt Greta opened the package Mr. Dorning had brought. Adriana crowded close, while Mr. Dorning perched on the edge of the basin.

"Mr. Hartley is spying, ma'am, plain and simple. He's no more interested in taking me to wife than Adriana is in learning Latin."

Adriana had begun to make strides with her Latin, provided she was taught every term that applied to centurions, chariots, legions, and conquests.

"Nothing says that Mr. Hartley's focus can't expand, Fenny. You are a lovely, dear, hardworking, frightfully well-educated, endlessly patient woman. Hartley probably underestimates you, but that doesn't mean you have to underestimate yourself."

Greta in particular would miss Fenny, but Fenny had two younger sisters in the governess line, and Margaret could likely hire one of them.

"Mr. Hartley is a hard worker too," Fenny said. "And he's not bad-looking."

"All I ask is that you remain lamentably ignorant about my estate business, Fenny. I don't want Bancroft getting greedy where Summerton is concerned, but neither do I want him thinking we manage so badly that he's justified in usurping my authority."

Fenny paused at the top of the terrace steps. "He'd do that? Take Summerton from you?"

"Bancroft would take the girls from me, knowing I'd part with Summerton, my right arm, or the heart in my breast to keep them safe and happy."

Now he was courting an heiress, which could only make acquiring sole guardianship of the girls easier. This was not the time to complicate matters with a husband who had little wealth, for all he was reliable, kind, industrious, and honorable.

And a very good kisser.

## CHAPTER TEN

The music box was a success, though Thorne mentally kicked himself for not bringing two.

Or three. Three would have been brilliant, but Dorning Hall's nursery had had only the one specimen, a relic of years past that yet played *Twinkle, Twinkle, Little Star*.

"I know this song," Adriana said, making a grab for the music box. "Fenny taught us." She put her hands at her sides and took a deep breath, like a soprano launching into her third-act aria. *"Twinkle, twinkle, little star, how I wonder what you are."*

The child had a prodigiously carrying voice.

Greta held the music box to her ear. "Hush, Dree. I want to hear the insides."

*"Up above the world so high, like a diamond in the sky! When this blazing sun is gone, when he nothing shines upon!* Aunt Margaret! Mr. Dorning brought us a music box! *Then you show your little light, twinkle, twinkle through the night!"*

Three more stanzas to go. Thorne joined in, lest the child start at the beginning. *"Then the traveler in the dark thanks you for your tiny spark. He could not see where to go, if you did not twinkle so."*

"HUSH," Greta bellowed, the music box pressed to her ear.

Adriana smiled at Thorne hugely. "I forgot that part. Aunt Margaret, Mr. Dorning can sing."

Margaret was smiling at Thorne too, which made the foolishness of nursery rhymes in the garden worth the indignity. But was her smile a yes-I-will-marry-you smile, or a you-do-me-a-great-honor smile? The answer mattered more than Thorne was comfortable admitting.

"Mrs. Summerfield." He bowed over the lady's hand. "Miss Fenner. Good day to you both."

The governess, a petite creature with a pointed chin and fine green eyes, dipped a hasty curtsey. "I fear Greta will sleep with that music box under her pillow."

"A music box can meet a worse fate," Margaret said. "Mr. Dorning, it's a pretty day for a walk. Fenny, we'll leave you with the angel chorus. Best of luck."

The women exchanged a look, partly humorous, partly long-suffering. Career soldiers probably knew that look, as did yeomen trying to wrestle a livelihood from tired ground. *Best of luck—you'll need it.*

"Let's enjoy your bluebells," Thorne said. "They have yet to reach their peak, but the blooms are gathering momentum." Margaret took his arm, and they wandered onto the path that led from the garden. Thorne let the silence stretch and tried to exude the patient confidence of a man worth marrying.

"Mr. Hartley has called on Fenny twice now," Margaret said. "He's spying for Bancroft, and Fenny knows it."

"Is Hartley spying, or pretending to spy the better to shield his masculine pride?"

"Perhaps both. Are you ready for shearing?"

Margaret Summerfield would be very good at any betting card game. "I am ready for shearing to be over," Thorne said. "Every year, I tell myself that I need not wield the clippers myself, but height gives me an advantage with the more surly beasts, and I cannot abide idleness."

"And every year, you end up with an aching back, sore arms and shoulders, a few nicks and bruises, and a great weariness that doesn't abate in time for haying. Do you apply comfrey salve?"

"I'm usually too tired after a day of shearing to apply anything but soap and water. You've had some of your deadfall cut up."

The woods had the open feel of an ancient stand, which allowed sunlight to reach the forest floor and paths to meander beneath shady boughs. In another two weeks, the canopy would reach its full glory, and the flowers would fade.

"I sent a load of wood to Hannah Weller," Margaret said. "She was my aunt's dearest friend and a great source of comfort to me before I married Charles. I've known her forever."

Thorne had not made the time to call on Mrs. Weller after their one encounter on market day. He'd been too busy getting ready for shearing and composing swainly speeches.

"If you're wearing a fragrance today," he said, "I can't detect it."

Margaret held out her bare hand. "Try near my wrist."

The forest had a scent—woodsy, of course, damp, green—and the path was downwind from the bluebells, which gave the air a light fragrance.

"Roses," Thorne said, holding Margaret's wrist beneath his nose. "And something else, something that leans toward raspberries?"

She sniffed her wrist. "Perhaps it does at that. This is my everyday soap, and I don't want it to have too strong a scent, because then it clashes with any fragrance I apply. The rose fades faster than a lavender or citrus scent would, and that can be an asset when one wants to be clean but not too aromatic. I am babbling."

"Don't be nervous, Margaret. I have little to offer, I know that, but I offer in good faith and genuinely want your happiness. If marriage to me doesn't suit you, then I will wish you well and take myself back to the shearing shed."

That recitation hadn't been among the swainly speeches Thorne had rehearsed, but perhaps it should have been. He'd been wishing

Margaret well for years—her, then her and Charles, then her, Charles, and the girls.

"My situation is complicated," she said, taking Thorne by the hand and drawing him down a different path than the one that led to the bluebells. "I believe you and I would suit wonderfully."

There was a *but* coming. *Well, hell and damnation.* "As do I."

"We are both practical people, not given to drama, happy to be useful. We are neither of us greedy or vain, and we're both loyal to those we love. My values and yours are compatible."

"You've given this considerable thought." Reason to be encouraged, perhaps?

"You are involved in an effort to make your family's botanical resources profitable, and that project matters to you greatly. I am similarly committed to raising my nieces."

From the direction of the garden, the first verse of *Twinkle, Twinkle, Little Star* had sounded several times, as had some yelling of an indeterminate nature. This was what marriage to Margaret would be like, domestic realities side by side with beauty and companionship.

Thorne's version of wedded bliss, in other words. "Your nieces appear to thrive in your care."

Margaret escorted him to a bench along the trail, a plain plank seat that had a view of the back gardens through the trees. The bluebells bloomed farther along the trail, the breeze dispersing their scent.

"Adriana would thrive anywhere she found a reasonable amount of kindness and common sense," Margaret said, patting the place beside her on the bench. "She is impossible not to love. Greta is a more complicated little person."

Greta, to be honest, was a somewhat odd little person. Thorne liked her, based on their limited acquaintance, because her oddness was of the honest, earnest variety, perhaps like his own.

"My brother Valerian is the complicated one in our family," Thorne said, sitting hip to hip with the lady. "He has hidden depths and has made appearing shallow and harmless his life's work. One crosses him at one's peril, though."

"Precisely the case with Greta. She can appear unperturbed by gale-force winds, but if her porridge hasn't been sweetened with honey, the nursery becomes the scene of pitched battle for the rest of the morning."

Margaret was directing the conversation toward some conclusion that related to Thorne's marriage proposal, but he could not for the life of him divine her strategy.

He twined his fingers with hers. "Would you like children of your own, Margaret?" She'd dodged the question the last time he'd posed it.

"I have forbidden myself to think in those terms. My loyalty now must be to my nieces. Charles's will provided that I be their custodian here at Summerton, though Bancroft is named a co-guardian, as you know. Charles had a better opinion of Bancroft than Bancroft deserves, but then, Charles had a generous and forgiving nature."

Margaret already had children, in other words. Nieces, not daughters, but children just the same. "Do you worry that becoming my wife would mean you'd have less to give to your nieces?" It would never have occurred to Thorne—or to his siblings—that marrying Margaret would mean he had less to give to Dorning Hall or any of its ventures.

"Something like that," she said. "Right now, the children are happy here. Any change in my circumstances, even a change for the better, and I give Bancroft a weapon to use against me. Marrying you would be a selfish choice on my part. I harbored a tendresse for you in my youth, you know."

She was refusing Thorne's suit, and yet, he was pleased with her admission. "I was likewise preoccupied with you. The other girls were loud, fluttery, and silly. You were mysterious and quiet. They idled in the market square. You took up a sturdy trug and struck off across the fields."

*And I followed you.* Thorne's dignity required him to keep that to himself—for now. Young Margaret had occasionally gone wading on hot summer days, and the sight of her ankles and calves had been the stuff of fevered adolescent dreams.

"I saw you swimming once, you know," she said. "In the mill pond at dusk. The other boys had gone home, and you stayed there, naked as Adonis, floating on your back as the stars came out."

"Margaret Summerfield, I'm shocked." Thorne was also—and this had not been on his agenda either—falling in love. Not merely smitten with the quiet, wandering girl, but overtaken by a slow, sweet rise of affection and tenderness for the sensible, calm woman at his side.

What an inconvenient time to succumb to the yearnings of the heart. Elements of youthful longing colored his feelings, but so, too, did a desire to share the rest of his years with the woman Margaret had become.

"Hawthorne, if marrying me meant you had to turn your back on your family, could you do it?"

His first reaction was in the negative—no man should turn his back on family—but like the lady, the question was complicated. "My family could find another steward for Dorning Hall, Margaret."

"That's not the point, though, is it? You and I would suit, I do have some experience with botanical scents, and our land marches. The union would be practical and would allow you to assist your brothers while taking on a wife and family. But if you had to choose, the Dorning family and its priorities or me and the girls, would you marry me?"

Thorne's brothers would tell him to marry and be happy, but his brothers, even Grey, had no idea exactly what went into stewarding Dorning Hall.

"I could not forsake my family," Thorne said, "but if you and I married, then you, Greta, and Adriana would become my family as well, and my brothers and sisters would not turn their backs on us either. Grey is an earl. Willow married an earl's daughter. Jacaranda married a nabob who came into a minor title, and his brother is also an earl. Marry me, and our children—and your nieces—can be presented at court, if you wish. I had not considered my connections to be of any moment to you."

Though, of course, they would and should be. Thorne wanted Margaret's recipes and her knowledge of fragrances and tisanes. If she hadn't had that expertise, he'd likely not have set out to court her, no matter how fetching her ankles. He would have sweated himself to exhaustion in the shearing shed, on the haystacks, and at harvest, wishing Margaret well and being a damned fool from afar.

"I had not considered your connections either," she said slowly. "I'm not a snob."

Thorne heard the unspoken words likely forming in her mind: *But Bancroft Summerfield is a snob.* A very great snob indeed, considering the man was nothing more than a country squire with more land than he could manage profitably.

Margaret, by contrast, was a countrywoman. She had some means, both inherited from her family and as a function of her marriage, but presentation at court would not have crossed her mind as more than a girlish dream.

For her nieces, she could aim higher—*if she married Thorne.* He'd been raised with the certainty that some fine day, he'd make his bow at a royal levee, and he could not have escaped that fate by any honorable means.

"We would suit, Margaret, and if you fear that I'd let Bancroft take the children without a fight, lay your fears to rest. When you marry me, your battles become mine, and your children become mine too."

Her regard was serious to the point of solemnity, as if Thorne had recited a vow that surpassed even the weightiness of the nuptial promises, but what did marriage mean, if not a pooling of resources and loyalties?

"Bancroft is determined and wily," Margaret said. "I have underestimated him in the past, to my sorrow. I had no idea Charles would involve him in the girls' situation, but the will is clear. If I were to marry you, Bancroft would be a constant threat to our happiness and our home. I need you to know that, because were the decision based on only my own wants, then I'd not have hesitated—"

Thorne wanted to hear whatever fears and misgivings Margaret had to share, but her *no*—she'd been intent on delivering him a no—had shifted to an *if I were to marry you*. That was worth kissing about.

Also worth taking the lady in his arms. Margaret acceded to the overture, draping herself across his lap and twining her arms around his neck. Thorne had meant to offer a happy pleasure, but Margaret was intent on more substantial fare.

She apparently liked kissing, or liked kissing him, and Thorne liked her boldness. She tasted him, traced his lips with her tongue, sank her fingers into his hair, and generally chased all thoughts of family feuds, worldly connections, and pretty speeches from his head.

She was a widow. She knew exactly where this sort of kiss could lead, and Thorne was overjoyed to be led there.

"Margaret, has anybody ever made love to you on a bench in a shady forest?"

She gazed up at him. "Has anybody made love to *you* on a bench in a shady forest?"

"Not until today. Are we to be married, then?"

Blast him for an idiot, because she sat up, scooted off his lap to place beside him, and straightened her skirts.

"Hawthorne, there are aspects of the situation I'm not sure how or whether to convey. They prevent me from answering easily."

Perhaps she could not have children? Maybe that was what drove her interest in herbs and flowers. Thorne was about to present himself as the most trustworthy confidant ever to hang on a lady's every word when a long shriek split the air.

"That's Greta," Margaret said, bolting off the bench. "That's Greta, and that is the start of an imperial tantrum." Margaret sprinted off down the path, and Thorne loped after her.

"DESPITE YOUR FAILURE TO warn us of your *visit*, Valerian,"
Grey said, "you are of course welcome for as long as you'd like to stay.
I am, however, at a loss to know how kicking your heels here in
London will further the project you profess to support."

For Grey, that casual inquiry amounted to a tongue-lashing. The
trip to London had taken Valerian longer than it should have as a
result of bad roads, a broken coach wheel, and an unwillingness to
expend funds sufficient to secure a place on a post-chaise. Valerian
had arrived the previous evening to find the earl and countess out at a
formal dinner hosted by Mr. Tresham and his lady.

Company that Bancroft Summerfield would not have been
admitted to, thank heavens.

"How is kicking your lordly heels in London supporting that
project?" Valerian retorted. The familiar painting of Durdle Door
now hung here in the family parlor, an airy, cheerful space compared
to the town house's estate office. Other changes were more subtle.

The Dorning London residence smelled better, less of muddy
boots and dusty corners, more of cinnamon, baking bread, and
sunshine. The servants moved about quickly, rather than idling to
chat with one another on the stairs. The flowers on the sideboard
were fresh, not drooping or scattering petals onto the carpet.

Grey was married. Valerian had been present at the ceremony,
but domestic details made the vows real in a way a formal ceremony
had not.

"The mercantile project is not mine to undertake," Grey said,
settling into a chair upholstered in lavender velvet. "I thought I made
that clear. You lot at Dorning Hall may have the use of any crop,
herb, acre, or resource the Hall possesses, but making the venture
profitable is in your hands."

Valerian would die for any one of his brothers, if they didn't drive
him to Bedlam first.

"We have no capital," he began, pacing the width of the carpet
and back again. "We have no labor, because Dorning Hall requires us
to literally put our hands to the plow, shovel, shears, hoe, and reins, as

ungentlemanly as those exertions might be. We have no management expertise, because as the ornamental fellows we've been raised to be, concocting perfumes and tisanes lies outside the limits of our education. In addition to land that is largely going to waste growing the various experiments and oddities Papa collected, you gave us nothing more than a good idea, Grey, and an impossible schedule. Good ideas, even brilliant ideas, are thick on the ground, as are impossible schedules."

Grey was in good looks, though he'd always been a handsome devil. He was rested, he was no longer gaunt, his gaze had lost the perpetual anxiety of a man with too many dependents and not enough cash.

That was all to the good, but the rest and rejoicing of marriage had also, apparently, rejuvenated Grey's stores of pigheadedness.

"The schedule, as you term it, is apparently meaningless," Grey said, pulling an embroidered satin pillow from behind his back and tossing it to the sofa. "You were to be shipping products to market by Yuletide. That was months ago, and I've yet to see a single sachet sent this way."

"Nor will you see any in the immediate future," Valerian countered. He fell silent while a footman wheeled in a tea tray. Not a footman Valerian recognized, but then, Grey's countess had brought some household staff to the union, and Valerian was now a *visitor* in a dwelling he'd always thought of as a Dorning family home.

"Thank you, Thiel," Grey said to the footman. "I will pour out for my brother."

A year ago, Valerian would have rung for the damned tea if he'd wanted any and poured out for himself. The change—Grey shifting from head of the family to host—was necessary, good, and infuriating. Perhaps this was why Ash and Sycamore dwelled elsewhere, why Willow remained in the country with his wife and his hounds.

"I've had breakfast," Valerian said. "No tea for me."

"Then you'll miss a treat," Grey said, lifting the lid of the teapot and sniffing at the rising steam. "Gunpowder with jasmine flowers. Beatitude favors it."

"Would she favor a perfume with that scent? Would she like your shaving soap to remind her of that fragrance?"

Grey replaced the lid. "Perhaps. She says it's both soothing and pretty."

"How does one capture a scent, Grey? How does it get from the flowers and the teapot into a lotion, say?"

Grey took the tea tray and shifted to the reading chair by the window. He set the tray on the side table and settled back, crossing his boots at the ankle. He moved more freely now, no longer the walking temple to manners and deportment he'd been before his marriage—another change for the good.

"How should I know? I'm an earl, not an apothecary."

"Now that is odd, for I'm not an apothecary either. To the best of my knowledge, none of my other brothers can claim an apothecary's skill, nor a perfumer's, nor an alchemist's. But should we stumble across, by an advantageous marriage perhaps, somebody who does have that arcane knowledge, somebody who is willing to part with it without compensation—for *we haven't any to offer*—then we have no venue from which to sell our tisanes and sachets, do we? We have no distillery or herbal sizable enough to produce goods in quantity. We have no wagons to transport our wares to London, save those vehicles needed for use on our farms.

"What we do have," Valerian went on, making another circuit across the parlor, "is an older brother who thinks snapping his fingers will result in a viable commercial venture, though the same older brother thought demolishing an entire dower house and a family wing while we also manage thousands of acres of arable land was the work of a few weeks."

"Months, Valerian. I had hoped the demolition could be finished over the course of the summer."

Grey poured himself a cup of tea, which Valerian dearly wanted to dump in his brother's lap.

"So we accomplished a near miracle, getting the dower house razed and the salvage sold without a single field of crops languishing. When we can't produce another miracle and get this botanical business up and running overnight, your response is to offer the best land we have for sale to the biggest buffoon in the shire. *Are you mad?*"

Grey added a dash of sugar to his tea, stirred gently, tapped the spoon twice against the cup, and took a sip. "Tell me about the advantageous marriage."

"Thorne has always harbored a tendresse for Margaret Summerfield."

Grey set down his cup and saucer. "Thorne? Our Hawthorne and Margaret Summerfield?" He appeared to consider the notion. "She's something of a free spirit, or she was before she married Charles. She put me in mind of Papa, always out among the hedges and stream banks, collecting mushrooms or mandrakes. She has nieces underfoot now. I don't see her as presenting Thorne many advantages." He smiled at his boots. "Beyond the obvious, of course."

*Well, well, well.* Grey Dorning was a paragon of manners, a walking testament to etiquette and gentlemanly deportment, but he was now a *married* gentleman, a creature able to admit of carnal joy.

About damned time.

"Margaret Summerfield has dwelled at Summerton with her nieces since Charles died," Valerian said. "She consented to the use of the stream to create our water meadow, and your hay yield went up twenty percent as a result. Your spring lambs weigh on average ten percent more, in part because we have early grass to put them on. You lose fewer ewes to lambing because our flocks are in better weight for having had superior fodder over the winter. You sell that water meadow, and Thorne might well disown you."

"I see."

Grey *hadn't* seen. He loved Dorning Hall with his whole heart, but he'd been drifting into the status of an absentee landlord, while Thorne had become his factor in Dorset. Grey had been more than overdue for a respite, and Thorne had thrived on the responsibility. Mostly.

"There's more," Valerian said.

"Yes, there is." Grey took up his cup and saucer for another leisurely sip of his tea. "Bancroft Summerfield is interested in acquiring the land. We ran into each other at Hatchards, where he found me browsing political treatises. He claims he can make the sale worth my while."

# CHAPTER ELEVEN

The tea abruptly turned sour in Valerian's belly. "Is Bancroft's coin of greater value than Thorne's happiness?"

"Of course not." Grey's answer was swift and certain. "But Dorning Hall has thousands of acres to its name. We can make another water meadow."

"No, Grey, *we* cannot. We have a plethora of winter burns at Dorning Hall, but only two year-round water sources, and a water meadow requires a steady, moderate flow across low-lying land during the coldest months. Think about our terrain, and you'll see that Thorne's use of the stream was ingenious, and also the only possible option."

Moreover, between the last of the demolition and salvage efforts on the dower house, the ongoing labor needed to keep the estate running productively, and this new botanical venture, Dorning Hall had no resources to devote to *creating* any more water features.

How could Grey not see that? "We need Margaret Summerfield," Valerian said, rather than haranguing the earl about his own land. "Selling the land to Bancroft would cost us her goodwill, and perhaps Thorne's loyalty."

Grey wrinkled his lordly beak. "Thorne is in love, then?"

"Do you recall when his mare was in foal to Greymore's stud?"

"A wife is not a broodmare, Valerian."

"That arcane fact has drifted within even my feeble cognizance, your lordship. Thorne went without sleep for weeks, fed the damned colt by hand, rigged a sling for the mother when she didn't show any willingness to stand. Slept in the barn for more weeks and never once complained or shirked other duties. You thwart his will at your peril, and I can assure you, I am not a viable candidate to take his place as your land steward, head farmer, layer of hedges, hay stacker, foaling expert, fence mender, ditch digger, engineer, head shearer, project foreman, and ambassador to the neighbors and tenants."

A fraught silence ensued, but Grey was a shrewd man. Valerian prayed marriage hadn't changed even that.

"I have been gone a fair amount in the past year, I know."

"You were a very involved landowner, and your absence has been felt." *While you expect your brothers to take up the slack, start a new venture, and keep a barely profitable estate running smoothly.*

Valerian could not say that, because he was fed, clothed, housed, and horsed for his labors, which amounted to being a house steward for an empty dwelling. So far, he'd done precious damned little to earn his keep, but he could at least champion Thorne's concerns.

"I made no commitment to Bancroft," Grey said. "I can put him off for a while, but the growing season is under way, Valerian. When will Papa's herbs and flowers be put to some use?"

"I honestly don't know. Thorne's closer acquaintance with Margaret Summerfield was inspired by the fact that she's a genius with scents."

"Nobody in the vicinity of Dorning Hall is a genius at anything," Grey said, popping a tea cake into his mouth. "All of England regards Dorset as the back of the great bucolic beyond, which it surely is, and may the Creator in His wisdom keep it ever thus."

"And yet, you became one of the foremost men of manners in the realm, and you hail from Dorset, or you used to. Then too, Lady

Casriel seems to think you more than passingly competent at being her husband."

Grey touched his left breast. "Touché. I fear I sent the wrong brother to read law."

He had, but Ash had needed to go somewhere and do something, and the family lacked the means for two brothers to spend years reading for the bar.

"You will not sell that water meadow to Bancroft Summerfield?"

"Not without consulting you and Thorne first, though I honestly might have to sell it. Bancroft has been sniffing about the skirts of Miss Emily Pepper, the Season's current darling. Her settlements are rumored to rival the national treasury, and Beatitude claims she's a lovely young woman."

"Why would such a lovely young woman marry a country squire?"

"Her father deals in cloth and seeks entrée into the landed gentry. He realizes Emily would be miserable among titled society and is willing to climb the ladder generation by generation, or that's what Beatitude says. I have the great luxury of not troubling my handsome head with heiresses and incomparables anymore. You cannot imagine my relief."

Valerian could see that relief in the casual pose Grey adopted, in his enjoyment of a simple tea tray, heedless of getting crumbs on the carpet. Even his cravat was a plain knot, a half-inch center, and the informality looked good on him.

"Oak is thinking of taking a post in Hampshire," Valerian said. "He was to write you about it."

"Correspondence is the bane of a literate man's existence. Will he be drawing master to somebody's talented progeny?"

If Oak had written, Grey hadn't read the letter yet. "He'll restore old paintings for a reclusive widow, assuming they can come to terms. I'll mention it to Beatitude, in the event she knows something of the widow. She has relatives in Hampshire, doesn't she?"

"The marquess. They correspond. I need this botanical venture to start producing revenue, Valerian. If you've delivered the scolding you were sent here to deliver, you are free to return to Dorset and start brewing up jasmine tea perfumes."

*Ye gods, I will kill him after all.* "Haven't you been listening? A jasmine tea perfume could take years to develop, for all I know. Thorne says scents change over time, they can lose fragrance while sitting on the shelf, or their odor can deteriorate once applied. We have no manufactory because we've been too busy removing the eyesore of a dower ruin from the foot of the drive. We have no commercial establishment here in London because where we open a business depends in part on what we sell and who we sell it to. *We are trying*, Grey, but you offer nothing in the way of support and everything in the way of judgment, ignorance, and indifference."

Valerian had raised his voice at a sibling for the first time in ages. He'd also earned Grey's undivided attention.

"Beatitude says I'm not to interfere. I'm to let my brothers sort out how to go on, because they are a capable and industrious lot who need only a chance to prove themselves."

"Then don't interfere, for God's sake. Don't threaten to sell the best land out from under us, don't impose ridiculous deadlines while you heap competing projects on the Hall's staff. Don't expect the impossible."

Grey rose and brushed at his cravat. "As you say, more is coming to bear on this situation than meets the eye. I haven't said anything to anybody else, though I'm sure Ash and Cam suspect."

"Suspect what?"

"Beatitude is expecting—not the impossible, but a child. My willingness to muddle along, an impecunious earl with more manners than money, is at an end. I understand your concerns, Valerian, but you must understand that I can be patient for only so long. The earldom needs funds, and I shall have them, one way or another."

*Well, of course.* Grey's refusal to leave Beatitude's side, his willingness to entertain the outlandish notion of selling acreage, his urgency about the botanical venture... Grey worried not for himself or his earldom, he worried for his family, as always.

"Congratulations," Valerian said, "but just as you cannot hurry Beatitude toward parturition, you must be patient with your siblings a while longer. Funds in the short term will be little consolation when your brothers can no longer trust you to manage the family resources sensibly."

A few years ago, that declaration might have been cause for fisticuffs, or at least a display of lordly temper from Grey. He merely nodded now, a show of understanding, but no sort of capitulation at all.

GRETA'S TANTRUMS TOOK a variety of forms. Over the winter, she'd developed a silent tantrum. She'd sit wedged into a corner, arms around her updrawn knees. Any attempt to pry her loose from her self-imposed ball of misery, and she'd screech like a demon until she was again left in peace.

Her usual stock in trade, though, was to shriek, cry, cast herself down, and kick viciously at anybody who attempted to approach her. By the time Margaret reached her, she was already on the ground by the garden fountain, howling like a banshee, while Fenny attempted to reason with her.

"It's not my fault," Adriana bellowed over Greta's dramatics. "I didn't do anything, and why does she always carry on like this?"

Why must she carry on like this before Hawthorne Dorning, who'd easily kept pace with Margaret on the dash back to the house?

"Miss Fenner, if you'd take Adriana inside, please?" Margaret asked, trying for a calm tone.

"She broke it," Adriana said, loudly enough to be heard over Greta's crying. "She broke the music box, and now it won't play *ever again.*"

That observation provoked even greater effusions from Greta, who kicked at the air as if beset by six press gangs at once.

"Greta, stop this nonsense immediately." Margaret moved closer, her boot crunching on something small and solid. The key to the music box lay on the paving stones, as did other mechanical parts. "Miss Fenner, to the house, if you please."

Fenny took Adriana by the wrist and led her away, leaving Margaret with one very upset little girl and a suitor who was doubtless rethinking his proposal.

"Greta, Adriana is gone," Margaret said, crouching beside the child. "Please calm yourself."

That admonition was pointless. Greta could carry on for an hour at full volume and then abruptly go silent, get up, and find a corner to sulk in. Margaret usually waited until the sulk had become a nap, then carried Greta up to bed.

Greta swiped at Margaret's chin with a small fist.

"No hitting." Hawthorne picked Greta up and sat with her on the edge of the fountain.

A battle ensued, with Greta flailing mightily, fists and feet flying, and Hawthorne easily containing her struggles.

"I'm not letting you go until you are calmer," he said, pleasantly enough considering a tornado in a dress occupied his lap. "You'll do yourself an injury, and that we cannot allow."

"It's *broken*," Greta sobbed. "Broken *forever*. Adriana *said*."

After a few more minutes of wailing and flailing, the struggles became mostly for show, reflexive attempts at freedom that had the agreeable effect of tiring Greta without risking her well-being.

"You're concerned for the music box?" Hawthorne asked.

"B-*broken*. F-*Forever*." No lament had ever been more heartrending, no sorrow greater. Margaret pulled out a handkerchief and passed it to Hawthorne.

He managed to grab the handkerchief without losing his hold on Greta. "We'll put it back together."

"But it's *broken*."

"My arm was broken once," Hawthorne said. "It mended. See?" He held out a long, strong arm. "The music box can be mended too."

He seemed to know that Greta did not respond well to petting and stroking. He held her securely, nothing more.

"You broke your arm?" Greta sniffled.

"Somebody else broke it. They stomped on it when I was lying defenseless on the cobbles. Hurt like the very devil. I would not like to see you hurt yourself, wee Greta."

"I hurt the music box. It's—"

"We will repair it, but first we must find every part that has come loose. Every spring and wire, every screw. If a part is missing, we will send to London for a replacement, or have the smith fashion a new one. You owe your aunt an apology."

Greta stared up at Margaret, her little tearstained face a study in puzzlement.

"For trying to hit me," Margaret said. "We don't hit the people we love."

"I didn't want to hit you. I wanted you to go away."

Hawthorne passed Greta the handkerchief. "If you want somebody to go away, tell them to go away or wave your hand at them. A closed fist will hurt whether you mean it to or not."

A sensible suggestion and utterly useless to Greta when a temper was upon her.

She wiped at her cheeks, blew her nose, and passed Hawthorne the handkerchief. He set it aside as if soiled linen was of no moment.

"Adriana hit me once at Yuletide." Greta shuddered out a sigh. "By accident. She was a pirate. It hurt."

"And she apologized," Margaret said. "Because she did not want you to be hurt, and she was sorry."

"But I didn't hit you." Greta wiggled off Hawthorne's lap, being careful not to step on any loose music box parts. "You moved away. I want to mend the music box. Mr. Hawthorne Dorning said." She pronounced Hawthorne's name as if it was one word, *Mr.-Hawthorne-Dorning.*

He looked like he wanted to argue the ethical logic of apologizing for unintentional harm that had not come to fruition, which with Greta could entail the rest of the morning wasted.

"Let's find the parts then," Margaret said. "Though I haven't a clue what we're looking for."

Hawthorne lowered himself to the paving stones, hunkering at Greta's side. He picked up what looked like the main gear, a little metal spool with tiny teeth at irregular intervals.

"We'll need the key that winds the mechanism," he said, "the wooden housing, and anything else that's come loose."

"I have the key." Greta snatched up the little metal knob and passed it to him. "What's the mech-nism?"

"If you two will excuse me," Margaret said, "I'll be back in a moment. I'd like to check on Adriana." Margaret wanted to hear from Fenny exactly what had happened, because the girls were not reliable reporters. Then she needed privacy.

"We'll be fine," Hawthorne said, not looking up. "The mechanism is what makes the music. Have you ever looked inside a pianoforte and noticed how the hammers strike the wires?"

Margaret left him to his explanations, though they might result in the pianoforte in pieces on the parlor floor. She made it as far as the back hallway before she pulled out her spare handkerchief, sat on the settle, and let herself cry.

Fenny found her there five minutes later, more or less composed, at least outwardly.

"Adriana suggested we start a puzzle, because Greta likes them so."

"Thoughtful of her," Margaret replied, folding up her handkerchief. "What happened?"

Fenny took the other half of the settle. "They were squabbling over the music box, which I should have put an end to, I know. Greta didn't seem too interested in the music, but she liked the sound of the insides spinning and turning, or maybe she liked the vibrations. Who knows with that child? Adriana grew impatient and tried to snatch the music box away, and the blasted thing fell on the stones. You heard the rest."

No sound came from the garden now, just blessed, sunny peace.

"He calmed her, Fenny. He took Greta in his lap, let her struggle to the limit of her strength, and never raised his voice."

"She's sometimes stumped by novelty. He might not have such good luck next time."

"He will teach her to fix what she breaks." A very important lesson. One Margaret had not mastered. "He wasn't disgusted, wasn't angry, wasn't anything but patient and kind."

Fenny patted her knee. "Was Greta's temper part of the reason you hesitated to marry him?"

"Part of the reason." Not all. By no means all, but a bigger part than Margaret could easily admit. Greta was different, often in a loud, unattractive, bewildering way.

*When you marry me, your battles become mine, and your children become mine too.* Hawthorne had meant those words, truly, honestly meant them.

"When Mr. Dorning and I conversed, he reminded me of something important," Margaret said. "His brother is an earl."

"Also a genuinely decent man, according to everybody who's had the pleasure. The Dornings seem like a fine family."

"I know them as neighbors, and you're right. They are so hardworking and unpretentious that I forget they are also titled. Lady Jacaranda married a minor title with significant wealth. Her husband is also an earl's heir. Willow Dorning married another earl's daughter. They are people of consequence, Fenny. Real consequence, not merely the local assembly variety."

"And Bancroft hasn't the standing to tangle with real consequence."

"Not at the moment, but if he marries wealth, he'll have the means to come after Summerton and the girls, and he'll be better situated to provide for them than he is now. Am I demented for fearing that he'll try?"

"Their settlements are substantial, and Summerton is lovely. Some people never have enough and will work harder to steal from others than they would to earn honest coin. Go tell Mr. Dorning you'll marry him."

"I wasn't intending to," Margaret said. "I thought to pretend to think about it for a while longer, so that I could find a way to... compromise."

"You're a widow." Fenny rose, her smile tired. "You can't be compromised. Marry him. He's steady, good-natured, reliable, and patient with shrieking children. Right now, I cannot conceive of a higher recommendation for an unmarried man."

*He's a good kisser, and he likes copulation a lot, but I have fallen in love with him because he's kind and honorable.*

"Is she getting worse, Fenny?"

"Greta is getting *bigger*," Fenny said. "If Mr. Dorning distracted her from her tantrum, perhaps she's growing up too. We can hope."

Fenny returned the way she'd come, and Margaret got to her feet. Greta's tantrums were draining for the whole household, also frightening. Bancroft had seen one, about a year ago at the village lending library and bakery, and been horrified. That display had been minor compared to Greta in a true taking.

Margaret smoothed her hair, put away her handkerchief, and prepared to tell Hawthorne that she'd become his lawfully wedded wife, provided he could procure a special license before Bancroft returned from Town.

# CHAPTER TWELVE

"My dearest Miss Pepper, you look ravishing." Bancroft assayed a bow at his own reflection.

*Too effusive. Too solemn.* Emily Pepper wasn't a featherbrain, but neither was she a Puritan.

"My dear Miss Pepper, a pleasure to see you, as always." Another bow, not quite as low.

Better, still not quite... Those blasted Dornings would know exactly how to greet a silk nabob's heiress daughter.

"Miss Pepper, you look splendid as always." A little more smile, a little less bow, so a fellow could gaze approvingly into the young lady's eyes.

"I do believe that will serve." Bancroft tapped his top hat onto his head. "Walking stick, Rutherford."

Bancroft's valet, who'd come with the highest recommendation from the most exclusive agency, passed over the required item.

"This is a veritable cudgel," Bancroft said, examining the plain brass handle. "Is this the best we've got?"

"I can look into procuring a more ornate version, Mr. Summerfield. For a morning call, the understated approach is often the most impressive." Rutherford exuded the cheerful calm of the gentleman's gentleman and was himself exquisitely turned out. He'd already proved useful spying below stairs, and Bancroft's wardrobe had never been so lovingly tended.

Bancroft looked himself over for the dozenth time. His attire was tastefully correct, according to Rutherford. The blue morning coat and cream waistcoat looked a little drab to Bancroft, like the country squire newly arrived in Town and not wanting to call attention to himself.

"I will look exactly like all the other admirers, which will not do."

"We have yet to choose your *boutonniere*, sir, and that coat does marvelous things for your eyes."

Blue eyes ran in the Summerfield family, true English blue, not that periwinkle-violet color that afflicted many of the Dornings.

"Have we a blue flower among the offerings?" Bancroft asked, accepting a pair of spotless kid gloves from Rutherford.

"I had thought pink, sir. The ladies favor the blushing quality of a sweet pea or carnation, and a touch of contrast enlivens daytime attire."

*Pink?* Bancroft had never worn pink in his life. Then too, a lisping fop in a pink waistcoat had relieved him of substantial blunt over cards the previous evening.

"You're sure, Rutherford?"

Rutherford was young for his post, probably not yet thirty, but his deportment was impeccable. Rather than take offense, which he really might have done considering his expertise, he instead appeared to consider Bancroft's question.

"Every gentleman's wardrobe will differ in its details, Mr. Bancroft, the better to represent the wearer in the manner he wishes to be represented. The proof lies in the impression made first upon you, yourself. You know how you'd like the world—and Miss Pepper and her father—to view you. I took the liberty of choosing three possibilities from among the options on offer at the market this morning. I will happily fetch three more, if that's what you desire."

"Let's have a look," Bancroft said, pulling on his gloves. They fit perfectly, not like the gloves sewn in Dorset by aging cottagers. Bancroft's boots shone exquisitely. His cravat was a work of art. Truly, London was the center of the civilized world for good reasons.

At the front door, Bancroft stopped to admire himself in the pier glass, for he made a splendid impression. No wonder the Dornings always looked so well turned out. Every one of them had the advantage of Town bronze and Town tailoring, in addition to undeserved standing because of their papa's title.

"I had thought this one," Rutherford said, holding up a tiny bouquet, a pink carnation bound up with a few violets and a sprig of something green.

"I don't care for the violets."

"They do tend to wilt as the day goes on," Rutherford said, selecting a plain white rosebud bundled with a tiny dash of lavender.

"Get rid of that wretched weed," Bancroft said. "Damned stuff stinks up an entire room. I like the rosebud, though."

Rutherford extracted the lavender without disturbing the rosebud and affixed the *boutonniere* to Bancroft's lapel. "Like so, sir?"

The third choice was pale blue, some little blossom Bancroft didn't recognize, but he'd seen it growing along country lanes and borders—a cheap hedge flower.

"Exactly," Bancroft said. "Roses have *élan*. I will once again make the perfect impression on Miss Pepper."

"I'm sure you will, sir." Said with enough good cheer to qualify as encouraging without shading into irony.

Bancroft jaunted the three streets to Miss Pepper's house, in charity with the world, despite last night's losses at the gaming tables. All gentlemen indulged in a few hands of cards, and nobody won all the time. Life in London was life as it was meant to be lived. Well dressed, well tended, well received, well entertained. Hartley had sent two dreary reports from Dorset, all about woolly sheep and sprouting corn, but Bancroft had given them only cursory attention.

Of more interest were the paragraphs relating to Summerton,

which apparently ran fairly well, considering the limitations of a widow's expertise when it came to managing property. That was all to the good, for Bancroft didn't want to take over yet another ailing estate when the time came to add Summerton to Hartley's responsibilities.

Which it would do, sooner rather than later, with the help of Miss Pepper's settlements.

That good lady received him cordially at the door, while another fellow, some baronet, took his leave of her.

Sporting of the baronet to cede the field, but then, Bancroft was not a panting puppy. He was a man of means and standing paying a call on a lady who enjoyed his company. Rutherford had summarized the situation thus, and Rutherford knew what he was about.

"Mr. Summerfield, how good of you to call." Miss Pepper beamed at him when he offered his you-look-splendid bow, clearly pleased to welcome him. "You take coffee, don't you? Please say you do, for I adore it."

Bancroft did not care for coffee. "As you wish, miss. Always exactly as *you* wish."

"If we did as I wished, sir, we'd be free of the crush and coal smoke of Town. Your acres are in Dorset, aren't they?"

She'd apparently done some research, a very encouraging sign. "Who told you that?"

"Perhaps you did?" She led him to a sunny parlor done up in green, pink, and cream. The wallpaper alone—a pattern of lush jungle vegetation, peacocks, and blushing orchids—would have paid for the enclosure of another five acres.

"Perhaps I did mention Summerfield House to you in a previous conversation," Bancroft said. "I confess an abiding affection for my family seat, and you would, too, were you ever blessed to see it. Thousands of acres of the most beautiful countryside in the realm." Beautiful for those who enjoyed smelly sheep, smellier bullocks, muddy ground, and hairy draft horses. The house itself was grand, if a bit drafty in winter.

And yet, Summerfield was home, and Bancroft appreciated that land alone gave a man true standing.

"And where are your family's holdings?" Bancroft asked as his hostess gestured him to a settee and—more encouragement?—took the place beside him.

"Papa has a number of properties, though I don't think he owns any in Dorset, not yet. He tends to find projects closer to Town. How do you like your coffee?"

"With a healthy tot of milk and a dash of sugar."

A companion sat over by the window, plying her needle like a spider waiting for a fly to happen by. She was young, as companions went, also pretty in an unsmiling way.

Miss Pepper passed over the coffee, which Bancroft only pretended to drink.

"So as a man of vast real estate holdings, what occupies you at this time of year?" Miss Pepper asked. "I'd think spring an inconvenient time to be parted from one's property."

"Not a'tall, my dear. I am fortunate to have good staff and good land. It practically runs itself. Our planting is done for the year, and the rest is in nature's hands." Hartley's reports had maundered on about shearing and haying, but Bancroft had heard the same hand-wringing and fretting since he'd hired Hartley upon Charles's death.

Agriculture had to be the most boring topic ever to pass for polite conversation.

"Good help is so important," Miss Pepper said, slanting a smile at her companion. "I would be lost without my dear Miss Briggs."

Briggs smiled at her embroidery hoop. "Thank you, miss."

"So Dorset is sheep country, isn't it?" Miss Pepper asked, taking a swallow of black coffee.

Bancroft nearly winced at the sight. "Our flocks thrive, so much so that we're looking into the acquisition of a water meadow, the better to increase our hay stores."

"Oh, really?" Limpid brown eyes made Bancroft wish he'd paid closer attention to Hartley's rhapsodies about that blasted water meadow. "I've never quite understood what a water meadow is, Mr. Bancroft. Perhaps you could explain it to me?"

"The concept is simple, my dear. Have you ever noticed how on the banks of streams, the grass remains green even into winter and is the first grass to show green again in springtime?"

"I can't say as I have. Miss Briggs, have you noticed this phenomenon?"

"As a girl in Sussex, ma'am. My grandfather maintained a water meadow."

"I own I am fascinated." The young lady topped up her cup of coffee. "The world is full of wonders, and I am barely cognizant of them. How does the rushing water keep the grass green?"

"A swift flow doesn't freeze as easily,"—or so Hartley had reasoned—"and thus the grass and the soil beneath are warmer than winter ground generally. The grass continues to grow longer into autumn and resumes spring growth sooner."

"Like having a brazier of coals beneath one's pasture. How ingenious. Do have some lemon cake, sir. And you say Summerfield has such a marvel?"

"We are in the process of acquiring one from another estate where the land marches with a Summerfield holding. One doesn't like to speak ill of one's neighbors, but the current owner of that water meadow is one of those infamously impecunious titles. A spot of cash will serve his lordship's purposes, while I, having the greater resources, can look toward wealth in the longer term."

The lemon cake was excellent, both moist and sweet. Miss Pepper prattled on about her papa's dabbling in the landowner's art, but having little true expertise when it came to crops, beasts, and *so forth.*

All the while, the companion sewed quietly in the corner, and Bancroft pretended to sip his coffee. The whole of London knew that Osgood Pepper sought to join the ranks of the landed gentry—who didn't among the mercantile class?—and yet, like most climbing cits, he'd have no idea how to go on.

Such a pity when a man took on challenges for which he was not suited by birth or education.

"Shall I ring for more coffee?" Miss Pepper asked, a good thirty minutes later.

"Please not on my account. Will you attend the Framleys' ball next week, Miss Pepper?"

Mrs. Framley was an ambitious hostess whose guest lists included anybody who was anybody, whether titled or not. Bancroft had an invitation because his mama and Mrs. Framley had been friends. Emily Pepper's settlements meant she'd be welcome at such a gathering, despite her lack of title or breeding.

"I do believe I have accepted that invitation, haven't I, Miss Briggs?"

"You did, miss."

"Then might I ask you to spare me a dance? Not the opening set, of course, but a turn down the room with you later in the evening would be most enjoyable."

Miss Pepper rose, signaling the end to the visit well after another hostess might have shown Bancroft to the door.

"I am still so new to Town," she said. "Do I offend protocol if I offer you my supper waltz, Mr. Bancroft?"

"Offend protocol? My dear young lady, you give me cause for rejoicing." He led her from the parlor, and the companion—clearly not a stupid woman—remained behind at her stitching. "The supper waltz ensures we'll have more time to converse, and nothing would make me happier, unless of course you'd like to ride out with me in Hyde Park tomorrow at the fashionable hour?"

Faint hearts never did win fat settlements, and besides, Bancroft liked Miss Pepper. She exuded a friendly, practical air without one slippered toe ever crossing the line of proper decorum. She'd do well in Dorset, where winters were long and dreary and assemblies were the only social gatherings of note.

"I so enjoy the carriage parade with a knowledgeable escort," she said. "If we happen upon some of your neighbors up from the country, will you introduce us?"

Oh, better and better. "Manners would require at least that much of me."

"Then I will look forward to our next encounter, Mr. Bancroft. Look forward to it very much."

Brown eyes were so expressive. "As shall I, Miss Pepper." He bowed over her hand, accepted his walking stick, hat, and gloves from a silent butler and was in the process of donning the hat when the knocker sounded.

Three fresh-faced gentlemen at once crowded into the foyer, making a lingering farewell impossible to execute. Bancroft merely touched his hat brim to the young sprigs and withdrew.

All three of the puppies had worn pink roses on their lapels, though each boutonniere had been subtly garnished with a different flower. Bancroft made a mental note to mention that fact to Rutherford, though clearly, Miss Pepper had selected her favorite, and what a fine choice she'd made too.

THORNE SPREAD his handkerchief on the paving stones around the fountain, and he and Greta placed every part of the music box they could find on the little linen square.

"That looks to be the lot," he said. The music box had held up to years in the nursery, and more damage had been done to the wooden housing than to the metal innards.

"Are you *sure?*" Greta asked, gaze on the bits and bobs on the handkerchief.

A glib assurance would not do for this child. For Adriana, perhaps. Not for Greta.

"Let's have a look, then," Thorne said, lowering himself to the walkway and sitting with his back against the dry fountain. "This is the heart of the business." He held up the metal drum with its array of tiny teeth. "If we opened this cylinder here, we'd find a spring, and winding that spring turns the barrel, here."

Greta slanted him another scowl. "How do you know there's a spring inside?"

"Because," Thorne said, picking up the key, "when you insert the key into this opening and twist, you can feel the resistance of the spring and hear it tightening." He gave it a twist.

"Oh. Can I try?"

"Not too tightly."

Greta gave the key a cautious half twist.

"A little more than that."

A full twist, and the barrel obligingly turned for a few tinny bars' worth of nursery rhyme.

"I can *see* it," Greta said, rapt. "I can see it making the music!"

Margaret came down the steps from the terrace. The child didn't look up, but Thorne certainly did. The lady's eyes were suspiciously shiny, and her posture had lost its starch. He rose while Greta remained crouched over the music box's mechanism.

"Aunt Margaret, come look. You can watch the barrel turn and the notes come out. The music box plays itself when you wind the spring."

The tune wound down, thank heavens.

"Why don't you show Adriana?" Margaret suggested. "She's working on a puzzle in the nursery."

Greta popped to her feet, the music box mechanism in her hand. "This is the most wonderful present ever, Mr.-Hawthorne-Dorning. Thank you."

Her smile reminded him of somebody, though it was gone as quickly as it had appeared, then she was scampering toward the steps.

"Greta!" Thorne called. "You'll need this." He held the key out to her.

She rushed back, snatched the key, curtseyed. "Thank you. I shall show Adriana. And Fenny. I will show Ambers as well, and

Cook and Mrs. Blevins." She disappeared into the house, adding to her list.

"Never has a broken toy brought one child so much pleasure," Thorne said. "Greta has a unique view of life."

"I worry for her." Margaret picked up the handkerchief and folded the edges over the pieces of wood and screws within. "She is very bright, very stubborn. She never forgets anything even when you wish she would, and as fanciful as she can be, she's also astonishingly logical."

"You love her," Thorne said. "You love them both."

"With my whole heart. What made you choose a music box?"

*Are we engaged?* That question plucked at Thorne's nerves as tautly as the pins of the music box cylinder plucked at its metal teeth.

"The breeze is picking up," Thorne said, "and you've come outside without your cloak. Shall we go inside?"

"I suppose we ought. I smell rain, though it's still some distance off."

Thorne couldn't smell anything other than a spring day in the garden—and possible defeat of his courting aspirations. "I brought the music box because Adriana struck me as a child who'd enjoy lively stories and detailed illustrations, while Greta... Greta likes other predilections. She has an engineer's instincts."

Margaret paused just outside the terrace door. "How could you possibly conclude that?"

"She knew to seek the high vantage point when defending the Asian steppes. She figured out how to climb a piece of furniture that's twice as tall as she is. She solves puzzles."

"While she creates mayhem," Margaret said, moving away from the door. "My sitting room is off the music room."

She opened a set of French doors and led Thorne to a small square room with a slightly worn blue sofa, a somewhat scratched desk, and a rocking chair positioned near a parlor stove that backed up to a low hearth. Before the rocking chair was a footstool, and opposite sat a reading chair.

Unique scents—cinnamon and honeysuckle, maybe a hint of cedar—gave the little sanctuary the air of a private retreat.

"We will be undisturbed here," Margaret said, closing the doors and setting the handkerchief on the blotter, "assuming Fenny can keep peace in the nursery. I have decided to accept your offer of marriage."

She might have been announcing the choice of vegetable on tomorrow night's dinner menu, so prosaic was her tone.

"Have you really?"

What followed was interesting. Margaret swept a hearth that was already clean, straightened correspondence that was tidily stacked, retied a curtain sash that had been in a neat bow.

"You are gathering your courage," Thorne said. "I'm learning the signs. Don't marry me unless you truly want to. I understand your speech about both of us being pragmatic, but I have long held you in esteem and look very much forward to being your husband. If you are not similarly enthusiastic about this union, then let's forget I proposed, and I will go back to my shearing shed, there to..."

Shear his way to utter oblivion, if such a thing were possible. If it were not, he'd start on the apple brandy Valerian had begun making several years ago. Wickedly potent stuff that went down as smoothly as a card sharp dealt a hand of piquet to a table full of college boys.

Margaret took him by the wrist and led him to the reading chair. She perched on the hassock. "Please sit. The problem is Charles."

"You love him still. I know. That's a testament to your—"

She shook her head. "He was not well." She tapped her chest. "Here. His heart was weakened by childhood illnesses, and though he looked hale and happy, he tired easily and was prone to palpitations and sweats."

Well, damn. A beloved deceased husband would likely always hold a place in his wife's heart. A beloved husband tragically struck down by illness, heroically facing his demise one brave smile at a time... Thorne could not compete with that. As a gentleman, he should not want to displace such a love.

"I'm sorry. I hadn't known he was ill."

"Bancroft put it about that Charles had eaten tainted meat, lest somebody conclude the ailment ran in the family. If anybody wondered why only one person in an entire household would succumb to food poisoning, they never raised the question."

"And you were too bowed down with grief to argue with him."

"I was sad, of course," Margaret said. "Very sad, but Charles told me when he proposed that his health was compromised. His death was a loss, though for him I think it was also a relief. I was not with him when he died. I do regret that, but he'd warned me that his ailment was unpredictable. He'd be fine for weeks and then bedridden for no apparent reason. Changes in weather affected him some years, not others. He'd spend all summer reading in a hammock, then be fit enough to dance a minuet with me at the autumn assembly. I could make very little sense of his illness, but I believed him when he said ours was likely to be a short, happy marriage."

"You were very brave to take him for your husband."

Margaret rose and went to the desk, opening a drawer. She withdrew a handkerchief and passed it to him. "To replace the one Greta has commandeered. I was not brave."

Thorne wanted to pull her into his lap, the better to have this difficult conversation, but just as he'd resisted the temptation to cosset a distraught Greta, he merely watched as Margaret squeezed the sachets dangling from the curtain rod and straightened the carpet fringe with the toe of her boot.

"You were as brave as any soldier. You went into the marriage knowing heartache would follow."

"I had my reasons, Hawthorne. I had to do something. My aunt was in poor health, my inheritance would be modest, and I was not a convivial young woman to attract suitors on the strength of my charm."

"You attracted me. You still attract me." *More than ever.*

"You were off at university, while I... I love our corner of Dorset, you see. I know every hedge and stream, every fairy mound and field.

I never want to leave it, while an earl's son is most likely to find his fortune in the military, the church, or diplomacy. Had you proposed, I might have turned you down."

*Or you might have accepted me, damn the luck.*

He took her hand in his. "I didn't propose, and you married your dear Charles. Now you are to marry me, though you still appear to have reservations."

She folded back down to the hassock, keeping his hand in hers. "You should have reservations, too, but you are too gentlemanly to mention them. Marriage to Charles was far from perfect, which is the point of my ramblings. He was increasingly weak, unable to leave the house, exhausted simply by the effort required to dress. Some days, he had to be carried up the steps, or his heart would start pounding before the first landing. After the first year..."

She brought Thorne's knuckles to her lips. "I was more nurse than wife," she went on. "I will make demands on you, Hawthorne. I will expect... fidelity. Certain attentions. A wife's due. You've said you enjoy intimate relations. You are to enjoy them *with me*, do you understand?"

What on earth was she trying to say? "I understand that our marriage will be physically intimate. I look forward to that." Even talk of such intimacies in this private parlor tempted Thorne's imagination in wayward directions.

"Not simply intimate, Hawthorne—this conversation is intimate. I want a husband with whom I can be enthusiastic. I want a husband who will bring passion and energy to bed with him. I want... I want lustiness and joy. Creaking bed ropes. Breathless kisses. *Sweat.*"

Margaret sat hunched in on herself, but her eyes blazed with determination, and her grip on Thorne's hand was fierce. Such a bundle of contradictions and so very, very dear.

"Passion is mine to give in abundance," Thorne said, rising. "Passion for you." He drew her to her feet, smoothed her hair back from her cheek, and took her in his arms.

After all her brave and unnecessary talk, he'd apparently

surprised her by taking action. She started slightly as Thorne wrapped her in an embrace.

"I could lift your skirts right now, Margaret Summerfield." He kissed her while that possibility sent mischief coursing through him. "Sit you on a corner of the desk and be inside you in two minutes. I could loosen your bodice and within one minute be adoring your breasts with my mouth and hands."

He permitted himself only a glancing caress to those breasts. "I could kiss you in shockingly intimate ways. Endure the same pleasure from you..." He fused his mouth to hers rather than expound on that luscious fantasy.

Margaret twined her arms around him and kissed him back with a voraciousness that nearly had him undoing his falls. She pressed near and pulled him closer, all the while deepening the kiss. Her hands were everywhere—his arms and chest, his backside, his *falls*...

*Ye cavorting gods of procreation. Ye heavenly choruses of matrimonial joy.* "Margaret." A warning, a plea for restraint.

She pulled him under again.

# CHAPTER THIRTEEN

Margaret went a little mad—more than a little. She flung her desire at Hawthorne the same way she used to charge up a hillside on the first beautiful day of spring, determined to reach the summit and drink in all the splendor of nature's glories.

Hawthorne was not Charles. A small, stubborn voice in Margaret's head tried to be sad about that, but the sentiment simply wouldn't wash. Hawthorne was a healthy, vigorous specimen in the prime of life, one who delighted in physical activity, and—apparently—in kissing.

Kissing *her*.

"I was half a wife," Margaret said, drawing back to rest her cheek against Hawthorne's chest. He could not know what joy his steadily thumping heart brought her, could not fathom how many times she'd heard Charles's heartbeat pattering a rapid, thready rhythm after the tamest of couplings.

"You were wholly devoted to your spouse," Hawthorne replied.

"I would kiss his cheek, but never ask for… for intimacies. When he made overtures, I was always worried that the exertion would cost him his life. I restrained desire, anger, sadness, even joy. His illness was like a fractious child who finally succumbs to sleep. Wake the child, and the whole household can be thrown back into an uproar."

For once, Margaret was glad to be indoors, glad to be where no prying eyes could see her in the arms of a man who delighted in a yeoman's exertions, a fellow who could pluck Greta from the furniture and casually carry her on his hip.

"I have another request," she said, stepping back enough to see Hawthorne's eyes.

"If it's anything like the first, I am a temple of masculine anticipation." He tucked a lock of Margaret's hair back into her chignon, and even that casual gesture made her hungry for more of his touch.

*I have been asleep.* The notion dropped into her head, whole and true, much as she had risen on summer mornings long ago, inexplicably certain that she'd find the feverfew at the edge of the village common in full bloom.

"You will think me forward."

"Margaret, I think you wonderful."

"I think you are wonderful too, Hawthorne Dorning."

They beamed at each other, and a glimmer of the girl Margaret had once been, full of joy and confidence, trickled through her.

"I want to be married by special license, please."

Hawthorne drew her close, his arms loosely around her shoulders. Oh, the scent of him... clean, masculine. A bit of horse and leather, a hint of meadows and tannin. All dancing beneath good old English lavender. She would change the sachets in this office to lavender before the day was through.

"You needn't wait to avail yourself of my charms, you know." He whispered this, his breath tickling her ear. "I can be persuaded to anticipate the vows. Shower me with kisses and flattery, make a few bold promises. I estimate that if you exert yourself to the utmost, my inherent shyness will crumble in at most four or five... seconds."

He was about as shy as a barnyard rooster.

"I want a special license, Hawthorne, so this marriage is a fait accompli before Bancroft returns from London." Before anybody could summon him back from London.

Hawthorne kissed her brow, a thoughtful sort of kiss rather than flirtatious. "And here I had hoped the prospect of my creaking bed ropes alone inspired your enthusiasm. Has Bancroft threatened to take the girls from you, Margaret?"

"Not overtly, not yet. He mentions that Summerfield House is larger and more commodious. He suggests that *one day* the consequence of a wealthy uncle will be a greater advantage to them than that of a widowed aunt. He'd probably settle for their money and Summerton, but I am their guardian, so ideally, he'll need control of me as well."

Hawthorne stepped back. "And to have control of you, he needs the girls."

The light of passion in his eyes had cooled, which for the best.

"I admire your devotion to a pair of helpless children," he said, sitting on the arm of her reading chair. "I promise you that their welfare will concern me every bit as much as it concerns you, but as long as we're being pragmatic, Margaret, can we clarify one more thing?"

*Pragmatic* had been Margaret's word to describe both herself and Hawthorne, though she regretted it now. Thorne was pragmatic, also apparently romantic. Margaret, by contrast, was ruthless where the children were concerned.

"We can clarify as much as you like," she said, "though perhaps we should continue this discussion on the terrace?"

Thorne took her hand and drew her closer so she perched upon his thigh. "I do hope a little friendly kissing in front of the children figures in your version of holy matrimony."

"It... does."

"Good." He pressed his lips to her knuckles, a brisk, affectionate smack. "I need your recipes for scents and tisanes, Margaret. My family needs them. Casriel is growing impatient, and he's like a

Congreve rocket with a ten-yard fuse. For the longest time, he merely mutters and grumbles, until you think that's all he'll ever do. Then the last two inches of that fuse burns down, and the results are loud, far-ranging, and unpredictable. He's the most mannerly of men until he reaches the limits of his patience."

"Like Greta. She has ten calm days together, and I think my dear little girl is finding some reserves of self-control. Then the cat goes missing—off to the barn for his frolics—or Adriana rearranges the toy chest without discussing it first with Greta. Pandemonium ensues."

Margaret yielded to the temptation to rest her head on Thorne's shoulder, for even the memory of Greta in high dudgeon was daunting.

"If I cannot convince Casriel that selling botanical products will be profitable," Hawthorne said, "pandemonium might well ensue. At least two of my brothers, possibly three, are depending on me to put Casriel's idea into action, and I cannot do that successfully if all we're peddling are the same sachets and scents already on offer. You mentioned a cure for baldness, for example."

Margaret pushed away, because she could not think when Thorne was stroking his thumb over her wrist.

"Not a cure, a treatment. Not one I've ever concocted." Though she knew two different recipes that claimed over a course of months to restore hair growth to the male scalp. Hannah swore by them, while Margaret suspected simply massaging the scalp vigorously three times a day for months brought about the intended result.

"Then we need a salve for saddle soreness, a patent remedy for those who overimbibe, a powder that restores manly vigor, something unique, effective, and available only to us because of the enormous collection the late earl amassed—"

Margaret held up a hand. "I cannot dabble in medications, Thorne. The herbalist's art has been denied me in that regard." Of all the deceptions and half-lies Margaret was prepared to weave, this truth stood on the solid ground of fact. "I have studied those remedies, true, but I haven't the gift of applying what I know. Hannah might be better able to help you in that regard. With scents, I am on much firmer footing."

Even Bancroft couldn't object to Margaret parting with a few recipes for shaving soap or hair pomade.

Thorne regarded her for a moment, his gaze putting her in mind of Greta. The child could leap over a dozen pieces of information to land on a conclusion that made perfect sense, but only after the course of her logic could be traced.

"Then we start with scents," he said. "The most luscious, precious, intriguing scents you can concoct using what Dorning Hall has to offer. Papa collected from all over the world, and he kept meticulous notes about what grows where on the property and the conditions each plant prefers. Casriel reduced the size of the conservatory, though, so Papa's careful system has grown ragged in some instances."

"I would love to help reorganize the conservatory, but what about that special license, Thorne?" This mattered, more than he could know.

"I have three brothers in London. I'll send an express, and we should have the license within a fortnight at most."

Margaret hugged him, the enormity of her relief creating a curious temptation to cry. "Thank you, Hawthorne. I have always admired your gift for industry. You accomplish a task while others stand about planning and procrastinating. That is a lovely quality in a man."

"When you have eight siblings, the planning and procrastinating can go on forever and tend to sound like bickering. Is there more you'd say about this, Margaret? If Bancroft has betrayed the trust Charles placed in him, I'd like to know that now."

*I betrayed Charles's trust.* The delicacy of Thorne's question sank in before Margaret could let old guilt swamp her.

"Bancroft has never made untoward overtures, if that's what you mean. He knows the law prevents him from marrying me, and he's not a man to exert himself for no purpose."

Some of the tension Thorne had been holding eased from his body. "You put my mind at rest. I don't favor dueling, but I'm entirely comfortable with a round of fisticuffs when the occasion warrants. I'll send a letter to London this afternoon, and Valerian should be at Doctors' Commons before sunset tomorrow."

He spoke with such assurance, such certainty that his plans would be carried out. "With Charles, everything we did was bounded by the limitations of his health. Any plans we made—for a picnic, for a drive, a call on neighbors, even a review of the household books while we sat before a cozy fire—were qualified by the postscript: depending on Charles's health. Depending on how he felt. Depending on if he was up to the exertion at that moment. If a nap restored some of his energy, I'd drop what I was doing to indulge his desire to walk in the garden. We lived for those good days."

"You have been through much," Thorne said, his hand moving slowly on her back. "I had thought you retiring, not particularly sociable. It never occurred to me that poor health might curb Summerfield's socializing. He was always affable, always cheerful when I saw him."

Charles's pride had been the other limitation on the marriage. Margaret had come to see that only recently, as Bancroft's pride—what sensible landowner eschewed turnips, for pity's sake?—had become more apparent as well.

"I look forward to becoming your wife," Margaret said, "but you must be patient with me. You are not Charles, but I am still me."

"We will be patient with each other," Thorne said. "And we will weather the storms together, for there will be storms."

Had he ordered the heavens for his own purposes, his comment could not have been better timed. Thunder rumbled gently from the south.

"Away with you," Margaret said. "Write to your brothers. I will read your father's notes and think on what scents you could produce in quantity that will be unique to the Dorning brothers' enterprise."

Thorne kissed her cheek—a prudent choice when they must part —and bowed. "May I call on you Friday?"

Margaret trailed a hand over his chest, stopping north of his waistband. "You may call on me any day."

"If the weather's fair on Friday afternoon, dress for an outing on foot. I'd like to show you some of my favorite corners of the estate."

*Oh my.* Said with that smile, in that particular tone, Margaret could be certain that the parts of the estate to be appreciated would be beautiful and absolutely, entirely private.

"I'd like to show you a few parts of my estate as well, Hawthorne."

He kissed her on the mouth this time, a smiling kiss. The thunder rumbled again, and then he was out the door and striding off across the terrace amid a rising wind.

"YOU ARE SITTING at Grey's desk." Oak sauntered into the Dorning Hall estate office, his cuffs turned back, smears of paint on his knuckles and forearms. "You look good there."

"I'm writing to Valerian, Sycamore, Ash, Willow and Casriel, but you can be the first to congratulate me. Mrs. Summerfield has done me the honor of consenting to be my wife."

Those stilted, formal words could not convey the blend of relief, glee, and anxiety the reality provoked in Thorne.

Oak came around the desk, grabbed Thorne's head in a wrestling hold, and scrubbed his knuckles hard across his crown. "Congratulations, best wishes, and I *will* kiss the bride, assuming the lady doesn't object." He kissed Thorne's brow and let him go. "Well done, Hawthorne. Have you set a date?"

Thorne ran his hands through his hair. "I'm writing to Valerian to procure us a special license. Margaret doesn't want any fuss."

"Does she want *you*?" Oak settled into the chair across from the desk, one every Dorning brother had occupied on those occasions when Papa had felt a lecture was necessary. Papa had not been much of a disciplinarian, but his disappointment could fell a naughty boy's pride in two minutes flat.

"Why would you imply she doesn't want me?" Thorne replied, sprinkling sand over the letter. "She accepted my proposal, and Margaret is a woman who knows her own mind."

"Mar-gar-et." Oak grinned. "You want her, clearly, but then, you always were a bit taken with her."

"How the hell would you know that?"

Oak rose and went to the window, where rain turned the view of fields and pastures into a fractured, dripping facsimile of a rural landscape.

"You are my brother."

"I have that honor."

"As do a herd of other worthies," Oak said. "You followed Papa around. I followed you. Papa loved the plants. Every little weed and wildflower fascinated him more than the little weeds and wildflowers he'd produced for the nursery upstairs. You loved the land itself, the abundant sustenance it provides. You and he at least had common ground, as it were, to discuss. I learned to love the whole of it, the entire pastoral pageant, though I will never capture the wonder of nature adequately on canvas."

*I followed you.* And Thorne had followed Margaret on many occasions. "One forgets that younger brothers can be devious."

Oak wandered from the window to the sideboard. "One never forgets that older siblings can be oblivious, as can parents. Sycamore refused to be ignored. I learned to enjoy my relative privacy."

While Valerian used a bit of both strategies. "Will you enjoy removing to Hampshire?"

Not so far away, and yet, Thorne understood why Valerian had balked at the notion. After years of rattling around Dorning Hall in a noisy, quarrelsome throng, most of the Dorning brothers seemed to be in a rush to leave home.

"No, actually. The lady I'm corresponding with sounds set in her ways, exacting, and dour, but she's in a position to provide me work that I enjoy."

"I will miss you." The realization tossed a damper on Thorne's pleasure at having become engaged. "You can talk sense to Valerian and Sycamore. Hell, you can talk sense to me on occasion. Why did you ask if Margaret wants me for a husband?"

Oak rummaged in the sideboard and produced a dusty bottle. "She is a comfortably well-off widow. She needn't marry anybody, but she's agreed to become your wife. Of course she wants you." He poured two servings and passed one to Thorne. "To marital bliss."

Thorne drank to that, the brandy spreading a comforting warmth on an afternoon grown dreary.

"There's wanting and there's wedding," Thorne said. "You asked your question for a reason, Oak."

Oak resumed his place at the window, drink in hand. How often had the late earl stood in the same place, gaze upon his lands, while a son or two or six tried and failed to earn their father's notice?

*I will be a good father to Margaret's girls, for that's what they need.* Not a step-uncle to carve the roast at the head of the table or to be an occasional visitor to the nursery or a dispenser of lemon drops. Those activities mattered, but they did not make a man worthy of the privilege of raising children.

Oak peered at his drink. "I always thought Margaret Mallory would end up with Lucas Weller."

"Hannah's grandson?"

"Great-nephew, grandson, I'm not sure which. He often foraged for plants with Hannah and Margaret and sometimes with Margaret alone."

"You mean, alone along the lanes, or alone where no one but my nosy brother could spy on them?" Why did this ancient history matter? Lucas hadn't lived to see his majority, and Margaret had accepted Thorne's proposal.

"We live in rural Dorset, Thorne. Even the lanes are hardly

thronged with traffic. Is that letter ready? I'll take it into the village and post it for you."

Oak had apparently said all he intended to say on the subject of Lucas Weller and Margaret Mallory Summerfield, but he'd said enough. Just as Thorne had dallied with Mrs. Plumley, Margaret might well have been infatuated with young Lucas. If Lucas had had any sense, he'd been infatuated with Margaret too.

"I can take the letter to the inn," Thorne said, pouring the sand back into the jar. "You don't really want to go out in this downpour."

"I like rambling in a good storm," Oak replied, finishing his drink. "The streams fill up, the sky commands attention, the wildlife leaves the stage for a time." He set his empty glass on the sideboard. "Will you live at Summerton?"

That question tossed another layer of practicality over the rosy glow of Thorne's new status as husband-in-waiting.

"I thought we'd set up housekeeping in the steward's cottage. The place is certainly large enough, and Margaret can lease out Summerton to earn additional rent." The idea of going to live at Summerton wasn't exactly repugnant—the house and grounds were lovely—but Dorning Hall was Thorne's home.

That Thorne had lived in the steward's cottage for only a few months meant Margaret would have a free hand in making the place into the dwelling best suited to her and the girls.

"I'm sure you'll sort it all out," Oak said, taking Thorne's glass and finishing his brandy. "You'll have the rest of your lives to get situated, after all. What's that?"

"A handkerchief." Thorne folded the letter around the square of linen Margaret had given him to replace the handkerchief Greta had used. He parted with Margaret's token reluctantly, but needs must when Casriel grew impatient.

"You are paying hard-earned coin to send a handkerchief to London by express?"

"I'm sending ammunition." Thorne finished folding the letter, sealed it with his signet ring, then tied a length of twine around it, not that twine would deter Oak if Oak was inclined to pry. "My thanks for posting it."

Oak took the letter and paused by the door. "Give some thought to the ceremony. Margaret married Charles by special license, too, you know. No villagers cheering the happy couple around the green, no bells rung for all to hear, no wedding breakfast in the assembly room. All very quiet, and then not long after, Charles whisked her off on a wedding journey that lasted months."

"We'll not be going anywhere until after harvest," Thorne said. "Margaret grasps that my duties require me to be at Dorning Hall, especially if Grey insists on cavorting about in London."

"Grey is married," Oak said. "I do believe Beatitude does the insisting."

"And Margaret insists on discretion regarding our nuptials, if you please. No whispering my good news to whoever's napping in the snug, Oak. We'll make an announcement once we're wed."

Oak drew his finger along the edge of the letter. "This has to do with Bancroft, doesn't it?"

"Yes."

Oak looked like he'd say more, but then he saluted with the letter. "I'm off to enjoy the elements."

"I'll go with you to the foot of the lane."

"Even a doting swain doesn't pay two calls on his intended on the same day, Thorne."

"How fortunate I am to have a brother well versed in doting swain-hood, though this same brother has never so much as serenaded a lady by moonlight."

Oak preceded him from the room and down the steps. "I've serenaded a few ladies. One doesn't have to finish university to make a fool of oneself."

Oak had tried a year at Oxford and promptly declared the exercise pointless. He'd been there without brothers, Sycamore being resistant to the notion, though Thorne suspected the real issue was family finances.

"I am not making a fool of myself with Margaret. She has reasons for remarrying, and I have made it plain to her that her expertise with scents will be a valuable asset to our new mercantile venture."

Oak went right at the bottom of the steps, in the direction of the back hallway. "Was that before or after you offered her a sonnet to her fine blue eyes? Did you tuck that declaration into the list of attributes you adore about her? Lovely smile, kind heart, excellent mustard plasters? Maybe you conveyed your tender commercial sentiment between verses of French poetry?"

"She knows I care for her."

Oak took down Thorne's cape from the peg on the wall and tossed it at him. "Oh, well, that makes all the difference. I *care for* my horse, Thorne. Even if the lady said yes to your proposal, you had for damned sure better figure out how to court her, or your marriage will be a field that lies fallow, year after year." He shrugged into his own cape, the hems swirling about his boot tops.

"You are in a temper," Thorne said, jamming an old felt hat onto his head. "You never get into a temper."

"I am always in a temper, but unlike you, I don't sweat off my ire wrestling livestock and hedges. I mostly trust you to be a decent husband to Margaret, Thorne, but have you thought that if you marry her, you are all but indenturing yourself to Dorning Hall? Grey snaps his fingers and expects us to turn his weeds and hedges into a profitable undertaking, when he was barely able to keep Dorning Hall afloat with all of us lending our aid."

"We also expected Grey to absorb our expenses, which are considerable."

Oak opened the back door, revealing a world gone damp, shadowed, and lush with spring rain. "I love Grey, as we all do, but he's the earl. Rescuing Dorning Hall is his responsibility, not yours, not ours. The exchange has been fair thus far in your case because you've worked your arse off to keep the estate producing. Grey has been free to take a wife, to leave the property at a whim. You don't owe him the rest of your life, much less your choice of wife."

"It's not like that, Oak. Margaret and I are well suited."

"Because you want her perfumes, and she wants you to keep Bancroft from wrecking Summerton the way he's wrecking Summerfield. I suppose good marriages have sprung from less." He marched out the door, Thorne following him. "Don't you trust me to deliver a letter to the posting inn?"

"I trust you, but I've been meaning to pay a call on Hannah Weller. Today is as good a day as any."

The crushed shells of the walkway crunched beneath Thorne's boots, a reminder to ask Margaret about the marling schedule at Summerton—between damned verses of French poetry.

"Will you stand up with me?" Thorne asked when they reached the front drive.

"Beg pardon?"

"When we speak our vows, will you stand up with me?" Because having at least one brother on hand for the ceremony seemed like a good idea.

"Thorne, I will be honored to witness your nuptials, even if I know you are a damned fool to rush into this without paying the lady court in the manner all women are due, much less without thinking through your own motivations."

"I'll take that as a yes."

Oak shoved him hard enough that Thorne very nearly fell on his arse amid a patch of bedraggled pink tulips. "Of course it's a yes, but you really should court your lady. Begin as you intend to go on, and all that."

Thorne thought back to kisses shared in a small, fragrant office, to the feeling of Margaret resting against him, her head on his shoulder.

"I can muster a little romance." Though—this bothered him—he also truly did need for Margaret to part with a perfume recipe or two.

# CHAPTER FOURTEEN

"I do believe London traffic is a foretaste of eternal damnation," Bancroft said. "Pardon my language."

"Our first and second coachmen are Scottish," Miss Pepper replied, twirling her parasol slowly. "It takes more than a mention of eternal damnation to mortify me, Mr. Summerfield."

Bancroft maneuvered his rented gig past a fish wagon, of all the affronts to fresh air, only to be halted by a manure wagon stopped in broad daylight in the middle of the street.

"I say there!" he called to the wagon master. "Let's get on, shall we?"

An enormous fellow in enormously dirty clothes lumbered over from the stopped vehicle. "T' off-hind wheeler's come up colicky. He canna pull nay mair t'day. Relief teams on t'way."

"Oh, the poor darling," Miss Pepper cooed. "A bit of the somnifera might set him to rights. Shall I have a look?"

"My dear," Bancroft muttered, "not the done thing."

"But an animal is in pain, and I do so love animals."

"A fine attribute, but I'm sure this fellow knows his cattle. Good sir, if you could assist me to back this team up enough to continue on to Hyde Park, I'd be obliged." The team was rented, too, a pair of glossy chestnuts with matching white stockings up front. The hostler had referred to them as his courting pair, no less, and, in honor of Bancroft's objectives, had let them out for a veritable song.

"Aye," the drayman said. "Have ye on yer way in a trice." He tugged his shaggy forelock at Miss Pepper and shuffled to the head of the team. Some foreign incantation ensued, which had the effect of coaxing the chestnuts to back up a few yards—no small feat when the street was becoming snarled with traffic—and maneuvering into a reversal of direction.

"Well done," Miss Pepper said. "I find London overwhelming, for all that the people seem friendly. Do you miss Dorset?"

No, Bancroft did not. Not in the least. He loved the bustle and hum of Town, loved that he could stroll two streets over and find a long evening of whist in the company of sophisticated gentlemen. He did not miss the scent of cow shite spread over the fields, or the bawling of new calves, or the company of his neighbors, who could discuss only marling, lambing, and other bucolic drudgery.

"I miss the beautiful scenery,"—he slanted her a smile—"though London hath charms that put any lowly shire to the blush."

"I would love to see your corner of Dorset, Mr. Summerfield. You speak of it so fondly. I believe you want to make the next right turn."

"Indeed, I do." Though having changed directions, Bancroft was in fact on uncharted ground. He took the turn, and at the end of the boulevard, the green expanse of the park loomed several streets on. "You seem to know your way about London well, for a lady new to Town."

"Because my father dabbles in property, I've seen maps and surveys and elevations since I was in leading strings. How many acres is Summerfield House?"

Bancroft launched into a fairy-tale description of his estate—the views! the charming neighbors! the heavenly peace of rural life!—which lasted until the vehicle was once again forced to halt amid the crowded confines of the park.

"You planned this, didn't you?" Miss Pepper said, touching his sleeve. "This same outing would have taken us a mere quarter hour at any other time of day. Very clever of you, Mr. Summerfield."

That touch on his sleeve, not quite a caress, but certainly friendly, made Bancroft bold. "You must call me Bancroft. All my friends do." Nobody save Margaret called him Bancroft, and familiarity from her could not be helped.

"Would that be proper? I don't think it would be. I will ask Briggs the instant I am home, but I will ask her where Papa won't overhear me. I will ask her if you might call me Emily. My name is hopelessly plain, but then, I am plain."

"You are the pattern card of feminine pulchritude, I assure you." Any woman boasting settlements like those rumored to attach to Miss Pepper could never be plain.

"Flatterer. You always know how to go on, *Bancroft*. Is there no blot upon your escutcheon? No youthful indiscretion that might make you a less intimidatingly perfect man?"

The entire carriage parade was halted, probably to allow some dowager to harangue her godson or show off her granddaughter, and yet, nobody was paying any attention to Bancroft and his guest.

Not now, *but they would*. "As a matter of fact, I have two youthful indiscretions, both boys. Charming lads who take after their papa in both mischief and looks. One isn't to mention such situations, though I trust I can be honest with you."

A calculated risk, but here in the park, what could even a sheltered young lady do? Demand to be taken home immediately? That would give Bancroft a good half hour to concoct apologies and protestations of remorse.

Though he wasn't remorseful. His boys were a pair of devils, and he liked them both tremendously. Their mothers were another story.

"Briggs warned me about this," Miss Pepper said, folding her parasol. The carriage was stopped beneath the maples, and afternoon shade blanketed the lane. "Gentlemen of means can afford to indulge their animal spirits, and I am not to remark upon it, but I shall, of course. Do you care for these children?"

"I provide for their every need, see them regularly, and monitor their well-being as any doting papa must." Charles had set up annuities for both lads, with the quarterly interest going to their mothers until the boys turned twenty-one, at which point each young man would come into his income. At the age of twenty-five, the principal would be turned over to him.

Bancroft had borrowed from his sons from time to time, though his solicitors had insisted he repay the loans with interest, of all the ridiculous posturing. He would make the repayments, if for no other reason than it irked him to have to send his own money to the mothers each quarter.

"How old are these little darlings?" Miss Pepper asked.

"They are both ten."

"Twins?"

"I'm afraid not."

Miss Pepper opened her parasol. "You were in the grip of young manhood, which Papa maintains is a form of dementia. That you are responsible toward your offspring speaks volumes in your favor."

The carriage ahead moved forward at a placid walk. The chestnuts, without any direction from Bancroft, did likewise.

"As long as I'm taking you into my confidence, you should know that I'm also responsible for a pair of nieces. My sister went too early to her reward, and her girls are now my responsibility."

Miss Pepper waved to a carriage passing in the opposite direction, which was not how a young lady conducted herself in public.

"Those girls must miss their mama terribly. They must be missing you right now almost as much."

What a softhearted creature she was. "Greta and Adriana are in the care of their widowed aunt for the moment. Margaret was married to my brother, but the union was not fruitful. I, by contrast, am a parent twice over, a man of means, and a dutiful uncle. Now that the girls are ready for the schoolroom, I'd like to take a more active role in their upbringing." And a very active role in handling their funds.

"That is noble of you, Bancroft, to be so concerned for a pair of orphaned girls. I'm sure their aunt will be relieved to see you take them under your wing."

*Bancroft* was relieved at Miss Pepper's reaction. Not every woman would have regarded a suitor with two dependent females underfoot so benevolently.

"The aunt is somewhat problematic," he said. "Margaret never quite got over Charles's death, and her approach to the children is one of duty rather than real warmth. She's something of an eccentric. She would never neglect their basic needs, but I fear for the girls if they're left with her much longer."

The carriage ahead turned off onto another lane, and—wonderous to behold!—no others blocked the way. Bancroft none-theless allowed the chestnuts to toddle along at the walk.

"You must rescue those girls, Bancroft. I had a few governesses growing up who were motivated solely by duty. Dragons, the lot of them. It's a wonder I lived to attend finishing school."

"Precisely. I must rescue the girls. I was hoping you'd see it that way, but mine is a bachelor household, and these are motherless girls. Even I would not take the children from all that's familiar to them without providing some sort of maternal figure to ease their transition."

"You will think of something." Another soft pat to his arm, more of a stroke. "You are a resourceful and intelligent man, and I know you care for your nieces. The solution will come to you. I'm sure of it. Tell me more about Dorset."

Bancroft regaled her with rhapsodies about endless sunlight, sparkling waterfalls, gay assemblies, and beautiful night skies, so much so that by the time he delivered Miss Pepper back into Briggs's scowling company, he was the tiniest bit homesick for Dorset himself.

"THORNE SENT YOU AN EXPRESS?" Casriel asked.

Valerian moved down the row of jars on the apothecary's shelves. "He assuredly did. He's writing to you, Sycamore, Will, and Ash separately, but I might as well tell you…"

A pair of ladies entered the shop, a mother and daughter from the looks of them.

"Does half of London subsist on True Daffy's Elixir?" Casriel muttered, peering at a blue bottle.

"The half that isn't stuporous from imbibing Godfrey's Cordial." The apothecary had pointed out that one concoction made the bowels seize, while the other inclined them to loosen, so the two remedies were often bought together.

"And the nature of Thorne's epistle?" Casriel asked, setting the bottle back among the two dozen like it on the shelf.

"Let's finish this discussion outside."

The apothecary was absorbed in listening to the older woman's recitation of symptoms, while the younger lady looked as if she wished to be anywhere but at her mother's side.

"I have never spent much time in apothecary shops," Casriel said when they'd gained the walkway. "What a lot of nonsense."

"That nonsense is profitable. People suffer with coughs, grippe, ague, headaches, boils, fevers, melancholia, wind, catarrhs, insomnia, dropsy, hay fever—"

"Valerian, that will be quite enough." Casriel set a brisk pace for the corner.

"Well, they do. Dances come in and out of vogue. The waltz might be all the rage at present, but two years from now, if the waltz is the only dance a fellow knows, he could well be sitting out every set. Human ailments are always in fashion, and Daffy's Elixir has been selling for more than a century. If we put Papa's botanicals into patent remedies, and one of them becomes popular, we could make a tidy sum." *Many* tidy sums.

"Selling opium or brandy by any other name, while avoiding taxes because the use is supposedly medicinal. I cannot believe Papa would want us to use his legacy thus. This is precisely why gentlemen do not engage in trade—because so much of what we call commerce is in truth deception wrapped up in pretty advertisements."

"You are more our father's son than you know."

They rounded the corner onto Jermyn Street, as if Casriel were anxious to leave behind even the sight of the apothecary—though doubtless, one or two streets on, another would come into view.

"Do you know there are entire warehouses of patent remedies?' Valerian asked.

"I read the newspaper. One can't help but see the announcements. A shipment of Lord Fremund's Celestial Tincture has newly arrived! St. Wigbert's Balsam to be had for a limited time! Lady Mary's Finest Black Cherry Comfort now available!"

"Some of which might even do a bit of good."

"If one is taking people's money, one ought to do so in exchange for the occasional bit of good. People become dependent on Godfrey's Cordial. They turn babies into little dolls that lie in their blankets, unmoving, for hours."

Jermyn Street on such a fine day was crowded with dandies and swells walking arm in arm. Traffic consisted mostly of handsome idlers at the ribbons of a flashy phaeton or yellow-wheeled curricle.

"Are these objections yours or your lady wife's?" Valerian asked. They were gentlemanly objections, but Casriel hadn't made them previously.

"Her ladyship's delicate condition predisposes a man to thinking."

"To worrying?"

"That too. Beatitude doesn't want to use an accoucheur. She's asked to use her sister-in-law's midwife."

"This is not a topic a bachelor from the shires discusses comfortably, Casriel. We're out and about to investigate our competition." More to the point, if Casriel got to airing his paternal anxieties, the entire excursion would likely be for naught.

"Do you think I am comfortable discussing it?" Casriel retorted. "I am to be a bulwark of masculine calm, a citadel of good cheer and husbandly serenity. Every time I see Beatitude put her hand on her belly, I am seized by panic. She nibbles her toast more slowly, and my own digestion feels tentative. Having a wife in this condition is a torment about which nobody offers any warning. One day, you're sailing along on a cloud of marital bliss—"

"Casriel, perhaps this is not the time."

"—in charity with all of creation and disrobing rather more frequently than before you spoke your vows. The next, you are wishing your manly humors to perdition, because the peril your dearest spouse faces is unfathomable, and but for your own damned rutting—"

"My lord, we are *in public*."

"We are in the heart of that masculine preserve known as club-land, and I may worry for my countess any blasted time and any deuced place I please."

"Perhaps you need a nerve tonic. I know where you can have your choice of a dozen."

"My brother is a wit. Who knew? What is that scent?"

Casriel came to an abrupt halt outside an emporium that styled itself as providing fashionable haircuts and accoutrements for men.

"They sell perfumes in there, as well as combs, brushes, shaving soaps, salves, and the like."

Casriel had darted through the door before Valerian could stop him. Inside, gentlemen conversed with fresh-faced clerks, all of whom were shaved, trimmed, brushed, and burnished to a high shine. Would a female shop clerk appeal to male customers the way a male clerk was often hired by modistes and milliners? Valerian made a note to discuss that possibility with Sycamore, who, alone among the Dorning brothers, seemed to have an instinct for commerce.

If a gaming hell could be considered commerce.

"I will smell like a flower seller when I leave here," Casriel said, sniffing at a bar of hard-milled soap wrapped in green paper embossed with gold violets. "Beatitude's sense of smell has become acute lately. She can tell whether I've been to the club, the lending library, to call upon Tresham or Sycamore..."

He trailed off, picking up one bar of soap after another and holding each beneath his nose. "Flowers," he muttered. "Lavender and jasmine, lavender and citrus, lavender and lavender... All quite lovely, but what if I don't care to smell like Provence in summer? I'm an Englishman."

"You're an idiot," Valerian replied, taking a whiff of a pomade that reeked of roses. "But you're an educable idiot. You expect your brothers to compete with this establishment, the apothecaries, with Truefitt, Harris, and the great Floris himself... And those families have all been in business for years, if not decades. Do you begin to grasp the complexity of the task you've set before us?"

"Let's get out of here." Casriel moved toward the door, when Valerian had thought to linger. "You never did tell me about Thorne's express."

They reached the street, and again, Casriel struck off, this time in the direction of home.

"I'll part from you at the intersection," Valerian said. "I must travel toward the City."

"Looking at properties for rent? If we're to cater to gentlemen, this is the neighborhood we need to be in, Valerian. Go where your customers are. Not a complicated concept."

"Exactly as I told you. We need to rent shop space in the most expensive quarter of the most expensive city on earth."

Casriel kept moving. "We don't need a large space. Perhaps Sycamore knows of something."

"I'll call upon him later today, just as soon as I finish my errand for Hawthorne."

"How is dear Thorne? Up to his elbows in bales of wool, I hope?" Casriel sounded wistful rather than teasing.

"You are homesick for Dorset. Admit it. Squiring your countess around Mayfair is all well and good, but you will be overjoyed to get back to Dorning Hall." Valerian was homesick for Dorset, which made no sense when he'd seized the first opportunity to leave the place.

His lordship examined the handle of his walking stick, a dragon of some sort done all in silver. "I miss home, true enough, but I'm trying to leave you fellows some privacy to sort yourselves out. I didn't want to hover as you took your personal effects from Dorning Hall, like a landlord evicting delinquent tenants."

Like an older brother who did not want to cast his siblings out into the world and might lose his resolve if he had to watch the spectacle firsthand.

"Smell this." Valerian passed him a plain square of linen with a sprig of bluebells embroidered into the corner.

Casriel glanced up and down the walkway, then took the handkerchief and sniffed. His brows rose. He took another whiff. "That is the smell of home. Of Papa's woods and meadows and... Dorset sunshine? How is that possible? There's even a hint of moss or ferns, cakes left to cool on a windowsill... Where did you get this?"

"Thorne sent it along. That is *one* of Margaret Summerfield's casual creations. If you entertain any more daft notions about selling off the water meadow, you will also—according to Thorne—lose access to the mind that made that fragrance and can make a dozen more just like it."

Casriel tucked the handkerchief into his pocket. "Hawthorne is threatening me?"

"He is talking *business* to you, Casriel. Explaining cause and effect, and I, for one, applaud his plain speaking. Now I'm off to Doctors' Commons."

"Valerian, have you news of a matrimonial nature?"

"In a manner of speaking, yes. Hawthorne has become engaged to Mrs. Summerfield, and the nuptials are to be celebrated by special license."

For the first time since Valerian had arrived at the London town house, Casriel seemed to truly focus. "Hawthorne is *marrying* Mrs.

Summerfield by special license? He's doing this to gain access to her perfumes?"

"Well, somebody had better do something, Casriel, because the owner of Dorning Hall is too busy fretting over his digestion to be bothered. Allow me to remind you, though, that Hawthorne will also accept responsibility for two small children when he takes a wife. He'll add Summerton to the properties he must oversee, at the same time he's stewarding Dorning Hall and minding the production of all the scents you seem to think will produce themselves before they magically fly through the air from Dorset to London at no cost."

Casriel took out the handkerchief and brought it to his nose again. "I need a nerve tonic made with this scent. Perhaps we all do. I will write to Thorne and tell him the water meadow won't be sold for the present."

"Lovely, and while you're about it, you might consider congratulating him on his engagement, but he wants no word of this development to trickle back to Dorset. The ceremony is to be very discreet."

"I don't like that, Valerian. When a Dorning marries, the world should rejoice. We have no need to sneak about on the way to the altar."

"With Bancroft Summerfield among our potential relations by marriage, I intend to respect Thorne's request for discretion."

The lordly beak wrinkled. "In-laws are like taxes. One understands why they exist, but one needn't like them. Discretion it shall be. What will you get up to while I'm congratulating the groom on his good fortune?"

"Thorne has asked me to keep a close eye on Bancroft and any lady who appears to have caught his fancy."

Casriel adjusted the angle of his hat. He was a little less buttoned-up since marrying, a little less an icon of conservative fashion.

"You'll need an introduction to Miss Emily Pepper. I'll consult with my countess and see that you become acquainted with the lady in the next twenty-four hours." He strode off, not the fashionable earl sauntering about Town, but once again a Dorning brother intent on a mission.

Valerian went the opposite way, already dreading the introduction to Miss Pepper. He knew two things about the lady sight unseen. First, if Bancroft was sniffing about her settlements, they were substantial settlements indeed. Second, if she seriously entertained Bancroft Summerfield as a suitor, she was not too bright and likely not too discerning either.

# CHAPTER FIFTEEN

"You will please keep the children indoors, Fenny." Margaret paced the length of the family parlor, which in the course of a pretty Friday morning had shrunk to the emotional space of a broom closet.

"They will not leave the house, I promise, ma'am. The girls are working on an illustrated book of adventures, and I doubt I could entice them into the garden if I wanted to."

Margaret had heard about those adventures on her visit to the nursery. An intrepid wise woman had fallen into an old mine shaft while foraging for parsnips, an accident that could all too easily have been taken from real life.

"What of sums?" Margaret said, her gaze straying for the hundredth time to the back garden below the window. "They haven't done any sums this week."

"Why should they?" Fenny set aside her embroidery hoop. "Both of them wrangle sums as if they had abacuses in their little heads. I suppose they get that from you."

The usual response—*But the children are not related to me*—seemed pointless. "Then they should work on subtractions, or perhaps it's time to introduce multiplication. Greta already seems to grasp the concept."

While Margaret could not hold a thought in her head. Spring fever afflicted her, or *Hawthorne fever*, more likely. The day was glorious, also *Friday*, when he'd asked her to dress for a walking excursion. This feeling halfway between glee and worry was new to her. Neither Charles nor Lucas had inspired anything of the kind, though she'd liked, been attracted to, and grown attached to both men.

"Mr. Dorning will be here soon," Fenny said. "Perhaps you should wait for him by the fountain."

"One doesn't want to appear too eager."

"You and Mr. Dorning are to be married. You are *allowed* to be eager. After all your years tending to Saint Charles, and more years tending to his nieces, the notion that somebody has come along to tend to *you* for a change rather pleases me."

"Thank you, Fenny. It's just that—"

There he was, emerging from the woods. Hawthorne wore riding attire—wore it very well—and was bareheaded.

"He is easy on the eyes, isn't he?" Fenny said, joining Margaret at the window. "Away with you, and enjoy your walk. I'll see how the intrepid wise woman has fared at the bottom of her mine shaft."

Margaret took one more moment to admire the sight of Hawthorne Dorning crossing the garden at an easy prowl, then whirled for the door. "Start on multiplication, Fenny. The girls are ready for it."

"Yes, ma'am."

And Margaret was ready to be free of the house, free from Fenny's knowing smile, free from everything. Hawthorne stopped by the fountain, his expression suggesting he'd caught sight of her as soon as she'd stepped out of the house. Margaret kept walking, down the terrace steps, along the paved path, straight into Hawthorne's open arms.

"Mr. Dorning, good day." Oh Lord, he smelled good. Of woods, leather, peppermint toothpowder, shaving soap, and springtime.

His embrace closed around her, secure and precious. "Mrs. Summerfield. I hope you're well."

The words were prosaic compared to the affection so freely given and so generously reciprocated. *I will love being married to this man.*

"I am in the pink," Margaret said, stepping back. "And in great good spirits too. Are we to take a walking tour of your property?"

"That would require far longer than the few hours I can spare today," Hawthorne said, drawing Margaret's arm through his. "But eventually, yes, I'd like to ride every acre of Dorning Hall with you and call on every tenant. I'd like to see every hedge and field of Summerton when you have the time to show them to me. Let's start by admiring your bluebells."

Margaret had been in the woods the previous day with the girls, but hadn't strayed as far as the bluebells. By scent alone, she could tell that they'd reached their full glory and would soon start to fade.

"To the bluebells, and you will please invite your brother Oak to sketch them in the next few days. This has been a good year for spring wildflowers." None of which Margaret had harvested, though she knew Hannah had been foraging all over the neighborhood.

"How are Greta and Adriana?" Hawthorne asked as they wandered from the garden.

"They are soon to embark on the wonders of multiplication. My babies are growing up. Some days that's a relief, others..."

"You wonder where the years go. I recall marching around our kitchen garden with little Tabitha on my shoulders. Now my niece is off to some fancy finishing school, speaking French like a native, whipping off entire piano sonatas by heart, and dreaming of candlelit ballrooms. How did that happen?"

The bluebells came into view, and surely they had never looked finer. Dappled sunlight winked down through trees gauzy with new leaves. The delicate scent perfumed the air—the fragrance of spring itself, according to the children—and pale violet flowers carpeted the grassy clearing.

"Hawthorne, is that a picnic basket?" Margaret tried not to step on any flowers, but they were too thick underfoot to avoid. "That *is* a picnic basket, and blankets, and wine... Oh, what am I to do with you?"

He'd arranged the scene like something out of a travelogue from a beautiful, exotic land. He'd spread not one blanket but three thicknesses, an oil cloth, a wool cooler, and then a quilt. A wicker basket sat at one corner of the blankets, a pillow at another. Just beside the blankets stood a small porcelain crock stuffed with tulips, bluebells, and a spray of French lilacs.

And this was for her. In the middle of the myriad tasks that went with managing a vast estate, Hawthorne had done this for her. Margaret sat on the nearest boulder and promptly began to cry.

For no reason, no reason at all.

Hawthorne came down beside her and passed her a handkerchief. "Margaret?"

She waved the handkerchief. "I'm being ridiculous. This is a *picnic*. In my bluebell wood, with the flowers... " Her own tears made no sense to her, but when Hawthorne wrapped his arm around her shoulders, that made all the sense in the world.

"Oak scolded me," he said. "Said I ought to court you, not simply snatch your recipes, mumble my vows, and go back to sharpening all the scythes in preparation for haying."

"Oak should mind his own business."

"He usually does, which is why I paid attention to his lecture. He's right, but you must not tell him I said so."

"Word of honor," Margaret said, dabbing at her eyes. "I'll never tell. You need not court me, but I'm glad you are. I've never had a picnic before, unless children were cavorting about, making a racket, and growing overly tired."

"I've never had a picnic either," Hawthorne said, "unless two brothers were arguing over the last bottle of wine, another was trying to steal my food, and a fourth was lounging over my half of the blanket. Will you picnic with me, Margaret?"

His eyes were so blue and his gaze so serious. Margaret had to kiss him. By virtue of great self-restraint, she kissed his cheek.

"We will share the bluebell wood with each other, and the blankets, and the wine." Margaret stayed right beside Hawthorne, reveling in a perfect moment. The day, the bluebells, the man... All was for once exactly as she pleased, and—most perfect of all—she sensed the moment was exactly as Hawthorne pleased too.

ONCE UPON A TIME, Thorne had been galloping homeward on Gowain, trying to outrun an autumn storm on the way back to Dorning Hall. Gowain had, as usual, attempted to leap the brook at one go and, as usual, made a huge splashing landing in the water instead.

And then the horse had lost his footing and gone down, knees to nose, tossing Thorne into a cold, rushing torrent. The whole ordeal was made harder for Thorne to comprehend by three-quarter ton of equine thrashing about just downstream. The shock of the horse going out from under him, the abrupt dousing, and the mental disorientation had stayed with him long after he'd shed his wet clothing and stepped into a hot bath.

Margaret's tears were a similarly unexpected development, as shocking to Thorne's heart as the cold water had been to his body, and somehow as painful too. Thorne hated to see her upset—*hated it.* Would have snatched up the blankets and cast the basket into the bracken to stop her crying. Margaret Summerfield was a sensible woman, independent in nature, and not given to sentiment.

Which was why her sniffling tore at him, and the feel of her curled against him, *leaning on him,* stirred all manner of tender feelings. He and Margaret were to be married, truly, intimately, forever

married. The reality was more complicated than Thorne had anticipated and more daunting.

A woman who cried at the sight of picnic blankets could be hurt.
*Probably had been hurt.*

"Shall we fortify ourselves before we go rambling?" Thorne
asked. "The fare is humble—chicken sandwiches, cheese, and apple
tarts. I stole some of Oak's French chocolates, but one never deci-
mates his brother's private stores, so my larceny was limited to a few
pieces."

Margaret regarded him through teary lashes. "You steal from
your brothers?"

"The property laws among my siblings are complicated and silly.
From earliest boyhood, we've each hoarded items of special interest
to us. Oak loves his chocolates. Sycamore had a penchant for a certain
type of sketch."

Margaret bumped her shoulder against his. "Naughty sketches?"

"Let's leave the fellow some pride. They were simply sketches
that appealed to him. Valerian treasured items of fashion—a pair of
gold sleeve buttons, an embroidered handkerchief. He even had a few
of Mama's earrings that had lost their mates. Willow scribbled adventure stories featuring intrepid hounds."

"What did you have?"

"Nosy brothers. Each boy attempted to hide his treasures from
the others, to no avail. We were an industrious lot when it came to
violating one another's privacy, but our intent was not to destroy
precious belongings."

"Your intent was to destroy one another's peace of mind. What
odd creatures brothers must be."

Odd and dear. "We had unwritten rules. If I found Oak's chocolates, I would take one or two, as a warning that his hiding place had
been discovered. To gobble them all would have been unsporting. If
Valerian came cross Willow's stories, he'd casually quote from one of
them at mealtime. Willow would know to move his hiding place.

Sycamore would find that an occasional moustache or eye patch had been added to the ladies featured in his sketches."

"But only to one or two. I see."

She didn't see—one had to have brothers to truly grasp this degree of nonsense—but neither did Margaret offer any judgment.

"I had an imaginary sister," she said. "Her name was Pamela, like the virtuous heroine of the famous novel. She was very kind and always certain of her moral direction. When I grew older, I told myself she had gone to finishing school, and I'd write letters to her, but once I turned sixteen, I stopped allowing myself even that fantasy. I daresay she would have disapproved of me by then."

Such wistfulness, and such a fanciful way to combat what must have been a lonely girlhood.

"Shall we eat?" Thorne asked, rising and offering Margaret his hand.

She stood and wrapped her arms around him. "I am glad we are engaged to be married, Hawthorne. I suspected we would suit. I'm sure of it now. You are a good listener and a romantic. I feel as if I've found the Dorning family's last, best treasure trove, and I intend to gobble him all for myself."

Thorne was already accustomed to the feel of Margaret in his arms, already sensed a familiar comfort in her embrace. He had no light, witty retort, though, just as he'd had no hidden store of boyish delights.

"I'm sorry your only friend was imaginary." Sorry she'd had no siblings to torment and protect, to fight with and fight for.

"I had books, I had the beautiful countryside, Hannah took an interest in me. One manages. Shall we investigate that picnic blanket?" She led Thorne by the hand across the glade, apparently happy to get on with the meal.

He was hungry—he was often hungry—but also unsettled. An exchange of boyhood family lore, a harmless confidence about Margaret's girlhood, a little affection... Nothing about the encounter should have left Thorne feeling off-balance, and yet, he was off-balance.

Perhaps what he was experiencing was the same sense of stepping into a different world that befell every traveler who found himself in an enchanted land. He was to be married to a dear, desirable woman of hidden depths and increasing preciousness. Perhaps he'd found a treasure trove meant only for him at long last.

MARGARET'S INTEREST in Hawthorne Dorning had progressed from a girlish infatuation with a youth of higher station to a widow's silent observation that someday some lucky lady would be his wife.

She was the last woman he ought to marry, and yet, that lucky, lucky circumstance was apparently to be hers.

"Would you say you were lonely growing up?" she asked, kneeling beside the hamper.

"I had a horde of siblings and both parents with me at all times," Thorne replied, sitting cross-legged on the blankets. "My grandmother dwelled in the dower house, and various uncles, aunts, and cousins were forever visiting. I should not have been lonely."

She found the apple tarts first, wrapped in paper and tied with twine. She passed them to Hawthorne, who produced a folding knife to cut the twine.

"You were usually alone when I spotted you out walking," she said. "Don't eat those yet."

"Why not?" He took a bite and held the tart out to her. "They're delicious."

Every difference between women and men, every difference between Margaret and her intended, was encapsulated in that simple gesture. Hawthorne ate when he was hungry. He shared from his abundance. He trusted his bodily urges and didn't apologize for sampling sweets before sandwiches. He was forthright, where

Margaret doubted herself, and he enjoyed his pleasures free of memories or misgivings.

Margaret took a bite of cinnamon, buttery pastry, apples, and sweetness. "Forbidden fruit," she said, sitting back. "You're right. It's good."

"Have some more."

"We shouldn't."

Hawthorne scooted closer. "How can somebody who was raised without a single nosy younger sibling have such a well-developed fear of being tattled on? We are private, Margaret May. In your own woods, not another soul to be seen. Enjoy yourself."

He held up the tart again, though Margaret was focused on the scent of him. He was near, he was to be hers, and they were private, as he'd said.

*Very private.* "If I'm truly to enjoy myself, then we should put the tart away."

He set the tart on the paper and leaned back on his hands. "Am I to enjoy myself too?"

The slanting sun turned his hair auburn and caught the shine of a cheek recently shaven. He was of a piece with the natural surroundings, and yet, he was also sophisticated enough to know when a woman needed—craved, longed for—wooing.

Margaret wanted to woo him too. Wanted to know him, to claim him, to be joined to him with a yearning that was physical and personal, but also anxious. Men disappeared. They had a bad habit of dying when Margaret needed them most. Other men—Bancroft—meddled, and only a woman with a strong male ally would be equal to the inevitable battle in which Bancroft would soon embroil her.

For that, she needed Hawthorne more than he knew. "You did say we could anticipate our vows, sir. I'd like to anticipate them now."

He slipped a sleeve button from his cuff. "I've been mentally anticipating our vows for the past three days,"—a second sleeve button disappeared into his pocket—"and nights." His cravat pin went next, followed by his pocket watch and chain.

How tidy and methodical. Why should these mundane steps toward disrobing turn Margaret's insides into a muddle?

"I can help you with your boots, if you like," he said, "unless you intend to ravish me with your boots on?"

"You're willing to be ravished, then?"

"Enthusiastically so. You?"

Margaret wanted to laugh, to pelt through the forest with Hawthorne in pursuit. "Likewise."

He tugged off one big riding boot, then the other, and set them side by side in the grass. "Valerian applied for our special license two days ago. I got his express this morning. The license should be ready by Wednesday or so and in our hands not later than Thursday. If we're to anticipate our vows, we're not anticipating them by much."

"We're to anticipate our vows, Hawthorne." The news about the special license was pathetically reassuring. Margaret had already forgiven herself for succumbing to Lucas Weller's charms—she hadn't known any better, hadn't even known that coitus outside of wedlock could result in conception, or what *exactly* coitus entailed. After hearing about Hawthorne's upbringing, rich in siblings and extended family, she forgave herself all over again.

Lucas had shown a very lonely, awkward girl some attention. He'd liked her. He'd told her she was pretty. If he'd asked her for the moon, she would have been pleased to snatch it from the sky for him. When he'd died, he'd asked more than the moon of her in ways she hadn't realized until several weeks later.

That lonely, bewildered, half-wild girl had deserved better than Lucas's heated fumblings, and now she was to have better. Much better.

"Hawthorne, stop."

He paused, his neckcloth undone. "You've changed your mind?"

A world of wary male forbearance colored that question, and again, Margaret felt herself falling more thoroughly in love. If she *had* changed her mind, Hawthorne would button up, finish his apple tart, and make no mention of her fickleness.

The opposite of Lucas with his importuning and cajoling. Also the opposite of Charles, who'd viewed moments of passionate arousal as precious gifts not to be squandered merely because his wife was in the middle of a rare and much-needed midday nap.

"I have not changed my mind. I need help with my dress." Margaret spun on the blanket, swept her hair off her nape, and presented him with her back. "If you'd oblige me?"

She had one instant's warning—a hint of warmth on her neck—before Hawthorne whispered in her ear.

"I will oblige you until we are both spent and dazed, then I will oblige you again. I might oblige you so thoroughly you'll ask me to carry you back to the house." He kissed Margaret's nape, sending shivers down her arms.

The pretty day became beautiful, the future luminous. "We will oblige each other."

Hawthorne was good with buttons, a fine quality in a man one intended to marry. His touch was brisk, he didn't snag Margaret's hair, and neither did his hands wander. The fresh air touched her between the shoulder blades, and then Hawthorne hugged her from behind.

"You must be honest with me to the point of ruthlessness, Margaret. Don't humor me if I'm going about matters in a manner not to your liking."

She kissed his forearm. "This is a beginning, Hawthorne, a place to start. I don't expect perfection, and neither should you."

"Practical," he said, kissing the top of her head and sitting back. "I do adore your level-headedness. Perhaps you'd like to undo my falls?"

Well, no. Margaret would rather have ripped them loose instead of carefully undoing each button as Hawthorne lounged on his back, not a care in the world. When she'd undone both sides, she sat back.

"Now what?"

He sat up enough to shrug out of his coat and drape it over the picnic blanket. "Waistcoat next?"

"Lie down."

Margaret had valeted Charles, as many wives did for their husbands. Charles had been self-conscious of his appearance, envying more vigorous men their muscles and appetites. Undressing Hawthorne was nothing *at all* like assisting Charles.

Hawthorne's frame was robust and in excellent condition. Supple muscles wrapped around big, long bones, and the whole came together in a testament to the species at its finest. Margaret ran her hand over Hawthorne's chest, sparing a thought for how justified Charles's envy had been. Illness had denied him so much, and for the most part, he'd borne his tribulations quietly until the end.

*But I did not die with him, and for that I am grateful.*

"Will you take your shirt off for me?" Margaret asked, undoing the last of Hawthorne's waistcoat buttons.

"Little would please me more." He pulled his shirt over his head, the muscles of his belly flexing as he sat up.

Margaret was still more or less fully clothed, though the buttons at the back of her dress were undone. Stupid of her not to have dressed for seduction. She'd dressed for a walk through the country-side, hoping Hawthorne might steal a few kisses or take her hand when they crossed a stile.

"I'm wearing stays."

"Not for long, you're not." Hawthorne got her dress off over her head and started on her laces, and in this, too, he was competent.

"You've undressed other women."

"A few, none recently. I got off on rather the wrong foot with a woman at university who presented herself as widowed, until having a large, jealous husband was a more lucrative status. One learns caution with the ladies after such an experience."

"There's more to this tale."

"Which I will happily tell you some other time. Suffice it to say, I made a gold-plated fool of myself, got my arm broken for my trouble, and didn't make the same mistake twice. Is that loose enough?"

Margaret had to stand to wiggle out of her stays. "I feel daring to be parading around in my chemise out of doors." Daring, but also, for the first time in ages, like her true self.

"What you are," Thorne said, tugging on her wrist, "is luscious. Make love with me."

Margaret had initiated this seduction, though where she'd found the courage was a mystery. Perhaps Hawthorne had given her the inspiration, with his combination of good humor, pragmatism, and roaring male vitality. For him, the situation was simple: They were to be married. They desired each other. They had privacy and time.

Margaret lowered herself to the blanket and kissed him, though for her, this whole situation was not simple at all.

# CHAPTER SIXTEEN

The most secluded path in the most secluded corner of Hyde Park was not nearly isolated enough for the thinking Valerian had to do. London was driving him mad, or perhaps close proximity to Casriel and his new countess was having that effect.

Sycamore was already housing Ash and hadn't invited Valerian to join them, which meant Valerian spent his days watching Casriel, a generally sensible and self-possessed man, make sheep's eyes at Lady Casriel for the duration of every meal, carriage ride, and casual encounter in the foyer.

"If I weren't so jealous, I'd find it amusing." That confidence could be safely placed in the keeping of Valerian's horse, a cantankerous bay gelding by the name of Clovis. The horse was no happier than Valerian to be cooped up in London, but a morning hack went a long way toward subduing Clovis's misanthropic tendencies.

They'd had their gallop for the day, and still, Valerian did not want to return to breakfast at the town house.

"More tea, my love?" he muttered, pitching his voice low. "Thank you, dearest," he replied in a soft falsetto. "Until I'm ready to cast up my toast and run howling from the premises. Hawthorne knows not what he's asked of me..."

Clovis's ears pricked forward as voices came from around a bend in the path.

"I tell you, Briggs, the wretched habit is the problem."

A female, and an annoyed female. Exactly what Valerian's morning did not need. The path ended at a fountain tucked away beneath the maples, so turning around would result only in Valerian being trapped without a means of escape.

"Onward," he whispered to his horse.

Clovis sauntered around the bend and came to a halt.

"Miss Pepper." Valerian tipped his hat. "Miss Briggs."

The companion sat upon a beast just above pony size. She and her mount wore identical expressions of martyrdom, and if they had a groom, he'd abandoned his duties.

"Mr. Dorning." Miss Pepper left off fussing with the skirts of her riding habit as her mare snatched at the reins. "Good morning. If you overheard my unladylike language, I trust you will ignore it."

"Not a chance," Valerian said, swinging to the ground. "Stand, Clovis, or we'll go home by way of the knacker's yard."

Clovis assayed his innocent-little-pony look, which he did nearly as well as Valerian impersonated a charming gentleman.

"Have you perchance misplaced your groom?" Valerian asked, approaching Miss Pepper's mare.

Miss Briggs sniffed, much as a horse might have snorted at the sight of an unwelcome pasture mate.

"I ordered him to leave us some privacy," Miss Pepper replied. "I want no witnesses to my humiliation. I also gave an order to cut out Briggs's tongue unless she swore a blood oath of silence."

"My lips are sealed," Briggs said. "Until we regain the privacy of the town house."

The girths were properly adjusted, the bridle as well. Valerian took hold of the nearest rein. "What's your mare's name?"

"Poppy. She came highly recommended as a lady's mount."

"She's not to snatch at the reins like that. Speak sharply to her the next time she does it." The habit of instruction came naturally, though usually Valerian was instructing young lads on how to survive the ordeal of asking a lady to dance.

Poppy snatched at the reins again.

"Madam," Valerian said in his most menacing tones, "your unseemly conduct disgraces your upbringing, brings shame upon your stable, and risks a dire fate. Cease immediately."

"Oh my." Miss Pepper took a firmer hold of the reins. "You have hidden depths, Mr. Dorning."

"She'll be good until my back is turned," he said, moving to Miss Pepper's side. "A gentleman typically aids a lady to adjust her skirts after assisting her to mount, the lady being necessarily concerned with control of the horse. A groom is not as willing to take such a liberty, which is foolishness when a woman's safety is at issue."

He tugged a length of fabric free of the stirrup leather and draped it straight down, then walked to the other side of the horse. "Stand up a bit in the stirrup. If all you can manage is to lean forward, do that."

Miss Pepper complied, and he pulled another wad of velvet from beneath her seat, then freed a fold from between the saddle and pad.

"More comfortable?" he asked.

"Thank you, yes. Now if only I can avoid the near occasion of death on the way home. I had my heart set on trotting today, but Briggs has forbidden it."

Valerian climbed back into the saddle and gave Clovis a pat for standing as if he routinely respected his rider's orders. Clovis would dispel that fiction sooner or later.

"Ladies riding aside generally avoid the trot," Valerian said. "They prefer to canter or walk, those gaits being smoother."

Briggs made a noise that probably translated from Companion into English as *I told you so.*

"But one must learn to stay on at the trot," Miss Pepper replied, "trots sometimes occurring between the canter and the walk."

A well-trained horse, especially a lady's mount, could transition smoothly from walk to canter and back again, provided the rider knew how to give the cues.

Valerian nudged Clovis forward, and the mare fell in step beside him. "You don't know how to ride." Miss Pepper was not a particularly gifted dancer either, though Valerian had stood up with her for only one minuet. Bancroft Summerfield had claimed a waltz with her on the two occasions that Valerian had observed.

The results had been uncomfortable to watch.

"I did know how to ride, once upon a time when a girl could sit astride her pony. I took a tumble and sprained my wrist when I was eight. I love horses, and I've spent many a happy hour with the grooms—I'm a competent groom myself—but then I was too busy learning French, deportment, algebra, German, Italian, pianoforte—"

The mare jerked her head up, which had the effect of pulling the reins from Miss Pepper's hands.

"Scold her," Valerian said as the mare took advantage of her own bad behavior and tore a mouthful of grass from the verge. "Shorten the reins and threaten her with mortal doom."

"Bad girl, Poppycock," Miss Pepper said in tones that might have got the attention of a particularly shy kitten. "Shame upon you."

Valerian reached over and took a firm hold of the mare's reins. "You shameless little baggage, if you misbehave in a similar fashion even once more, I will sit upon you myself and deliver a course in etiquette you will not soon forget."

"You sound like Briggs on the subject of unruly lapdogs."

"Briggs is clearly a woman of intelligence, for horses and dogs both benefit from sensible rules consistently enforced."

"I do not benefit from sensible rules consistently enforced," Miss Pepper said. "I cannot blame the mare for testing the limits on her freedom."

"Poppycock is not a well-educated, self-possessed, articulate young woman. She is a domestic animal with a job to do. She can test limits all she pleases when she's in a nice cozy stall, knee-deep in straw, a pile of hay at her hooves."

Miss Pepper fiddled with her reins. "You think I'm self-possessed and well educated?"

In a ballroom or at a card table, that question might have been flirtatious. From a lady perched awkwardly in the saddle, nobody to overhear her but a loyal companion, Miss Pepper's query suggested a hint of uncertainty.

"I have firsthand proof that you are a gifted conversationalist, witty, and astute. Think, though, of the demands of the waltz. When your partner knows what he's about and conducts himself with confidence and tact on the dance floor, your role is much easier to fulfill. When your partner fumbles about, can't find the beat, and nearly tramps on your hem... life is much more difficult. You must be the leading partner in the dance with Poppycock. She will be a happier horse when that is clear to her."

Clovis took leave to debate that theory on occasion, lest a rider get overly confident. Brothers were another reliable source of humility in Valerian's life, and sisters... sisters were a realm of complexity unto themselves.

So why did he miss both of his?

"You've seen me waltzing with Mr. Summerfield," Miss Pepper said, letting Valerian hold back a branch for her. "I am not exactly a paean to grace."

"The gentleman takes responsibility for the dance as the partner who leads. I myself have attempted to teach Mr. Summerfield the rudiments of the waltz. He has not been gifted with natural ability in some regards." Bancroft had brought neither humility nor humor nor tenacity to the endeavor either.

Briggs had allowed her cobb to fall several yards behind, though Valerian wasn't sure if that was by design or default.

"You and he are neighbors," Miss Pepper said. "He mentioned that. Are you cordial?"

"The Dornings are on good terms with all and sundry. We're not exactly impoverished these days, but as a family, our stores of charm are more reliable than our fortunes."

"So you don't have a profession or occupation?"

What an uncomfortable, insightful question. "As it happens, I do have responsibilities. My family is developing a legacy of botanical treasures into a commercial enterprise. My brother Hawthorne will be in charge of producing the goods in Dorset, and my other brothers and I will see to the London end of things." A suitably vague but honest response.

"My legacy is fabric," Miss Pepper said, as if that inheritance was a sentence of transportation. "Silks and satins, wools and linen. I can tell you the value of a bolt of velvet to the penny, and my eye for lace has made Papa more than one fortune. We avoid cotton, because the best quality is to be had from the Americans, and Papa says their situation is unstable and morally repugnant. In fact, the whole cloth business can turn on a whim of fashion, which is why Papa is so keen to enter the propertied classes."

"Land has its challenges too. Agriculture is a vast and changing science, and rents are not what they once were."

And this was not idle chitchat. But then, Miss Pepper studied algebra, an unusual addition to a lady's curriculum. Chitchat probably bored her witless.

They had reached a wider path, where a fellow in workingman's garb sat atop a hairy, unrefined hack that probably did double duty hauling the cook to market.

"Your groom?"

"The long-suffering Diller, who prays nightly for me to be married off. I am a trial to his nerves."

"And mine." That, from Briggs, who rode past Miss Pepper to join the groom.

"I'll wish you good day," Valerian said. "If you'd ever like a few pointers about how to remain in the saddle, or make a better impression when turning down the ballroom, I am happy to oblige." He usually charged for those instructions, but in her case...

"Thank you, but I believe my dancing is hopeless, Mr. Dorning, and if Bancroft Summerfield is to be my partner, I am not much motivated to improve. You aren't perchance returning to Dorset anytime soon, are you?"

"I am charged with finding a commercial property here in London for my family to acquire or rent, the better to further our business interests. Until that task is complete, I am doomed to bide in London. Why?"

"I have a job too, Mr. Dorning." She spoke softly and not happily. "Mr. Summerfield has invited us to return to Dorset with him. While I enjoy the countryside immensely, the journey will be long."

With marriage as its destination? Was that her *job*, to become Mrs. Bancroft Summerfield? Valerian did not know her well enough to ask that, and her plans were none of his business, except insofar as Bancroft Summerfield appeared to be courting her, and Bancroft was very much his business.

"Dorset is beautiful, Miss Pepper, and Summerfield House is situated in the midst of congenial neighbors. Has Mr. Summerfield offered a general invitation, or something of a more specific nature?"

"We're to leave on Wednesday of next week, weather permitting, and he will escort us to Dorset himself. In deference to my supposed delicacy, we'll take the journey in easy stages, but Papa is determined to have a look at the property before the situation progresses further."

"You are not looking forward to this journey."

She turned her face up to the morning sunshine. "We do what we must, Mr. Dorning. Perhaps we'll be neighbors one day soon."

Valerian did not want to be her neighbor, not if that meant she had to marry Bancroft Summerfield.

"Summerfield House is a lovely residence." The equivalent of telling a woman, *You could do worse.* It struck him that his circumstances were something like hers: He was attempting to ignite a spark of commercial potential on the dry tinder of his father's botanical obsession. The task was one he neither enjoyed nor intuitively grasped, and yet, he must make the attempt.

*We do what we must.*

"I have a lovely residence, Mr. Dorning. Several of them, if I'm to be honest. You should call upon my father. He holds title to all manner of odd properties here in London. He's a conscientious landlord and a sound businessman. He might know of something suitable for your family's enterprise."

"Thank you." She had opened a door Valerian might have pounded on in vain for weeks. He was an earl's son, but that did not guarantee him any entrée among the merchant classes. Just the opposite, in fact.

"You didn't laugh at me," she said, gathering up her reins. "All of polite society had a great joke at my expense when Mr. Bancroft attempted to waltz with me. Your eyes held only kindness."

And then he'd looked away. "I can teach you to waltz, Miss Pepper. I'm accounted something of a dancing master." The words spoke themselves, but really, how else could he thank her for the invitation to call on her father?

"Perhaps when I return from Dorset."

*If she returned from Dorset?* "You're leaving Wednesday next?"

She nodded.

"I might see you in Dorset after all, Miss Pepper." He touched his hat brim, and she guided her mare over to the waiting groom.

MAKING love with Margaret in the bluebell wood felt by turns daring, presuming, ridiculous, and perfect. Hawthorne had thought to woo her with a fine meal, or a ride around the prettiest of Dorning Hall's many views. In his braver moments, he'd contemplated reading her some of Wordsworth's blatherings. None of those gestures had rung with the sort of authenticity that he wanted for their marriage.

A picnic amid the flowers had struck him as a place to start, to use Margaret's phrase, a place to talk and touch.

That Margaret desired him was reassuring, that she'd peel down to her shift and stockings and undress him was... His mind stopped forming complete sentences when she straddled him.

"I don't know what's normal," Margaret said. "Charles was ailing, and especially after the first year of marriage, our intimacies were limited."

Hawthorne shaped her breasts through the fine linen of her shift. She was wondrously well made, her curves full and round.

"I'm told relations three times a day would qualify as normal," he said, undoing the bow that held her décolletage together. "Four, if you're feeling frisky."

"Three times *a day*?" She looked intrigued rather than amused. "What about at night? I thought—"

Hawthorne kissed her, because her puzzlement was that dear and because she seemed oblivious to the effect of her proximity to his breeding organs.

"I am unaware of any rules, Margaret. We make love whenever we please to, though if you summon me to the bedroom morning, noon, and evening, my duties at Dorning Hall will suffer."

"Can't have that," she said, wiggling her shoulders.

The neckline of her chemise fell lower, and Thorne spent a few moments acquainting himself with the glory of her bare breasts. Her skin was pale and traced with blue veins. Her nipples smallish and puckered.

Thorne took a taste. "Flowers." Rosy, sweet, luscious...

"What are you...? Is that...? *Gracious, everlasting...* " Margaret's hands fluttered tentatively about his shoulders, then she sank her fingers into his hair. "I like that."

Thorne spared a thought for poor Summerfield, who'd apparently been sicker than anybody had known. "What else would you like, Margaret?"

"Don't rush me."

Thorne switched breasts, letting his palms trail down around Margaret's waist to her hips, then to her backside. He moved slowly, in part because she had asked him to and in part because this was a beginning to savor.

She kissed him, hovering above him. "We'll get freckles."

"We could get a baby too." An inane observation, and yet, this coupling was different for Thorne. As a bachelor, the thought of siring a child had been worrisome. He'd limited his recreations to women who knew what they were about, but still... to think of his progeny being raised under any roof but his own was uncomfortable. To consider marriage to a woman who'd been interested in him only as a passing fancy had been equally unappealing.

His solution had been to work himself to exhaustion, choose his partners carefully, and indulge in self-gratification as needed.

With Margaret, what had been a worry became a wonder. To raise children with her, to be not only her lover and husband, but also the father of her children would be a privilege and an adventure.

"A baby," she said, folding down onto his chest. "With Charles ailing so badly, a baby would have been a complication. I like babies."

"I will like our babies exceedingly," Thorne said, wrapping her in his arms. *I like you exceedingly.* Rather than admit that foolishness, he occupied himself with searching for the pins in her hair. A few minutes' effort and her braid slipped free, brushing against his arm. Desire hummed insistently, but Margaret had asked not to be rushed.

Thorne stroked her back and waited.

"I have been married," she said, trailing her fingernails through the hair on Thorne's chest. "I grasp the nature of the institution, and I am all but naked in your arms, and yet... I cannot focus. I cannot think or plan or worry. I am tipsy with some sort of disorientation that I can only attribute—"

Thorne put two fingers to her lips. "No thinking needed, only loving." He liked being on his back, liked having his hands free, but he also sensed that Margaret wanted fewer decisions and distractions. He rolled them so she was beneath him on the blankets.

"Will this do, madam?"

"I can smell the flowers. When we move, they give up more of their fragrance. This is... decadent."

Her smile was decadent. She wrapped her legs around him, boots and all, and Thorne made himself take the time for a deep, carnal kiss. By the time he rested his forehead against her chest, Margaret was moving beneath him in a slow, erotic rhythm.

"You asked me not to rush you," he said.

"I told you not to rush me, and you haven't."

When she moved like that... "Would now be acceptable?"

She brushed her hand over his chest, her fingertips teasing at his nipple. "Now would be lovely."

*Thank God.*

*Not* rushing—specifically and imperatively *not rushing*—added a layer of arousal beyond the usual restraint Thorne believed his partners were owed. He nearly came undone when Margaret wrapped her hand around him and showed him exactly where she wanted him.

A slight flex of his hips, and he began the joining. Margaret went still at first, her hands beside her head on the blanket. The only sounds were the whisper of the greenery beneath the blankets and the distant murmur of the stream. All of nature seemed to be holding its breath, the better for Thorne to focus on his lover.

And then Margaret began to move. She caught the rhythm, then picked up the tempo.

"Margaret, I'm trying not to—"

"Hush."

*Oh, ye blooming pleasures.* She locked her ankles at the small of his back and became insistent, then demanding. Thorne focused on the feel of her boots against his backside, then on the sting of her nails digging into his arms. That didn't help at all, because every sensation somehow became so much more arousal, until his control was a frayed, burning rope tied around rampaging desire.

"Hawthorne..." His name was nearly a growl as Margaret became a woman possessed by passion. She bucked, flailed, panted, and groaned until Thorne was drowning in a roaring tide of pleasure.

The phrase *to lose one's wits* made a new kind of sense to him as he hung panting over the woman who was to be his wife. Thoughts drifted past, just beyond his mental reach, and cogitation was a series of impressions.

*Her chest is flushed.*

*Her chest is lovely.*

*Keep your mouth shut lest you say that aloud.*

*Maybe she'd like me to say that aloud.*

*What fool left my handkerchief in the pocket of my breeches an entire yard beyond my reach?*

Margaret lay beneath him, eyes closed. "I never did take off my boots."

Thorne tucked closer, resting his cheek against hers. "I like swiving you when you have your boots on, Margaret." He liked it perilously much and liked her even more. Quiet, self-contained, proper Mrs. Margaret Summerfield had not subdued the wild soul of Miss Margaret May Mallory. In all of creation, Thorne was doubtless the only man privileged to know that.

"And we're to do this three times a day, Hawthorne? Four, if I'm feeling frisky?"

He could *feel* her smiling. He was smiling, too, inside and out. "You mock me when I'm in no condition to defend my manly dignity." The spring sunshine pleasantly warmed his back, and the beginnings of hunger muted stirrings of renewed arousal. Life could not be any sweeter, and never had a lover been as precious as Margaret was to him then.

"My womanly dignity went begging into the wilderness. I'm trying to decide if I mind."

"Don't mind," Thorne said, kissing her temple. "Not with me, Margaret. Not ever."

She studied him, her gaze serious. "I wish I had married you first, Hawthorne."

*Why didn't you?* But then, why hadn't he asked her to? "We can be married next week, assuming I've recovered the ability to walk by then."

That earned him a smile. "Let's restore our energies with some apple tarts. Married by next week sounds lovely, though I warn you, sir, that spring weather does have a tendency to make me frisky."

"Then spring just became my favorite season." He lifted himself off of her and crawled across the blanket to retrieve his handkerchief. Getting dressed was a leisurely exercise punctuated by a wander down to the stream. Margaret apparently liked to hold hands, as did Thorne—who knew?—and what he'd intended as an hour's respite over a humble meal stretched into the sweetest afternoon of his life.

# CHAPTER SEVENTEEN

Making love with Hawthorne Dorning had unleashed a side of Margaret she'd abandoned when she'd agreed to marry Charles Summerfield. From that day forward, no more wandering the fields and hedges. No more losing track of time over a pot still or a new treatise on the medicinal qualities of chocolate. No more blending scents for the sheer pleasure of wearing a fragrance no other woman in the shire—perhaps no other woman in the world—had worn before.

Charles had needed her close at hand in case his health took one of the sudden turns that had become increasingly frequent the longer she and he were married. Her time had no longer been her own, and her perfumes had been limited to the tame scents that didn't aggravate Charles's digestion.

Week by week, she'd become less the young woman who'd loved storms and delighted in arguing with Hannah over treatment options and more Mrs. Charles Summerfield, a widow-in-waiting.

Since her picnic with Hawthorne five days ago, she'd spent hours out of doors every day. She'd dusted off her collection of treatises, and she'd even set a pair of footmen to scrubbing out her herbal.

"Excuse me, ma'am." The head maid, a petite, energetic young woman by the unlikely name of Calpurnia Higgins, stood in the doorway to Margaret's office. "You have a caller. Mr. Dorning awaits you in the family parlor."

"He doesn't bite, Higgins," Margaret said, rising from her desk. "You need not look as if he's here to steal the silver." *He has merely purloined my wits.*

Higgins had joined the household on a recommendation from the vicar, though she lacked the lilting, characteristic speech of the local populace. Her f's did not glide into v's, and when a word began with a vowel, she did not affix a gratuitous w at the front. She might have been an escaped slave, which Margaret considered none of an employer's business.

A lady's past was private, after all.

Higgins's expression remained dubious. "Ambers says the Dorning menfolk are long on charm and short on coin."

Now what sort of domestic mischief was this?

Hawthorne had walked with Margaret to the foot of the lane after services on Sunday, a courtesy the neighbors were bound to have remarked. With Adriana and Greta clamoring for piggyback rides, the time spent together had been far from romantic.

And yet, Hawthorne had kissed Margaret's cheek before he'd bid her farewell, and both girls had dissolved into peals of giggles. Then he had offered to kiss them, too, which silliness had had Adriana preening for the next hour and Greta looking distracted. Ambers had seen the entire exchange.

"Ambers knows better than to spread talk," Margaret said. "Mr. Dorning is a perfect gentleman." And a very skilled kisser.

"If you say so, ma'am. Shall I bring in a tea tray?"

"Tea would be appreciated, and some sandwiches."

Higgins looked like she wanted to say more, though Margaret was eager to join her caller. When was the last time she'd been eager to do anything, other than share a walk through the woods with Hawthorne?

"What is on your mind, Higgins?"

The maid stared at her boots. "Will things be changing here, Mrs. Summerfield? I know it's not my place to ask, but Ambers is friends with the Dinwiddies' housekeeper, and Mr. Dorning has walked you home twice. Now he's calling again, and you've never had a gentleman caller before."

That speech was extraordinary, not only for its presumption, but also for its length. Higgins was a quiet soul who made up in industry what she lacked in loquaciousness.

"I cannot go back to London, you see," Higgins went on. "I did not do well there. London is too big and busy and... I cannot return."

When Margaret might have scolded a domestic for getting above herself, she instead restrained the urge to offer reassurances. How many seemingly contented young women were coping with pasts made difficult by circumstances about which they remained silent? And yet, Margaret had not discussed the details of a shared household with Hawthorne. Perhaps his visit was an occasion to do just that, among other things.

"Ambers's gossip disappoints me," Margaret said, though it certainly didn't surprise her. "You may be certain, Higgins, that if my domestic arrangements change, my staff will suffer as little disruption as possible. You are a hard worker, and your conduct has been exemplary. If you'd like to leave, I'll write you a sincere and glowing character, but I would be sorry to see you go."

"Thank you, ma'am." Said with a shy smile. "I'll see about the tea tray."

"And the sandwiches."

"And the sandwiches."

Higgins bustled off toward the steps, though Margaret's delight at the prospect of spending time with Hawthorne was muted by the issues a simple exchange with a maid had raised: Having Hawthorne join the household would mean changes. The male servants would compete to look after the master of the house's wardrobe and private rooms. The butler's consequence would rise more clearly above the housekeeper's. The nursery staff might be caught up in the attendant drama.

Something as simple as who sat where in the gig on the way to market would be renegotiated.

The sight of Hawthorne in riding attire inspired Margaret to set aside those concerns and revel in her intended's embrace.

"I've missed you."

"You saw me on Sunday." He kissed her on the mouth, an almost-chaste little peck. "I've missed you too. I dropped a hammer on my foot yesterday because I was too busy missing you, and this morning I cut myself shaving. You are a force to be reckoned with and a dangerous woman to court, Margaret Summerfield."

"Thank you. I haven't been a force to be reckoned with in far too long." Margaret detected something earthier beneath his usual lavender, starch, and peppermint scents. "Did you ride a different horse today?"

"I rode a great slug of a beast whom Oak claims has some relation to the equine. A mastodon under saddle would be more elegant than my brother's gelding. My own mount was having his shoes reset, and I felt some urgency to see you." Hawthorne's tone was more distracted than flirtatious.

"I take it the special license has yet to arrive?"

Higgins interrupted with the tea tray, though Cook had apparently mistaken Hawthorne Dorning for a regiment on the march.

"My compliments to the kitchen," Hawthorne said as Higgins curtseyed and withdrew. "As it happens, I am hungry."

Margaret was assailed by memories of Hawthorne feeding her bites of apple tart. Hawthorne draping his shirt over her bare shoulders, to preserve her from the near occasion of freckles, while he showered her with kisses. Hawthorne laughing as he'd joined his body to hers for the second time.

"If you're hungry, let's sit."

He took the wing chair, which was a disappointment. Margaret took the corner of the sofa nearest to him and poured two cups of tea.

"I should know how you prefer your tea," she said, the small awkwardness taking another bite out of her happy mood.

"The same way you do: a dash of sugar, a dollop of milk. My dear, we have a problem."

Margaret set down the teapot. *My dear* was lovely, but *we have a problem* had her insides aflutter in the wrong way. "Do we have a special license?"

"We do, which is fortunate. Valerian tucked in a note along with the license. Bancroft is leaving London today and bringing guests back to Summerfield House. If you seek to be married before Bancroft returns, our nuptials have acquired some urgency."

He reached for a sandwich, which was another slightly jarring reminder that life was changing. As a guest, Hawthorne would have waited to be served. But he wasn't a guest. He was her fiancé, her lover, and soon to become her husband.

"Bancroft travels in style," Margaret said. "His coach is enormous and turns into a veritable bed on wheels. I've known him to make the journey from London in as little as one long day."

"Have you said anything to the girls?"

"About?"

"You becoming Mrs. Hawthorne Dorning."

"I wanted to wait until the special license was in hand."

Hawthorne put down his sandwich, untasted. "You did not trust me to make good on my proposal?" The question was merely curious.

"I have learned not to count chickens, Hawthorne. Charles was in good spirits and, for him, relatively good health when last I saw him. Three days later, Bancroft sent me a note—a damned, wretched, blasted note—informing me that my husband had died."

Hawthorne shifted to sit beside her and looped an arm around her shoulders. "I'm sorry. That's one more reason not to like Bancroft. He's been cutting up your peace for some time, hasn't he?"

"Terribly." Margaret was put in mind of the vase Greta had broken. One minute, the little heirloom had sat serenely above all the noise and bustle of the household. The next, it had lain shattered on the carpet. News of Bancroft's precipitous return felt exactly like that. "Can we be married today, Hawthorne?"

He kissed her forehead. "We can, though I suspect we have at least until tomorrow morning before Bancroft arrives. He's bringing guests, a Miss Emily Pepper and her father. I gather Bancroft is being considered for matrimonial honors where Miss Pepper is concerned, and she's quite the heiress. He won't travel at a breakneck pace with the lady sharing his coach, not if he wants to impress her favorably."

This was not good, not good at all. "If he has a wealthy wife, he's in a better position to take on care of Adriana and Greta."

"If he has any sort of wife at all, other matters will likely occupy him at least until the wedding journey is complete."

A comforting thought, but Margaret could not afford to put her faith in it. "Tomorrow morning, then. Early and without any fuss. Fenny will be my witness."

"Oak has agreed to attend me. I'll see the vicar on my way back to Dorning Hall. Where would you like to hold the ceremony?"

One of the benefits of a special license was that the vows could be spoken at a location other than the parish church. "I hadn't thought that far ahead."

"I have an idea," Hawthorne said, passing her a sandwich. "We can discuss it while you help me do justice to this food. You will need your strength, Margaret. You are soon to be a married woman."

He was teasing her, and in return for that kindness Margaret could find a smile. That she and Hawthorne were to be married—tomorrow, bless him being such an accommodating fellow—was in truth a reason to rejoice. She ate the sandwich and wondered what sort of well-dowered woman would even consider marrying Bancroft Summerfield.

ONE OF CASRIEL'S recent economizing measures had been to reduce the size of the Dorning Hall conservatory by one-third, selling the glass and framing to a neighbor who'd come into an inheritance. Casriel had included in the price some of the less exotic inventory, but the remaining space still bore the quality of an overgrown grotto.

"This is an unusual choice of chapel," Oak said, batting at Hawthorne's hair. "Papa would approve."

"He would have approved of life in a tent, provided the surrounding flora was of interest to him. Stop fussing me."

"Fine, then," Oak replied, giving Hawthorne's hair a final pat. "Get married with your hair sticking up like some village lad who has just finished cavorting around the maypole. Are you nervous?"

Oak was nervous, which was touching and annoying as hell. "Hard work has never deterred me in the past. Where can she be?"

"By now? Either halfway to London, on her way to Cornwall, or maybe taking ship from Bournemouth. Do you truly consider holy matrimony to such a lovely woman *hard work*?"

"Margaret and I have not had a chance to discuss how we will move her and the children to my house. What furniture stays at Summerton, what furniture comes with Margaret as her dowry? How will her staff be divided up, and what becomes of Summerton when she's moved? We have not worked out the settlements, so to speak. She's a woman of means, and I... I am willing to work hard."

Oak sauntered over to the bench and took a seat. He was a handsome devil when he took the time to don morning attire. His hair was too long, and he needed more meat on his bones, but his very indifference to appearances gave him an enviable air of self-possession.

"I would opine that you've been working *too* hard," Oak said, resting an arm along the back of the bench. "We haven't shared an evening meal for the past week. You're gone by first light, and you look like you could use a three-day nap."

Thorne felt like he could use a three-day nap, preferably in the same bed with Margaret, and yet... "I had not reckoned with the changes marriage will bring."

Oak patted the bench. "Tell Brother Oak all. I will thrash you for your stupidity, and you will feel much restored by my kindness."

If only the usual boyhood rituals still worked. Thorne remained on his feet. "I am, in a sense, marrying Papa's botanicals when I marry Margaret. I am committing to make a go of Casriel's venture in a way I didn't before. Margaret will expect it of me, and having a family to raise, I must expect it of myself."

This train of thought had invaded Thorne's mind after he'd spoken with the vicar. Margaret had been understandably distracted by the news that Bancroft was already returning, but perhaps she was also realizing the magnitude of the upheaval marriage would bring. A woman expected to leave her parents' house when she became a wife. She did not expect to leave her own house, towing two children, staff, property, and means.

"As if," Oak said, "no man has ever tried his hand at a venture, given it his best effort, then decided his interests lie elsewhere. Have you whistled up the fairies to steal your legendary common sense, Thorne?"

"Children are not a *venture* one can undecide."

"Children can be moved. They can follow marching armies. They can go away to school. I've heard wives are somewhat portable too."

But were dreams portable? Hawthorne had dreamed that Casriel might one day deed him one of the more modest tenancies, a place needing care and knowledge to bring it 'round. That dream was passing away, replaced with the job of making the botanical venture successful. The trade included having Margaret for a wife—a delightful consideration—but also taking on two children to raise and possibly many more.

Thorne liked children, and in particular he liked Adriana and Greta, but did they like *him*? "Will you be going to Hampshire?" *Say no. Not now, not yet.*

"I have taught all the local squire's daughters and son their water-colors and sketching. I have painted every scenic view on the property. I have completed more labels and advertisements for Casriel's queer start than he could ever need, assuming we eventually have products to wear the labels. I am of age, and I have skills. As the saying goes, it's time I made my way in the world."

"Please wait until after haying." That would give Thorne a few weeks to... what? Settle into married life?

"I'm still haggling with the widow, but if she does not hire me, I will continue to look for a post. I'm advertising as far away as the Lakes."

The Lakes were beautiful, also too damned distant.

The door opened, letting in a gust of cool air. "The ladies have arrived," the vicar said, beaming. "If you gentlemen are ready, we can begin shortly."

"I'll fetch Hannah from the parlor," Oak said, rising. "You are a lucky, lucky man, Hawthorne Dorning. See that you make Margaret Summerfield a lucky woman." He squeezed Thorne's shoulder and strolled off, not a care in the world.

Oak was right, not that Hawthorne would tell him that: Margaret was putting her entire trust into Hawthorne's hands, in addition to the well-being of two children she loved dearly. Hawthorne *was* a lucky man, and if he'd had his doubts, Friday afternoon had banished them.

Mostly.

"Margaret." He held out a hand to his bride. "You look lovely."

She'd styled her hair softly, with a long honey-blond skein curling over her shoulder. Her dress was a pale lavender, the cut simple and old-fashioned. A shawl of white lace was draped over her shoulders, and she'd affixed a little corsage of bluebells to her wrist.

Thorne bowed over her hand when he wanted to kiss her witless. Time enough for that later.

She curtseyed. "Mr. Dorning."

"Mrs. Summerfield." Probably the last time she'd be addressed thus. Did that bother her? "Miss Fenner, thank you for joining us. I think you know my brother Oak, who will be along—"

Oak ushered Hannah Weller into the conservatory. "Is my timing not impeccable? Ladies, a pleasure. Ma'am, you will take excellent care of my brother, please, and if he in any way proves a disappointment, you will apply to me, and the matter will be addressed."

That bit of banter had Margaret looking confused.

"He's implying," Thorne said, "that a man who has never entertained the notion of holy matrimony, a man incapable of remembering to remove his muddy boots before setting foot in the parlor, can beat some sense into a fellow blessed with a lovely wife. Don't worry, though. Oak is applying for posts as far away as the Lakes. We likely won't see much of him."

"I'll miss you, Master Oak," Hannah said. "Miss Margaret, you look radiant."

Embraces followed, though to Thorne's eye, Margaret also looked worried and perhaps a bit short on sleep.

"Shall we begin?" the vicar asked. "I must say, the surrounds are unusual, but quite lovely."

Thorne had stayed up late wrestling trees and potted plants, ferreting out the varieties in bloom, and making a list of what he'd moved from where. Papa had made a map of the conservatory, though who knew to what extent it still reflected the current configuration?

The vicar arranged those present, with Hannah taking the bench and the witnesses standing on either side of the bride and groom. Though Thorne had attended many weddings, he was still not prepared for the brevity of the ceremony, nor for the moment when he produced a plain gold band and found that Margaret's fourth finger already wore a pair of rings.

"Sorry," she muttered, twisting the rings free. "I hadn't thought..." She passed the rings to Miss Fenner, who held them along with the single glove.

"No matter," Thorne said, sliding the plain band onto her finger. The ring was too big, having been among the late earl's collection and given to Thorne at the time of his father's passing. "We'll have it resized when next we're in London."

That occasioned an uncertain smile, then the vicar was blathering on about worldly dross and heavenly rewards. A ceremony that had seemed too short droned on now, until finally, finally, Miss Fenner congratulated Hawthorne with a shy hug, and Oak kissed the bride before Hawthorne could punch him aside.

The wedding breakfast was mercifully reduced to a modest luncheon, though the Dorning Hall staff had trotted out the good silver, and then Oak was offering to see Vicar, Miss Fenner, and old Hannah home.

"We are man and wife," Margaret said, unpinning the corsage from her wrist when Oak had ushered the guests from the dining parlor. "Are you as tired as I am?"

Was that an invitation? A confidence? Did a husband rise from the wedding breakfast and carry his wife off to bed? Not that Hawthorne's old room at Dorning Hall had been aired out.

"I was up late in the conservatory. Perhaps you'd like to return there?"

She put her corsage in the water glass. "Honestly, the scents in the conservatory were somewhat overwhelming. You have a sizable library. Shall we take a tour?"

All that wrestling of trees and rearranging of shrubs, and the conservatory had been *somewhat overwhelming*. "I'd be happy to show you the library."

"Thank you for inviting Hannah. That meant a lot to me, and I would have regretted the oversight for years."

"She is as close to family as you have. I wish more of my family had been able to attend."

Margaret looked up from wrapping her shawl about her shoulders. "I'm sorry they couldn't be here. I'm very glad to be married to you."

*Well, damn.* "And I to you." He held her chair, wondering where the ease they'd shared on Friday had gone, because every other word from his mouth landed amiss today. A few of Margaret's were landing amiss too.

They'd taken off their gloves to eat, and before Margaret could put hers back on, he took her hand. "I mean that. I have long esteemed you, Margaret Dorning, and I look forward to being a good husband to you."

Her brows drew down. "Margaret Dorning." Thorne had watched while she'd signed her name thus on Vicar's registry, but the form of address seemed to confuse her.

"Margaret May Mallory Summerfield Dorning," Thorne said. "The library is this way." He led her through the house, with Margaret peering about at portraits, busts, dried flower arrangements, and other appointments Thorne had stopped seeing decades ago.

"You are the son of an earl," she said at length.

"Some things can't be helped. Fortunately, I am also the son of a passionate amateur botanist and the brother of eight formidable and worthy siblings. Welcome to the Dorning Hall library."

Margaret stopped just inside the door. The place was chilly and probably needed a good dusting, but it was a pretty room and full of natural light.

"You know, I'd best not look around here after all, Hawthorne. If your father was half the botanist I knew him to be, I will start reading his collection of treatises, and we won't get back to Summerton until next spring." She let go of his hand and went straight to the shelves where the late earl's collection of medicinal monographs was arranged alphabetically by author. The rest of the library might be all topsy-turvy, but Papa's treatises had been carefully cataloged.

Margaret pulled one from the shelf while Thorne was torn between bemusement that she'd so readily ignore her new husband for the sake of musty tomes and appreciation for the picture she made in her pretty dress, head bent over her reading.

Then the import of her words sprouted among the other dislocations, regretted exchanges, and awkwardnesses of the day.

"Get back to Summerton," Thorne said slowly. "To retrieve your trunks?"

She looked up. "My trunks?"

"For removal to my house." The steward's house, to which Thorne did not have title, though he had possession.

Margaret closed the monograph and held it against her chest. "Your house?"

"Where I live." *Where I thought my family would live now that I'm married.* "I assumed that marriage meant cohabitation, and that means you and the girls remove to my dwelling."

She shelved the treatise. "I assumed marriage meant cohabitation as well, but I did not conclude we'd be uprooting the children, closing up Summerton, letting my staff go..."

And she wasn't offering to undertake those efforts now.

"We are married," Thorne said, approaching her.

In the space of a few steps, he saw her gaze become troubled, and on her wedding day, she should not *be* troubled.

He stopped directly in front of her. "We have time to sort this out. You haven't even seen my house, and the children barely know me. Let's not rush this."

Finally, he'd found the right thing to say, for Margaret's relief could not have been more apparent. "We do have time. Thank you, Hawthorne. There's much to consider."

No, there wasn't. Man and wife should live together, and the steward's house was a reasonably commodious place to do that. Summerton could be let out, the staff could all retain their posts, and *married life* would go on.

"Let me show you the rest of Dorning Hall," he said, taking her by the hand and leading her from the library. "If you're willing to valet me, I can change out of this folderol and take you back to Summerton when we've finished our tour."

Though what was marriage without a wedding night?

"Would you consider joining me for another picnic later today?"

As consolations went, a picnic with Margaret would do nicely. "I would indeed." He stopped at the foot of the main staircase and framed her face with his hands. "I really am very, very glad to be married to you, Margaret."

She kissed him, a thoroughly married kiss that had Hawthorne thinking thoroughly married thoughts, until somebody cleared his throat.

Hawthorne looked up to find Valerian standing in the foyer, wearing an enormous smirk. "Timing is everything," he said. "Mrs. Hawthorne Dorning, I presume?"

# CHAPTER EIGHTEEN

Memories of Margaret's first wedding day intruded on her second.

She hadn't known when she'd married Charles exactly how sick he truly was, or how soon his illness would become the driving force in their relationship. They'd had one year before his health had become precarious, time enough to realize that in many regards, they suited very well. Time for gratitude and mutual esteem to grow into a quiet, accepting sort of love. Time enough for a protracted journey with Charles's sister and her husband, and then to return home to the corner of Dorset that Margaret had missed terribly.

The wedding day, though, like this one, had been rushed, awkward, and exhausting. *Please, God, don't let that be a portent of things to come.*

"Perhaps we should tell the children of this day's developments," Hawthorne said, handing Margaret down from a gig. He'd changed out of his formal attire and seemed more relaxed for it, if not more cheerful.

She remained standing with him before the Summerton front terrace, her hands on his arms. "I'd rather wait." Were they to have their first quarrel before she'd even taken off the dress she'd been married in?

"I apologize for Valerian's interruption. He's supposed to be finding us a place to do business in London."

Margaret embraced her inten—her husband—though they stood in plain sight of the house. "I suspect Oak summoned him. That seems the sort of thing your siblings do. They were very friendly."

She'd been acquainted with Oak in the manner of two people whose paths used to cross out among the fields and hedges. He'd always had a friendly wave for her, but then he'd resume sketching and she'd go back to her foraging. She'd stood up with Valerian a time or two at the local assemblies, but now those men were among her family, as was the earl himself.

It was all a bit much, even as Margaret admitted that Hawthorne's family and their consequence had been part of her motivation for marrying him.

"Perhaps we need a schedule," Hawthorne said, his arms wrapping Margaret gently. "A list of priorities and tasks. With haying coming up, my time will not be my own, though you are my wife—my new wife. My time should be at least partly yours."

*I hate lists and schedules.* At the end of his life, Charles's whole day had been a list of medications, tisanes, and tinctures, all administered on a strict schedule. Greta's day was bounded by a looser framework, but one that still constrained the household beyond the nursery. Even Adriana grew restive without some semblance of a routine, while Margaret...

*I want to take a long walk, by myself, to no particular destination.* She did not dare admit that. A groom with a perfectly good set of eyes and ears hovered by the horse's head.

"Shall we take advantage of the weather and tarry on a certain bench?" she said, stepping back.

"You can take the carriage back to Dorning Hall," Hawthorne said to the groom. "I'll walk home."

The man climbed aboard and, with a touch of his cap in Margaret's direction, guided the horse down the drive.

"You refer to the bench in the woods where I kissed you?" Hawthorne asked.

"The very one." While Hawthorne referred to Dorning Hall, where he no longer lived, as *home.*

Margaret linked arms with him and crossed the drive. The children were doubtless watching from the nursery windows and half the servants from other vantage points. Fenny had been instructed to say nothing to anybody, other than that she had accompanied Margaret on a social call to Dorning Hall.

When they'd gained the privacy of the woods, Hawthorne handed her onto the bench and came down beside her. "Where shall we start?"

Gracious of him to even ask. By law, the husband was a domestic tyrant, and all a woman could hope for was that he'd be a benevolent dictator. Margaret should have anticipated that Hawthorne would expect his wife to remove to his domicile.

"I'd like to start by doing nothing," Margaret said. "I need some time to think about our options, discuss them, perhaps try them on. The children are easily upset, Bancroft will descend any day, and his reaction to our nuptials will matter."

Hawthorne sat forward, resting his elbow on his knees. That posture accentuated the breadth of his shoulders and the long line of his back. "I did not marry Bancroft, Margaret."

*I married you because of Bancroft,* though that was not entirely honest. Hawthorne was attractive in his own right, and for much more than his broad shoulders.

"You did marry me in haste, for which I will be forever grateful. I would rather we deliberate on our course for a short while than strike out in a direction that becomes hard to reverse once embraced. Children can adjust to much, but not if changes are thrown at them haphazard."

He sat back and ranged an arm along the bench. "I want a

wedding night." His tone was half determined, half self-conscious, and all dear.

"I want that too. Did you have tonight in mind?"

"Part of me has this very moment in mind. Part of me knows that you're right. We must consider our next steps carefully, and that you'd think of the children first is one of the many reasons I esteem you. I'm also aware, though, that I now have two brothers underfoot, both doubtless willing to tell me how to be a husband, how to manage acres and acres of haying—though I've been managing the haying in this shire for ten years—how to get the damned botanical venture launched. And I honestly do not care what Bancroft Summerfield has to say to our nuptials. Your consequence now exceeds his, and that should be an end to his meddling."

"Your brothers will give you some peace, or I will have a word with them."

Hawthorne took her hand and kissed her knuckles. "*A word*, Margaret? Should I be concerned for my siblings?"

"You are newly wed, entitled to some privacy about your affairs, and much concerned with projects that benefit Dorning Hall generally. Your brothers will either respect that you are a busy man with much on your plate, or I will correct their misapprehensions."

His arm came around her shoulders. "They don't correct easily."

"I have amused you. Listen to me, Hawthorne: When I joined Charles's household, everybody—from his housekeeper, to his butler, to his physician, to the gardener—thwarted my attempts to keep Charles healthy. Bancroft scoffed openly at my expertise, even though the physicians Charles consulted supported my recommendations. Nobody thought he was well enough to travel, but he desperately wanted to see something of the world beyond Dorset before he died. Every time I ordered my husband a hot bath, I got mutterings from the footmen about cold baths being healthier, as if the footmen knew more than I did."

She rose, propelled by old anger. "Bancroft belittled me in front of the staff, referring dismissively to the *potions* I plied my husband with. The butler went so far as to remark in my hearing that Mr. Summerfield continued to decline, proof that I had nothing of value to contribute to my husband's care. I had Charles sack the rotter the next day, with little severance and a very sparing character. Your brothers will learn to respect my wishes where you are concerned, or I will make them rue their inconsideration."

Hawthorne got to his feet. "I did not mean to vex you, and I'm sorry Charles's situation was so challenging for you. Haying lasts only a month or so, but for that duration, I will ensure my brothers are too exhausted to cross swords with you."

A month... a month of Hawthorne being exhausted, spending his days in this or that distant field, lending his strength to neighbors and tenants alike, while Margaret hadn't even thought as far ahead as the wedding night. Damn meddling Bancroft and his schemes anyway.

"May I show you something?" Margaret asked.

Hawthorne cocked his head and smiled a very husbandly smile.

She smacked him on the chest. "Not that sort of something. Come along." She waggled her fingers at him, and he took her hand.

"I do so enjoy a woman who enjoys self-confidence. Rather like a lover who leaves her boots on for the duration of the picnic."

"I promised you a picnic this afternoon. I think I have something better to offer you."

Hawthorne held her fast when she would have started for the back garden. "At the risk of starting our first argument, allow me to say that you could not possibly have anything better to offer me than the picnic we enjoyed last week."

"Oh yes, I have. Much better."

Hawthorne came along as docilely as a pet lamb.

"DID you find us a stall from which to peddle our wares?" Oak asked, passing Valerian a glass of brandy.

Valerian took a sniff. "This is the good stuff."

"Hawthorne is a good brother, and this is his wedding day. Had I known how precipitously he intended to act on that special license, I'd have told you to bring it home in person."

Dorning Hall was still home. That realization had smacked Valerian in the face as he'd turned his horse up the drive. That Thorne had chosen to speak his vows in the conservatory—a tidy, inviting, bowery version of what was usually a hodgepodge of potted plants and dirty flagstones—spoke volumes about the Hall's place in his heart too.

"I nearly did deliver it in person," Valerian replied, "but Mr. Osgood Pepper deigned to see me the same afternoon I posted the license."

Oak was serving this celebratory tot in the family parlor, which felt too big with only the two of them to share it. "Osgood Pepper is related to the famous Miss Emily Pepper?"

Emily Pepper ought to be famous. She was among the most self-possessed young women Valerian had encountered. He was all but certain her dealings with Bancroft were more convoluted than she wanted anybody to know.

The poor woman had no sense of rhythm, though. None at all. "Osgood is her father, and she's his only offspring."

"Hence the heiress status. Why marry Bancroft when she could buy a title?"

"Why waste your money on a title when you can instead spend far less to become gentry? From that vantage point, buying titles becomes a less costly proposition for all of your future progeny. Besides, titles worth buying are in short supply."

"So Mr. Pepper is shrewd. What did he think of our venture?"

Oak was still in his wedding attire, and damned if he didn't clean up nicely. Of all the brothers, he was hanging on to the lanky, lean proportions of youth the longest. Perhaps he always would.

"Mr. Pepper was a conundrum. Miss Emily is the only reason I got onto his calendar at all. He's clearly very busy, and genial once he decides to converse, but somebody should take the time to teach him a few manners."

Oak propped his boots on a hassock, for which somebody ought to scold him. "We can't all be high sticklers, Vanity Dearest. Pepper has been busy making money. Would that we Dornings were as accomplished in that regard as we are at small talk."

The boyhood nickname made Valerian sad, as had seeing the way Hawthorne and Margaret regarded each other. If they weren't lovers, that oversight was being corrected while Valerian swilled brandy and wondered pointlessly about Emily Pepper.

"Mr. Pepper has barrels and cisterns full of money," Valerian said. "I don't think it's made him happy. He did not even stand when I entered his office, he was so preoccupied with some ledger or report."

Oak leaned his head back and closed his eyes. "Have our good manners and blue blood made us happy?"

"Hawthorne seems pleased to be marrying his lady." He'd also seemed nervous and impatient, a novel departure from Thorne's usually taciturn and stoic disposition.

"Can Osgood Pepper find us a fashionable address for our emporium?"

"He can. The question is, will he. He struck me as harried, for all that he listened cordially. He also made inquiries about Summerfield House that I was not well prepared to answer."

Oak opened his eyes and took a sip of his brandy. "What sort of inquiries?"

"How many acres? How many sources of fresh water flowing year-round? Tenancies? Any timber? The facts and figures Hawthorne knows without thinking about them."

"The ones we ignore because,"—Oak saluted with his glass—"we are not Hawthorne. I might be getting a bit tipsy."

"You're allowed. The ranks of the bachelor Dorning brothers are thinning, and Hawthorne's courtship was precipitous. What do you hear from the art collector in Hampshire?"

"I have promised Hawthorne I will not depart the Hall until after haying."

Valerian rose to refresh both drinks, then resumed his place on the sofa. "Every sane citizen of England hates making hay."

"Except Hawthorne. He glories in all that sweat, dust, and exertion. Then too, the ladies who catch sight of him without his shirt probably love a good hot haymaking."

Yes, Oak was getting tipsy. Not a bad idea. "Pepper said he'd think about our situation and get back to me after he'd paid this visit to Summerfield House."

Valerian had wanted to pass that bit along, about Mr. Pepper possibly having a property to rent in Town, but Hawthorne hadn't turned loose of the new Mrs. Dorning long enough to give a brother a chance for a private word.

Tomorrow was soon enough to be the bearer of mercantile tidings.

Oak slouched more deeply into his chair. "Let's hope Miss Emily can bring Bancroft up to scratch directly, then. Casriel is losing patience with us, Hawthorne's becoming distracted, and I'm increasingly willing to take the first post that provides me an income. If Papa's legacy is ever to do us any good, we need to move forward with it soon."

"I'm all for that." Though Valerian was not exactly in favor of Miss Pepper bringing Bancroft up to scratch. She'd be a lovely addition to the neighborhood, but the thought of all that vitality and humor consigned to a lifetime at Bancroft's side...?

"If we're getting drunk, we should switch to cheaper brandy," Valerian said.

"Drunk? The Dorning menfolk hold their liquor quite well. Tipsy is possible, but today of all days, I'm not switching to cheaper fare. Neither should you."

Oak had always been the still-waters-run-deep sort. When he bothered to speak with conviction, a prudent man listened. Valerian propped his boots on the hassock and settled in to become tipsy.

"We should drink a toast to the happy couple," Valerian said. "Several toasts."

"Splendid notion. Send for another bottle, why don't you?"

HAWTHORNE HADN'T HAD specific expectations of his wedding day beyond vows, formal attire, a good meal, and the ceremonial loss of his bachelorhood. He'd had *general* expectations, though.

A wedding night would have been nice.

A happy scene in Margaret's nursery where he promised to look after Adriana and Greta as if they were his own daughters had been on his list.

A pleasant walk in the woods with Margaret, the talk turning to matters both mundane and marital wouldn't have gone amiss.

And if all of that was too much to ask, the simple absence of discord would have been appreciated.

Instead, Margaret led him to a whitewashed cottage sitting just inside the tree line at the back of her garden. The roof was made of shingles gone gray with age. The windows were mullioned and framed by blue shutters. A few daffodils yet bloomed near the door, while tulips looked to be a week or so from displaying their colors.

He'd seen this place on his rambles in her woods and not given it a thought. "A gardener's cottage?" he asked as Margaret produced a key from beneath a blue ceramic pot of purple and white heartsease.

"Probably at some point. I took it over when I married Charles, though I haven't used it to speak of since he died. This is my herbal." She worked the key in the lock and pushed the door open.

Thorne's first impression was of a place taken out of time, such as happened in fairy stories. The entire cottage was a single room, perhaps twenty feet by twenty feet, with ample windows on all but the north side and large fireplaces on both the north and south walls. Dried herbs hung from dark exposed beams, and sunlight formed a lattice pattern on the slate floor.

The corners held no dust or cobwebs, and the hearths were spotless. Somebody had folded blankets just so at the foot of the plain oak bed occupying one corner. The table and chairs in another corner were arranged symmetrically. The books shelved in a third corner were neatly arranged in order of height.

The fourth corner was a kitchen of sorts.

"Those are stew stoves," Hawthorne said, peering into the open grates over what had been designed to hold charcoal fires. A counter of stout oak, much scarred, sat beneath a window, and a cistern full of water, apparently piped from the roof, took up the space at the end of the counter.

All of that was interesting, mostly because it belonged to Margaret, but the scent of the place was more interesting still.

The herbs were dried to greenish-gray or brown, and their scents had faded as well. A hint of rosemary, lavender, rose... Thorne could not parse them all, but they added to the sense of a space that hadn't been abandoned so much as it had been waiting under some enchantment for Margaret's return.

"You had this cottage fitted out to your specifications," he said, "then you ceased to come here. Why?" And why bring her new husband here?

"The girls needed me. They were grieving for Charles, as was I. Don't touch that."

He'd been reaching for a bundle of leaves dangling from the rafter. Three more bundles just like it hung before the nearest window.

"What is it?"

"Foxglove. Every part of the plant is poisonous."

"*Foxglove*? The pretty summer flower? But I've picked it without coming to harm since childhood."

"Probably because your mother made you wash your hands when you came in from playing. Touching the plant is unlikely to result in anything more dangerous than a queasy stomach, and that would take sucking your thumb, or trying to suck the nectar from the flowers. It's still dangerous. If a dog were to drink the water you'd put the flowers in, death might result."

And to think he'd brought bouquets of wild foxglove home to his mother and sisters. Thorne ambled away from the window to peer at the bound volumes and treatises on the bookshelf.

"Is that why your herbal is here, rather than in the house? Because you worked with dangerous plants?"

"Summerton has no herbal, and I could not use the kitchen to make the medicine Charles relied upon most often." She joined Thorne before the books and took down a journal bound in green leather. "This is what I wanted to show you. Come sit with me."

She had the most agreeable habit of taking him by the hand. She towed him to the bed, where they could sit side by side.

"This is one volume. I have others like it. By necessity, I spent significant time making the medicines Charles needed, and the perfumes became more of a pleasure and less of a science. I tried all manner of combinations. Lemons and roses, citrus and cedar. Some worked, some... There's a reason this cottage has so many windows."

She paged through the journal as if it were a girlhood diary recounting halcyon summers long past.

"You worked very hard at this," Thorne said, though reading over her shoulder, he could hardly understand what she'd written. *A cold decoction from a cold extract using butter rather than lard to pull the scent.* What did that mean?

"I loved time spent in here mixing up Charles's medication. Gathering up flowers for my scents gave me an excuse to wander alone. Summerton was not always a joyous house. Charles tired easily, and try as he might, he did resent his indisposition."

Thorne closed the journal and set it aside. "Did he resent you?"

"Of course, and I resented him. We learned to take short holidays from each other, and that eased tensions somewhat. Charles bided at Summerfield House on occasion, while I remained here. After the first year, we rented Summerfield House out and dwelled at Summerton. The pretext for our periodic separations was that he was overseeing preparations for the next tenants' arrival, but Bancroft could have done that. He had his own apartment at Summerfield House even then."

Thorne had the sense this recitation was important and that Margaret was most comfortable offering it here in the one place that had been hers alone during her first marriage. Even so, they were sitting *on a bed*, and it was their *wedding day*.

Maybe that was important too? "Were you having one of your periodic holidays when Charles died?"

She nodded. "I've wondered if Charles did that on purpose— went away to die—but his health had been precarious for ages. He was ready to go, or so he claimed, but I would rather have been with him."

What a grim way to be married. "I hope perfumes are a more cheerful undertaking for you than medicinals were." And no wonder she eschewed medical practice now, given Charles's situation.

"Perfumes are a delight by comparison." She leaned into him as if imparting a confidence. "I want you to have this journal. I have a dozen others, some containing recipes your father collected, some based on what I wrote down from Hannah's memory. Look over this group first and see if anything strikes you as appealing to a gentleman's nose."

A body part other than Thorne's nose was well aware of Margaret's proximity. "I won't know what I'm looking at. You mention blending rose and lemon, but I lack the imagination to conceive of what the result would be."

She took the journal from him, set it on the table, and returned to the bed. "Imagine garnishing lemonade with a blooming damask, as some people garnish their lemonade with mint or lavender."

Margaret could apparently do that—imagine scents. Thorne's mind boggled at the prospect.

"Can we agree to avoid foxgloves in our recipes?" he asked, wrapping an arm around Margaret's waist. "You keep this cottage locked, but small children climb in windows, find keys, and otherwise defeat common sense."

"Shall we also avoid lily of the valley? Daffodils? Rhododendrons? Azaleas? Hydrangeas? Oleander?"

"I don't even know what some of those are." While Margaret probably knew their every property and variety.

"Most toxic plants are more of a risk to pets than people, though there are a few specimens whose sap alone can cause blindness. Your father always kept extensive notes on the exotics he collected, so you need not worry that my safety is at risk here."

So confident, and yet, Thorne was worried. "Why all the foxglove?"

She burrowed against him as if seeking warmth. "Because in small quantities, a decoction from the dried leaves can slow the heart. Used carefully, it's very effective for combating dropsy and similar conditions. To be sure I was mixing up a consistent dose, I harvested what I needed all at once in the spring, dried the leaves, and made the medication as Charles needed it. This is not what I want to discuss on my wedding day, Hawthorne."

He wrapped his arms around her. "What would you rather talk about?"

"Whether you'd like your new wife to keep her boots on when she makes love with you this time."

# CHAPTER NINETEEN

---

"What have you learned in my absence, Hartley?" Bancroft kept his tone pleasant, though two days of meandering along the roads with Emily and her father had driven him nearly daft. He'd left his intended—for Bancroft most assuredly did intend to get his hands on Miss Pepper's settlements—forty-five miles up the road. Emily had promised to *make good time* for the rest of the journey, which Bancroft took to mean a leisurely trot that began after noon.

"Learned, sir?" Hartley took a seat without being invited to do so. His boots were less than spotless and his cravat askew, though the day wasn't nearly over. This slovenliness would never do if the man was to be introduced to Mr. Pepper.

"Regarding dear Margaret's inability to properly manage Summerton. About the lack of discipline with which my nieces are being raised, about the resources going to waste on the only property the little dears are likely to inherit."

Hartley found it necessary to consult his watch. "Hepatica Freeman, for some reason I cannot fathom, informed me that her son threw rocks at the windows of Hannah Weller's cottage. Mrs. Weller is seeking restitution for the cost of repairs."

Bancroft's eldest was apparently overdue for a birching, though really, what normal boy hadn't felt compelled to test his aim against an inviting square of glass?

"What has that to do with me?"

"You asked what I have learned, and Miss Freeman did request that I pass this news along to you in my next report. She isn't one of your tenants, but she said you'd want to know of the incident."

"It's not my fault if a woman of loose morals and an old witch can't come to terms over a boyish prank. I have other concerns pending, and important concerns they are. Miss Freeman ought to keep a closer eye on her offspring, and you will please tell her as much."

Hartley put his watch away. "One of the rocks struck Mrs. Weller on the shoulder. She's eighty-three years old. Had she fallen, broken a bone, and gone into a decline, the boy might have been liable for charges of assault or worse."

Bancroft rose from behind his desk. "Hartley, a man of my station tries to remain above the petty dramas of the village square. I'd advise you to do likewise. I am to host distinguished guests, and all must be in readiness for their arrival."

Hartley got to his feet as well. "I'll send the housekeeper to you, then, sir, or the butler. Perhaps both? Haying is due to start next week, and I'm sure you'll want me to bend my energies to the success of that venture."

"I don't give a bloody bent copper about damned haying, Hartley. Mr. Osgood Pepper and Miss Emily Pepper should be here by the day after tomorrow, Monday at the latest if they eschew travel on the Sabbath. When I've needed you to keep a close eye on the doings at Summerton and prepare the way for my management of that property, you've been involving yourself in spats over broken windows. I am not at all pleased with your performance."

Bancroft never raised his voice with his subordinates, but he never threatened idly either.

Hartley apparently did not grasp that last point, for he strode across the office, stopping only when he had one hand on the door.

"Half your farm wagons need new axles," he said. "Your scythes haven't been sharpened in two years, because when I gave the orders last summer to see that done, your tenants failed to heed me. One of your teams is threatening to founder because the spring grass came in too quickly and your most experienced grooms have all retired or quit. Three of your tenants are feuding with the other five, so you can expect haying to be a slow, contentious undertaking. One good thunderstorm, and you could lose an entire field's worth of fodder. Two thunderstorms, and you'll be buying hay for half the winter. If you'll excuse me, I must pick up the scythes from the smith, who agreed to sharpen the lot for half what he should have charged."

That was the longest speech Hartley had ever made, also the most disrespectful. Bancroft had spent down his ready cash at a perilous clip in London—needs must when a gentleman goes up to Town—and he wasn't in the mood to humor a fractious employee.

"Hartley, your problem is you haven't learned to delegate. Haying never goes well. Thunderstorms always ruin at least part of the yield. Tenants always feud, but I rarely entertain such illustrious guests. I am hopeful that Miss Pepper will look with favor upon my suit. If you expect to keep your post in that event, you'd be well advised to moderate your tone."

Hartley was the best paid of any employee at Summerfield, and housing for him as well as stabling for a horse were part of that compensation. No bachelor without means could afford to turn his back on lucrative employment, and yet, no man with any pride liked to be verbally thrashed.

Watching Hartley struggle with that dilemma was the best entertainment Bancroft had had in weeks.

"Have you anything more to say, Hartley? For you are correct: I need to meet with both the butler and the housekeeper, and you will please send them to me." An errand fit for a junior footman.

"Yes, sir, I have one more thing to say. The scythes at Summerton are all sharp. The farm wagons and teams are all sound. The tenants all get along, and as far as I know, Mrs. Summerfield is not so daft as to invite fancy guests down from Town at the busiest time of year for her staff and dependents. You may rely on that information, because I all but beggared my honor to verify it."

"Do you imply that Margaret is a better steward than you are, Hartley?"

"Her tenants and staff respect her, and she benefits from proximity to Dorning Hall. The earl's family is known to aid any neighbor in need, and if her tenants failed to tend to their responsibilities, one or the other Dorning brother would call on them and set the matter to rights. And Mrs. Summerfield *is* a very competent manager who also takes excellent care of the children. Good day."

Hartley closed the door softly, leaving Bancroft to ponder whether he should dismiss the man with a character or without one after the Peppers' visit was successfully concluded. A character that damned with faint praise could be more damaging than no character at all.

"No need to make that decision today." Bancroft resumed his seat at the desk, assembled pen, paper, ink, and sand, and dashed off a note to Margaret. If the Peppers' arrival was still two days off, tomorrow would be time enough to collect the children and install them at Summerfield.

MAKING love with Hawthorne was magical. He brought a sense of deliberateness, of focus and savoring, to all that he did. For Margaret, his unhurried touch was balm to a soul that had been too often involved in hurried couplings or attempted lovemaking that ended in disappointment for all concerned.

The bed was cramped for a man of Hawthorne's proportions, particularly when the agenda was something other than a quick nap.

"Can you sit up?" Margaret asked, scooting back over his thighs. She was still in her shift, while he—magnificent beast—wore not a single stitch. He'd troubled to close the drapes on every window before he'd disrobed, turning the cottage into a shadowy retreat full of peaceful memories and happy intentions.

He hoisted himself back on his elbows and propped himself against the pillows at the headboard. "Like this?"

"Exactly like that." Margaret recommenced kissing him, mentally assuring herself that in the next month, they'd make love in every possible position, at every conceivable time of day or night. What Hawthorne's hands on her breasts did to her was the stuff of large families and cheerful unions.

"You drive me... I want to make you as frantic as you make me," she said, pressing her forehead to his shoulder. "More frantic even than that."

He brushed his thumbs over her nipples, slowly, back and forth. "You do, Margaret. You most assuredly do."

He was aroused, wonderfully so, but he didn't *sound* aroused. He wasn't panting, gasping, and heaving with need. Between one caress and the next, Margaret grasped why that should be: Hawthorne's heart was sound. He was not a man slowly losing a fight with death. He was hale and whole, *and hers.*

Thank every benevolent power, Hawthorne Dorning was *hers*. She sank down over him in one glorious undulation of her hips, physical pleasure blending with profound joy.

"I'm delighted that we're married," she said, going still. "I will be the very best wife to you that I can be."

They were eye-to-eye in this position, and what lovely eyes Hawthorne had. They would always remind her of the bluebell wood, where this marriage had truly begun.

"I will be the very best husband to you, and the best father figure to the girls, that I can be. We will be like the seeds you've learned to collect so carefully. The ceremony that joined us was small and humble. With time and care, the marriage can be magnificent."

He kissed her sweetly, and Margaret understood why tears of joy might befall a woman. The relief of intimate commitment to a man of such dear and honorable intentions was enormous, like a reprieve from a life-threatening diagnosis.

Hawthorne gave her no time to ponder particulars, but began moving with the sort of quiet intensity she could not outlast. He brought her pleasure upon pleasure, until she lay spent, naked, and drowsy in his arms.

"Is that what you meant by three times a day?" she murmured, kissing his chin.

"Of course not. I only spent the once, so this only counts as once. Male math."

"What is male math?"

"Female math says 'help yourself' means take no more than three biscuits, even if the rest will get stale and be wasted on the hogs. Male math says so long as I leave at least three uneaten, I've stayed within the parameters of 'helping myself.' Female math is exact but has little logic, and its adherents advocate for it passionately."

"In this instance," Margaret said, "male math will suffice. I'd like to open a window."

Hawthorne kissed her temple. "Because I've loved you into a swither?"

"Because I want fresh air in here." *And in my life. Wonderful Hawthorne-scented fresh air.* "This herbal has been shut up and unused for too long. I need to burn that damned foxglove or send it to Hannah. The footmen didn't do a thorough enough job of cleaning the stoves, and—" She fell silent as she climbed off her husband and gained her footing beside the bed. "I need to store a few snacks here. Making love with you leaves me famished."

Hawthorne half sat, half lay against the pillows, resplendent in his nudity. "We'll be making love here often?"

"Three times a day, according to my husband, whom I esteem most earnestly. Where is my shift?" Hawthorne had drawn it off of her at some point when Margaret had been ready to pitch the last nod to her modesty into the nearest ocean.

"On the table. I aimed for the chair, but somebody distracted me.

Spoiled my accuracy." He smiled at her, the most naughty, pleased, masculine smile she'd ever seen a man aim at a woman.

Dorset had a long tradition of wise women, though in unenlightened times, some had called them witches. They danced naked under the moonlight and worshiped the deities of the fields and forests. When Hawthorne smiled at Margaret like that, she felt a kinship with her pagan sisters.

A happy kinship. "Will you lie in the altogether before me all day, Hawthorne? I'd like to get something to eat, then visit the girls in the nursery."

He rose from the bed and took up Margaret's shift, tugging it down over her head. "You didn't eat much at the wedding breakfast, Mrs. Dorning. How will you have strength enough for your marital exertions if you neglect your tucker?" He pulled her braid free from her shift, buttoned the top two buttons—Margaret had no memory of them being unbuttoned—and kissed her nose.

"You are so casual about these joys," she said, tossing him his shirt for the sake of her own dignity. "I am unused to a man of such an affectionate nature." Such a vigorous, healthy, straightforward, affectionate nature.

"I am affectionate with those I care for," Hawthorne said. "I desire you, I esteem you, and I also like you exceedingly, Mrs. Dorning. One hopes you will soon hold me in similarly warm regard."

How brave he was to put those sentiments into words, and how careful.

"I already hold you in warm regard. I'm just not used to it yet. Such happiness is an adjustment."

Hawthorne assembled his clothing into a pile—breeches, stockings, waistcoat, cravat. "Give it a week. By the end of the first day of cutting hay, you won't be able to stand the smell of me, and I will have to stand upwind of myself lest I faint from my own stench. Thank God the mill pond is always good for a peaceful swim at the end of a hot day."

He was worried about haying, and Margaret delighted in being able to deduce that from his grousing. She delighted in the way they helped each other to dress and in the obvious glee with which both girls greeted Hawthorne when Margaret took him up to the nursery.

Adriana told him her story about the woman who'd tumbled into the mine shaft. Greta simply held his hand and studied the pocket watch he'd passed over for her examination.

While Margaret fell in love with her husband. Thank the good angels that Bancroft had yet to return, because this marriage to Hawthorne was, indeed, a gift to be savored.

MARRIED LIFE HADN'T STARTED off quite as Hawthorne had envisioned. His first assumption had been that the steward's cottage would turn into a family home. He'd anticipated the laughter of children greeting him when he returned from the fields at the end of the day and Margaret's affection making those days more pleasant than bachelorhood could ever be.

The *more pleasant* aspect was off to a spectacular start, if yesterday's interlude in the herbal was any indication. Today, Hawthorne was taking Margaret with him on calls to the Dorning Hall tenants, a day-after-the-wedding-day courtesy necessitated by the haying that would commence on Monday.

The visit to the nursery also hadn't gone quite as planned. Thorne had been waiting for Margaret to say something to the girls about the wedding. Something simple and honest.

*Mr. Dorning and I have married, and I hope you can be happy for us.* Too grown up.

*Mr. Dorning has fallen madly in love with me, and I'm Mrs. Dorning now.* Too daft.

*Mr. Dorning would like to be a papa to you, though he knows he can never be your true papa.* Too honest. Also complicated.

Perhaps Margaret was waiting for inspiration, but children could not acquire a step-uncle, change abodes, and hear their aunt's form of address altered all without an explanation. Then too, Margaret might be waiting for an infusion of courage, because clearly, certain topics related to the nursery would require that she and Thorne come to an understanding, the sooner the better.

But those discussions could wait at least until haying was done.

Thorne brought the gig to a halt at the foot of the Summerton front steps and wrapped the reins. A groom took the horse by the bridle.

"I won't be long. Offer him water and let him blow."

"Right, Mr. Dorning." The groom's smile was particularly cheerful.

Did the fellow suspect that Hawthorne had married Margaret yesterday? The servants at Dorning Hall had known that a ceremony had taken place in the conservatory. Before Margaret had quit the premises, the senior staff had lined up in the foyer to wish her and Thorne well, while Valerian and Oak had smiled like the pair of fools they were.

Envious fools, most likely.

"We want to come with you!"

That childish demand reached Thorne's ears even before he knocked on the door. Adriana was apparently in a taking.

Thorne rapped softly, then let himself in. "Good day." Margaret, Miss Fenner, and both girls were in the foyer, Margaret with a bonnet in her hand.

"You're going with him again." Greta did not sound pleased. "You were with him yesterday. In the herbal."

Margaret aimed a look at Miss Fenner. "Somebody was spying out of windows."

"Daydreaming," Miss Fenner said, grabbing one of Adriana's hands. "Let's wish your aunt a nice outing, shall we, girls? We have multiplication to do."

"I don't like multiplication," Adriana said. "It's hard and stupid. I want to ride in the carriage with Aunt and Mr. Dorning."

"I like multiplication," Greta muttered. "I don't like you, Dree."

"Let's not be rude," Margaret said.

Thorne eased her bonnet from her grasp and set it on her head. "I would love to take all of you fine ladies for a carriage ride, perhaps even for a picnic. Today, though, I brought only the gig. It's too small for the whole family, and the seat is hard. When I take you out driving with me, I'll bring the vis-à-vis, and we can have a nice visit while we take the air."

Adriana shook her hand free from Miss Fenner's. "What's a veez-ah-vee?"

"Use your French," Miss Fenner said as Hawthorne took Margaret by the hand and tugged her toward the door. "It means facing or at opposites. Now can you puzzle out what it might be?"

Greta fingered Hawthorne's watch chain. "Why didn't you bring the big carriage today? Then we could all go now."

For the children to interrogate adults was surely unacceptable, and yet, Hawthorne had seen one of Greta's tantrums. Perhaps he was about to witness another.

"I did not bring the big carriage because next week will be furiously busy. The entire neighborhood will be involved in this year's haying, and as many horses as possible need their rest today. They will work to the limits of their strength soon, so I took the smallest, lightest carriage and hitched only one horse to it. Mrs. Dorning, shall we be on our way?"

Greta stepped back as if shocked by an electric spark. "Why did he call Aunt that?"

"A mistake," Margaret said. "He meant Mrs. Summerfield."

*No, I did not.*

"What's this?" Adriana asked, picking up a folded and sealed piece of paper on the sideboard. "It's for Aunt."

Miss Fenner took the note from her and passed it to Margaret. "That came yesterday. I meant to mention it at supper, but I forgot."

"You can read it in the gig," Hawthorne said, reaching to tie Margaret's bonnet ribbons.

She batted his hands aside. "This is from Bancroft. I recognize his penmanship."

Miss Fenner, Greta, and Adriana all looked worried, while Hawthorne felt his temper rising. Why the hell should a note from blasted Bancroft ruin the new Mr. and Mrs. Dorning's first outing as a couple? Why couldn't the newlyweds even get out the damned door without strife and accusations barring the way? Why couldn't Margaret simply tell the children she was the new Mrs. Dorning?

She tore open the note, which looked to Hawthorne to be a mere few lines.

"Fenny, please take the children back up to the nursery."

"Right," Hawthorne said. "We'll return this afternoon, and I'm sure many multiplication problems will have been accurately solved by that time."

Margaret passed him the note. "*Now*, Fenny, if you please."

Greta looked as if she were holding her breath. Adriana began to hop on one foot. "I don't *want* to go back to the nursery. We are *always* in the nursery, while Aunt gets to go for a *carriage* ride. She *never* has to do multiplication, and multiplication is stu—"

"Enough," Hawthorne said. "You heard your aunt. Begone and behave." He'd sounded exactly like his father, whose patience was rising in Hawthorne's esteem by the moment.

Adriana stopped hopping. Greta took her by the hand, sent Hawthorne a dirty look, and towed her sister toward the stairs, while the governess brought up the rear.

The peace and quiet was lovely.

"Read it," Margaret said as the children's footsteps faded. She ripped her bonnet from her head and caught a lock of hair in her hatpin. "He's coming to take the children. I'm barely married a day, and already, he's coming to take my children."

The note was terse:

*Dearest sister-in-law,*
*In anticipation of changes in my own situation, I've decided the time*

*has come for my nieces to at last remove to the family seat. I'll be by*
*tomorrow morning to collect them, so please have their effects packed*
*when I arrive. You will of course be free to visit them, though I'd*
*suggest you wait a decent interval to allow them to settle in before you*
*call upon my nursery.*
*I remain most sincerely your brother-in-law,*
*Bancroft*

"You were right," Hawthorne said slowly. "I thought perhaps you were overreacting or borrowing trouble where Bancroft is concerned, but you were right."

Margaret whipped off her cloak. "Of course I was right. I've dealt with him for years, and he's not the pompous fool everybody takes him for. He's lazy, mean, greedy, and determined. You will write to him this instant and explain that his foolishness is at an end. You and I are man and wife, this is the only home those girls have known, and I won't allow that vile—"

A clatter of wheels on the driveaway interrupted what might have been a blossoming tantrum.

Hawthorne peered through the window beside the front door. "He's here, and he's brought his traveling coach."

"So he can steal them and their worldly goods. Call him out, Hawthorne. Beat him to flinders, or threaten him with a press gang. Just make him go away."

Margaret had married Hawthorne precisely so he could defend the Summerton nursery from Bancroft's machinations, and yet, the tactics she proposed were outlandish.

"We are married, true enough, and this might well be the only home the children have known, but that Bancroft is taking an interest in them is not entirely bad. He doesn't know you have a husband now, doesn't know you've allied yourself with a titled family. I suggest we invite him in for tea and alert him to your good fortune."

"You still don't believe me," she said, snatching up the note and waving it. "You have proof of his perfidy in his own hand, and you don't believe me."

Hawthorne had heard too many of his parents' quarrels not to recognize an impasse when confronted with one. Nothing he could say or do, short of smuggling Bancroft in chains onto a vessel bound for New South Wales, would appease Margaret.

Nothing she could say or do would persuade him to take such drastic measures. The problem came down to one meddling relation who simply needed to be reminded of his place. A short conversation over tea ought to see the situation put to rest, and then Thorne and his new wife could get on with their tenant calls.

# CHAPTER TWENTY

Hawthorne meant well, but Margaret knew in her soul that he did not grasp the seriousness of the threat Bancroft posed to the girls—or to her. That Bancroft would stage this ambush should not have surprised her, but it did. Oh, it did.

"I was too busy being married," Margaret said as she stalked into the family parlor. "Too busy pretending we had time to sort out strategies and maneuver artillery into place."

Hawthorne closed the door behind them. "Your hair," he said, waving a hand near his ear. "When you took your bonnet off, the pins..." He approached as if he'd tidy her up, the same way Fenny tidied up Adriana's braids after too much hopping on one foot.

Margaret turned from him and used the glass of the window to examine her reflection. She affixed the errant curl to her chignon, jamming pins against her scalp.

"I cannot allow Bancroft to have the children, Hawthorne. He's doubtless planning to court some lack-witted heiress and put on a show of avuncular affection for her sake. Once he's netted his trout, he'll pack the girls off to some awful school, and I will never see them again."

"We shall not allow that."

The very calm that Hawthorne exuded only upset Margaret more. "Greta won't deal with even the upheaval of moving to Summerfield, and when she can't manage a girls' school, he'll send her someplace far worse. Someplace cheap and awful. I won't even know where she is."

"Margaret, you've spiked his guns. He hasn't the legal authority to keep the girls from you. You are their guardian."

"Co-guardian," she said. "Damn Charles for leaving me only that."

"You don't mean that."

Footsteps in the hall signaled the enemy's approach.

"Yes, Hawthorne, at this moment, I mean that. Don't let Bancroft take my girls." She wanted him to promise her that he'd prevent that outcome, to swear an oath, to offer assurances backed up with promises of violence.

"We'd best order a tea tray," he said as a knock sounded on the door. "We have good news to share with Bancroft, and in light of our nuptials, he'll want to re-evaluate his plans for the girls."

"You underestimate him."

"Enter," Hawthorne called, as if Summerton were his house, though his presumption was well timed, for civil discourse was beyond Margaret.

Bancroft strode in, and the footman closed the door behind him. "Margaret, good day. Mr. Dorning, greetings. I'll have to ask you to excuse me and Mrs. Summerfield. We have family business to discuss. I'd be happy to chat away the morning at another time, but as it happens, my errand is somewhat urgent."

He smiled that simpering, self-satisfied smirk that made Margaret want to smash a heavy pot over his head.

"As it happens," Hawthorne said. "I am now family, and Margaret's business is my business. She did me the great honor of marrying me yesterday. I'm sure you'll want to wish us both well." Hawthorne apparently knew that in Margaret's present mood, husbandly displays of affection were not well advised, though he did send a smile in her direction.

"Mr. Dorning speaks the truth, Bancroft. He and I are man and wife. We were married before witnesses at Dorning Hall yesterday."

"A special license, then," Bancroft said, seating himself uninvited. "My, my. I do hope the course of true love was not precipitous of necessity."

"The only person being precipitous—" Margaret began, but Hawthorne gestured her to a seat.

"Let's ring for tea," he said, his tone excruciatingly reasonable. "I'm sure Bancroft was making a jest. Our happy news has surprised him."

Bancroft didn't look surprised. He looked impatient.

"Tug the bell-pull," Margaret said, "though I'm sure Bancroft won't be staying long. He never does." She ought not to antagonize him, but she wanted to do much more than merely insult him. She wanted him jailed for being a horrible human being, a miserable brother, and a terrible uncle.

"I am a busy man," Bancroft replied. "I need tarry only long enough to collect my nieces, and I'll leave you two to your wedded bliss."

"How are your preparations for haying coming along?" Hawthorne asked, in all apparent seriousness.

"Splendidly. Hartley has all in hand, as usual. Are the girls packed? Looking forward to new surrounds in a more commodious household?"

The problem with Bancroft was not simply that he was evil, but that he excelled at looking and acting genial and reasonable while being evil. For that alone, Margaret wished him to perdition.

"Surely," Hawthorne said, "you don't mean to uproot the children now. This week has seen a significant change in their lives, and while I am overjoyed to consider myself family to them, I know their welfare must take precedence over my own selfish concerns."

Bancroft blinked, then his smile was back in place. "It's you who bring the upheaval, then, Dorning. I am their doting uncle, offering them a haven at the family seat where they've visited many times. You are all but a stranger, and you'd take them off to some dingy cottage let at your brother's sufferance. Perhaps you expect them to rattle around at Dorning Hall, half of which is scheduled for demolition, if the talk is to be believed. Even Margaret would agree that the situation I offer the girls is superior to your circumstances."

"What matters the number of unused bedrooms in a home," Margaret began, "when the only person to love these children—"

The footman interrupted with the tea tray. Margaret didn't bother offering to pour out, lest she smash the teapot in the process.

"That's part of the problem," Hawthorne said. "You expect the girls to leave the only home they've known, no explanation to them, no assurances that their aunt, the one constant in their lives, will remain in the role of guardian, as she's legally responsible to do."

"Co-guardian," Bancroft countered. "An unusual arrangement easily attacked in court given my brother's precarious health at the time he revised his will. Summerfield is the family seat, and the children belong with me. They are ready for the schoolroom, for the care a devoted uncle can give them, and I'm not prepared to belabor that point with a fellow whose abode is nothing more than a large tenant cottage."

*Limb of the Imp. Hell-spawned blight upon decent society. Vile, posturing, manipulative, affront to masculine honor.* In her head, Margaret began concocting a strong purgative, one sufficient to ease the bowels of the most costive patient.

"Forgive us," Hawthorne said, pouring out a cup of tea, "for not acquainting you with the details of our situation sooner. Margaret and I will be making our home right here, and we chose this dwelling specifically to spare the children from a change of abode."

He added milk and sugar to the tea and passed the cup and saucer to Margaret. She did not dare take a sip while Bancroft's cheap bay rum scent was befouling the whole parlor.

"You're moving here?" Bancroft asked.

Despite her ire, despite her terror, Margaret knew a moment of pure respect for her husband. Hawthorne presented his intention to dwell at Summerton as a fait accompli, the choice any gentleman would make when it was in fact an enormous gesture of goodwill.

"Of course I'll bide here," he went on, "though rather than spring that addition to the household on the children all at once, I'd thought I'd ease gradually into their lives. We've made good progress getting to know each other in a short time, and for you to yank them away, remove them from the staff who cares for them and from the very beds they've slept in for years, makes no sense. They are thriving in Margaret's care, while you have no experience raising children, as best I recall. Would you care for some tea, Summerfield?"

For an instant, Margaret thought Hawthorne's concession might have won the battle. He would not claim he was moving to Summerton and then reverse course later, not with Bancroft circling the children's settlements like a stray dog lurking near a knacker's yard.

"You have not, though, made Summerton your residence yet," Bancroft observed. "I prefer my tea plain, by the way."

Hawthorne passed over a steaming cup. "I plan to wait until after haying to join the Summerton household. Have you a nursery staff in place?"

"Any maid can make a bed." Bancroft took a sip of his tea, made a face worthy of Adriana, and set down the cup and saucer. "We have inside maids by the dozen at Summerfield. Any one of them can keep two little girls stitching samplers or whatever it is little girls do."

"They are too young to stitch samplers," Margaret said.

"What of a governess?" Thorne asked pleasantly. "Both children are avid readers. They are proficient at sums, picking up a little French, and making a rudimentary attempt at drawing. I'm fairly certain Margaret has started them on the pianoforte and natural science and perhaps a few Latin phrases too."

Hawthorne made it sound as if Fenny taught a well-planned

curriculum, rather than scrambling to keep one step ahead of the girls.

"What do a pair of girls need with all that?" Bancroft retorted. "I admit the French, pianoforte, and drawing have a place, and every lady needs to know how to tote up her pin money, but the rest of it seems excessive."

"They are heiresses," Hawthorne said. "They need to be able to do more than tote up their pin money, and they are also quite bright. Education should not be denied them and certainly not merely on the basis of their gender."

Bancroft wrinkled his nose. "You've brought up many girls, that you'd know all about that, Dorning?"

"I saw my sisters educated. I watched the earl's daughter brought up at Dorning Hall until her recent move to a finishing school as she approached her presentation at court. I've seen my nieces raised, and—"

"But like Margaret, you are not a parent, while I can claim that honor twice over. I do believe my status as a father rather over-shadows all your good intentions and rhetoric. I am grateful to Margaret for doing what she could, but the girls no longer need female coddling. They can take their places under my roof, and my wife—should the lady see fit to accept my suit—can see to their further education."

Bancroft shot a bland smile at Margaret and reached for a tea cake. His words held a veiled threat, for his parenting experience probably hadn't extended five minutes beyond the act necessary for conception.

"You see the wisdom of my reasoning," Bancroft murmured, dusting the carpet with crumbs. "I thought you might. Newlyweds should have a bit of privacy, eh, Dorning?"

He was so pleased with himself, pleased to wreak havoc on the lives of innocent children. Perhaps even Hawthorne sensed some-thing of Bancroft's true nature, for he remained silent, while Margaret bit back curses.

"I'm glad that's settled," Bancroft said, taking another tea cake and rising. "I can take the girls now, and you can send along their things later."

He was smiling at Margaret again, his lips curved, while his eyes regarded her with a reptilian focus. The sheer menace in his gaze stopped the protests boiling up inside her.

"That won't suit," Hawthorne said, getting to his feet. "If you've no nursery maid and no governess, you aren't prepared to host the children for even a short visit. They thrive on a familiar routine, and you haven't given the first thought to how they're to remain occupied. Idle children get into mischief, as you must know based on your vast experience as a father. You wouldn't want the girls to make a bad impression on your fiancée, would you?"

Something unspoken passed between the two men, while Margaret remained seated and entertained a whole new list of fears.

"You have a point," Bancroft said. "Margaret, perhaps you'd be good enough to lend me your nursery staff. In the short term, that would allow the children to enjoy the benefits of moving to Summerfield while maintaining familiar associations. I'm surprised I didn't think of this arrangement sooner."

Everything in Margaret longed to fly at Bancroft and do him an injury, and yet, that look—that one venomous, malevolent glance— stopped her. Three years ago, he'd accused her of neglecting Charles, of treating him with quack remedies, of longing for his death.

That look promised renewed accusations, and then how would the children fare? Would she even be allowed to see the girls?

Hawthorne was watching her. Rather than exert the authority that was now his by law, he was apparently waiting for Margaret to decide whether the nursery staff would accompany the girls.

"The staff will need time to pack," Margaret said. "The children must choose which belongings to take with them on this visit, and I warn you, Bancroft, if you or your servants raise a hand to either girl, I will not answer for the consequences. Charles did not believe in striking females, and you violate his wishes at your peril."

"Spare the rod," Bancroft began, "and—"

"Mrs. Dorning has reared these children from infancy," Hawthorne said. "She hasn't merely dropped around once a month to pass out licorice candy while pretending such behavior qualifies her to call herself a parent. Hannah Weller is considering bringing charges against your son, Summerfield. If criminal behavior is the fruit of your paternal guidance, then the girls are far better off here. You either agree that the girls will not suffer corporal punishment at Summerfield, or you'll need the magistrate's authority to pry them loose from our care."

Hawthorne was angry. At long last, he was in a temper when a temper was needed. Bless him for that.

"Then I will make that assurance," Bancroft said, "but don't complain to me when they end up as prone to wandering as Margaret was in her youth. Charles was not well, and Margaret exerted undue influence over him as his health declined. She should never have been given any authority over these girls, and if I must, I will go to court to rectify my brother's error. I bid you both good day, and I'll expect to see the girls at Summerfield tomorrow."

Hawthorne sent Margaret a look she could read all too well: Let me pound him to flinders. Not a hand would be raised without her permission. As much as she longed to see Bancroft put in his place, she could not risk him involving the magistrate over a round of fisticuffs.

And neither could Bancroft bring the courts into the matter in the near term, not while he was trying to impress his guests. In that regard, he had yet to maneuver his own artillery into place.

Margaret rose to stand beside her husband. "The girls will join you at Summerfield for a visit, Bancroft."

Hawthorne took her hand, as if he knew she might let fly with her own fists. "A visit only."

Bancroft merely grinned, bowed, and snatched another tea cake. "Right, a visit. Until tomorrow. No need to see me out."

He jaunted for the door, while Hawthorne's grip on Margaret's hand became quite firm.

"We will call on the girls frequently," Hawthorne said to Bancroft's retreating back. "And when Casriel returns from London, I'd like to bring him to meet your prospective bride as well. He's the ranking gentleman in the neighborhood, and acknowledging your London guests would only be polite of him and his countess."

"Do the pretty all you like, Dorning, but bring those children to me tomorrow."

Margaret was in tears before the front door had even closed, and thus Bancroft had the last word.

HAWTHORNE HAD BEEN AMBUSHED ONCE BEFORE, in a dark, fetid alley behind a tavern in Oxford. One moment, he'd been pleasantly tipsy and contemplating a soft bed, the next, he'd been facedown on the cobbles, while a pair of bullyboys had whaled on him with their clubs.

As Bancroft's coach clattered down the drive, the sheer distance between Hawthorne's gleeful anticipation at the prospect of showing off his new wife to the neighbors and the sound of her quiet tears put him in mind of that experience.

"Please don't cry," Thorne said, trying to wrap her in a gentle embrace. "We'll find a way—"

"Don't cry? *Don't cry?* That man, that wretched, smirking, foul excrescence on the face of humanity has just decided to *take my children*, Hawthorne. If ever tears were appropriate, it's now." She stomped across the room, a handkerchief pressed to her nose.

"He's taking them for a visit only," Hawthorne said, trying to strike a balance between sweet reason, for which Margaret would likely fillet him, and a simple statement of fact.

"No, he's not. He will never give them back, and then he'll tell the solicitors that I need not be given a courtesy copy of the quarterly reports because the girls are no longer in my household. He'll squander their inheritance or leave them to the charity of his new wife. God help those children if Bancroft is marrying a harpy, for I know every noxious plant growing wild in this shire. Don't think I won't resort to drastic measures to protect Adriana and Greta."

"Talk like that won't help us regain custody of the children, Margaret."

She turned her back on him. "If Bancroft had announced plans to whisk *your* niece away from her only home tomorrow, would you be reasonable?"

"I'd be trying to talk Casriel, as the girl's father, into being reasonable."

"And you'd be wasting your breath."

The line of her back and set of her shoulders announced that any husband presuming to approach had best do so cautiously. Hawthorne took two steps closer nonetheless.

"What will we tell the children?"

Margaret turned to face him, her expression flat, despite her cheeks being blotchy and her eyes sheened with tears. "*We?*"

"I promised you that your troubles would become my own, and that means this situation isn't one you will face alone."

"I don't know what that means, Hawthorne. In less than twenty-four hours, my worst fear will come true. I will leave the children at Summerfield, only Fenny and Ambers to protect them, and the children will think it's only for a visit, but I'll know in my heart that I've lost them forever."

Margaret had convinced herself of that, which was puzzling. Another woman might have clung to the hope that a fortnight's visit would see Bancroft engaged to his heiress and the children returned home. Another woman would have been consulting the calendar to ensure that she could make the time for a trip to Summerfield every other day. Another woman would have been putting on a brave face.

The bleakness in Margaret's eyes put Thorne in mind of Demeter, wandering the world in search of her lost offspring, heartbroken, beyond all consolation. Though, if Zeus had been any sort of damned father, Hades would never have been able to interfere with Persephone.

Thorne risked another two steps closer to his bride. "You have not lost the children forever."

"Everybody thinks Greta is the fragile one," Margaret said, as if Thorne hadn't spoken. "She is different, but not as delicate as it might seem. When Greta is upset, the entire household knows about it. Adriana has never had a single tantrum, not once. Not even when she was small."

"She's an agreeable child." Somewhat prone to making noise. A lot of noise.

"She's so fiercely protective of Greta, she's never *allowed* herself to have a tantrum. She blames herself when Greta is out of sorts. She tries everything to jolly her sister along, and the first time Fenny insinuated that Greta should be caned for having a tantrum, Adriana climbed out a window to fetch me from the herbal. She wasn't four years old, and I could hear her shrieking for me from the back terrace."

Difficult questions begged to be asked, but the sheer desolation in Margaret's voice prevented Thorne from asking them.

"You're saying Bancroft will separate them?"

Margaret stood two feet away, gaze on the back gardens. "Hawthorne, he will break them into a million pieces and delight in doing so. He will tell himself they have been coddled and indulged and that his version of discipline—which will only start at separating them—is for their own good. I loathe those words."

"I'm none too fond of them myself."

She crossed her arms, even as a lone tear tracked down her cheek. "Bancroft struck Greta once, in the church yard. We'd just resumed attending services after Charles's death, she was hot and tired, and the sermon had gone on forever. She snapped at me as somebody was offering condolences, and before I'd even realized Bancroft had heard her, he'd slapped her."

The image of a grown man striking a small, bewildered, grieving Greta left Thorne nearly breathless with a rage so pure, his hand shook when he touched Margaret's shoulder.

"I'm sorry."

"Oh, half the parish was likely sorry. The vicar hurried over, but nobody—not Vicar, not the curate, not Hannah—dared remonstrate with Bancroft. He hit Greta because he could, and he was letting me know in as public a manner as possible that my time with the girls was at his sufferance. He's a truly nasty man, Hawthorne, and I have just agreed to yield the children to him."

Perhaps Margaret was being dramatic, but nothing Hawthorne knew of his wife supported that theory.

"You are the children's co-guardian," he said, "and you can force this matter into litigation before the children are sent to any schools. If an appeal to the courts is the course you prefer, I'll support it." He'd dread having to explain to his family why such a scandal was necessary, but he'd made Margaret a promise.

"Thank you, but litigation will beggar me, bring scandal down on the children, and likely achieve the same result. If Bancroft is boasting of his parental accomplishments now, how much more will he have to boast of when the case goes to a hearing two years from now? Bancroft will be wealthy by then and likely have a baby or two in his own nursery."

While Hawthorne would still be wielding a hayfork and trying to peddle lavender water. "I'll move a few things over from the steward's cottage," he said, because once haying began, there would be no time for personal errands.

"Why?"

"Because we're married? Because Bancroft will exploit any deviation from the plan we set forth? Because that plan does make sense, in light of recent developments?"

"Thank you," Margaret said, moving toward the door. "I am off to have a difficult discussion with Ambers. Pray hard that she and Miss

Fenner are willing to remove to Summerfield with the children, or my sanity is entirely forfeit."

She closed the door quietly, leaving Thorne alone.

Bancroft could break the children, to use her term. That was horror enough from Thorne's point of view, but after less than a day of marriage he also knew that if Bancroft's scheme regarding the children was allowed to prosper, so too would Hawthorne's new marriage be broken beyond any possibility of repair.

# CHAPTER TWENTY-ONE

Margaret told herself over and over that the children were merely to visit at Summerfield. That Hawthorne's family was her family now, and even Bancroft would hesitate to drag somebody with titled connections into court. That Bancroft would put on a show of avuncular duty for his prospective bride, and then he'd discard the girls like stage props.

Margaret's rational mind repeated those observations over and over, as if repetition might eventually smooth off the jagged hurt making every moment ache with loss.

"We are going for a visit," Adriana informed her stuffed dog. "We will stay at Summerfield in the nursery, which we used to do when we were babies. Aunt, did you stay with us when we were babies and we visited Summerfield?"

"I lived at Summerton with Uncle Charles. Your parents would come with you when you visited." And how Margaret had relished those visits.

Greta stood by the window, gazing down the drive. "Summerfield is cold."

"Miss Fenner and Ambers will make sure you're warmly dressed and that you have plenty of blankets."

"And you will come see us," Adriana added, a frequent refrain since Margaret had broached this topic yesterday. Hawthorne had mostly kept quiet during that discussion, but his very calm had seemed to reassure the children that the visit was to be enjoyed rather than dreaded.

"I will come see you often," Margaret said. "And you will get to meet Uncle Bancroft's friends, who came all the way from London."

Adriana, of course, began hopping on one foot. "London is very, very, very, *very* far away. Why can't we go to London?"

Margaret had lain awake for most of the night contemplating wild schemes—take the children away, refuse to allow the visit, disappear with the children—but Hawthorne had shared the bed with her, and stealing off into the darkness wouldn't solve anything.

He was a quiet sleeper, and Margaret had awoken plastered to his side, her head on his shoulder.

"He's here!" Adriana shrieked. "Mr. Dorning is here!"

The clatter of coach wheels on the drive confirmed Adriana's announcement. Fenny and Ambers had gone ahead with a first load of trunks. Hawthorne had insisted that the Dorning coach and four be pressed into service to deliver the girls to Summerfield.

"This coach ride will be longer than when we merely trot into the village," Margaret said. "We could be in the coach for an hour. Both of you visit the necessary before we leave."

Adriana tore off down the corridor. Greta remained at the window as Hawthorne let himself into the house without knocking.

"Mr. Dorning, welcome."

He swept off his hat. "Margaret. Greta. Has Adriana run off to join the Navy?"

"She's using the necessary," Greta said. "I don't want to go."

"Try, Greta," Margaret said. "An hour is a long time to sit in a coach."

Greta was rubbing the hem of her pinafore between her thumb

and forefinger. "I mean I don't want to go to Summerfield. Uncle Bancroft isn't nice."

Hawthorne set his hat on the sideboard, while Margaret cast around for something to say. *Uncle is nice in his way... You will like him better when you know him better... You have to give him a chance...*

"I don't like him much either," Hawthorne said, crouching down to Greta's eye level. "He pays calls here at Summerton, but never thinks to stop by the nursery. He's always in a hurry, and he barely gave you a day to pack and prepare for this visit. Not very nice of him."

Margaret would never have uttered those truths. Not in a million years of despising Bancroft would she have been that honest with Greta.

"He smells," Greta said. "Like Mr. Jeffers."

"Bancroft smokes a pipe," Margaret said. "He won't smoke around you children. That's a rule."

"You don't have to like him," Hawthorne said, "but you must show him your good manners nonetheless."

"Why?" Greta aimed that question at Hawthorne, which was fortunate, for Margaret hadn't an answer.

"I think it works like this," Hawthorne said. "If we are nasty to somebody, they are entitled to be nasty back. If we are courteous and respectful, then they are more likely to be courteous and respectful back."

"And we want Uncle to be courteous and respectful?" Greta asked.

"We do," Hawthorne said. "I expect he'll be a slow learner, so you must be patient. If you are at the end of your tether, you tell Miss Fenner or Ambers that you need a nap. They will make sure you have the peace and quiet of the nursery to settle your nerves, as is any young lady's right."

"What is at the end of my tether?"

"Ready to make a royal fuss," Margaret said. *As I have been for the past day.*

Adriana cantered up the hallway. "I'm ready! Greta hasn't used the chamber pot. She should use the chamber pot before we go, because Summerfield is far away."

"As long as we sit in church," Hawthorne said, "that's how long we'll sit in the coach."

Greta appeared to give that helpful observation some thought, then scampered off in the direction of the stairs.

"I'll come with you!" Adriana bellowed, running after her.

Hawthorne stepped closer, but did not take Margaret in his arms. "How are you?"

"I believe the phrase is *bearing up.* I want this to be over with, and I want to find every possible excuse to delay our departure."

"You did not sleep well. I'm sorry for that." He was asking a question, though Margaret had only half an answer.

They hadn't made love. Hawthorne had kissed her good night—on the cheek—and she'd rolled over and pretended to go to sleep.

"I'm glad you stayed with me last night." She could say that much honestly. "I hate that Bancroft has done this, and I am angry that the girls must endure his machinations, but thinking clearly is beyond me right now. You will please get us to Summerfield and keep me from proving that Bancroft's low opinion of me is justified."

Hawthorne's smile was wan. "We will mind our manners, not because we approve of him or like him, but because the children learn from our example."

The girls charged back into the foyer, and then Hawthorne was tossing them up into the coach.

"You brought Captain," Greta said. "He isn't muddy this time."

The dog sat up on the box, looking like the coachman's eager assistant.

"I thought he could use a change of air," Hawthorne said. "Shall we be off?"

He was smiling, calm, and relaxed, for which Margaret nearly hated him and also loved him dearly. She climbed into the coach, Hawthorne followed, and when the children finished arguing over who sat where, he rapped on the roof. The coach lurched forward, and Margaret swallowed past a lump in her throat bigger than all of Dorsetshire.

Hawthorne entertained the children for most of the ride, pointing out manor houses, an occasional oak tree claimed by the Royal Navy, and other landmarks. He mediated squabbles about seating, answered the endless *how much farther?* questions, and launched into a description of London that made an excessively dirty city seem like a place of enchantment.

The miles rolled by, and all too soon the coach pulled up before the Summerfield main entrance. The children burst from the coach almost before the horses had halted—rather, Adriana burst from the coach, and Greta climbed down after—while Margaret sat beside her husband, wanting to shout at the children to get back in the carriage.

"I cannot do this, Hawthorne."

"You should not have to do this. Before we leave, I will negotiate with Bancroft an end date for this visit. He can tell his guests whatever he pleases, but the children will be returned to you."

Margaret could not allow herself to hope, but she did appreciate that Hawthorne believed what he said. He left the coach and turned to offer her his hand. She emerged into a sunny afternoon and beheld an anxious Fenny standing on the steps.

"Ambers took the children upstairs," Fenny said. "You should come see them settled."

Hawthorne offered his arm.

"Was the nursery at least clean?" Margaret asked, accepting her husband's escort.

"They burn coal in the nursery here," Fenny said. "I had a word with the butler and the housekeeper, and we've been airing the nursery since I got here. The whole place is at sixes and sevens because of the London guests arriving tomorrow or Monday. I suspect the children will be largely left in peace."

Hawthorne held the door, though where was the butler? The first footman? Anybody to mind the front door?

"I told Greta that if she's feeling overwhelmed, she can ask to be taken to the nursery for a nap," Hawthorne said. "I don't know as that tactic will help, but it can't hurt."

"I'll pass the same suggestion to Adriana," Fenny said, starting up the main staircase. "This really could be a lovely house, but the housekeeper says it hasn't fared well since the current Mr. Summerfield took over."

Margaret did not care that Summerfield was dusty and—as Greta had said—chilly. She really should care that the children still did not know of her nuptials, but at that moment, she could not muster one iota of concern on that score either. Climbing the steps to the nursery felt like climbing the scaffold to a gallows, where all of Margaret's hopes and happiness would be snuffed out to suit Bancroft's greed.

"Is Bancroft too busy rehearsing his flirtations to greet his nieces?" Margaret asked.

"Mr. Summerfield had to meet with his tenants," Fenny said. "Something about a hay wagon that broke down on the way to a field that's to be cut Monday morning. Mr. Hartley was quite vexed."

"If Bancroft isn't home, so much the better," Margaret said. "I'll take the children on a tour of the premises before he gets back, and we can part at our leisure without Bancroft hovering and gloating."

Fenny winced. "Mr. Summerfield is most anxious to make a good impression on his Town guests. Ambers and I intend to keep the children out of sight as much as possible."

Hawthorne paused outside the nursery door. "Do we know when Bancroft will return from his meeting with the tenants?"

"Mr. Hartley didn't tell me that."

"Which means," Margaret said, "we cannot negotiate an end date for this visit today, can we?" She hated her peevish tone, she hated that Bancroft had likely outmaneuvered her, and she hated worst of all that good manners prevented her from collapsing into a screaming, kicking heap right there on the floor of the corridor.

"NELSON IS NEW TO THE JOB," Oak said, taking off his straw hat, and swiping a forearm across his brow. "Can't really blame the lad."

"The *lad* has been driving teams since King George went mad," Hawthorne retorted. "How in the hell anybody can overturn a hay wagon on a field that's all but level..." The wagon sat halfway down the windrow, the hapless driver now at the heads of the team. The horses stomped at flies and whisked short tails about their quarters, as if they too were out of patience with human incompetence.

The crews that should have been raking were instead knotted around the wagon, pointing and chattering as if somebody had dropped an elephant carcass in their midst.

"We didn't lose the team," Oak said. "That's something."

"Because the singletree snapped loose from the wagon carriage," Hawthorne retorted. "Now we have a useless wagon, a load of hay scattering itself on the breeze, and grounds for arguments that will last the next fortnight."

Hawthorne risked a glance at his watch while Valerian sauntered over with the water bucket and dipper.

"Only the third day of haying," Valerian said, "and already the Millers and Rileys are exchanging threats and curses. Nothing like country life, is there?"

He took a drink and passed Oak the bucket.

"So why, Vanity Dearest," Hawthorne said, "aren't you ensuring that the Millers and the Rileys work at opposite ends of the field?"

Valerian shaded his eyes and regarded the overturned wagon. "They love to bicker. It's entertaining."

Ye gods, why did it seem as if haying grew more difficult every year? "And when they are bickering, they aren't working, but those rain clouds come closer nonetheless. Then too, their bickering occasionally descends into fisticuffs, and then nobody works while the spectacle unfolds."

"That's why you're here," Oaks said, taking a good long slurp from the dipper. "To keep us all sorted out." He grinned, as if he'd made a joke.

"I should be leaving," Hawthorne said. "Margaret asked that we pay a call on Summerfield this afternoon, and I will have to disappoint my wife. The alternative is to leave one of the most important jobs I do in the hands of a pair of fools who should be righting that damned wagon instead of placing bets on the Rileys and Millers."

Oak had the grace to look sheepish, Valerian stepped closer. "You cannot leave now, Thorne. If anybody can get the Millers and Rileys sorted out, it's you. If anybody can make an overturned wagon a slightly humorous triviality, it's you. If anybody can gauge when the damned rain will get here, it's you. This is no time for a social call."

Haying did this. It shortened tempers, blistering more than just hands and backs. Haying frayed scarred neighborly relationships, incited violence, and tried nerves.

"I promised my wife," Hawthorne said. "The one thing she asked me to do—to keep the children from their uncle's meddling—and I have failed her. Now she makes an even more reasonable request, and you want me to instead sweat away my afternoon playing nanny to a parcel of bumblers."

Oak plopped his hat back on his head. "The hay crop was short last year. Playing nanny to a parcel of bumblers might be all that stands between them and another very hard winter."

"You can pay the call on Bancroft tomorrow," Valerian added. "Go first thing in the day and you can be back in the fields before noon."

*I do not want to be back in the fields.* The thought landed between Hawthorne's temper and his devotion to duty as something of a revelation.

"Where else in the entire realm," he said, "are three earl's sons sweating like beasts, getting blisters on their blisters, and earning headaches to go with their sore backs?"

Oak had the courage to answer. "Nowhere."

"Casriel himself would be here too," Valerian said, "if he wasn't in Town."

"But he is in Town, *with his wife*. As I should be with mine."

Something in Thorne's tone must have communicated itself to Valerian, for he offered the bucket and dipper. "We'll apologize to Margaret, Thorne. We'll explain to her that the day turned rotten on you. We'll make your excuses."

Margaret was doubtless pacing the parlor at Summerton, dressed for paying a call, and fretting herself senseless because after less than a week of marriage, her husband was rehearsing excuses. Hawthorne hated that picture, and hated himself for adding to her disappointments.

"We can make our excuses to her in person," Oak said, gaze on a gig that had turned into the field by way of a break in the tree line.

Margaret held the reins, and her posture suggested she was ready to hold forth on the topic of tardy husbands too.

"Explain about the overturned wagon," Valerian said. "She has to see that's not a problem you can walk away from."

"And the rain clouds," Oak added. "Closer by the minute."

While Oak and Valerian were backing away. "Cowards."

Their expressions went blank, then they turned their backs and retreated in earnest.

"Get the damned hay wagon righted," Thorne called after them. "Fill it up and push it by main strength to the haystack. Stop scything until that's done and maybe the rain will pass us by."

Valerian waved an arm without turning.

"And separate the damned warring factions."

Another wave, while Margaret drove the gig directly across the field. She halted the horse so a mere six feet separated her from her husband.

"You are late," she said, and throughout the entire history of marriage, no wife had ever packed more disapproval into those three words.

More hurt.

"I lost track of the time and things here rather went to hell." As Hawthorne's marriage was going to hell, day by day. The draft team that had been pulling the wagonload of hay was now snacking on the pile of cut, dried grass dumped between the windrows.

"Get those horses away from that uncured hay!" he called. "They'll colic before sundown otherwise."

"Hawthorne, you said we'd call on the girls today."

In truth, he'd said on Monday that they'd pay a call Tuesday, once the haying had commenced. Yesterday, he'd put Margaret off until today.

"Would you care for a drink of water?" he asked, mostly because he hadn't anything else to offer her.

"I would care to see the children." She was outwardly composed, her words calm, but her eyes told a different tale.

He was breaking her heart, plain and simple. "I'd like to see them too, but in some ways, these people are my children. They rely on me, and I have allowed them to."

Margaret regarded him as somebody led the team away from the pile of new hay and Oak and Valerian organized men along one side of the wagon.

"You cannot rely on your brothers to tend matters here for one afternoon, Hawthorne?"

"My brothers are half the reason that wagon is on its side. Half the reason the Rileys and the Millers got within feuding distance, half the reason nobody takes any initiative but instead stands around hoping the hay will make itself."

She blinked a few times and then gazed off across the fields. "They've disappointed you. I see."

"More than that," Hawthorne said, waving away a fly. "They know our situation and they aren't taking it into account. I expected better from my own brothers." The actual feeling, the one Hawthorne didn't want to name aloud, was *betrayal*. "The heat is making me irritable."

Beyond irritable. Ready to knock heads and curse and tell the lot of them to go to perdition—over a few acres of hay?

"You are needed here," Margaret said, taking up the reins. "I see that. I will pay my own call on Summerfield."

She would not reproach him, would not scold or plead, and what was at stake for her was much more precious than a load of hay. If Valerian and Oak's lack of understanding rose to the status of betrayal, what must Margaret be feeling toward a husband who did not keep his word?

The hot breeze wafted more of the spilled load away as the men got the wagon righted with a shout and a loud clatter. Some of them began forking up the loose hay, while others heeded Valerian's direction to get back to the raking.

They had known what to do, they had simply wanted somebody to reassure them before they did it.

"Margaret, do you smell rain on the way?" Hawthorne asked.

She closed her eyes for a moment. "Not rain, just humidity. An hour from now I might give you a different answer, but no rain on the way at present. Why?"

"Because I would not want us to get a soaking on the way to Summerfield." He climbed into the gig, leaving the bucket and dipper between two windrows.

Margaret sat for a moment, the reins in her hands. "You're sure you can spare the time?"

"I'm sure that you were wiser than I. You asked me how I'd cope if I ever had to choose between my new family and my old. I choose you and the girls, Margaret. If my brothers and neighbors cannot manage without me for an afternoon, then I have not helped them, I have held them back from developing their own abilities."

Perhaps that was overstating the case, perhaps the matter was one of allowing habits to form—the habit of relying on Hawthorne and the habit of being relied on. Maybe Casriel's arm's length attitude toward the botanical venture was an attempt to right a similar error.

Hawthorne did not much care to parse the philosophical questions, he cared only that his wife know she had his loyalty.

"You'll need a bath," Margaret said. "I daresay you'll need some comfrey salve too."

*I need you.* Rather than say that, Thorne kissed her cheek. Their hat brims mashed against each other, and somebody hooted from halfway across the field.

"A bath and some salve sounds heavenly."

Oak and Valerian watched them go, and it seemed to Hawthorne that both of his brothers were smiling. Of a certainty, Margaret was smiling, and so was Hawthorne.

# CHAPTER TWENTY-TWO

"I do hope you're enjoying your visit," Bancroft said as Miss Pepper donned a straw hat adorned with blue silk flowers. She had a knack for tying a bow off-center under her chin that drew Bancroft's notice. Was it purely by chance that her bonnet ribbons curled ever so fetchingly against her breasts?

He thought not. Emily Pepper was clever in the way women were meant to be clever, meaning she knew how to hold a man's notice and make him feel appreciated.

"Dorsetshire is delightful," Miss Pepper replied, taking up her parasol. "Summerfield is delightful. Papa is much taken with your property."

"May I tell you a secret?"

She sashayed out the door ahead of him, and Bancroft took a moment to admire the view before following her onto the back terrace.

"I'd rather you didn't," she said. "Secrets want keeping, and that takes effort. Let's stroll, shall we?" She opened her parasol, a lacy blue confection that matched her bonnet ribbons.

Such fashion sense, she had.

"This isn't that sort of secret," Bancroft said as she took his arm. "I had Hartley move the hay crews to the fields closest to the house because I thought you and Mr. Pepper would find the sight of the yeomen at their labors charming."

The lads made a happy picture, swinging their blades. Bancroft had told Hartley that a song or two wouldn't go amiss, but so far, the tenants hadn't obliged in Bancroft's hearing. Perhaps haying songs were naughty.

"Everything about Summerfield is charming," Miss Pepper said. "That gazebo, for example, just begs for a lady to escape for a few hours with a book or some sketching paper. If I were Greta or Adriana, I'd be planning tea parties for my dolls there."

Of all topics, Bancroft did not want to discuss his nieces. "That pair won't be blighting my garden anytime in the near future. Until they can conduct themselves like ladies, they will be confined to the nursery."

Miss Pepper dropped his arm and bent to sniff a pot of purple flowers. "I've always thought hyacinths were too sweet, too overpowering, but these have a lovely scent."

Which was probably part of Margaret's legacy. She had been permitted to meddle inordinately with the gardeners and groundskeepers.

"Are those hyacinths? They do lovely things for your eyes, my dear."

"Flatterer." She resumed her progress toward the gazebo, which was a hexagonal, open-sided little temple to architectural vanity at the foot of the garden. "Was your late sister confined to the nursery as a child, Bancroft?"

"My sister was a much-wanted daughter, and the only daughter. She was overindulged from infancy." Charles had enjoyed the role of doting big brother where their sister had been concerned, and Bancroft had always wondered if he'd been denied some critical sibling sentiment. Siblings were simply there—usually getting most of the parental attention and resources. Siblings weren't particularly useful, and they did tend to complicate one's aspirations.

"Were you and your brother confined to the nursery?"

What did any of that matter? "I spent a fair amount of time with my books. Charles was the heir, though—the oldest and the favorite. Charles and Papa frequently rode out together, Charles sat between Mama and Papa at services, and Charles went to public school and did two years of university." A complete waste of funds and attention, as it turned out.

"While you toiled away with some droning tutor, you poor thing." She took the steps up into the gazebo, and it occurred to Bancroft that perhaps—possibly? maybe?—the lady was inviting him to steal a kiss.

He hadn't so far. He'd come close yesterday in the conservatory, but then Greta had emerged from behind a potted fern, and Miss Pepper had gone into raptures about the child's lovely quiet manner.

"This is the perfect place for a doll's tea party," Miss Pepper said, twirling with her parasol propped on her shoulder. "I wonder if that was perhaps the very purpose for which the folly was built. I must have the girls down here this afternoon, dolls and all. I'm sure the nursery staff would appreciate a break from their duties."

She settled onto one of the cushioned benches that ringed the interior. "Sit with me, Bancroft. Tell me more of your childhood." She patted the cushions and closed her parasol.

He came down immediately beside her. "My childhood was unremarkable and happy. Because Charles was off at school, I drew closer to the land itself. I followed Papa and his steward everywhere, got to know the tenants as if they were extended family, and longed for the day when I could support my brother in his management of this fine property."

Bancroft's childhood had been a misery. Never as important as Charles or as dear as their sister, he'd been relegated to the company of somnolent tutors. The local boys had taunted him for his status, and as he'd matured, the local girls had flirted with him in hopes of earning his coin.

Ignorant yokels, the lot of them. Whopstraws whose greatest delight was wandering the square on market day, cramming meat pies into their maws. A far cry from the gentlemen in Town with whom Bancroft had whiled away many a friendly hand of cards.

"How lovely it must be," Miss Pepper said, "to find the purpose in life for which you were born. Summerfield is that for you, isn't it?"

Bancroft took her hand. "If I say no, you will know me for a dissembler. If I say yes, then I'm admitting to a very humble ambition —to simply tend my acres, to see my tenants and neighbors prosper along with me, to manage a happy household. In fact, I aspire to more."

The moment held potential for gestures beyond a stolen kiss. The warm breeze, the golden sunshine, the scents of flowers and cut grass combined to create a perfect romantic opportunity. Miss Pepper seemed to grasp his intent, because she closed her fingers around his, her gaze solemn.

"What more could a man ask for, Bancroft, than a life of contentment, husbanding his acres and enjoying the friendly society of his neighbors?"

Bancroft leaned closer, and still Miss Pepper held his gaze. "Summerfield is lovely, but it's an enormous dwelling for one man."

"Ah, but you have your nieces now to add joy to your days. I can see, though, that their aunt has been allowed to dampen their high spirits. You were right to take them under your wing, Bancroft. They will soon blossom in your care, and their laughter will add to your joy."

Not if he could help it. He'd already sent inquiries to his solicitors about boarding schools that didn't charge much, or pride themselves on turning out overly educated females. Even a brief sojourn to the capital left a man with expenses and debts of honor to pay, and coddling a pair of nieces was not in Bancroft's budget.

"The years the girls have spent with Margaret have doubtless taken a toll. But won't you tell me about your aspirations? Surely a young lady as sensible, pretty, and wise as you are has a few dreams as yet unrealized?" He stroked her hand, and though they were wearing gloves, she had to feel the caress.

"I do like children."

A promising admission, though one Bancroft would never share. He took pride in his boys, but they were a pair of noisy, rambunctious lads.

"And?"

"You clearly care for children, too, or you wouldn't be so conscientious toward your nieces. Surely you are taking such good care of Summerfield with an eye toward the future?"

The hope that Bancroft had been harboring since he'd laid eyes on Miss Pepper unfurled into a solid sense that she was determined to winkle a proposal from him. The minx, the dear, charming, *well-dowered*, utterly obvious minx.

Bancroft was debating the wisdom of sliding to one knee when a shout from the terrace intruded.

"Captain! Captain, come! You naughty dog! For shame. Come now!"

"Oh, that's Adriana and her doggy," Miss Pepper said, withdrawing her hand from Bancroft's. "I do wonder that you lack a country squire's regiment of panting canines, Bancroft. I so enjoy the companionship of a noble hound. Let's greet the children, shall we?"

She was off down the steps, waving to the girls, whom Bancroft did not want to greet. Not in the slightest, and his sentiments toward the dog exceeded the bounds of all profanity. He nonetheless slapped on his most gracious smile, caught up with Miss Pepper, and took her by the arm.

MARGARET HAD STEELED herself to tell Hawthorne the truth—about the girls, about the whole mess that had resulted in her marriage to Charles—but Hawthorne had fallen asleep before she'd driven the gig to the foot of Summerton's drive. He'd fallen asleep in the bathtub as well, though weeks of haying lay before him. Had no one ever explained to her husband that a steady pace had much to recommend it over tearing forth into every task?

Margaret turned the gig onto the lane that would lead to the Summerfield gateposts. "I will have a word with your lordly brother if he ever crosses my path."

"We both will. He's preoccupied lately, but if I wait for him to stop fawning over his countess, we will all be elderly."

"Did the comfrey salve help your sunburn?" The scent had accompanied them all the way from Summerton.

"It did. Thank you. What are my orders for this visit?"

Margaret could not read Hawthorne's mood. If he resented this obligation, he hid it well. He'd said he missed the children, and she believed him. She certainly missed them, and through two long days of haying, she'd also missed Hawthorne.

"My orders for myself," Margaret said, slowing the horse to a walk, "are not to cry. I am to be cheerful and calm. Pleased to see the children, of course, but not... not upset." *Upset* didn't begin to describe the stew of frustration, grief, rage, and worry she'd been enduring since reading Bancroft's note.

"Cheerful and calm." Hawthorne took the reins from her, as if he knew she needed her handkerchief now. "That sounds like me at the start of haying. Also me at the start of lambing, foaling, shearing, planting, harvest, hedging, calving, penning..."

"It's hard, isn't it?" Margaret said, dabbing at her eyes with her linen. "Always being cheerful and calm."

Hawthorne switched the reins to one hand and wrapped an arm around her waist. "You miss them terribly."

He hadn't answered her question, probably because the answer was obvious.

"Of course I miss them, but more significantly, I worry for them. Bancroft knows nothing about caring for children, this Miss Pepper person knows even less, and the girls can be difficult. I'm glad you left Captain with them."

"If they have to walk the dog, then they get outside several times a day. You want to kidnap the children, don't you?"

Even in the midst of what felt like an honest, private conversation, Hawthorne's air was slightly distant. "Why do you ask?"

"Because *I* would like to kidnap them. Damned Bancroft knew exactly what he was doing, snatching the children as haying began, and I let him get away with it."

"*We* let him get away with it."

Hawthorne glanced over at her, then urged the horse back to the trot. "Is there a reason *we* let him get away with stealing the girls?"

A carefully neutral question. Margaret could answer with only half of the truth. "He ambushed us. The law isn't against him, and if he's to marry Miss Pepper, the children should get to know her."

"They can get to know her after she's assumed the burden of being Mrs. Bancroft Summerfield, assuming she's that lacking in sense." Hawthorne turned the gig onto the Summerfield drive. "Are you looking forward to this visit or dreading it?"

"Both. What if they love it here, Hawthorne? Bancroft can be charming." Was Margaret's worst fear that the children would be consigned to some miserable school in the cold and distant north, or that they'd be taken in by Bancroft's pretense of doting?

"Give them more credit than that, Margaret. They know who loves them and who puts on a show for his own gain."

"You asked for your orders regarding this visit." Margaret turned her face against Hawthorne's shoulder and took a good, deep sniff of him. Lavender, comfrey, a hint of lanolin, meadow grasses... all good things and all him. "Keep doing what you're doing. Reminding me of the truth, reminding me what matters. Haying matters, too, Hawthorne, I know that. I just... I needed to be here."

"Haying matters," he said, steering the horse into the circular drive before the Summerfield façade, "but being your husband matters more. I'm sorry you had to remind me of that, and I will try to do better in the future. I'd do it, you know."

His apology was so sincere and so welcome, and it left Margaret feeling equal parts reassured and guilty. "You'd do what?"

"Kidnap them. In fact, I might enjoy that. Is your calm, cheerful smile in good repair?"

"Good enough."

He brought the horse to a halt before the front door. "As is mine. Mrs. Dorning, let the visit begin."

A BATH, a nap in the gig, and a chance to think in peace had done much to restore Hawthorne's equilibrium. Perhaps he had been in the sun too long, or perhaps being married took getting used to. Regardless of those factors, now that Margaret had taken him in hand —and applied salve to his blisters and sunburn, forced him to eat a decent meal, and valeted him into clean clothes—he could focus on the problem that was Bancroft Summerfield.

The man couldn't manage property worth a drover's fart. Fields more than ready for the scythe were still standing, while a shorter crop closer to the house was being harvested. A flock of sheep near the manor house had yet to be shorn, leaving the animals miserable in the heat. Fences had been painted on one side—the side facing the drive—which only made the boards warp more quickly.

Hawthorne handed his wife down from the gig and stole a kiss to her cheek. "If Bancroft was half as good at managing an estate as he is at managing appearances, Summerfield would be awash in coin."

"Every time I come here, I am a little sadder at what I see," Margaret replied. "If it's not livery going dingy at the cuffs, it's ruts in the drive or windows overdue for glazing. Charles would despair of the place now."

From a distance, Summerfield looked like a grand old stately home. Three stories of gray limestone—Chilmark, from the looks of it

—held pride of place atop a slight rise. An alley of lime trees flanked the drive, and pastures extended on either side of the trees. Windows on the first and second floors were trimmed in white, while the third floor looked to be taken up with attics. The front terrace was elevated above the drive and ran the length of the façade, with urns of red salvia set at regular intervals.

"Do you miss having such a grand home?" Hawthorne asked, rapping on the front door.

"Charles and I lived mostly at Summerton—fewer stairs. I don't miss this place, and I can't see that it's a better location for raising children than Summerton is."

"I hear Captain," Hawthorne said when the housekeeper had escorted them to the family parlor. "If Captain is in the garden, then the children will be there too. Mrs. Dorning and I will join the children out of doors."

"Mr. Summerfield is in the garden as well," the housekeeper said, "as is Miss Pepper. Mr. Pepper is above stairs at his letters, but we'll let him know that company has arrived."

The housekeeper withdrew on a curtsey.

"Calm and cheerful," Margaret said, looking tense and determined.

"I have a suggestion," Hawthorne said, drawing her into his arms.

"Suggest away, particularly if it involves kidnapping small children."

Hawthorne kissed her brow. "Let's divide and conquer."

Margaret peered up at him. "Whatever do you mean?"

IN MARGARET'S OPINION, the children were coping, to use Fenny's words. Adriana hopped on one foot for the length of the garden. Greta hadn't said more than two words. When Hawthorne had passed her his watch, she'd pressed it to her ear as if its ticking held the secrets to eternal happiness.

The dog stuck close to Greta, as did Ambers, while Fenny chased after Adriana. Margaret longed to take Adriana by one hand and Greta by the other and bolt for the gig, though Hawthorne had advised against it.

"I am so pleased to meet you, Mrs. Dorning," Miss Emily Pepper said as Adriana came hopping up the walkway on a return circuit. "My, that child has impressive stamina."

"The girls are accustomed to spending some of every day out of doors when the weather's fine," Margaret replied. "Sunshine is good for their spirits, and if they can have an hour to do as they please— within limits, of course—they settle more effectively to their studies."

Miss Pepper closed her parasol and passed it to Adriana as she hopped by. "You can shade your sister while your auntie and I have a chat in the gazebo."

Adriana looked at the parasol, then at Margaret.

"A fine notion," Margaret said, when she'd rather be exploring the gardens with the girls than making small talk with Miss Pepper. "What do you say to Miss Pepper?"

"Thank you, Miss Pepper!" Adriana brandished the parasol and skipped off toward Greta's bench. "Miss Pepper gave me a lance! We can joust like knights of old, Greta, and Captain can be our noble steed!"

"I used to have an imagination like that," Miss Pepper said. "Per-haps children without many siblings develop the knack of inventing adventures to make up for a lack of playmates."

The young lady's scent was not the overly sweet rose water or neroli many women her age wore. Those fragrances had all the subtlety of harbor cannon, booming over all other contenders by sheer force of impact.

Her choice started off lemony and blended down into warm spices, like a good, rainy-day tisane well suited to a touch of honey. Margaret liked the scent, though she didn't particularly want to like the woman.

"I was an only child," Margaret said, "and joined the household of elderly relatives at a young age. I was allowed to wander over most of the shire, often by myself. That sufficed to occupy my imagination."

They'd reached the gazebo, a structure Charles's father had built so his boys could play buccaneers and knights and whatever else caught their fancy on fine days. Charles had found those memories painful as his illness had progressed.

"You'd rather spend this time with your nieces, wouldn't you?" Miss Pepper asked.

This young lady could become the mother figure in Greta and Adriana's lives. Margaret did not want to offend her, but neither did she see any point in dissembling.

"I miss them terribly. I'm trying not to convey to them that they should be missing me just as much, but a part of me..." A part of Margaret had been weeping for days. "Promise me something, Miss Pepper."

Miss Pepper took a seat on the gazebo steps, a perch that meant they could keep the children in sight. Margaret took the place beside her.

"I don't make promises lightly, Mrs. Dorning."

"Nor do I ask for them lightly, but where the children are concerned, I have no pride. If you join Bancroft's household, please take care of my nieces. Care for them. They are wonderful children, and life has not been easy for them. They lost their parents, then their Uncle Charles. Bancroft would take them from Summerton now, and while I'm sure you are all that is worthy, they are little girls, and they will need time to adjust to yet another change."

Adriana took Greta by one hand and brandished the parasol with the other. Captain loped along with them as they charged across the garden, Adriana bellowing, "*A moi, mes* knights! *A moi!*"

"*Chevaliers!*" Margaret hollered. "*Mes chevaliers!*"

Adriana took up the cry, Captain barked, and Miss Pepper's expression remained hard to read.

"You are not a dried-up old besom who forces the children to memorize Scripture by the hour, are you?" she asked.

"I beg your pardon?"

"Bancroft paints himself as rescuing the girls from a drafty garret where they are condemned to drudgery by their widowed auntie's eccentric notions."

"The same Bancroft who has yet to visit the nursery this week?"

Miss Pepper's smile was slight. "The same Bancroft who they all but hide from when I insist he notice them. I do like children, Mrs. Dorning, and Bancroft can offer them the status of a wealthy landowner's household. He has servants, London connections, and vast acreage, while from what I understand, you are essentially married to a steward who has no property of his own, and you dwell on a glorified farm."

Greta took a turn wielding the parasol, though she used it more like a rapier than a lance.

"Did Bancroft neglect to tell you that my farm has several tenancies paying good rent and that my Hawthorne is the son of an earl? He manages many more acres than Bancroft does, and I believe you might be acquainted with his brother Valerian."

Miss Pepper's composure slipped. "Valerian Dorning? I assumed there was a connection, but at some remove. Like all the Joneses in Wales might be related, or all the Trengrouses in Cornwall."

"Hawthorne and Valerian are brothers. All the siblings have botanical names, and unlike Summerfield, the Dorning estate has been well managed."

"But stewardship is not comparable to owning Summerfield. What do you have to offer the girls that Bancroft can't offer them?"

Only a woman without children would pose such a question. "Love, Miss Pepper. I love those girls to the depths of my soul. All the liveried servants and London connections in the world are no consolation to a child being raised without love."

"Maybe I could love them too."

"If your love is only a maybe, that's not good enough. Particularly when Bancroft has never loved them in the years of being their uncle and merely seeks to gain control of their wealth."

Miss Pepper took off her bonnet and turned her face to the sun, something a young lady was taught to never do. "Bancroft has Summerfield. He need not steal from children, or are my perceptions in error?"

Margaret suspected Miss Pepper's perceptions were astute and well guarded. Hawthorne had devised a strategy, though, and so far, his approach was working.

"Do you understand what enclosure is, Miss Pepper?"

"Fencing off land attached to an estate, even though that land was in common use previously. The land can be better managed by the owner, though the results for those who lose access to it are harsh."

"The results are devastating, which is something both Bancroft's father and brother recognized, so they enclosed only a portion of Summerfield's common land. Enclosure is also very expensive and requires significant materials and labor. Charles had barely paid off the debt resulting from his father's enclosures, and then Bancroft inherited and began more enclosures. Other debts came with the estate, and Bancroft does not manage well."

Miss Pepper drew up her knees and wrapped her arms around them. "I haven't spent enough time in polite society's country seats to know if Summerfield is well maintained. The house seems dusty and drafty, and the servants look harried rather than happy."

Margaret forced herself to recite facts. The staff was smaller by one-third than it had been three years ago. The fields hadn't been marled in all that time. The crop rotation scheme was decades behind the best practices, and Bancroft had to buy hay every winter because he regarded turnips as the crop of peasants. The house was drafty because the windows should have been regularly reglazed, and the farm lanes at Summerfield were in poor condition because Bancroft didn't bother to clear his drainage ditches between planting and harvest.

By contrast, Greta's and Adriana's funds, which were managed by solicitors, were growing steadily.

Miss Pepper appeared to listen, as she also watched the siege going on across the garden. Margaret learned two things from the conversation. First, Emily Pepper was in no way smitten with Bancroft Summerfield. If she was considering his suit, her reasons were practical rather than romantic. Second, Miss Pepper would do her duty by Greta and Adriana at least, and she might even come to love them, but she longed for a family of her own, however well she kept that longing out of sight.

Miss Pepper's father eventually appeared on the back terrace, then made his way slowly across the garden. Captain greeted him enthusiastically and left off being a noble steed to remain beside Mr. Pepper throughout the introductions.

Simply by looking at the older man, Margaret learned a few more things about the Pepper family.

Mr. Pepper was dying. She didn't have to smell his breath to confirm that diagnosis. He was pale, and for a thin man, he none-theless looked puffy about the eyes and hands. He moved with little energy, and most significant of all, his gaze held that combination of courage and resignation Margaret had seen in her late husband.

Emily Pepper's father was gravely ill, and Bancroft was presenting her with a family ready-made and in need of love. Bancroft would gain control of a large fortune, and Margaret would lack the resources to battle him in the courts if he chose to never return the children to her.

# CHAPTER TWENTY-THREE

Hawthorne had counseled that he and Margaret use the visit as a reconnaissance mission, though the urge to grab one girl under each arm and bolt for the gig was making it hard to focus on Bancroft's blatherings.

Bancroft was that most detestable of creatures, a man with more wealth than decency. He was also a coward, meaning he would not steal the children unless he was confident his scheme would succeed.

Given that Summerfield was going to seed, the staff appeared to resent their master bitterly, and Miss Pepper was far from ensconced as lady of the house—settlements and all—Bancroft's confidence made little sense.

"Shall we have some brandy, Dorning?" he asked, crossing to the family parlor's sideboard. "I realize it's early in the day, but with the brats shrieking in the garden, Margaret glaring daggers at me, and the staff in an uproar over a mere two guests, a man's nerves need steadying. A few glasses of wine at lunch were not adequate to that challenge."

Hawthorne accepted a serving. "To a successful haying."

Bancroft lifted his glass, which was full to the brim. "To a successful haying, in every sense of the word. I think Miss Pepper is much impressed with Summerfield, as is Mr. Pepper."

*I'm fine, thank you, how are you?* "She seems a pleasant lady. Country life will be an adjustment for her."

"Country life? My dear fellow, if she sees fit to accept my suit, I can guarantee you we'll let out the ancestral pile and spend most of our time in London. I'm told Paris is lovely in spring, and Lisbon's winters have much to recommend them."

The brandy had been watered, likely by the staff. The adulteration was minor, though the vintage hadn't been first quality to begin with.

"I'm sure the children will adore hearing about your peregrinations when you return," Hawthorne said. "You must write to them regularly as you travel."

"Write to the children? They are girls, Mr. Dorning. Perhaps your father wrote occasionally to his sons when he was away on his botanical expeditions, but girls are another matter entirely. They can be packed off to boarding schools until they are old enough to be married advantageously. That's how it's done."

Bancroft tossed back a bumper of inferior brandy, while Hawthorne set his nearly full glass on the dusty mantel.

"You've raised a number of girls, then, to be an expert on their upbringing?"

"It's a simple undertaking," Bancroft said, refilling his glass, "though it takes more coin than it ought to. Any fool can see that much."

"Given that they are such a burden, when do you plan to return them to us?"

Hawthorne plucked a C major on the spinet—also dusty—but the instrument was so out of tune that the result was minor. G major and F major were equally harsh to the ear.

"Dorning, I regard you as a man of sense, though your taste in wives is questionable. Why would you want a pair of girls underfoot as you're trying to thaw the widow's ice?"

That Bancroft would fence rather than dismiss the question outright was encouraging. That he would insult Margaret to Hawthorne's face suggested inchoate inebriation.

"The lady is my wife, Summerfield. Mind your tongue." Hawthorne spoke mildly, when he wanted to plow his fist into Bancroft's face. Pounding a man to dust when he was half drunk wasn't sporting, nor—in this case—was it good strategy.

"I keep the pianoforte in the guest parlor tuned," Bancroft said. "No point bothering with an instrument that's only for show."

"So the girls practice their music in the guest parlor?"

"The girls, the girls, the girls... You are not their father, Dorning. You aren't anything to them, and I suggest you keep out of a matter you know little about. That's a friendly bit of advice you'd do well to heed. I waited to intervene as long as I dared, but I know my duty. What can those women be discussing?"

Out in the garden, Margaret and Miss Pepper were sharing a bench. Mr. Pepper was conversing with the girls, Captain at his side. Miss Fenner and Ambers occupied another bench. The scene should have been cheerful and relaxed, but was anybody in that garden happy?

"Maybe the ladies are discussing fashion. Miss Pepper's attire is quite stylish."

"She's the old man's only child, set to inherit an obscene fortune, and she's most favorably inclined toward me, Dorning. I can afford to do with the girls as I please."

"You mean Miss Pepper can afford to do with the girls as you please, but why bother with your nieces at all? Margaret loves them, she has taken excellent care of them, and I am not without a few connections of my own."

Half of Bancroft's second serving of brandy was already gone. He was either taking inordinate measures to steady his nerves, or he was overly confident of his aims.

"I had a duty to rescue those girls, Dorning. You might think me heartless, taking them away from Summerton, but nobody is safe in

Margaret's care. She fancies herself quite the healer, or she did, but she's learned humility on that score. Did you know she killed poor Charles?"

No, she hadn't, but the glee with which Bancroft served up his poison was appalling. "That is a serious charge. You will please explain yourself."

"Serious indeed, and the statute of limitations on murder will not run out for quite some time, will it? She poisoned him with her quackery. Poor sod had a bad heart. The best physicians in London pronounced his case hopeless. Told him to go home and put his affairs in order, for the end was nigh. He married Margaret instead, of all the damnable notions. Then he changed his will, and what should have been mine ended up going to a bloody lot of worthless females three very long years later."

Bancroft's recitation answered some questions and raised others. "You have all of Summerfield House, when as a younger son, that legacy was never guaranteed to be yours."

Bancroft gestured with his drink, sloshing brandy over his knuckles. "I have a bloody

lot of damned debt, while those wretched children rack up tidy interest every year on sums larger than they'll ever need. It's not fair, and a murderess pretends that she's a better influence on my nieces than I am."

So Bancroft was not only greedy, he was vengeful toward females who'd done nothing to harm him.

What a charmer. Margaret had withstood the threat of Bancroft's accusations for years, raised the girls in a peaceful and loving home, and set aside everything she knew about medicine rather than call Bancroft to account.

Thorne passed Bancroft his handkerchief. "This is an interesting tale, but if I'm to believe it, it wants details. How exactly did Charles die?"

Bancroft mopped at his hand with Thorne's linen. "I have your attention now, I see. I don't blame you for marrying Margaret—she's comely enough, and younger sons must get on as well as they can—but be careful around the tisanes and potions. Charles trusted her, swore by that damned decoction of hers. Made from flowers. Foxgloves or hollyhocks or some such. Vile stuff.

"Charles was here at Summerfield," Bancroft went on, "getting the place in order for the next tenants, or taking a few days away from the harpy he'd married. He wasn't doing well, so I gave him a bit of his magic potion, all to no avail. Gave him a bit more, and he fared even worse, so I gave him more... The footman went in to rouse him in the morning, and he was gone. The medication—if you can call it that—did him in, no question about it."

That sad recollection apparently necessitated that Bancroft consume the rest of his brandy.

Hawthorne made himself focus on the scene in the garden as a sort of tonic against violent impulses. No, not violent impulses, honorable impulses. Before he could act on those impulses, he wanted to confirm facts and strategy with Margaret.

"You've kept this sequence of events to yourself," Hawthorne said. "Why not bring charges at the time of Charles's death?"

"I was grief-stricken, Dorning. Felled by sorrow. I did not want to believe the evidence of my own eyes. That a woman would marry a man, knowing him to be in delicate health, then finish him off... It's a sad old tale from a Gothic novel, not a drama one expects to extinguish the life of one's only brother. Then too, one doesn't want to bring scandal down on one's house. By the time the medical men finished bickering over the cause of death, who knows what might have happened to my inheritance? Chancery could have tied up the whole estate for eons."

"A daunting prospect." For an heir who had likely been trading on his expectations for years.

"You see why the children cannot be raised in Margaret's household?" Bancroft asked. "I must do my dooby... my doo-ty by them."

What Hawthorne saw was self-delusion and greed on a virtuosic scale and a man drunk at midday. "And you timed your rescue of the girls for the moment when they could help you win Miss Pepper's hand—and fortune."

Bancroft smiled at his drink. "What can I say? Fortune favors the audacious, and Charles's will did make the situation unnecessarily complicated, but all is as it should be now."

"Not quite," Hawthorne said. "But soon. Let's have another brandy, and then I'll bid farewell to the children."

"I knew you'd see the way of it. Margaret will grumble about parting with her little charges, so I suggest you distract her with a baby or two, and it wouldn't hurt to remind her of the risk she runs if she seeks to thwart my authority on this matter. I regret to admit that Charles never took a firm hand with her—an oversight you can remedy, hmm?"

"Margaret will insist that we call on you again," Hawthorne said. "Friday suits. Perhaps by then you and Miss Pepper will have reached an understanding."

"Let's drink to that happy thought, shall we?"

"None for me," Hawthorne said, "but help yourself while I rejoin my family in the garden. No need to see us off, and do expect us back at the end of the week."

Assuming Hawthorne did not kidnap the children first.

MARGARET'S calm good cheer was shredding by the moment. The children had walked with her and Hawthorne around to the front drive, as had Miss Pepper. Bancroft, thank a benevolent providence, was nowhere to be seen. Ambers and Miss Fenner waited a dozen yards away, chatting with Miss Pepper.

"We will write to you after you leave," Adriana said. "We were going to write to you today, but then you visited."

"We were going to run away," Greta muttered.

"Were you?" Hawthorne asked, scooping Greta onto his hip.

"Twelve miles is a great distance to run. How would you have found your way?"

Greta cuddled onto his shoulder, which had to be about the dearest and most heartrending sight Margaret had ever beheld.

"Captain knows the way," Greta said. "We would have taken him with us and worn our boots."

"We saved our toast and jam from breakfast," Adriana added. "Miss Pepper is nice, but Uncle..."

"He smells bad," Greta said. "His breath stinks. His clothes stink. I don't like him."

"He acts all smiley and sweet when Miss Pepper is around, but then he goes like this,"—Adriana made a shooing motion with her hand—"when her back is turned, and Fenny takes us back to the nursery. We only get to go outside if Captain needs a walk."

"We want to go home," Greta said. "We want to go home now."

That particular tone, that emphasis on the word *now*, could presage a grand tantrum. Margaret sorted through replies—leaving without notice would be rude, Bancroft's feelings might be hurt, nothing was packed—but in her heart, she knew those lies for the excuses they were.

Bancroft had the girls, Miss Pepper was charmed by the prospect of becoming an aunt, and Bancroft would never cede that bargaining chip—much less the funds that came with it—now that he controlled it.

"I want to take you home with us," Hawthorne said, "but instead we will content ourselves with calling again on Friday."

That was news to Margaret—good news. "The day after tomorrow," she said. "Not long at all."

"Here." Hawthorne passed Greta his watch. "With every tick of that watch, the next visit comes closer. We can wind the watch together on Friday."

"May I have a watch?" Adriana asked.

Hawthorne set Greta on her feet and stroked a big hand over Adriana's head. "You are in charge of Captain, who looks to be thriving in your care. You must not, however, allow him to sleep in your bed."

Adriana exchanged a look with Greta. "We know. He's a filthy hound who has no business in the nursery."

"A filthy *damned* hound," Greta said, nose in the air, hand on her hip in a manner reminiscent of Bancroft. "But Fenny said Captain slept in the nursery at Summerton—he did for one night, so that's not a lie—and Miss Pepper said Captain should stay in the nursery with us here. I want to go home."

"Be patient until Friday," Hawthorne said. "We will all be patient. I urge you both to practice the pianoforte in the family parlor, take Captain out frequently for a *loud* game of bold knights, and wear your boots at all times indoors."

What on earth was he up to?

"And no running," he added, "not indoors anyway. Uncle Bancroft cannot abide the noise of running feet overhead."

Oh... *Yes, of course.* "Inside voices," Margaret said, slipping her arm through Hawthorne's. "Inside voices at all times, especially around Uncle Bancroft."

Another look passed between the girls.

"Until Friday." Hawthorne swept the children a silly bow, then aimed a more formal courtesy at Miss Pepper, Fenny, and Ambers. "Ladies, a pleasure. We'll see you again soon."

Margaret approached Miss Pepper, while Ambers and Fenny collected the girls. "Miss Pepper, a pleasure to have met you." *Do you know your father is dying?* In Margaret's experience, family usually knew the truth of a hopeless case, even when they didn't acknowledge that truth.

"I'll look forward to seeing you again," Miss Pepper said, dipping a curtsey. "Mr. Dorning, should the occasion arise, please give my regards to your brother Valerian."

And then the moment of parting was over, and Hawthorne was steering the horse down the lane.

"Thank you," Margaret said, leaning into him. "Thank for you making the time to pay this call, thank you for keeping Bancroft away from me, and thank you for agreeing to return on Friday. I want to leap from this carriage and run up the drive to hug my girls one more time. Bancroft will never let us have them back. I know that now, but I also know the girls are bearing up, and that's... that's something."

Maybe heartache was like this—cresting and ebbing, never quite resolving, and never obliterating all reason. Grief certainly fit that description, and in her first marriage, Margaret had developed an intimate acquaintance with that emotion. The prospect of more grief—a parent's grief rather than a spouse's—had her wrapping her hand around Hawthorne's arm.

He had been right to view this visit as a reconnaissance mission, but the facts in evidence were discouraging.

Hawthorne remained silent until he'd turned the gig through the gateposts. "We will return on Friday. I meant that."

"Despite haying?"

"To perdition with haying. Let's pay a call on Hannah Weller, shall we?"

HANNAH TOOK one look at Hawthorne and Margaret and set her kettle on to boil. "Trouble afoot?" she asked, taking down a tin of herbs.

The scent of the little cottage was a revelation to Hawthorne, a blend of everything from mint, to anise, to roses and honey. Margaret could probably list twenty different aromas without trying.

"We've paid a call on Bancroft," Margaret said, unpinning her bonnet. "The visit went well, which was both lovely and awful. I don't want my girls settling in at Summerfield. I want my girls home."

A look passed between the women that put Hawthorne in mind of the glances exchanged between Greta and Adriana. Someday, he and Margaret would be able to communicate like that, but not with secrets lying between them and Bancroft getting up to mischief.

"We both want the children home," he said, "and the girls want to be home."

"Bancroft has London guests." Margaret hung her bonnet on a hook on the back of the door. "He's courting a Miss Emily Pepper, and I regret to admit that she seems kind and intelligent."

"You'd rather she were a horror?" Hannah asked, setting out tea cups with a pattern of blue flowers glazed around the rim.

"Margaret would rather Miss Pepper not be so fabulously wealthy," Hawthorne said.

Across the cottage, Margaret paused before a portrait that looked to have been done in Oak's hand. The framing was rough wood, which suited the rustic fellow portrayed. Hannah's grandson Lucas had been a merry, friendly youth, taken too soon, and...

An odd shiver passed over Hawthorne's nape. He knew those eyes, knew that impish smile, but where...?

The kettle sang, and Hannah poured the water into the teapot, then set out a strainer, sugar, honey, and milk. "Are we in the mood for biscuits?"

"Made with butter?" Margaret asked, though what that had to do with anything, Hawthorne did not know.

"Yes, missy." Hannah set another tin on the table. "Made with butter. Some people like to experiment with a recipe from time to time."

"I'd like to talk to you about experimenting," Hawthorne said, "with medications."

"Sit." Hannah patted a chair. "Have a spot of chamomile tea, and we can chat all you like."

Hawthorne held the ladies' chairs, then took his place at the little table. Maybe the scent of the herbs was soothing his temper. Maybe the notion that he was getting closer to the truth gave him patience. He liked this place, liked it better than the high ceilings and gilt pier glasses at Dorning Hall.

Hannah poured the tea, the pot handle wrapped in a towel. "You are trying to tell yourself that the girls will manage at Summerfield if they must," she said. "I do not accord Bancroft nearly that much goodwill where another's interests are involved. He'll send the children off to spite you, Margaret. He's that hard-hearted."

She put a lump of sugar into Margaret's cup. "How do you like your tea, young Hawthorne?"

"Perhaps a drop of honey?"

"Good choice. Have a few biscuits." Hannah poured out for herself. "You too, Margaret. I can see you trying to make peace with a bad fate. You're good at that."

Margaret cradled her tea cup in her hands. "Sometimes we have to be."

"Not this time," Hawthorne said, "not if I have anything to say to it. Tell me about foxglove, ladies, and about Charles Summerfield's illness."

Margaret hunched over her tea cup and remained silent.

"The case was simple enough," Hannah said. "He had the classic symptoms of dropsy. Failing energy, could not get his breath, swelling in the face, hands, feet... such a shame in a decent young man. Margaret put him on a regular dose of foxglove dissolved in hot water, and his symptoms subsided. Showed those London doctors a thing or two."

"Is foxglove a cure?"

Margaret passed him a biscuit. "For some people, it apparently is, at least for a time. Not for Charles. He eventually got less and less relief from the same dose. We increased it, and again, some relief for some time."

"He lived for years the London doctors said he'd never have," Hannah added. "Good years, mostly comfortable because Margaret took such good care of him."

"He took care of me, too, Hannah, and of the girls."

"What happens when the foxglove stops working?" Hawthorne asked. The biscuits were simply butter biscuits with a touch of cinnamon, a perfect complement to the chamomile brew, though as to that, the tea wasn't simply an infusion of chamomile. Other flavors subtly complemented the chamomile, turning the tea into a rich pleasure.

"For Charles, the medication still hadn't ceased giving some benefit," Margaret said, "not entirely. Charles could get out of bed most days. He could still manage the coach ride to Summerfield from Summerton on a good day."

"But he was losing ground," Hannah said. "I don't think it much bothered him, except that he'd be leaving Margaret and the girls. His affairs were in order—he told me that himself—but he had a sweet life, and leaving it had to be a sorrow for him."

Hawthorne helped himself to another biscuit. "He wasn't ready to go, then?"

Margaret looked up from her tea. "No. He wasn't, not really, and I wasn't ready to let him go, but with a bad heart, the timing is always unpredictable. A patient can appear to be improving, and then pass away while enjoying a quiet hour at the end of the day. Another patient looks to be at death's door, but then rallies and can resume life at a normal pace."

"Does foxglove ever become dangerous? Margaret has mentioned that the plant is poisonous, but is the medication ever a hazard to the patient's health?"

"Yes," Hannah said when Margaret remained quiet. "Foxglove is both angel and devil. The difference between a dose that takes down the swelling and a dose that causes bellyaches and worse is perilously close. For some people, those two overlap."

"How do you manage such a medicine?"

Margaret rose from the table. "You experiment. You start with a small frequent dose and level off as soon as the symptoms of dropsy begin to subside. For the first year of our marriage, Charles never once had ill effects from the drug."

"And then?"

She shifted to study the portrait again, her back to Hawthorne. "Then it became more difficult. Charles needed a higher dose, but we had to space them farther apart, or his belly troubled him, his heart fluttered, and his head hurt. As time went on, the balancing became delicate, but Charles was stoic, and when he argued with me, wanting more of the drug despite evidence the dose was too high, I argued back until he saw reason. Misery can make even the most sensible man difficult."

Hawthorne went to stand behind her. "How do you think Charles would have reacted if, instead of your sensible, knowledgeable, conscientious self to speak reason to him, he instead had a brother pouring the medication down his throat, dose after dose?"

Margaret turned. "Such a course would have resulted in suffering, if not death. Once the medicine has begun causing mischief, the only thing to do is withhold it until the patient's condition improves. That's well documented in the medical literature, and Hannah and I have both seen cases where the medication must be temporarily stopped."

Hannah bit into a biscuit. "So Bancroft killed his brother? Can't say that surprises me."

Margaret listed into Hawthorne, her weight sagging against his chest. "Bancroft is lazy, selfish, underhanded, mean, and greedy, but he wouldn't.... he didn't..." She looked up at Hawthorne. "Bancroft said the medicine was worthless, that Charles should have stuck to the cold baths and plasters prescribed by the physicians."

The hurt in her eyes, the self-doubt, nearly had Hawthorne galloping back to Summerfield to call Bancroft out.

"Bancroft told you that you killed Charles, didn't he? Not your medications, but you, personally. Your care." A pained silence bloomed while Hawthorne wrapped Margaret in his embrace. If she dissembled on this point, he'd... He'd be patient and understanding and try again and again until the truth was exposed.

"After the funeral service," Margaret said quietly. "The men were going off to see to the burial. The women were coming back to Summerfield House to lay out the food. Bancroft helped me into the carriage and told me—plain as the crepe on the coach windows—that I killed my husband, and I had best put aside any notion of *dabbling* with herbs ever again. I could not believe my ears. I wasn't even with Charles when he died, but Bancroft is good at intimidation."

"And you've been waiting for him to renew that threat ever since."

"He could," Margaret said, subsiding into her chair. "He could easily have an inquest called. The local squires may not respect him, but they don't cross him, and for the most part, they serve as our magistrates."

Hawthorne sat next to her and took her hand, which was cool in his. "And you hoped that marrying me might at least give Bancroft something to think about before he grew too confident with his schemes. He was with Charles when Charles died, or under the same roof. I do not believe Bancroft intended to kill his brother, but he at least hastened Charles's death."

Hannah poured herself more tea. "What happened?"

"Charles apparently had a bad day. He asked for more medication in the evening, and Bancroft gave it to him—several doses in quick succession. Charles did not last the night."

"He wouldn't have," Hannah said. "Most patients can survive a dose or two beyond what's helpful, but not several nearly at once. Even a healthy man could succumb to that much foxglove."

"Oh, my poor Charles." Margaret bowed her head. "My poor, dear, ailing... I should not have let him go to Summerfield without me, but being able to travel on his own, to see to his various properties without me fussing at him and reminding him... I should not... Oh God. God help me. God..."

Hawthorne scooted his chair closer and wrapped an arm around her. She began to weep, then to keen and sob. Hannah rose, patted Hawthorne's shoulder, and went out the front door, while Margaret's tears wet his shirt.

She cried a good, long, loud, messy while. Hawthorne held her until she was sitting in his lap, arms around his neck, her nose pressed to his throat.

"Bancroft told me I married a murderess," Hawthorne said,

stroking Margaret's hair. "Told me to be careful around the tisanes. I have never been as tempted to do a man violence as I was in that moment."

"Good," Margaret said, her voice raspy. "He deserves a sound thrashing. When Charles grew cross, he became impatient. He would have demanded more of the medication, but the Summerton staff knew to fetch me when that happened. You're sure Bancroft didn't kill Charles on purpose?"

"I am certain he did not, but Charles is just as dead, isn't he? And Bancroft inherited the bulk of the estate."

Margaret raised a pink, blotchy countenance to Hawthorne, then extricated herself to take her own chair. "I must look a fright."

Hawthorne kissed her. "I tell you that you not only had nothing to do with your husband's death, but that you've been unfairly bullied by the man who did send Charles to his reward, and your first reaction is to cry for Bancroft's *other* victim. I love you, Margaret Dorning, especially when you look a fright, especially when your hair is coming undone, especially when you trust me to guard your dignity in a moment of heartbreak."

She tucked a lock of hair behind her ear. "Foxglove poisoning is a bad way to go, Hawthorne, usually. Maybe for Charles it was quick, because he was so weak, but still..."

Was she blushing? Her splotchy complexion made it hard to tell. "Bancroft was half-seas over when he recounted his actions, and as you said, he doesn't appear to have known how dangerous the medication could be. Is this why you haven't fought him yet for the girls?"

Margaret nodded, took a sip of her tea, and chose a biscuit. "Bancroft's accusation—that I was responsible for Charles's death—hung in the back of my mind like the sword of Damocles. He still hasn't renewed his threat outright, but one doesn't forget being labeled a medical incompetent. I feel relieved, angry, disoriented... I don't know what I feel."

Hawthorne felt tremendous admiration for his wife's fortitude, and rage at Bancroft for his sheer meanness. Charles Summerfield had gained years of good, loving life thanks to Margaret. Rather than be grateful that his brother's suffering had been eased, Bancroft had resented Charles's marriage. Not a man worthy of the term *brother*.

Mostly, though, Hawthorne was in the throes of a determination so powerful as to make the way before him as clear as a scythed row down the center of a ripe hayfield.

"The children will come home to us on Friday," he said. "Send Miss Fenner a note to see to the packing on Friday morning."

"You're certain? You don't want to wait until your brother returns from London?"

His brother, *the earl*. "I do not. I've asked Grey to come back to Dorning Hall, but he has not replied to my letter."

"So we wait until Friday," Margaret said. "I never knew waiting would take such courage." She rose and collected the tea cups and plates onto a plain wooden tray, then set the tray on the counter by the window. Her herbal bore a resemblance to this cottage, now that Hawthorne studied the appointments, probably as close to a home as she'd known growing up.

Hawthorne wrapped her in his arms, and she tucked close. "You have been so brave for so long," he said. "But this time, your bravery got you married to *me*. That means you don't have to deal with these consequences alone."

She returned the embrace, the feel of her perfect in his arms. She had put down a heavy burden of self-doubt and sadness, and Hawthorne could feel the difference in her.

"I love you too, Hawthorne Dorning."

As much as he rejoiced to hear those words, as much as they meant to him, that was not all he'd hoped to hear from her. He kissed her and led her out to the gig, but on the journey back to Summerton, Margaret said nothing more.

# CHAPTER TWENTY-FOUR

"From your brother Valerian." Margaret passed Hawthorne the note, so weary she could have gone straight up to bed. She was appalled at Bancroft's stupidity and his sheer nastiness, also terribly relieved to know that his threats regarding Charles's death amounted to nothing.

Less than nothing, because Bancroft himself had unwittingly hastened Charles's demise. God help Miss Pepper if she became Mrs. Bancroft Summerfield.

"Valerian asks for the pleasure of my company at Dorning Hall." Hawthorne took Margaret's cloak and hung it on a peg near the front door, then unpinned her hat.

She let him undress her as if she were a tired child, sliding her gloves off and dropping them in the crown of her bonnet. "You don't want to go?" she asked.

"If somebody had an accident in the hayfield, I'd go, but a mere summons..." He passed her the note. "No. Not now. They can learn to wait."

*Join us at the Hall at your earliest convenience. Much to discuss. V.*

"Rather cryptic, but it doesn't sound urgent." Hawthorne wasn't muttering about returning to his blasted hayfield either, which was fortunate. Margaret had taken comfort simply from sitting beside him in the gig, and she wasn't ready to lose sight of him.

He unbuttoned his coat and hung it on the peg that had become dedicated to his garments.

"I want to take you upstairs," he said, "and make love to you until we're both exhausted and at peace. Spending time at Summerfield was less than pleasurable, though I'm glad the girls are well."

"They are well," Margaret said, taking off his hat and brushing her fingers through his hair. "They are not happy."

Neither was she, exactly. Relieved, of course. Very relieved. Angry with Bancroft, though her anger was edged with both physical and emotional exhaustion. How dare Bancroft behave so wretchedly? So stupidly? She could not make her mind focus on what was to be done next, though.

"Did you really mean you want to go upstairs with me, Hawthorne?"

He brushed his thumb over her lips, a casual intimacy that nonetheless sent desire trickling past the welter of emotions the day had brought.

"I meant it. Supper isn't for some time."

"Send a note to your brothers to meet you here in two hours, then. If they have something important to say, we can both hear it."

Hawthorne took her hand and kissed her fingers. "I like that idea. I like it a lot. They can gallop across the fields at my summons for a change. Take me upstairs, Mrs. Dorning. I've missed you."

"I've missed you too." Margaret did take him upstairs, leading him by the hand and ignoring a smiling Higgins when they passed her in the upstairs corridor.

Marriage to Hawthorne was proving more complicated and more rewarding than Margaret had envisioned. He was a good man, putting her in mind of Charles. Both of her husbands were honorable, devoted to family, courageous in a quiet way, and practical.

But, oh, Hawthorne was so blessedly robust. Margaret helped

him out of his clothes, and he did the same for her, though she left her shift on. Some habits would take time to conquer. Maybe by candlelight…

"Come to bed," Hawthorne said, scooping her into his arms. "We are married, and by God it's time we enjoyed some of that bliss everybody's always snickering about." He tossed her onto the mattress as if she weighed no more than a velvet pillow, then came down over her and nuzzled her temple. "I wanted to kill Bancroft. Wanted to wrap my hands around his skinny neck and watch him gasp for air, but I thought you'd disapprove."

"Not entirely, but we must be mindful of the example we set for the children. Nonetheless, I appreciate the sentiment that—kiss me again."

Hawthorne obliged, though the dratted man had stores of patience that made Margaret forget all about her trying day. She kissed him back, reveling in the sheer delight of being private with her husband. Hawthorne was spectacularly aroused in no time—a *fine* quality in a husband—and then Margaret got the inspiration to tickle him.

To laugh and love felt wonderful. To join her body to his and let the glory of erotic pleasure eclipse all else was a joy beyond description. She had not known pleasure could be so exuberant and lusty, had not foreseen that physical intimacy could be at once sublime and simply human. When she lay panting on Hawthorne's chest—the tickling had escalated to wrestling—she found she was indeed exhausted and at peace.

Almost.

Hawthorne drew patterns on her back, his breathing a gentle tide beneath her. "I should get dressed," he said. "Tell me to get dressed."

"What's the rush?" The rhythm of his breathing, full and deep, slow and calm, lulled her toward sleep. And toward profound gratitude for the man she'd married.

"We have serious matters to discuss, my dear, and I'm to summon my brothers as well. If I don't summon them, they might well come calling uninvited, and the teasing we will endure if we're caught literally napping..."

"Not teasing." Margaret kissed her husband's brow. "Envy. They will be so envious of us, they will gallop off to find spouses of their own. I do love you, Hawthorne. Very much."

She could make that admission while he was caressing her back, her cheek pressed to his. She bid a silent farewell, not to Charles's memory, but to the shadows on that memory that had prevented her from proper grieving and from letting go.

"I love you, too, Margaret-mine, but I meant what I said when I referred to serious matters that must be discussed."

Margaret sat up, hoping to see humor lurking in her husband's eyes, but no teasing light leavened his words. "We've discussed accidental death and even murder, Hawthorne. What could be more serious than that?"

He gathered her close, so they were again skin to skin. "I'll tell you what could be more serious than murder." He put his lips near her ear. "Motherhood."

$\sim$

HAWTHORNE FELT the shock of the word—*motherhood*—go through Margaret as a shiver. He drew the covers up over her and prayed for fortitude.

"Greta has her papa's eyes and his smile," he said. "What I cannot puzzle out is how she came to be called your niece rather than your daughter."

A fraught silence gathered, while Hawthorne traced a four-leaf clover on Margaret's back.

"Lucas died without knowing I was expecting."

"I'm sorry." How much loss was one woman to endure? "How did he die?"

"Measles. I had measles as a child. I recovered. Lucas was an adult, in the pink of health, but the disease progressed to lung fever, and there was no saving him. It's worse for babies and adults, apparently. I was so upset, so surprised and unprepared. I did not realize that I had conceived until the situation became obvious even to me. Lucas told me I could not conceive, not from a few encounters, and I was too embarrassed to ask Hannah for particulars..."

Perhaps Lucas had been that ignorant, but Hawthorne doubted it. Hannah would likely have provided a better education than that to her grandson.

"But you did conceive."

Margaret nodded, her hair tickling Hawthorne's chin. "Charles came upon me out gathering spearmint. I was crying—the scent of spearmint still makes me sad—because I missed Lucas, because I did not know what to do, because soon everybody would know what a fool I had been. I had little in the way of means to support a child, and I felt... I was tired all the time, food had no appeal, and my aunt was threatening to cast me out."

"The same aunt who didn't teach you enough basic biology to protect yourself from handsome young men—that aunt?"

For the first time since they'd embarked on this topic, Margaret peered at Hawthorne. "You blame her for that?"

*I certainly don't blame you.* "You had no papa, no brothers, not even cousins who might have protected you from charming bounders. Of all young women, you should have been equipped with a factual understanding of conception. Maybe Lucas Weller meant to marry you, but he neglected to tend to that detail before he went walking with you in the beechwood, didn't he? And from what I recall, Lucas had only a laborer's skills, though he could have learned medicine from Hannah, as you did."

"He was learning, and he was a hard worker."

What the hell good, what damned good at all, was a young man's capacity for hard work when he'd left a woman alone to fend for herself and for a child she hadn't known could come along?

"My ignorance is no excuse," Margaret said. "I should not have let Lucas so much as kiss me. I knew better."

"For all your herbal expertise, you apparently knew next to nothing. Tell me about Greta."

Margaret rolled away so she lay beside Hawthorne on the bed. "The London doctors told Charles that he hadn't long to live. I knew him because he consulted with Hannah regularly, and when he proposed marriage—his name in exchange for my medical care—the bargain seemed heaven-sent. The only difficulty was that Greta would arrive at such a time that Charles would have been away in London when she was conceived. Then too, Charles did not expect to live long enough to be any sort of father to her. His sister was expecting, and placing Greta with her seemed like an ideal solution."

Hawthorne did not care for this heaven-sent, ideal solution at all. "Charles talked you into the notion that Adriana and Greta could be his sister's twins." Why not allow the mother and child to remain together, for God's sake?

But then, Charles had been facing death, and Margaret would have suffered all manner of judgment if it had become known she'd married Charles while carrying another man's child.

"Charles's sister had been trying for years to start a family," Margaret said. "She leaped at the chance to become a mother twice over, and I hadn't the backbone to insist that Charles give me his name and accept a cuckold's horns at the same time. His illness robbed him of much dignity, and to be honest, my feelings regarding a baby were mixed. I can see in hindsight that I was infatuated with Lucas—only infatuated—and for a time, I was infuriated with him too."

Hawthorne longed to take Margaret in his arms, but settled for linking his hand with hers beneath the covers. "Your feelings aren't mixed now. You would die for those children."

She turned on her side so she faced him. "I want to steal them away and disappear to darkest Peru with them, Hawthorne. I let Greta go once, and it nearly killed me. We had a few months together while Charles's sister finished her confinement, but before Greta could crawl, I had to leave her. I hate that. I hate knowing I left her in another's care when I was on hand to love her, but now Adriana has been left with me and has no mama at all."

"They have you. They both have you." *And you all have me.*

Margaret withdrew her hand from his. "How did you know?"

"You will recall that I did not come to our union in a state of ignorant chastity."

That earned him a small smile. "Thank the Deity for that."

"Thank a certain Oxford widow, among others. Mrs. Plumley was a mother. She was not a widow. Childbearing can change a woman's body."

"But I keep my shift..." Margaret closed her eyes. "In the herbal. You took off my shift, and I forgot to slip it back on before I left the bed. You saw the marks on my belly."

"I saw all of you, naked as the day you arrived in the world. A more fetching sight I have yet to behold."

She sat up, tucking the sheet under her arms. "I've lied to you, Hawthorne. Married you under false pretenses. I am sorry for that, but I didn't think you'd wed a woman who'd conceived an illegitimate child and given that child to another to raise. Your family has significant consequence, while I'm... I married above my station, both times." She folded the sheet in a careful crease. "Are you angry?"

Hawthorne sat up too, so they both had their backs to the headboard. "I am enraged."

She ducked her head. "You are entitled to your temper. If you'd like to establish your household at the Dorning Hall steward's cottage, I will understand, but I hope that the girls—"

A soft tap on the door to the sitting room adjacent to the bedroom had Margaret drawing the sheet up higher.

"Go away!" Hawthorne bellowed. "Mrs. Dorning is resting."

"Callers, sir. Your brothers are here."

Margaret flopped back against the pillows. "Higgins would not disturb us unless your brothers were being insistent."

"They are always insistent, but you and I are not done with the discussion. Nobody will be moving anywhere just yet, *Mrs. Dorning.*

Our first priority is to return the children to Summerton, and for that, my brothers might be of some use."

She was off the bed before he could kiss her, and maybe that was for the best. Valerian and Oak would be delighted that Hawthorne and his new wife were unable to immediately receive callers in the middle of the afternoon, but given the day's events, Hawthorne was not in the mood to be teased.

"THE PHYSICIANS SAID a change of air would do you good," Emily said. "The trip down here has left you more exhausted than you were in London."

Papa watched her pace, his expression bemused. When had he grown so pale? The afternoon sun slanting into the guest parlor revealed not only dust on the piano, but a further decline in Papa's health.

"Stop fretting, Daughter. Anybody would need time to recover from more than a hundred miles of the king's highways."

No, they would not. Not when those hundred miles were taken at a snail's pace in the most luxurious traveling coach ever commissioned.

*Papa is losing ground, and I am losing my wits.* "So now that we're here, what do you think of Summerfield?"

"The acreage is considerable, the neighborhood pretty. The house is structurally sound, and you've the money to kit it out any way you please."

Emily had the money to kit out half the country manors in England however she pleased, but she had only the one father.

"The steward is evasive when I ask him about marling, crop rotation, tenancies, and the like."

Papa shifted as if uncomfortable, though the sofa was well upholstered. "Hartley is a man, in case that detail eluded your notice. He's probably unused to females interrogating him. If ever a woman was suited to the post of magistrate, you are she."

Emily stuffed a pillow behind Papa's back. "I am not inclined to take on Summerfield." Papa believed that land was the bridge that, when crossed, could make a cit into a squire. In Emily's experience, a cit with a huge country estate was a laughingstock, at best.

"You have turned up your pretty nose at the past four possibilities I have paraded past you, Emily Catherine. Is your objection to the property or to Bancroft Summerfield?"

She took the place beside her father on the sofa. "Both. The front drive needs a fresh load of shells if the ruts and pits aren't to become worse. The growing season is well under way, and he hasn't even finished shearing. I went riding with him this morning, and I can tell you his hedges are overgrown, his ditches haven't been cleared in several years, and his tenant cottages need repairs."

That bothered Emily. The tenants could not by law make their own repairs to a rental property, and those families had children. A smoking chimney, a persistent draft, a leak that encouraged mold... Those evils were to be expected in London slums, not in the "pretty" countryside.

What bothered her even more was her conversation with Margaret Dorning.

"Child, you want too much," Papa said. "You want a perfectly run estate that yet turns a healthy profit, but I tell you, that's not how farming works. The land is a jealous mistress. She will take all of your profits and give you a flood or drought in return. A prudent man makes only those improvements necessary to wrest a good crop from his acres, and he saves his coin for the lean years. Bancroft is shrewd enough to see how intelligent you are and lazy enough to let you have the running of the place. You can manage him and Summerfield easily."

When had life come to such a pass that Emily must consign herself to a shrewd, lazy husband? "I never aspired to be a country squire's unpaid steward or his intimate convenience. You and Mama were a love match. Is it too much to ask that I esteem my husband?"

Papa patted her hand, his fingers cold against her knuckles. "Such blunt speech won't win you any man's regard. You will be miserable married to a fellow you cannot manage, and Bancroft is all but begging for a female to put him to rights. He's already notorious for leaving Town without paying his gambling debts. Next, he'll mortgage this property and end his days in debtors' prison unless an obliging horse tosses him headfirst into a ditch betimes."

"And for the pleasure of letting him raid my settlements, I'm to take on the job of nannying a grown man and raising his children?"

Valerian Dorning sprang to mind, a younger son without property or means. He would never turn into a sot, much less end his days in debtors' prison or leave a debt of honor unpaid. Bancroft had been given so much, and he was doing so little with it. He was handsome, but fortune hunters were supposed to be handsome.

Papa said nothing. Emily at first thought he was nodding off, which had begun to happen since coming to Dorset. He had taken to sitting in the garden when the children exercised the dog, and invariably, the hound greeted him and ended up reclining at Papa's feet.

His gaze went to the window, where a beautiful spring day was ripening into its afternoon glory.

"Emily, we are running out of time. My businesses are in the hands of good managers, and I know they will consult with you on any major decisions, but you—my most precious daughter—cannot wait for a perfect match. Bancroft can frolic with your settlements all he pleases, and you will never know want. The lawyers will keep him in check to that extent. As an unmarried heiress, you are vulnerable. I would like to go to my reward at peace in the knowledge that your situation has been settled."

Emily subsided onto the piano bench rather than debate the truth. If Papa himself acknowledged his ill health, arguing with him would be unkind and a waste of breath.

But, oh, to lose him. To lose the only man who treated her as if she had half a brain, the only man she could trust to take her interests to heart. And now he, too, was counseling her to compromise, to settle, to yoke herself to a husband whose greatest claim was that she and her lawyers could manage him.

"I will think about your advice, Papa, but you are wrong. You say I can be happy only with a man I can manage, as a governess manages an unruly toddler. I suspect the opposite is true: I can never be happy with a man I must manage, and surely Bancroft Summerfield is such a creature."

A dog barked in the garden, a happy, exuberant noise suggesting Captain was playing tag with the children.

"The faithful hound is exercising with his charges again," Papa said, pushing to the edge of the sofa cushion and then to his feet. He kept hold of the arm of the sofa for a moment before straightening. "Perhaps you'd fetch my cane and see me to the garden. I've a mind to sit in the sun for a bit."

Emily complied, and as she offered her father her arm for the journey down the terrace steps, she considered Margaret Dorning's words. Bancroft did not love the beautiful, lively, wonderful children throwing a stick for the dog. He did not love his estate. He had affirmatively misrepresented his sister-in-law, and he didn't care enough for his sheep to see them comfortably shorn as hot weather approached.

Emily seated Papa on a sunny bench, then continued on to the folly at the foot of the garden. The day was lovely, not quite hot as long as the breeze blew, and the scent of scythed grass added a pleasant tang to the air.

"I cannot manage a fool who loves only himself," Emily muttered when she had the privacy to express herself honestly.

And yet, where would that leave the children if Bancroft refused to send them back to their aunt and Emily declined to become Mrs. Bancroft Summerfield? Was she to accept his proposal for the sake of a pair of girls she barely knew?

Maybe. They were very dear, and very small, and had neither mama nor papa to love and protect them.

The dog snatched up the stick Miss Fenner had pitched over the greening flowerbeds and loped off with it to drop his treasure at Papa's feet. Papa made no move to pick it up, but remained, chin on chest, dozing in the brilliant sunshine.

# CHAPTER TWENTY-FIVE

Hawthorne was prepared for Oak and Valerian to greet him in the family parlor. Instead, the room was crowded with Dornings.

Grey, Earl of Casriel, looking natty but tired, occupied the reading chair. Valerian lounged by the window, Oak examined the portrait over the mantel—three small children seated on some steps—and Sycamore was sniffing the stoppers of each decanter on the sideboard.

"My dear," Hawthorne said, taking Margaret by the hand and drawing her into the room, "we've been invaded. Gentlemen, may I present to you my wife, Mrs. Margaret Mallory Summerfield Dorning. I will soundly thrash any brother who gives my Margaret cause to regret marrying me."

In order of age, each brother bowed over her hand. Sycamore had put on muscle during his sojourn in London, and he'd acquired a modicum of manners too. Before leaving Dorning Hall for the greater world, he would have sampled the contents of the decanters without benefit of a glass.

"Mrs. Dorning," Sycamore said, "a pleasure. If yonder handsome lummox gives you any cause to regret marrying him, you may apply to any of us, and we'll apply our fists to his person. Works a treat every time."

"He means that," Hawthorne said, cuffing Sycamore on the back of the head.

"Shall I ring for tea?" Margaret asked. "And some sandwiches too, I think."

"I have a special power." Sycamore finally released Margaret's hand. "I can make sandwiches disappear. I'll demonstrate if you order us a tray."

"But can you shut your mouth for five minutes?" Valerian mused. "Let's find out, shall we?"

Oak consulted his pocket watch. "Starting now."

Grey and Sycamore were in riding attire, while Valerian and Oak looked like they'd come in from the fields and done a cursory washing up.

"My brothers have a unique charm," Hawthorne said, "best enjoyed in small doses."

"Small, frequent doses," Valerian said. "Might we be seated? Several days of haying have heightened my appreciation for any cushioned surface."

"Heightened your need for a bath too," Sycamore said.

"Seventeen seconds." Oak snapped his watch closed. "Cam, London has not been a good influence. You used to be able to go twenty consecutive seconds without sounding off. We must assist you to regain the self-restraint you've lost."

Hawthorne had missed Sycamore, the youngest of the brood, and worried for him. He'd also missed Grey and, in a different sense, worried for him, too, but at the present moment, all he wanted was for his brothers to state their business and leave him and Margaret to finish the conversation they'd started upstairs.

"Let's be seated, shall we?" Hawthorne suggested.

The room held just enough furniture to accommodate six adults. Margaret took one of the reading chairs, Grey the other. Oak, Valerian, and Sycamore occupied the sofa, and Hawthorne took the chair from behind the escritoire and set it next to Margaret's seat.

"I received your letter," Casriel said. "At the risk of making a bad impression before the new Mrs. Dorning, I will eschew the pleasantries. How do matters stand with Bancroft Summerfield?"

"You wrote to your brothers?" Margaret asked.

"To inform us of the happy news," Casriel replied, "so we might welcome you to the family. My countess will follow me down from London with our brother Ash as her escort, and Dorning Hall will host a proper ball in your honor. I gather a few details need tending to first."

Bancroft Summerfield would have an apoplexy to hear himself referred to as a detail in that bored drawl.

"Bancroft invited Margaret's nieces for a visit," Hawthorne said, taking his wife's hand. "His aims are twofold. First, he seeks to impress a potential bride with his avuncular devotion. Second, he is moving into position to add the girls to his household so he can plunder their fortunes without any interference from me or Margaret. We don't particularly care about the fortune. We will have the girls back, come what may."

"You should care about the fortune," Casriel observed. "When the girls are young ladies, those fortunes could be the difference between choosing a fine young man for a spouse, or facing altogether different options."

"The fortunes matter," Valerian said, shooting his cuffs. "Oak?"

"Bancroft has wealth of his own. He cannot be permitted to steal from orphans. Bad form. We take a dim view of bad form."

Hawthorne kissed Margaret's knuckles. "Margaret, what have you to say?"

She looked bewildered.

"You state your opinion," Sycamore said. "You air your perspective in the company of family, and if you're full of wrong-headed notions, we'll convince you to see the error of your ways. Or Hawthorne will. He's obnoxiously reasonable when a fellow wants to burn down the tavern or turn a neighbor's cattle loose. Has no flair for drama whatsoever."

"I want the girls home and home to stay," Margaret said. "The funds are important, but not nearly so important as having the children home, where they are loved and protected."

"Then we don't bargain away their inheritance," Hawthorne said, not that he'd been considering such a course. With his brothers on hand, though, wading through discussion of a problem was part of ensuring that the solution chosen had the support of all involved.

"I could steal the little dears," Sycamore said. "Climb into the nursery and spirit them away in the dead of night."

"Captain would chew you to bits before you got halfway through the window," Hawthorne said, "though we appreciate the sentiment."

"A show of force?" Valerian suggested. "Pound the miserable sod —I mean, fellow to a pulp? Let him know we look after our own?"

Hawthorne heard in that suggestion a veiled apology for disloyal conduct in the hay field.

"No pounding," Margaret said. "He could hit back in a lawsuit."

Oak studied the ceiling, as if entreating the heavens for patience. "More bad form."

The trays arrived—three of them—and Hawthorne's brothers did what Dornings did best, demolishing the food as quickly as good manners allowed. The puzzle of how to put Bancroft in his place once and for all apparently worked up prodigious appetites.

Hawthorne passed Margaret a sandwich. "Eat something. They won't leave enough for a pair of crows to fight over."

"Are we fighting, Hawthorne?" Her quiet question passed unnoticed by the Vandals ransacking the trays.

"No, nor will we. Not about the situation that led to you marrying Charles. You managed as best you could, and I'm benefitting from your choices."

"Is it as simple as that?"

Probably not, and complications would arise as the years unfolded. Greta was legally a cousin to Adriana, born to Mrs.

Charles Summerfield during her marriage to Adriana's uncle. In reality, the girls shared no blood relation, and yet, they believed themselves to be sisters. The potential for hurt feelings and burdensome secrets was significant.

And yet... "Did you mean what you said upstairs?" Hawthorne asked.

"About?"

He leaned near enough to whisper. "Your regard for me."

She nodded. "Did you mean it? When you said the same thing about me?"

"Of course I meant it." He bussed her cheek, optimism blooming in the face of long odds. "We'll contrive, Margaret-mine. Come fire, flood, famine, or family, if we care for one another, we shall contrive."

"No whispering," Sycamore called. "Grey and Beatitude are forever whispering and smiling, and it's enough to make one bilious. These are good biscuits. Don't suppose the kitchen has any more?"

"His name should have been Locust," Valerian said, snatching the last biscuit from the tray. "As in plague of, not the tree."

"Honey Locust Dorning," Sycamore replied, plucking the biscuit from Valerian's hand. "Just a growing boy."

Oak smacked him and took the biscuit, breaking it in half and sharing it with Valerian.

"In answer to the question you are too much of a lady to ask," Hawthorne said, "yes, they are always like this, but we are married now, Margaret. 'Your brothers are disgraceful' is not grounds for an annulment. What's to be done about Bancroft?"

Hawthorne had a few ideas, and he was prepared to announce them, but first he'd allow his brothers to finish spouting their nonsense.

"If I might make a suggestion?" Margaret said.

The bantering and near-brawling stopped. "Please," Casriel said. "We are all ears."

Of course they were, now that the food was gone.

"We could simply retrieve the girls on Friday," Margaret said.

"March in, smiles at the ready, collect the girls, and thank Bancroft for his hospitality."

"And six weeks from now," Valerian said, "what's to stop him from doing the same thing, particularly when he has acquired a *wealthy, charming, pretty sensible* wife—whom he does not deserve and whose funds will make Bancroft an even better choice of guardian for the children?"

"Precisely," Margaret said, "so what we need is a means of striking where Bancroft is vulnerable. He needs funds. The girls, like Miss Pepper, are a means to that end. But doesn't Bancroft's lack of funds put him at a disadvantage as well?"

Brilliant woman. She'd anticipated the direction of Hawthorne's own plans.

"More biscuits, please," Sycamore said. "Plotting a bounder's comeuppance is hungry work."

He winked at Hawthorne, and the last vestige of doubt fell from Hawthorne's heart. Bancroft's scheme was doomed, and the girls would soon be home.

"I MARRIED A BRILLIANT MAN," Margaret said when Hawthorne's brothers had been sent on their way.

"You married a man with a lot of family," Hawthorne replied. "I was surprised to see Casriel and Sycamore."

"They love you." Margaret looped her arms around Hawthorne's waist, leaning into the solid wonderfulness of him. "I love you." She liked saying the words, liked feeling the warmth in her heart that even the thought of Hawthorne brought. Wanting to trust someone, longing to trust them, was not the same at all as having that trust simply given, whole and unasked for, to keep forever.

"I love you too, Mrs. Dorning. Do you realize Casriel didn't once bring up his damned botanical scheme?"

"He didn't mention haying either, or shearing, or the plans to demolish a wing of the Hall. I expected him to be, I don't know, more imposing."

Hawthorne wandered with her from the front door back through the family parlor, which looked like it had hosted an entire village assembly. Plates, cups, saucers, table napkins, and trays littered the room, and the scent of various soaps lingered, along with the cut-grass fragrance wafting in from the hayfields. The aroma of the Dorning menfolk planning a future for the Summerfield girls.

"I think I know why Emily Pepper is considering Bancroft," Margaret said, collecting dishes onto a tray.

"Because she's kind to dumb beasts?"

Margaret had the oddest impulse to smack her husband. "Because her father is dying."

Hawthorne popped a last uneaten bite of sandwich into his mouth. "Dying? Pepper looked a little travel-weary to me, but dying?"

"He has all the symptoms of dropsy, though a liver ailment might be to blame. He's under-weight, has no energy, can't catch his breath, and is puffy about the face and hands. I suspect his ankles and feet are swollen, and he's not sleeping well." Then too, his daughter watched him with a particular sadness in her eyes.

Hawthorne drained the last of what had been Casriel's tea cup. "Can you help him?"

The question was unremarkable. Four words offered while tidying up after company, and yet, Margaret felt their impact like a powerful tonic.

"Help him?"

Hawthorne gestured with the empty tea cup. "Brew up some of that tisane you made for Charles. Foxglove leaves dissolved in hot water. Small doses at first, and so on. You knew as much about the business as Hannah Weller, if not more. Though I daresay if you could find a way to blend the tisane with the chamomile brew Hannah served... Margaret, are you well?"

She had taken the reading chair, groping for the arm as she'd lowered herself to the cushions. "I could help him."

"You gave Charles years of life he would not have had otherwise. The girls will recall him fondly, and if it hadn't been for the poor man's idiot brother—I suspect most brothers are idiots, though Bancroft wins the sweepstakes in that regard—who knows how many more years Charles might have had?"

Hawthorne moved on to another brother's tea cup, while Margaret felt an odd lightness in her chest.

"I can help him, and I *will* help him, and then Miss Pepper won't have to marry that bleating buffoon."

Hawthorne knelt before the chair, wrapped his arms around Margaret's waist, and rested his cheek against her thigh. "I doubt she'll want to have anything to do with Bancroft after Friday."

Margaret smoothed her hand over Hawthorne's hair. "Unless her father can be restored to some sort of health, she'll just settle for the next fortune hunter to come sniffing around."

"Valerian is sweet on her. He nearly came out of his chair when her name was mentioned. That Oak and Cam didn't tease him suggests his sentiments have been engaged."

How lovely this casual cuddling at the end of the afternoon was. How precious. "I haven't treated anybody for anything since Charles died. I let Bancroft intimidate me out of using my skills and alleviating what suffering I could."

"Hannah has been on hand for those truly in need."

"She's too old to march all over the shire in all weather, Hawthorne. Will you come out to the herbal with me?"

He got to his feet, his hair sticking up on one side. "The herbal with that damnably small cot?"

"We can have a large bed moved out there, but I'd like to consult my notes."

Hawthorne drew her to her feet and looped his arms over her shoulders. "You were patient with my brothers. Thank you for that."

For no reason at all, and because she absolutely had to, Margaret kissed him. He kissed her back, and then they slipped out the French doors to the terrace, and from there they walked, hand in hand, to the herbal.

~

HAWTHORNE WOKE up early on Thursday out of habit, but rather than rush off to the hayfields, he lingered over breakfast with his wife.

Actually, he lingered *before* breakfast with his wife and then again *after* breakfast. Time spent in the herbal the evening before had also resulted in some lingering with Margaret and in immediate orders to replace the cot with a proper bed.

Margaret had gone wandering over the wilds of Thorne's body, exploring every intimate hollow and shadow, until he'd forgotten the day, the month, the year, and the challenge looming at Summerfield.

Almost. The business to be conducted there on the morrow was foremost on Hawthorne's mind as he made his way to the hayfield. If he couldn't flatten Bancroft literally, he could at least take out his frustrations in hard work.

"You look rested," Casriel said. His lordship had been working with the team loading the dried hay into wagons. From there the crop would be added to the stack taking shape at the far end of the field. Oak and Valerian were forking—moving the hay from the wagons to the stack—and normally, Hawthorne would have been at the top of the stack. That hot, grueling job one of the most dangerous, because the risk of falls was greatest, but also one of the most critical.

A haystack that hadn't been properly packed and built was at risk for rot and fire.

Hawthorne finished the pear tart he'd been munching. "I look rested because I am rested. You look like you'll have a proper set of blisters by sundown. Welcome home."

"Blisters, sunburn, the occasional bee sting for variety, and a sore back that lingers for days. How one misses the splendors of the countryside."

Casriel was the most scientific pugilist of Thorne's brothers. Landing a solid blow on him was difficult, and what few punches he threw could do significant damage. Hawthorne had the sense the earl was spoiling for a fight.

Bless his misguided heart. "Margaret will disapprove if I lay you out before half the village for your whining, but she will also patch up the combatants. She has this marvelous comfrey salve that makes you want to breathe through your nose and write poetry. Takes away at least half the ills of haying under the hot sun."

Casriel rested his rake across his shoulders, all languid grace and lordly composure, despite the battered hat and lack of a coat.

"Valerian said you'd gone daft. Oak didn't argue with him, and Sycamore said you were overdue for an outburst of some sort. You summon me here posthaste, then I find you aren't even living on Dorning property anymore. You've taken on another estate to manage, acquired a wife and children, embroiled yourself in this nonsense with Bancroft, and I'm told you abandoned the hayfields for the sole purpose of paying a social call on a pair of children."

"Walk with me," Hawthorne said, for he did not want to pummel his brother to smithereens in public, but apparently, pummel him, he must. Some of the jobs Hawthorne took on were both a duty and a pleasure.

Casriel stalked at his side and left the rake by the water bucket. "Even at this hour, the shade feels good. Perhaps it will cool my temper."

Hawthorne kept walking down the hedgerow, acorns crunching beneath his boots. "And what, precisely, has you in a temper?"

"Not a what, a who. My brother—the sibling usually referred to as the sensible one—was tasked with stewarding the family acres, and he's off socializing with his wife. He's supposed to be putting a botanical business together, and yet, here we are, months later, without a single sachet to sell. He's to be a good influence on Valerian and Oak. The one has fallen top over tail for a woman he can't have. The other is threatening to take up work in some Hampshire garret.

"I leave my brothers to sort themselves out," Casriel went on, "and I come home to... sheer chaos."

And Casriel did so abhor chaos. Hawthorne was equally torn between the impulse to hug his brother and to cuff him on the back of the head, so he did both.

"What is that supposed to mean?" Casriel said, pulling away and dusting at his clothing.

"Am I the Dorning Hall steward, *my lord*? I don't believe anybody ever hired me for that post. My wages were never discussed, nor were the terms of my employment. You haven't been in the field for two hours, and you're whining, while I have been managing the haying since Papa died. There,"—he gestured at the youth driving the hay wagon—"that's Martin Weller's oldest. I was his age when I took on this job, and I have never shirked, and I am not shirking now."

"You come strolling along when the morning is half—"

"I have not finished. Margaret's children are now my children, and they are at risk of harm in a manner that is not to be borne. Your hayfields can rot, our brothers can become entangled with all the wrong women, and your botanical scheme can bugger itself until I know those girls are safe."

"Then tell me how in the hell Dorning Hall—"

"You maunder on about your damned botanical scheme, but the sachets and tisanes don't grow, harvest, or package themselves. I watched Margaret in her herbal yesterday evening, brewing up a tincture that can save a man's life. It's exacting work, taking patience and skill that require years to develop. She is better at concocting medications and blending scents than you or I have ever been at anything. If you want her expertise and my support, then you will need to hire a steward for Dorning Hall. Hartley might be interested, though he'll require supervision."

Hawthorne hadn't arisen that morning intent on delivering an ultimatum, but the words were overdue. If Margaret hadn't come along to literally pluck him from the hayfields, he would likely have gone on for years exhausting himself for the sake of grown siblings and bawling sheep.

Casriel's gaze was on the field, on the Weller lad driving the wagon slowly down the windrow.

"Is Margaret better at her simples than we are at arguing?"

"We're having a discussion," Hawthorne said. "When the fists fly, then we're having an argument. You are frustrated with the lack of progress regarding your brilliant idea—and it is a brilliant idea—but I refuse to be like our papa."

"The late earl was held in high regard, Hawthorne."

"So is the present earl, but Papa was more concerned with the damned Latin name for pennyroyal than with whether his family missed him. That's all we saw—a man always leaving, always wishing to leave, always eager to go away and find another damned exotic fern. I don't want to be that man. He wasn't happy, his family missed him, and he was a fool to value his ferns over his family."

"He had a passion," Casriel said, though the words sounded as if they'd been memorized.

"I have a passion now too," Hawthorne said, "and her name is Margaret Dorning. She gave me her perfume recipes, Grey, gave them to *us*, but I can't make sense of them any more than Margaret would know how to shear a sheep. What she does is art, and we need her, and she needs me, and that means you don't get to need me anymore."

That verbal punch connected. Hawthorne saw the impact of the blow in the consternation in Casriel's eyes.

"I can't need you as a brother?"

"Don't be an idiot. You can't need me anymore as your underpaid and overworked land steward, salvage manager, chief farmer, mender of fences, blacksmith, veterinarian, head shearer, digger of ditches, layer of hedges, et cetera, et cetera. I will help whoever you eventually hire any way that I can, and you can always need me as a brother. I will certainly prevail upon you in the same capacity, but I need to be Margaret's husband now and a papa to Greta and Adriana."

Hawthorne did not want to lose his oldest sibling's regard, did not want awkwardness or hard feelings, but how he and the earl went on was partly in Casriel's hands.

Casriel took out a flask and tipped it to his lips. "Beatitude told me I should tread lightly." He passed the flask over.

"She told you not to be an ass." The brandy was good quality, not like the watered spirits Bancroft Summerfield served. Hawthorne enjoyed a good, long pull and passed the flask back.

"Your Margaret really has a miracle salve that can soothe the injuries of haying?"

Casriel was choosing truce over discord. Wise of him, though a round of fisticuffs wouldn't have gone amiss either.

"She has such a salve, and yes, we can package it for sale. She and I discussed that last night. Margaret favors recipes with simple ingredients because they have predictable results, but those results also rest on consistency in the preparation. If, for example, you harvest a plant after a heavy rain, the recipe might not be as effective as if you harvest in the midst of a dry spell. Plants growing in a water meadow can have different properties than the same species growing in a shady wood. The same flower—"

Casriel pitched the flask at him. "You've made your point. Are you ready for tomorrow's call on Bancroft?"

"I am." Thanks in part to his brothers, who would always be his brothers. "Margaret is sending a note today asking Miss Fenner to pack as discreetly as she can."

"Then I would appreciate it if you'd take a look at the stacking job Martin Weller is doing. He's seen you do it for years, but that's not the same as earning your seal of approval."

They retrieved Casriel's rake and walked side by side across the field, and then Hawthorne climbed the ladder to the top of the haystack. The whole of the shire rolled away in gentle green undulations, while the scything crew took up a lilting, happy song suited to the rhythm of their labors.

# CHAPTER TWENTY-SIX

"Calm and cheerful," Hawthorne said, kissing Margaret's cheek as he handed her out of the coach on the Summerfield front drive.

Oddly enough, she did feel calm and cheerful. Hawthorne really could make love three times a day, or three times a night, and that was after spending hours in the fields and taking her for a family supper at Dorning Hall.

"I have never had such an escort before," she said as grooms led away the horses that Valerian, Sycamore, and Oak had ridden. Casriel had made the journey with them in the family's crested traveling coach pulled by a foursome of matched grays.

"We are retrieving our lost lambs," Hawthorne said. "Let my brothers make their little displays, for if Bancroft respects anything, it's appearances."

"And money," Margaret muttered.

"For which,"—Hawthorne winged his arm—"God be thanked."

Hawthorne had anticipated that fact, much to Margaret's relief. The Dornings individually hadn't much money, but they'd pooled resources for the sake of the children and were about to exert their collective influence in Bancroft's direction.

"Speak of the devil," Hawthorne murmured as Bancroft emerged from the front door, Miss Pepper at his side.

"If it isn't our local luminary," Bancroft said, bowing in Casriel's direction. "I do apologize for quitting Town without taking a proper leave of you, my lord. I will be sure to return this call forthwith, so we can tidy up that little matter of the water meadow." He patted Miss Pepper's arm in a manner that made Margaret's flesh crawl.

Hawthorne, looking every bit as lordly as his titled brother, bowed to Miss Pepper. "Miss Pepper. Given that Mr. Summerfield's manners are apparently on holiday, allow me to make the *requisite introductions* to several of my siblings. I believe you already know Valerian, so may I make known to you Grey, Earl of Casriel, whom it is my pleasure to call brother."

Bancroft turned a shade of pink reminiscent of wilting carnations.

"Perhaps you could order some refreshment for your guests, Bancroft," Margaret suggested when the introductions were complete. "The roads are dusty this time of year."

"I could use a lemonade," Miss Pepper said. "Shall we repair to the garden? That way, the children can join us."

Or perhaps Bancroft's complexion was more the color of the salvia in the urns on the front terrace.

"We will have ample time with the children on the coach ride home," Margaret said. "But refreshment would be appreciated. I've also brought some medication for Mr. Pepper."

"Margaret," Bancroft said, "marriage has apparently addled your wits. I have not given permission for the children to leave Summerfield, and your little potions and poisons aren't welcome here." His smile was positively venomous.

Margaret curled her hand around Hawthorne's arm and smiled back. Honestly and happily, because for once Bancroft's games were doomed to fail.

"Might we," Casriel said, studying the handle of his walking stick, "continue this discussion inside, Summerfield, like civilized adults?"

"Of course," Bancroft said, offering his arm to Miss Pepper, but that good woman had already taken the place at Valerian's side. "Inside, then. The formal parlor will do, and if the ladies would like some lemonade, then by all means, I will ring for lemonade."

His tone was a touch too jovial, his manner too bluff.

"What manner of medication have you brought for my father?" Miss Pepper asked when the assemblage had crowded into Bancroft's guest parlor. Hawthorne remained standing beside Margaret's chair, there being inadequate seats for so many guests.

"Digitalis," Margaret said. "It's made from the foxglove, and—"

"And it's the very tincture that killed my brother," Bancroft said. "Really, Margaret, must we air this linen now?"

"It's the very tincture," Margaret went on, *calmly and cheerfully*, "that gave my Charles several more years of reasonably good health. The dose must be administered carefully, under the direction of somebody knowledgeable. Unfortunately for Charles, Bancroft was not such a party, and misuse of the medication resulted while Charles was here with Bancroft at Summerfield."

Miss Pepper slanted a glance at Bancroft. "You weren't with your husband when he died, ma'am?"

"I was at Summerton with the girls," Margaret said. "Bancroft was here at Summerfield with Charles. Though I'm sure it was an accident, Bancroft had no idea how dangerous the medication can be and gave Charles far more than was safe. Bancroft admitted those sad facts to my current husband, but I don't think we need to go into that now. Charles was not doing well, and with a heart ailment, the end can come suddenly."

Bancroft was on his feet. "Margaret, I will not permit you to slander me in my own home, to cast aspersions and falsehoods on my name, when it was your confounded concoction that cost Charles his life—I have never in all my days beheld such gall. If you think I will allow a pair of innocent children to resume residence under your roof, you are much mistaken. Much mistaken, *indeed*."

He was so skilled at dancing on that edge between outrage and hurt feelings, and such a credible liar.

"Bancroft," she said gently, "it was an accident. You were trying to do as Charles requested, I'm sure. You needn't castigate yourself for a human mistake. Trained physicians are still learning how to use digitalis safely."

"But I had nothing to do—"

Casriel cocked his head. "Are you implying that my brother is a liar, Summerfield?" The earl spoke softly, even cordially.

"I'd take exception to that," Valerian said with equal good manners.

"As would I," Oak added. "Pity, when family can't be honest with each other."

"I don't particularly care if Summerfield wants to spout lies," Sycamore said. "I'll leave that to you lot, but I would prefer that those who frequent my gaming establishment pay their vowels before they leave Town on short notice. I do believe these are your notes of hand, aren't they, Summerfield?"

He withdrew a sheaf of folded papers from his pocket and set them on the low table.

Bancroft was no longer choleric, but rather, a greenish-pale color. "How did you...?"

"I am the proprietor of The Coventry," Sycamore said. "You enjoyed my hospitality for several nights not long ago, and then I find that you've decamped for an extended repairing lease at the family seat. You apparently do this every spring and rotate your custom to a different club when next you come up to Town. Fortunately for you, I've made a wedding gift of these debts to my brother and my new sister-in-law. They will doubtless be more forgiving about collecting than I would be. Was somebody about to order some lemonade?"

Sycamore's brothers beamed at him as if he'd just recited the entire royal succession perfectly. Margaret beamed at him too. The sum owed was substantial for a man who had little cash, and debts of honor were to be paid promptly. At Hawthorne's request, Sycamore had ferreted out gentlemen holding Bancroft's notes and purchased them at a discount with funds Hawthorne had put together with some aid from his brothers.

Money very well spent.

Bancroft wasn't beaming. In fact, he was looking a touch dyspeptic.

Miss Pepper picked up the piles of IOUs and leafed through them. "You left London without paying these, Bancroft?"

"I wanted to show you my home, to escort you here personally and see that all was in readiness for your visit."

"It takes two minutes to write a bank draft. How will you pay these?"

"He can't pay them," Margaret said. "Because Bancroft was late to get his sheep shorn, the prices dropped by the time he moved his wool to market. He's behind on his tenant repairs. His crop yields are down because he refuses to marl. He's fallowing a third of his acres rather than a quarter because he still won't shift to a four-crop rotation, and his drainage ditches back up after every heavy rain, so he's lost some corn to flooding."

"And," Hawthorne said, "he won't plant turnips for winter fodder."

Miss Pepper's gaze was pitying. "And you think you can manage *children*, Bancroft?"

Bancroft for once had no glib lie, no charming deception to offer in reply. Margaret had scooted to the edge of her chair, intent on gathering up the children and leaving, when Bancroft spoke.

"I am the legal guardian of those children," he said, making no pretense of pleasantness. "I have ample authority to do with them as I please."

This was the weakness in the plan. The idea had been to air the truth regarding Charles's death, wave the debts around, snatch the girls, and hope that—without Miss Pepper's good offices—Bancroft would desist from his foolishness.

No such luck, apparently.

"Bancroft," Hawthorne said, "don't be a bigger fool than you already have been. You are merely a co-guardian, an unusual situation, but there's royal precedent for leaving a woman in charge of young children. Margaret was Charles's choice to raise the children, while you are an impecunious bungler with airs above his station. The children can either be raised by a lady of true distinction, or they can suffer your ineptitude. You will have to take us to court to settle the matter, because the girls are already waiting for us in the garden. Their luggage is strapped to the coach."

Was he bluffing? Margaret went to the window and saw Fenny, both girls, Ambers, and Captain strolling between the flowerbeds.

"I sent a note to Miss Fenner as well," Hawthorne said. "An afterthought to your epistle."

A brilliant afterthought.

"You stoop to purloining children?" Bancroft sneered. "You are nothing to those girls, Dorning, and as long as I—"

"As long as you owe me a considerable sum," Hawthorne said, "you'd best guard your tongue. Casriel is on good terms with your magistrate, and you can bound over for debt as easily as I can."

"Debts of honor," Bancroft shot back, "are not actionable in a court of law."

Sycamore tugged the bell-pull. "Don't I know it, but Casriel and I had a little chat with your London landlord, a few of the better establishments on Bond Street, and the coaching inns that rent out teams to you between here and Town... At the risk of offending the ladies, Summerfield, your arse is waving in the breeze. If we must, we'll buy up those debts as well—the rest of those debts."

Two footmen and two grooms in Dorning livery had joined the party in the garden, stationing themselves at the compass points like an armed escort.

*I love you, Hawthorne Dorning.* To have married a man who could think ahead, plan for contingencies, and achieve an objective was wonderful.

Miss Pepper rose. "If everybody will excuse me, I'd like to... look in on my father."

"Take this," Margaret said, extracting a corked bottle from her reticule and a folded sheet of foolscap. "I've written out detailed instructions. The medicine is safe enough if used as directed. I'm happy to call again if you have questions, or you can pay us a visit at Summerton."

"You can't do this," Bancroft said when Miss Pepper had left. "You cannot march into my house, make off with my nieces, threaten me with dire consequences over a few minor obligations, and expect me to docilely yield to your threats."

"Why not?" Margaret asked. "I yielded to your threats, and you backed them up with nothing more substantial than lies, greed, and meanness. You are in debt up to your ears, and that is a poor reflection on your fitness as a guardian of house pets, much less of your nieces."

Ash Dorning, the brother who had read law, had opined in a letter to Hawthorne that Bancroft should never have been given authority over the children's funds. Bancroft was in theory his nieces' heir, and thus his interest in the money was conflicted.

Margaret would have happily raised that issue, but Hawthorne put a hand gently on her shoulder.

"Bancroft, you are taxing my wife's considerable patience. Here is how we will proceed. You will consent to have me appointed as co-guardian in your stead, of the girls and of their funds. When the courts have issued the appropriate orders, I will, with Margaret's permission, tear up your notes."

"That's blackmail," Bancroft spat. "That's trading my legal authority for—"

"That's the best offer you'll get," Margaret said, marching up to him. "And the best idea I've heard all day. Charles would be ashamed of you, and you should be ashamed of yourself. You either yield to Hawthorne on this, or you will lose Summerfield and whatever credit you still have. If I have to call an inquest into Charles's death, I will call an inquest."

Casriel, Oak, Cam, and Valerian were on their feet as well.

"Relax, gentlemen," Margaret said. "Bancroft can't hurt anybody except himself now."

Hawthorne smiled, the most pleased, contented, proud smile Margaret had ever seen on an adult male. "My dearest darling Mrs. Dorning, I believe my brothers rose in order to intervene if Bancroft needed protecting from you."

Valerian winked, Oak smiled, Sycamore shot his cuffs, and Casriel looked bored.

"Oh."

"We will send the appropriate legal documents around, Bancroft," Hawthorne said as Sycamore scooped up the notes. "You will sign them before witnesses, and then, as far as I'm concerned, you may go straight to perdition. My love, it's time we took the children home."

The gentlemen waited for Margaret to precede them from the parlor. No queen had ever felt more esteemed by her courtiers, and no mother had ever hugged her children with greater joy or relief.

Adriana chattered the whole twelve miles back to Summerfield, Greta sat beside Hawthorne, listening to his pocket watch, and Margaret fell in love with her husband for the third time that day.

# EPILOGUE

The summer lull had arrived, a sweet time when Margaret saw more of her husband and more of the blooming countryside. She took Greta and Adriana with her on her shorter walks, pointing out interesting plants when the girls were between rounds of Brave Explorers or Questing Queens. Hawthorne occasionally joined them, and picnics by the stream figured into every week's schedule.

This quiet mid-afternoon hour in the estate office had also become part of Margaret's routine with her husband. They dealt with business matters and correspondence, caught up on issues relating to the property, and exchanged the casual bits of information that made a marriage both real and intimate. "Valerian needs more arnica salve," Margaret said, setting his note aside. "Miss Pepper's dancing lessons are taking a toll on his toes." Hawthorne had moved a second desk into the room, so Margaret sat facing her spouse while he gently pried the housing from a new music box.

Hawthorne looked up, chisel in hand. "Miss Pepper is taking a toll on his sanity, but I hear she's doing wonders for Pepperidge."

She'd purchased Summerfield outright—or Mr. Pepper had purchased it for her—changed the name of the estate, ensconced her papa in a first floor apartment, and set up regular appointments for him with Hannah Weller. Two days after the sale had concluded, and one week after Hawthorne had been appointed as successor to Bancroft as co-guardian of the girls, Bancroft had disappeared with the proceeds of the sale on a fast packet to Calais.

A host of disgruntled merchants—and gentlemen—were still sending dunning notices down to Dorset. Miss Pepper returned each one with a polite note that Mr. Summerfield could likely be found in Paris.

"Do you think Bancroft is truly in Paris?" Margaret asked, slitting open another note.

"Casriel says he is, which means Beatitude has consulted with her various friends and confirmed the theory. Hand me that pen tray, would you?"

"You aren't merely removing the case from that one." Margaret passed over the elongated silver dish, and Hawthorne deposited a tiny screw in it.

"It's time Greta and I built a music box. Adriana can be our amanuensis, documenting our efforts. When Greta has mastered music boxes, we can find a simple clock to start on."

Margaret put down her mail and came around the desks to hug her husband. The children had been delighted to learn he was to be their uncle, and had nominated his brothers as honorary uncles as well.

Hawthorne hugged Margaret back, kissed her cheek, then pulled her into his lap. "To what do I owe the honor, Mrs. Dorning?"

How she loved being called that. When she'd communicated her joy adequately, she resumed her seat at her own desk. The estate office had seen its share of connubial bliss, but Hawthorne was intent on his music box, and talking with him was in its way as great a pleasure as the lovemaking.

"I wandered the fields and lanes around here for years, Hawthorne, but nobody saw me. They noticed that odd Mallory girl out wandering again, but they didn't really *see* me. You see Adriana and Greta and that makes an enormous difference."

Hawthorne dropped another screw into the tray. "Greta has such a hearty laugh for such a little person. Who would have guessed?"

Greta's laughter had been a surprise, one of many. With Bancroft gone, the children safe, and Hawthorne to share both estate matters and the business end of the botanical products, Margaret had emerged into an emotional springtime. She'd cast off worries that had grown heavier than she'd realized, and embraced hopes and dreams for the first time in years.

Not merely plans, but dreams too.

"How much longer do you think we'll have Fenny at her post?" Hawthorne asked. "Mr. Hartley has a certain determined gleam in his eye."

Hartley had begun walking Fenny home from services the same week he'd accepted employment at Dorning Hall. Miss Pepper had hired one of the Wellers as her steward, though Margaret and Hawthorne made it a point to drop by Pepperidge regularly. Thorne divided his calls between Mr. Pepper, who'd proven to be a godsend regarding London's mercantile habits, and the new steward.

Margaret also called upon the neighbors, often in the company of Lady Casriel. Margaret knew everybody, and everybody wanted to claim acquaintance with her ladyship. The result was a gradual easing of resentments that Margaret had once again married above herself—and to one of the handsome Dorning men, too—and an easing of Lady Casriel into local society.

"Fenny has two sisters who are governesses," Margaret said. "She will likely stay on until one of them can join our household. Hawthorne, I know not why this should be, but I am overcome by an urge to nap."

The lassitude was more than just a summer afternoon's drowsiness. Margaret felt as if she could close her eyes and nod off in her very chair.

"Then let's nap. You've been in the herbal morning, noon, and night when you aren't calling on neighbors or consulting with Hannah. If anybody deserves a little respite in the middle of the day, it's you."

Hawthorne wasn't a hovering sort of husband. He still had half a hand in the running of Dorning Hall. He'd made two trips up to London to look at properties Mr. Pepper recommended for the botanical business, and he'd taken the time to become thoroughly acquainted with Summerton's land and tenancies.

But he made time for Margaret too, and insisted she make time for him. He'd show up in the herbal with a picnic lunch, join Margaret as she explored the specimen plots at Dorning Hall, and occasionally declare a holiday for two.

"Hawthorne, I mean I truly want to nap." Could barely keep her eyes open in fact.

"That's what you said last week." He rose and came around the desks. "And we did nap—at first."

He was reminding her that this sudden fatigue had happened previously, about five days ago. A notion formed in Margaret's mind as to the cause, but she would wait to be sure before sharing her suspicion with her husband.

"Then let's to bed," Margaret said, taking Hawthorne by the hand. They climbed the stairs hand in hand, and they did, indeed, nap—at first.

I was surprised to learn that we still make medication to slow and more powerfully contract the heart using the actual foxglove plant. The molecules with the medicinal effect are apparently hard to replicate synthetically, and thus we have another example of the old ways still being the best ways.

English physician William Withering FRS (1741-1799) in the course of his medical practice in Shropshire came across an herb woman's recipe for treating dropsy (edema, often resulting from congestive heart failure). Patients claimed the recipe yielded significant relief of symptoms when other interventions were unavailing. Withering took it upon himself to investigate, and realized that foxglove was the active ingredient.

Withering kept careful notes from more than 150 cases, and soon concluded that a toxic dose and an effect dose could vary by a slim margin. He advised using a dilute mixture made from a dried powder of the leaves, and administering small, frequent doses until symptoms abated. He learned that London physicians were administering the drug without reference to careful dosing, and in 1785 published *An Account of the Foxglove and Some of Its Medical Uses*, which in essence summarized his many case histories. You can find that document online, and it makes for interesting reading, in that Withering was absolutely honest about his successes and his failures, patient by patient.

In 1776 Withering published the first widely read English language flora, *The Botanical Arrangement of all the vegetables naturally growing in Great Britain*, which earned him the epitaph, "The English Linnaeus."

Withering's medical education was completed at the University of Edinburgh, where botany was part of every medical student's training. His uncle was a physician, and his father an apothecary, while his wife was an amateur botanist who did many of the illustrations for his *Botanical Arrangement*. He was well educated, well mentored, and well partnered for his profession, but the spark of curiosity that eventually led to a medical breakthrough we still benefit from today belongs to him.

That said, do not EVER allow a pet to drink from the water in a vase that's held foxgloves. Margaret was telling the absolutely truth that it's a dangerous plant in careless hands!

Happy reading,
   Grace Burrowes

# TO MY DEAR READERS

To My Dear Readers,

I hope you enjoyed Hawthorne and Margaret's story. For me, this tale was a particular treat to write because Dorsetshire is an absolutely gorgeous place to research. Why is it, my bucket list gets longer the more books I write?

I hope to have another **True Gentlemen** ready for publication soon, (Ash and Della, can you hear me now?) but I'm also adding to the **Rogues to Riches** series with the November release of **Forever and a Duke** (excerpt below). If you don't want to wait until then for your next HEA, in June I'm releasing **How to Ruin a DukeHow to Ruin a Duke**, a duet with writin' buddy Theresa Romain. I hesitate to call that story a novella, because it crossed the finish line at about 40,000 words (excerpt also follows below). Somebody kept moving the goal posts, which often happens when I'm having fun with a story.

If you want a quick email alerting you to my new releases, sales, and pre-orders, follow me on **Bookbub**. If you'd like a few more details, my **newsletter** is a good option. I will never sell or share your personal information if you sign up for the newsletter, promise, and I only publish when I have something newsworthy to say.

Until our next HEA, happy reading!

Grace Burrowes

Read on for an excerpt from *When His Grace Falls*, in **How to Ruin a Duke**, coming out June 11, 2019.

# EXCERPT FROM HOW TO RUIN A DUKE

*Thaddeus, Duke of Emory, is the butt of a satirical novel,* How to Ruin a Duke, *a tale reminiscent of Lady Caroline Lamb's* Glenarvon, *aimed at Lord Byron. His Grace suspects his mother's former companion, Lady Edith Charbonneau, authored* How to Ruin a Duke. *He has confronted her over a meal, but she's clearly not enjoying the financial security the author of such a successful tome ought to be enjoying... Nor is Lady Edith enjoying Emory's company.*

A pot of strong tea and some real victuals had taken the edge off Edith's foul mood, enough that she could make a dispassionate inspection of the man across the table.

His Grace of Emory carried a vague air of annoyance with him everywhere, a counterpoint to his luscious scent and fine tailoring. He doubtless had reason to be testy. His mama was a restless and discontented woman by nature, given to meddling and gossip. His younger brother was the typical spare waiting to be deposed by a nephew.

"Perhaps your mother didn't write the book herself, but a co-author bears thinking about," Edith said. "The duchess's circle includes the set at Almack's, and they've all but banished Lady Caroline for her literary accomplishments. If Her Grace wrote *How to Ruin a Duke*, she could hide behind the skirts of a collaborator or hack writer."

His Grace next began slicing up the uneaten portion of Edith's steak. Perhaps he was one of those people who had to keep his hands busy, though in two years of sharing meals with him, she'd never noticed that about him.

"Lady Caroline had worn her welcome thin in polite society long before she took up her pen," Emory observed, "and for the viciousness of her satire, she deserved banishment. At least whoever decided to lampoon me left the rest of my friends and family unscathed."

"Which again suggests your mother, a cousin, or a rejected marital prospect. The author's ire is personal to you, Your Grace."

He finished slicing the meat and set down the utensils. "Sir Prendergast made a scene at Tattersalls." This recollection inspired Emory to a slight smile, more a change of the light in his eyes than a curving of his lips. The only time Edith had seen him truly joyous was on the occasion of becoming godfather to some new member of the extended family. No man had ever looked more pleased to have his nose seized in a tiny fist. No baby had ever been more carefully cradled in his god-father's arms.

The ceremony had gone forth, with the duke caught variously by the nose, the chin, or the gloved finger, and Edith feeling oddly enchanted by the sight.

"Perhaps Sir Prendergast is your culprit."

"He found another fortune to marry. Once his bruises healed, I made it a point to introduce him to a few cits who wouldn't mind seeing their daughter on the arm of a gallant knight."

Edith's lemon cake was half gone. She stopped eating, lest she regret over-indulging. "Generous of you."

"Prudent. He dwells in the north now, far from Cousin Antigone's notice."

"Which does not rule him out as your nemesis."

His Grace raised a hand and the serving maid scampered over. "If you'd be so good as to wrap up the rest of this food, I'd appreciate it."

A common request, but the maid looked as if she'd never been given a greater compliment. "Of course, sir. At once."

"All of it," he said. "Every morsel, and some plum tarts and cheese wouldn't go amiss either. You know how hunger can strike two hours after a decent repast, and good food shouldn't go to waste when a man of my robust proportions is on hand to enjoy it."

"Quite so, sir. Exactly. Ma says the same thing at least seventeen times a day. Eighteen, possibly."

The maid gathered up the plates while Edith tried not to watch. This was the best meal she'd eaten in ages, and Emory wasn't having the leftovers boxed up for himself.

"Thank you," she said, when the maid had bustled off to the kitchen.

He looked at her directly, something Edith could not recall happening previously. Emory stalked through life, intent on pressing business. At the ducal residence he'd often been trailed by a secretary, solicitor, footman, steward or butler, all of whom followed him about as he'd lobbed orders in every direction.

At table, Emory tended to focus on the food, the wine, the appointments in the room.

On the dancefloor, he was so much taller than most of his partners, he usually gazed past their shoulders.

The full brunt of his gaze was unnerving. His eyes were brown, the deep, soft, shade of mink in summer. They gave his countenance gravity, and Edith well knew those eyes could narrow on the deserving in preparation for a scathing setdown.

His gaze could also, apparently, be kind.

Order your copy of **How to Ruin a Duke**, and read on for an excerpt from **Forever and a Duke**...

# EXCERPT FROM FOREVER AND A DUKE

*Eleanora Hatfield, who excels brilliantly as a financial auditor, is trying to impress upon Wrexham, Duke of Elsmore, all that a thorough review of his books will involve. Rex needs to get his ledgers in order before somebody suspects accounts gone amiss, but just at the moment, he's a bit pre-occupied...*

Rex took up one of the pencils from the silver tray and drew a sheet of blank paper near. He crossed an ankle over a knee, used a ledger book for his easel, and began sketching the woman who boldly lectured him on the topic of petty domestic graft.

Corrected him, rather.

"Do you know the insult my butler will suffer if I impugn his integrity?" Rex paused to take another sip of tea rather than launch into a lecture of his own. Mrs. Hatfield could not possibly grasp the delicate workings of a large, wealthy domicile. "An affronted butler can set off a cascade of burned toast, sour wine, feuding housemaids, and warring footmen. The upheaval would rival the English civil wars."

Mrs. Hatfield's eyebrows were her most interesting feature. Most people's eyebrows were not perfectly symmetric. Hers were two exactly matched swoops that added elegance to the intelligence in her gaze.

Why had such a woman—competent, well mannered, even pretty —no husband? She hadn't said she was widowed, simply that she had no husband.

"Your Grace, please attend me."

He glanced up to find her gaze had grown quite severe. "You have my undivided attention." *And you have eyes that should not be hidden behind a pair of spinsterish spectacles.*

"You observe that you have no privacy, and yet, if I asked you which clubs your cousins belong to, could you tell me? If I asked you which tailors, modistes, or bootmakers they use, would you know?"

"Not in the usual course." Howell and James favored Hoby boots, but then, most of fashionable London did. Rex had sponsored James for membership at some club or other—the Explorers, or was it the Charitable Knights?

"Nonetheless," Mrs. Hatfield said, "those cousins all know your movements, your preferred merchants, your schedule, your clubs. Your servants know details far more personal than those. People who have less, who *are* less, keep a close eye on people who have more. Children are more observant about adults than conversely. Women are vigilant regarding the actions of men because we have to be. The same is not true in the opposite direction, not in any flattering sense."

Her words resonated with his experience and, more than that, organized a vague sense of frustration into cause and effect. Rex had responsibility—he had *power*—but not privacy. When had he chosen to strike that bargain with life? Had he even *had* a choice?

"You are saying whoever is fleecing me has had long acquaintance to learn my habits. That describes most of my staff."

She folded her arms. "And all of your family."

Rex sketched the curve of her jaw, which angled cleanly then flowed into a firm chin. "There, I must protest, madam. You will not impugn the honor of my family again, lest you inspire me to a display of temper." Not that he'd had any such displays since the age of about, oh, six?

"I would *at least* raise my voice if a family member betrayed my trust," she retorted. "I'd not be sitting on my elegant backside, swilling tea, and doodling. I'd throw fragile objects, provided they weren't worth much. I'd kick the wall and curse. To entrust another with money is an intimate act of faith. One's security, one's future, one's...I needn't tell you."

She thought his backside elegant. He could venture a similar opinion about hers, except that he sought to live to a vigorous old age.

"Don't forget that my dignity will also suffer when I find out which employee has been dipping a hand into my coffers. Dukes are supposed to have endless reserves of dignity."

"Dukes are people," she said, taking up her pencil of doom. "I thought that condition applied only to His Grace of Walden, a rarity of among his peers. My theory no longer fits the available facts, for you are nearly as stubborn as he is."

Rex took a moment with her nose. Noses were easy to get wrong, easy to relegate to an afterthought, but a whole countenance could be rendered either noble or ridiculous by an artist's handling of the nose.

"Did you just pay me a compliment, Mrs. Hatfield? I daresay you did. You admitted me into membership in the human species, a very exclusive club indeed. I cannot recall when last I was so cleverly flattered."

He finished the tea and realized he'd finished the shortbread as well. Mrs. Hatfield put her glasses back on, but Rex decided not to draw her wearing them. The lady on the page was intriguing, even beautiful, but she was not smiling. Glasses would make her look too severe, too unhappy.

"We must consider your family members among those responsible for mishandling your funds, sir."

"Who is stubborn now, Mrs. Hatfield? Do you think I wouldn't notice if my sisters were padding accounts? Am I so oblivious to my own cousins that they could steal from me, abuse my generosity, and have me none the wiser?"

Rex might resent his family, find their company tiresome, and even nip out to Ambledown occasionally to escape them, but he knew them well enough to trust them.

"You need not feel ashamed, Your Grace. Your holdings are vast, your family large. We'll find the source or sources of the irregularities and then you can decide what to do about them."

Sources, *plural*? "My family is above suspicion, Mrs. Hatfield. I'll grant you that errors occur, miscalculations can be carried forward, but I pay sufficient attention to my loved ones that the misbehavior you suspect them of could not happen. Give me that much credit, at least. We limit our investigations to retainers, employees, and factors."

On her chart of money paid and received, she drew another arrow that ended in a question mark and then two more. One for each sister? *Preposterous.*

"We can start with your staff, Your Grace."

A prudent cease-fire on her part, and doubtless not the last time Rex would have to limit her zeal with an application of common sense.

"I applaud your thoroughness, Mrs. Hatfield, and your diplomacy. More tea?" The brew, the shortbread, and the passage of time had apparently routed his megrim.

She drew another outward arrow on his money chart and labeled it with yet another a question mark. "Will you purloin my next cup too?"

What in creation was she—? Rex looked at the cup in his hand. *Hers*, the one he'd fixed with milk and sugar. Empty. He, who professed to know his family so well, to be able to vouch for their inmost motivations and private actions, had drunk from her cup and finished her tea without even noticing his own error...

Order your copy of **Forever and a Duke**!

Lightning Source UK Ltd.
Milton Keynes UK
UKHW031354010622
403836UK00002B/613

THE AFTERLIFE OF POPE JOAN